"Every bit as exciting, entertaining and humorous as the first volume. . . . Cox has produced a story so dramatic that the reader truly feels as if they are immersed in a Star Trek myth-inspired overview of the political upheavals of the mid-1990s. . . . This is a novel not to be missed by even the most casual Star Trek fan."

—Jacqueline Bundy, *The Trekker Newsletter*

"Worth the wait. . . *The Eugenics Wars,* Volume Two is an audacious, fast-moving conclusion to the Eugenics War duology, one-upping the considerable dramatic intensity and inventive accomplishment of the first volume, and bringing the story to a remarkably smooth, coherent conclusion, complete with an unequivocal (if surely controversial) moral. . . . Cox's electric, fun-loving style of storytelling is the perfect medium to take the reader into the twenty-first century and beyond. . . ."

—Kilian Melloy, Wigglefish.com

"Fans of the first *Eugenics Wars* will love this sequel. . . ."

—Michelle Erica Green, *Trek Nation*

STAR TREK®
THE EUGENICS WARS

The Rise and Fall of Khan Noonien Singh

VOLUME TWO

GREG COX

Based upon STAR TREK and
STAR TREK: THE NEXT GENERATION®
created by Gene Roddenberry,
STAR TREK: DEEP SPACE NINE®
created by Rick Berman & Michael Piller,
and STAR TREK: VOYAGER®
created by Rick Berman &
Michael Piller & Jeri Taylor

POCKET BOOKS
New York   London   Toronto   Sydney   Singapore

This book is a work of fiction. Names, characters, places and incidents are products of the author's imagination or are used fictitiously. Any resemblance to actual events or locales or persons, living or dead, is entirely coincidental.

 POCKET BOOKS, a division of Simon & Schuster, Inc.
1230 Avenue of the Americas, New York, NY 10020

Originally published in hardcover in 2002 by Pocket Books

 STAR TREK is a Registered Trademark of
Paramount Pictures.

This book is published by Pocket Books, a division of Simon & Schuster, Inc., under exclusive license from Paramount Pictures.

ISBN: 0-7434-0644-3

First Pocket Books paperback printing March 2003

10 9 8 7 6 5 4 3 2 1

POCKET and colophon are registered trademarks of Simon & Schuster, Inc.

For information regarding special discounts for bulk purchases, please contact Simon & Schuster Special Sales at 1-800-456-6798 or business@simonandschuster.com

Printed in the U.S.A.

Dedicated to the people and city of New York,
who have survived worse than the Eugenics Wars

Acknowledgments

Thanks, most of all, to my editor, John Ordover, for waiting patiently for the manuscript while I moved my entire life from New York to Pennsylvania. And to the rest of the gang at Pocket Books—Scott, Marco, Jessica, John, and Elisa—for invaluable assistance during the Eugenics Wars.

Thanks to David Weddle and Jeffrey Lang for describing Khan's flag in their recent Deep Space Nine novel, *Abyss,* and for alerting me to the reference. And to Dayton Ward, whose story in *Strange New Worlds III,* tying together a few relevant threads of Trek history, appeared in time for me to reference it here. (Let's hear it for inter-author cooperation and consistency!)

And special thanks (since I forgot to mention them last book) to Gene L. Coon and Carey Wilbur, who wrote the original Star Trek episode, "Space Seed," for creating Khan in the first place, and to Art Wallace and Gene Roddenberry, who created Gary Seven and associates in the episode, "Assignment: Earth."

Finally, as always, thanks to Karen, Alex, Church, and Henry for moral support on the home front.

"A prince should therefore have no other aim or thought, nor take up any other thing for his study, but war and its organization and discipline, for that is the only art that is necessary to one who commands."

—MACHIAVELLI, *The Prince*

PROLOGUE

Captain's log, stardate 7004.1.

Our diplomatic mission to the Paragon Colony on the planet Sycorax has erupted into a full-scale crisis—and a potential disaster.

Dr. McCoy and I were visiting Sycorax, home to a unique society of genetically-enhanced men and women, to assess the full implications of the colony's recent application to join the Federation. Human genetic engineering is, of course, strictly forbidden throughout the Federation, but recently this centuries-old policy has come under review. With humanity being confronted throughout the galaxy by alien races such as the Klingons and Romulans, many of whom are more physically powerful than the average human, Starfleet has quietly begun taking a second look at the potential risks and benefits of modifying human DNA. With this in mind, my own top-secret mission is to develop a firsthand impression of what such practices have yielded on Sycorax.

Unfortunately, upon arriving at the colony, we discovered that Starfleet was not the only organization interested in what Paragon had to offer. A Klingon delegation, led by my old adversary, Captain Koloth, has also appeared on the scene, eager to claim (via veiled threats and innuendoes) the colonists' considerable expertise at genetic engineering.

Not surprisingly, Koloth and his men soon wore out their welcome, but not before sabotaging the vital force field projectors that helped to protect the domed colony from the toxic and corrosive atmosphere of the planet. Now, with the protective dome facing imminent collapse, it looks as though no amount of genetic enhancement will be enough to save the superhuman inhabitants of the Paragon Colony from total catastrophe. . . .

CAPTAIN JAMES T. KIRK URGENTLY ADDRESSED Masako Clarke, the Regent of the Paragon Colony. "How long," he asked softly, "can your dome hold up against the pressure, without the additional protection of the force field?"

The regent, a silver-haired Asian woman whose trim and fit physique was a testimonial to the distinct advantages of designer DNA, shook her head ominously. She had the somber dignity of a ship's captain fully prepared to go down with her vessel. "Hours," she said. "At most."

Kirk frowned. Sycorax was a Class-K planet, not unlike Venus, with an atmosphere composed primarily of carbon dioxide laced with gaseous sulfuric acid. As if this noxious combination wasn't lethal enough, the atmospheric pressure outside the dome was nearly one hundred times that of Earth's, more than enough to reduce even genetically strengthened bones to pulp. Without the dome, Kirk realized, *these people are as good as dead.*

"Oh my God, Jim," Leonard McCoy whispered. The *Enterprise*'s chief medical officer stood a few feet away, his medical tricorder still draped over the shoulder of his blue dress uniform. He and Kirk had been enjoying a state dinner with the regent and her advisors when the disaster struck, in the form of an explosion that had destroyed much of the colony's primary deflector array. Now the elegant outdoor plaza where they had been dining had become the launch site for a frantic exodus, as assembled dignitaries and food servers rushed out of the plaza, hurrying to either their emergency posts or to the questionable safety of their homes. "We have to do something!" McCoy exclaimed.

Easier said than done, Kirk thought grimly. He craned his head back to stare at the vast green dome arching high overhead. Like so much of Paragon, the dome was a product of advanced genetic wizardry. It was, he had learned, a living organism whose roots extended deep into the planet's surface. Chlorophyll-based, the immense translucent hemisphere absorbed carbon dioxide from the atmosphere outside, converting it into the very oxygen that Kirk and the others were now breathing. As impressive as it was, however, the dome still required the reinforcement of a powerful force field to withstand the awesome heat and pressure forever threatening to break through the gigantic green blister. And now that force field had been seriously impaired. Already, bright blue flashes of Cerenkov radiation crackled along a sizable segment of the dome, providing dramatic proof that the structural integrity of the force field was weakening in spots. Large portions of the dome grew black and discolored, as its living substance succumbed to the pernicious effects of the planet's hellish atmosphere. Kirk sniffed the air. Was it just his imagination, or could he already detect the acrid scent of sulfuric acid? He feared that toxic gases had already begun leaking into the suddenly fragile biosphere.

Kirk had no doubt that Koloth was behind the explosion that had damaged an entire bank of deflectors. *Is he just trying to scare the colony into submission,* Kirk speculated, *or would he rather see the colony completely destroyed before letting it join forces with the Federation?*

Either way, Kirk wasn't about to let that happen. Hundreds of lives were at stake. His communicator beeped, and he flipped it open with a practiced gesture. "Kirk here."

The steady voice of Mr. Spock, who was currently holding down the fort aboard the *Enterprise,* emerged from the compact handheld device. *"Captain, our sensors are detecting an emergency situation upon the planet. Are you in danger?"*

"Most definitely, Mr. Spock," Kirk answered, "along with everyone else in the colony." He quickly filled his first officer in on the situation, while simultaneously trying to come up with a workable solution. "Is Koloth's battle cruiser still in orbit around the planet?"

"I'm afraid so, Captain," Spock reported.

Damn, Kirk thought. Evacuation, it seemed, was not an option; not only was there no time to transport the colony's entire population to the *Enterprise,* but the continuing presence of the Klingon vessel made any sort of rescue attempt too risky to attempt.

"Maintain Yellow Alert status," Kirk advised Spock. In his mind, he could readily visualize the heavily armed D-7 battle cruiser hanging in space above Sycorax, like a vulture circling wounded prey. "Don't even think about lowering the shields long enough to beam me or Dr. McCoy back to the ship."

Spock accepted Kirk's instructions without debate. *"Understood,"* he replied, no doubt recognizing the logic behind the captain's decision. *"What do you intend to do?"*

"I'm not sure," Kirk admitted, exchanging a glance with McCoy, who was listening to the exchange with a worried expression upon his weathered features. Lieutenant Seth Lerner, the sole security officer among the Starfleet landing party, also stood nearby, phaser in hand. "If I think of anything, you'll be the first to know," he promised Spock. "Kirk out."

Returning his communicator to his belt, he racked his brain for some way to save the colony. *There has to be an answer!* he thought emphatically; he didn't believe in no-win scenarios. But what?

"Captain," Lerner suggested, "perhaps you and the regent and a few others should attempt to escape in the shuttle?" The red-shirted crewman maintained a stoic expression. "One of the regent's people can have my seat."

Kirk admired Lerner's willingness to sacrifice himself, even as he rejected the idea. The maximum capacity of a Starfleet shuttlecraft was no more than a dozen humanoids; Kirk refused to save merely a handful of lives when an entire population was in jeopardy. "I appreciate the thought, Lieutenant, but we haven't quite reached that point yet."

"Well, if we do," McCoy said dryly, raising a bemused eyebrow, "let me know if I'm deemed expendable or not."

Lerner blushed, no doubt realizing that he had neglected to include the doctor among his proposed list of escapees. A relatively new addition to the *Enterprise*'s crew, he was also unfamiliar with McCoy's customarily mordant sense of humor.

Kirk ignored the security officer's discomfort. Something Lerner had said caused a light to blink on at the back of his brain. *The shuttle,* he thought. *Of course.* Because of the colony's protective force field, the landing party had not been able to beam directly to Paragon, but had been forced to ride a shuttlecraft down to the planet's surface instead. It had been a bumpy ride, he recalled, with the shuttle's own shields being severely tested by Sycorax's turbulent atmosphere.

A plan rapidly formulated in his mind. *The shuttle's deflectors!* he thought excitedly. His heart beat faster at the prospect of taking positive action against the oncoming disaster. *That just might work!* . . .

"I have an idea," he announced, hastily explaining his impromptu scheme to McCoy, Lerner, and the regent. "Lerner, you're with me. Doctor, you stay behind and look after the regent and her people. Contact Spock, too, and let him know what we're up to." He turned toward Masako Clarke, whose ashen countenance now displayed a faint spark of hope.

"Quickly," Kirk pressed her. "What's the fastest route to the landing bay?"

A short ride through the colony's underground subway system brought Kirk to the cavernous hangar where he had left the shuttlecraft several hours ago. "This way," directed one of the regent's aides, whom Clarke had instructed to guide Kirk and Lerner back to their shuttle.

Emerging from the deserted subway tunnel, now closed to all but emergency traffic, Kirk spotted the *Columbus-2* resting upon the floor of the hangar, surrounded by a wide variety of Paragon scout ships and cargo haulers, all the vehicles heavily armored so as to withstand the fearsome conditions outside the dome. He sprinted across the pavement, the planet's weak gravity, less than ninety percent Earth-standard, providing a little extra spring to his stride. A burning sensation at the back of his throat added urgency to his headlong dash for the shuttlecraft; the colony's atmosphere was obviously growing more contaminated by the second.

As he neared the *Columbus-2,* Kirk couldn't help noticing that the shuttle's white ceramic exterior showed signs of wear and tear from their earlier descent through Sycorax's stormy atmosphere. Lightning strikes had left carbonized scorch marks on the starboard hull, partially obscuring the *Enterprise*'s name and registry number. Acid rain, from the ferocious thunderstorms high above the planet's surface, had pitted the duranium plating over the engine modules. *A bad sign,* Kirk acknowledged ruefully, especially considering what he had in mind. . . .

He and Lerner left the regent's aide behind them as they scrambled into the shuttle's front seats. Kirk took the pilot's seat while the security officer manned the control panels to Kirk's right. "Preparing for takeoff," Kirk stated as he strapped himself into the contoured black seat. He rapidly pressurized the cabin, engaged the impulse engines, then pulled back on the throttle.

The *Columbus-2* lifted off the pavement and began cruising toward the dock-size airlock at the southern end of the hangar. Automated doors slid open to permit the shuttle's passage and Kirk waited impatiently for the airlock to release them from the insecure confines of the colony. The atmosphere within the cabin was purer than the tainted air inside the landing bay, but the shuttle's artificial gravity felt somewhat oppressive compared to the lightweight pull he had been experiencing since his arrival at Paragon.

Within minutes, the outer doors opened and Kirk steered the shuttle out into the intense heat and pressure of Sycorax's lower atmosphere. "Brace yourself," he warned Lerner. "This could be rough sailing."

The scenery was just as desolate as he remembered. Night had fallen on this part of the world, but the shuttle's high-intensity searchlights exposed a lifeless landscape, completely devoid of moisture and vegetation. Aside from the enormous green dome, which stretched entirely over a colossal, preexisting crater, the surrounding terrain consisted of basaltic ebon plains broken up by gigantic craters and fissures. Rocky, snowless mountains loomed in the distance. The heavy cloud cover, roughly sixty kilometers overhead, blocked out any glint of starlight, so that the still and silent night was as a black as a quantum singularity.

"Exterior conditions?" Kirk requested, as the shuttle ascended at less than a quarter-impulse power.

Lerner consulted the sensor gauges. "Outside temperature, approximately 470 degrees Centigrade. Atmospheric pressure, approximately 8,500 kilopascals."

Not exactly picnic weather, Kirk thought wryly. That was the sort of pressure you'd expect to find at the bottom of Earth's oceans, and more than enough to crush both him and Lerner to crimson specks. "How's our structural integrity?"

"Shields at maximum, but holding," Lerner reported.

Kirk silently thanked Starfleet engineering for the quality of their work. He realized, however, that there was worse to come. If his desperate plan was to succeed, and if he and Lerner had any hope of coming out of this alive, then that same legendary engineering would be tested to the utmost. "Very well, Lieutenant," he said. "Let's see if we can perform a little first aid on the Paragon Colony."

Lit from within, the translucent green dome glowed in the dark of night. The *Columbus-2* rose until it was nearly a kilometer above the colony, then turned its prow toward the beleaguered dome. Struggling to maintain a stationary position above Paragon despite the powerful winds buffeting the shuttle, Kirk was alarmed to see that the massive biosphere looked severely injured by its partial exposure to the Class-K environment outside the dome. Although a faint blue aura still crackled intermittently over maybe three-fourths of the living dome, indicating that the colony's crippled force field had not yet collapsed completely, a large patch of the dome, at least two kilometers across, was blackened and blistered by what looked suspiciously like a third-degree burn. As Kirk watched in horror, the ugly discoloration spread outward, consuming more and more of the dome. Charred sheets of genengineered cellulose, the size of a ship's bulkhead, flaked away from the dome, raining down upon the barren lava plains below. Thick green sap boiled and bubbled away, reduced to vapor by the tremendous heat. The damaged tissue swelled inwardly, forming a large, concave depression that threatened to tear apart catastrophically at any moment.

Kirk knew he had to act quickly. "Divert deflectors to the dome," he instructed Lerner. "Try to patch the holes in the colony's own force field."

"Yes, sir," Lerner said with a gulp. He carefully adjusted the shield controls and, seconds later, a luminous blue beam shot forth from the shuttle's deflector array. At the speed of light, the beam crossed the distance between the *Columbus-2* and the roof of the colony, focusing on the injured region of the dome. At first, the radiant energy didn't quite mesh with the tattered remains of the colony's disabled force field, but Lerner kept at the controls, a look of intense concentration on his face, until the outer edges of the deflector beam intersected with the expanding frontier of the blighted area. *That's it,* Kirk thought, avidly watching to see if the extra shielding had any effect. Had the burning slowed its advance? Kirk thought so, perhaps. "Keep it up," he advised Lerner.

Easier said than done, Kirk realized. Lerner's brow furrowed and he bit down on his lower lip as the security officer gave his full attention, and then some, to the challenge of implementing the captain's plan.

Let's hope he's up to the job, Kirk mused. Lerner was an able crewman, but the captain couldn't help wishing that Scotty were here in his place; if anyone could pull off the delicate task of supplementing the dome's defenses with the shuttle's own limited deflectors, then the *Enterprise*'s cagey chief engineer was the man Kirk would have preferred to tackle the job. Unfortunately, Scotty was still aboard the *Enterprise,* which couldn't safely lower her shields while Koloth's battle cruiser remained in the vicinity.

Not that the captain would have enjoyed asking Scotty to beam onto the shuttlecraft under these particular circumstances; the Achilles' heel of Kirk's plan was that, while the shuttle's deflectors remained directed at the dome, the *Columbus-2* had to survive the surrounding heat and pressure without any electromagnetic shields. Now, only the shuttle's insulated bulkheads, duranium hull, and outer ceramic plating stood between the two men and the unrelenting wrath of Sycorax's deadly climate.

"Here's where we find out exactly what this bird is made of," Kirk warned his copilot. The searing heat began penetrating the shuttle's bulkheads almost immediately, rapidly raising the temperature within the cabin. Keeping one hand on the throttle while fighting the cyclonic winds shaking the shuttle from side to side, he tugged at the constricting collar of his dress uniform. The shuttle's interior already felt like a Vulcan sauna; perspiration glued the back of his tunic to his spine, while sweat streamed down his face. He licked dry lips, tasting salt.

Lerner looked just as hot and miserable. He wiped the sweat from his eyes with the back of his hand as he continued to make constant adjustments to the deflector controls. Kirk feared that both of them were on the verge of heatstroke.

The alarming sound of creaking metal filled the cabin, making Kirk wince in anticipation. Clearly, the overwhelming pressure outside was making itself felt upon the unshielded structure of the shuttle. Kirk knew they were in trouble; Starfleet shuttlecrafts were built to last, but the *Columbus*-2 couldn't endure these conditions indefinitely, and neither could he or Lerner. The best he could hope to accomplish was to buy enough time for someone down in the colony to come to the rescue of the besieged dome.

But was there even a chance of repairing the dome in time? "C'mon," Kirk muttered to the imperiled colonists down below, his sweat-slick hands struggling to maintain a firm grip on the throttle. "Show me just how genetically superior you all are!"

The command bunker was located a half kilometer beneath the colony proper, excavated deep into the bottom of an original volcanic crater. McCoy wondered how long they all could survive here if and when Paragon's big green umbrella burst into flames? *Not long enough*, he thought morosely.

Regent Clarke and her top people had retreated to the bunker in order to coordinate their emergency efforts from a location of relative safety. McCoy had been brought along as well, although, since arriving at the bunker, he had felt pretty much like a third wheel. Despite his persistent offers to help in any way possible, he had been politely rebuffed, then more or less ignored by the busy regent and her aides. *Guess they figure that there's nothing a plain, old, ordinary human being, with distinctly old-fashioned DNA, can do in a crisis.*

"Typical," McCoy groused. Although hospitable enough, there had always been something faintly condescending about the way Clarke and the other colonists had treated their visitors from the *Enterprise,* even before the current emergency erupted. McCoy had picked up on the regent's mildly patronizing attitude almost as soon as he and the rest of the landing party had touched down on Sycorax, and so had, he suspected, Captain Kirk.

Still, the colonists hardly deserved the ghastly calamity befalling them now; McCoy wouldn't wish this sort of catastrophe on a Denebian slime-devil, let alone a city of well-meaning (if insufferably smug) human descendants. *Those blasted Klingons!* he thought angrily. *Why can't they ever take no for an answer?*

Reduced to standing in an unoccupied corner, doing his best to stay out of the way, the frustrated doctor inspected his surroundings. Like the rest of the so-called Paragon Colony, where creative bioengineering was literally a way of life, the cramped bunker was furnished almost entirely with organic materials. Polished teak panels covered the walls while a dry, spongy material carpeted the floor. Even the desks and computer consoles at which the regent's staff now anxiously worked appeared to have been crafted from some sort of petrified coral, with knobs, switches, and keyboards made of polished bone or ivory. The overall effect was somewhat charming, McCoy granted; certainly it made the bridge of the *Enterprise* look cold and sterile by comparison.

On the other hand, decades of relentless focus on applied biological science had left the colonists backward in other respects. McCoy was a doctor, not a technician, but even he could tell that the bunker's computer hardware was fairly primitive by Federation standards. Why, they didn't even seem to have basic duotronic technology!

Then again, he reflected, a trifle reluctantly, *how much computing power do you actually need when every one of your citizens has a genetically enhanced super-brain?*

McCoy watched wide-eyed as the emergency team bombarded the regent with constantly updated information on the developing crisis, every one of her advisors casually displaying unbelievable powers of comprehension and memory. Aghast and amazed, he shook his head in wonder as a young aide, who couldn't have been more than twenty years old, somehow managed to derive meaning from what appeared to McCoy to be a swiftly scrolling screen of incomprehensible, densely packed numerical data. "CO_2 levels rising," the speed-reading prodigy called out, "at roughly .987529 percentage points per second."

"Damn," Clarke murmured in response. The regent sat upon an elevated stool at the northern end of the bunkers, surrounded by aides who rushed to give her all the bad news:

"Increasing traces of H_2SO_4 in the colony's overall air supply. Ventilation and filter systems working at 115.87452 percent and failing. . . ."

"Repairs to primary deflector banks going slower than expected; it seems the damage caused by the explosion was even more extensive than it first appeared. Estimated time for repairs currently unknown, pending further inspection of the debris. . . ."

"Most nonessential personnel, 96.4724 percent, now sequestered in their homes. The rest are en route or unaccounted for. Calls to emergency services increasing exponentially. A psychosocial communications team is currently drafting Executive Addresses for all eventualities, including worst-case scenario. . . ."

"Extensive and continuing tissue damage to the chlorodome. Rate of morbidity: 17.5535 percent and increasing. Catastrophic environmental breach anticipated. . . ."

God help me, McCoy thought, not entirely sure he approved of all this obscenely extreme precision, *it's like being trapped in a bomb shelter with a dozen or so Spocks!*

Clarke herself absorbed the barrage of ill tidings with remarkable calm, allowing only an occasional scowl or sigh to betray her emotional response to the distressing unanimity of the reports. She took no notes and never asked for any information to be repeated, seemingly quite confident in her ability to retain and process all the information being given to her.

Curious, McCoy discreetly scanned the regent with his medical tricorder. To his surprise, he found her blood pressure, heart rate, and endocrine levels remarkably steady; there was little physical indication of the incredible strain she had to be under. He whistled appreciatively, impressed despite his own profound opposition to human genetic engineering.

"Divert more resources to the deflector repair team," she instructed her staff, betraying no trace of hesitation or indecision. "Put out a call for civilian volunteers if you have to." Aides scurried to carry out her directives. "The same goes for dome maintenance, if not more so. Pump more nutrients and growth hormones into the dome. Starve every garden, orchard, and lily pond in the colony if you have to. We can't let that geneforsaken hell out there break through our dome!"

The regent didn't seem to have much faith, McCoy noted, in Captain Kirk's plan to reinforce the colony's shields with the shuttlecraft's deflectors. Another example of the way she consistently underestimated standard-model humans, or was she simply planning for the worst, the way any sensible leader would? *To be fair,* he admitted, *Jim's plan alone isn't going to be enough to save the colony.* One way or another, they needed to protect the living dome from the planet's harsh environment, or else increase its ability to defend itself.

"Wait a second," he murmured as a wild idea occurred to him. Snatching up his Starfleet medical bag, he rushed across the bunker. "Madame Regent," he called out. "Ma'am!"

Clarke looked up from a whispered consultation with Gregor Lozin, her chief security advisor. She looked puzzled by the Starfleet officer's interruption. "Yes, Doctor?"

"Cordrazine," he blurted, clutching the rumpled, black bag against his chest. "Do you have any cordrazine?"

Both Clarke and Lozin gave him blank looks. "Of course not," the doctor rebuked himself, lightly slapping his forehead with his free hand. "It wasn't developed until after your ancestors, the original Paragon colonists, left Earth."

McCoy took a deep breath before diving into his explanation. "Cordrazine is a powerful stimulant, which, coupled with the right anabolic steroids, promotes tissue growth and healing. In theory, a large enough dose of such a compound might be enough to accelerate the dome's own natural recuperative abilities." He hastily checked the contents of his medical bag. "Blast! All I have is about 150 milliliters." He needed a lot more cordrazine than that for a "patient" the size of the dome.

But Clarke seized on his idea eagerly. "If you have a sample, Doctor, that's all we need. We can quickly design an organism to produce the compound you speak of, then use our industrial cloning tanks to reproduce the organism—and the cordrazine—in any quantity you require."

Could this be true? McCoy wondered, mildly horrified at how easy the regent made it sound. He wasn't going to look a gift horse in the mouth, though, even if that horse was the product of scarily proficient genetic engineering. "Here," he stated, deftly preparing a compound that he prayed would do the trick. He handed the loaded hypospray to Clarke, who quickly dispatched a messenger to deliver the sample to the appropriate laboratory, along with an executive order to manufacture as much cordrazine as possible as fast as possible.

But would that be fast enough? McCoy was impressed with the efficiency of the regent's staff, but worried that the embattled dome wouldn't last long enough to get the medicine it so desperately needed. Everything was happening so quickly! . . .

"Regent Clarke!" Stationed in front of a coral monitor, an excited colonist beckoned to her leader. McCoy heard a tinge of hope in the junior staffer's voice. "It's the dome," the young woman explained breathlessly. "The morbidity rate has slowed by nearly 72.0091 percent! The damage has stopped spreading . . . almost."

McCoy laughed out loud, diagnosing at once what—and who—was responsible for the sudden improvement in the dome's prospects. "It's Kirk," he explained to Clarke and the others. "By God, his plan is working. He's actually pulling it off!" *Way to go, Jim,* he thought silently. At times he suspected his friend and captain had more lives than an Andorian wildcat. *You've done it again.*

"For the moment, at least," Gregor Lozin added ominously. Irked by the man's negative tone, McCoy tried to remember that the security chief's paranoia and pessimism had been deliberately built into his DNA, the better to fulfill his designated role within the colony. Not that this made him any more likable.

Still, McCoy admitted, Lozin had a point. A single shuttle's deflectors weren't going to keep Sycorax's merciless environment at bay forever. *What's keeping that cordrazine?* McCoy thought impatiently, even though his precious sample had disappeared only moments ago. *Just how fast were those cloning tanks, anyway?*

"Do you really think we have a chance, Doctor?" Clarke asked him, lowering her voice so as not to damage the morale of her hardworking staff. McCoy was relieved to see that she wasn't completely above relying upon a mere human being in an emergency.

"I've seen cordrazine therapy work wonders with victims of Klingon disruptor blasts," he reassured her. "As far as I know, there's no medical reason why it shouldn't help your homegrown dome as well." *Provided the shuttle's deflectors don't conk out first. . . .* He reached over to rap his knuckles on one of the polished teak panels covering the walls.

"Knock on wood."

Forget Vulcan saunas, Kirk decided, feeling the sweat soak through his once-pristine dress uniform. Right now the shuttlecraft's sweltering cabin felt hotter than a Klingon's temper.

Feverish and dehydrated, he craved a glass of cold water. Instead he kept his sweaty palms wrapped around the throttle of the *Columbus-2* as he battled Sycorax's searing, violent winds to keep the shuttle hovering where it could do the most good. At the same time, he kept one eye on the emerald city below, where a faltering blue beam continued to protect the living dome from the worst the angry planet had to offer.

It was ironic, in a way. Recently, Kirk had been researching the infamous Eugenics Wars of Earth's late twentieth century, the better to understand the promises and potential pitfalls of human genetic engineering. Back then, he recalled, humanity had nearly been destroyed by the likes of Khan Noonien Singh and his megalomaniacal siblings. Now, nearly three centuries later, here were he and Lerner, two

standard-model humans, risking their lives to save another batch of allegedly superhuman men and
women.

But what else am I supposed to do? Kirk thought. Genetically enhanced or not, those were people down
there in that dome. *I need to rescue them now—and
worry about what they mean to the Federation later.*

Steel bulkheads creaked alarmingly, fighting a losing battle against the colossal pressure outside. Kirk
heard Lerner gulp dryly, and wished he hadn't had to
drag the lieutenant along on what was starting to
look (and sound) like a suicide mission. At least the
Enterprise was safely in Spock's hands. . . .

"Captain! Look!" Lerner croaked hoarsely. "The
dome!"

Lifting his gaze from the navigational controls,
Kirk saw what the security officer was reacting to. A
kilometer below, the injured region of the dome suddenly began to repair itself. Fresh green tissue billowed outward, displacing charred and blackened cellulose. The depression, where the toxic atmosphere
had almost burst through the dome's protective skin,
now filled up with moist and shining new life, bright
chlorophyll-green. Miraculously, the huge biological
organism appeared to have received some sort of re-
juvenating boost—and none too soon.

Intuitively, he knew that Dr. McCoy was responsible. *Good work, Bones,* Kirk thought, a smile upon his
parched and cracking lips. *That's what I call a house call!*

He shared a grin with Lerner, which ended abruptly
when the portside wall of the cabin crumpled inwardly,
forming a wedge-shaped protrusion into the passenger
area. Twisted duranium shrieked in protest, and the en-

tire shuttle lurched sideways, throwing the two men hard to the left, so that only their safety straps kept them from tumbling out of their seats. Bright red warning lights flashed all over Kirk's control panel, reporting damage, both major and minor, to nearly every system.

"Attention!" a strident computerized voice announced. "Hull integrity compromised! Repeat, hull integrity compromised."

Tell me something I don't know, Kirk thought in exasperation, silencing the annoying voice with the flick of a switch. He hauled himself back into an upright seated position and wrestled with the throttle until the shuttle tilted back into what felt like a level orientation. Just as he succeeded at righting the craft, however, another red light flared to life before his eyes. Kirk's stomach turned over queasily as up and down realigned themselves by about forty degrees. *Well, there went the artificial gravity,* he realized.

Switching gravities was the least of his problems. He caught a sulfurous whiff in the air, and looked back over his shoulder to see a thin tendril of brownish-yellow vapor creeping into the cabin through an infinitesimal crack in a rear upper corner of the passenger area. A burning sensation rapidly developed in his nostrils and throat.

At least we don't have to worry about explosive decompression, he thought with a touch of gallows humor. The pressure outside was so intense that the shuttle's atmosphere couldn't escape if Kirk wanted it to; the problem was keeping Sycorax's unforgiving climate from crushing the shuttle like an eggshell.

"Captain!" Lerner yanked his hands back from the deflector controls as a fountain of white-hot sparks erupted from the panel. Through the forward window, made of reinforced transparent aluminum, Kirk saw the shuttle's diverted deflector beam flicker weakly before evaporating completely. "We've lost the deflectors," Lerner reported, choking on the caustic fumes contaminating the air. "They're—gone, sir!"

"Acknowledged," Kirk coughed back. With luck, he hoped, maybe they're not needed anymore. He stared at the freshly healed area upon the dome, now roughly the shape of Jupiter's famous spot and glistening with renewed strength and resilience. For the time being, the dome seemed capable of defending itself; he could only pray that its growth spurt would last until the colonists got their all-important force field working at full capacity again.

He and Lerner were in the most danger now; unfortunately, there were no longer any deflectors to divert back to the shuttle. "Prepare for emergency beam-out," he ordered Lerner, shouting to be heard over the sound of warping metal. A tube ruptured within the shuttle's ceiling, spraying vaporized coolant into the cabin, further polluting the increasingly unbreathable air.

"Warning!" the computer wailed again, the extreme conditions overriding the captain's previous attempt to mute its Cassandra-like prophecies of doom. "Hull integrity failing. Ten seconds to total structural collapse."

If we don't move quickly, Kirk realized, *then our remains are going to end up compacted together in a very small duranium urn.*

"Coordinates?" Lerner asked, batting away smoke and sparks to get at the transporter controls.

Kirk's gaze stayed fixed on the fresh, verdant spot in the dome below them. With the *Enterprise* still shielded against a possible Klingon attack, there was only one escape route available to them: the one part of the dome still unprotected by a force field. "Straight ahead," he ordered Lerner. "Right through that big green doorway."

This should work, he thought, *provided the colonists don't repair the shield in the next ten seconds.* And as long as the shuttle's transporters were working better than the gravity or the deflectors.

"Five seconds to structural collapse," the computer informed them helpfully.

"Locking on," Lerner reported. "Transporting . . . now!"

As the familiar static tingle of the transporter beams swept over him, Kirk considered the weak spot in the colony's force field; in a way it was not unlike another dangerous wound in a planet's defenses: the gaping hole in Earth's ozone layer that Khan Noonien Singh first discovered back in the 1980s.

The hole Khan later turned to his own advantage. . . .

CHAPTER ONE

ONE HUNDRED AND SEVENTY FEET ABOVE THE CON-
crete launch pad, Roberta Lincoln crawled out onto
one of the horizontal swing arms of the towering
rocket gantry. A small green gecko scurried out of her
way as the fortyish American woman clambered on
her hands and knees across the steel bridge toward
her target: an Ariane rocket primed for takeoff.

*The more things change, the more they really do stay the
same,* Roberta thought wryly. Twenty-five years ago,
her longtime friend and supervisor, Gary Seven, had
crept across a similar elevated platform to sabotage
another rocket launch. His mission then had been to
prevent a weapon of mass destruction from being
launched into orbit, initiating a full-scale outer space
arms race. A quarter century later, Roberta's agenda

was pretty much the same. *The only difference is that this time I'm the one performing without a net.*

Just to play it safe, however, she clipped one end of a safety cord to the metal grating beneath her, keeping the other end securely attached to her belt. A cool, dry wind rustled her honey-blond hair as she came within reach of the powerful European booster rocket, designed to place commercial satellites in orbit high above the Earth. Roberta briefly wondered what kind of bribes and/or extortion Khan had employed to get his hands on the Ariane, let alone transport it to this remote launch site in the South Pacific, previously occupied by the French government's now-defunct nuclear testing program.

From her lofty perch upon the gantry, Roberta could look out over the entire atoll: a circular ring of greenery surrounding a large moonlit lagoon. Leafy palm trees and mangroves covered much of the island, although she could also spot the lights of the Mission Control center, nestled amidst the lush tropical flora.

"Let's just hope they don't spot me," she whispered to herself, acutely aware that her green camouflage shorts and tank top, which had blended perfectly with the tropical shrubbery on her way here, now clashed alarmingly with the industrial-red paint job on the rocket gantry. According to their most recent intel, Khan himself intended to be present for this launch, and Roberta sincerely hoped to get in and out of Muroroa without actually running into the man himself.

The last thing I need right now is a reunion with that smug, so-called superman, she thought. She and Seven had their hands full these days, coping with the crisis in Bosnia, not to mention all the other international mischief stirred up by Khan and his genetically engineered siblings. In their eagerness to assert their self-proclaimed destinies as rulers of the Earth, the Children of Chrysalis, as Roberta still thought of them, had sparked civil wars and unrest all over the globe, in Eastern Europe, Liberia, Somalia, Peru, and elsewhere. This had not made her and Seven's primary mission—preventing World War III—any easier. *And to think that, after the Cold War ended, I had briefly thought that Seven and I could retire!* If anything, their job had gotten even more complicated since the Berlin Wall came down.

And now Khan had to up the ante with this stunt! Roberta scowled and glanced toward the horizon, glimpsing a faint rosy tint where the night sky met the Pacific. The Ariane was scheduled to launch at dawn, so Roberta knew she had to act soon; the sun rose very quickly this close to the equator.

Her all-purpose servo device, cunningly disguised as a silver fountain pen, projected a beam of white light onto the outer casing of the Ariane's main rocket, which was flanked by two solid-fuel boosters, intended to provide the initial thrust upon lift-off. According to the diagrams she'd memorized earlier, the rocket's primary guidance system was just behind the metal panel directly in front of her, bearing the snazzy blue logo of Arianespace, the French manufacturer of the rocket. Roberta's plan was to tweak the controls so that the rocket would self-destruct harmlessly in the upper atmosphere, taking its insidious cargo with it. With any luck, Khan's latest scheme would be over before it even began.

That was the plan, at least. Trying hard not to think about the twenty-five tons of liquid hydrogen stored beneath her, just waiting to be ignited, she switched the servo to laser mode and began cutting a hole in the side of the rocket with what she hoped was surgical precision. The ruby-red beam traced a charred black line around the company logo, quickly forming a complete loop. Roberta gave the melted metal a few minutes to cool, then carefully lifted the newly created circular segment away from the rest of the rocket, revealing the intricate circuitry beneath.

Pretty smooth, she congratulated herself. A few deft moves and—*voilà*—Khan's high-tech hardware was more exposed than Sharon Stone. Grinning triumphantly, she cautiously laid the displaced metal disk aside, making sure it wouldn't topple off the edge of the gantry, and turned her servo back into a flashlight. She gripped the slender silver instrument between her teeth, to keep the incandescent beam focused in front of her, then reached carefully into the electronic innards of the Ariane satellite launcher.

A high-voltage jolt caused her entire body to stiffen in shock. A moment before she lost consciousness, she thanked heaven for the safety cord binding her to the steel platform. At least she wasn't going to fall to her death! . . .

"She's waking up, Your Excellency," a gruff male voice intoned, penetrating the fog receding from her brain. Roberta struggled to lift her eyelids, half-surprised to find herself alive and not electrocuted.

She suspected the good news ended there.

"Thank you, Joaquin," a familiar voice replied, confirming Roberta's worst expectations. *Oh no!* she thought, genuine apprehension sending a chill through her recently dormant body. As far as she could tell she seemed to be lying sideways on some sort of couch or cushion. *Not him!*

Blinking, she opened her eyes to see a tall Indian man looking down at her with an amused expression on his strong, handsome features. Piercing brown eyes inspected her as they might an exotic animal securely caged in a zoo; that is, with total confidence and an unchallenged sense of superiority. He was clean-shaven, with thick black hair tied neatly behind his head, and wore a spotless white Nehru jacket with matching cotton slacks. "Ah, Ms. Lincoln," he greeted her with a mocking pretense of warmth. "How good of you to rejoin us!"

"Hello, Khan," she said icily. Raising herself to a seated position, she tried to stand up, but found her legs still a little too wobbly. A quick glance around revealed that she was in a luxuriously appointed office decorated with traditional Polynesian art. An original Gauguin hung on one wall, while an authentic Melanesian wood carving of a cruising shark sat atop an executive-size desk. A colorful mat, woven from dyed pandanus fibers, carpeted the floor. Roberta did her best to meet Khan's gaze defiantly, despite a profusion of tropical butterflies in her stomach. "Long time, no smirk."

Looming a few feet behind Khan, a large, muscular brute with a sullen expression and light-brown hair glowered at Roberta. A plain black T-shirt was stretched tautly over a Schwarzenegger-size torso, above a pair of simple gray slacks. Compared to Khan's crisp, snow-white suit, the scowling bruiser's attire was dull and unremarkable, except for a large brass belt buckle that bore the visage of a snarling grizzly bear. "You will address His Excellency with more respect!" he warned her balefully, raising a meaty hand as he stepped toward her ominously. She flinched in anticipation of the blow, which would no doubt carry the full force of genetically augmented bones and sinews.

But Khan shook his head, dismissing his hench-man's concerns with an airy gesture. "No need to stand on formality," he insisted. "Ms. Lincoln and I are old friends." He smiled coldly at her. "Isn't that so?"

In a manner of speaking, Roberta admitted silently. She had first met Khan Noonien Singh eighteen years ago, in a vast underground laboratory hidden beneath the scorched sands of India's desolate Great Thar Desert. Khan had only been four years old then, one of hundreds of genetically engineered children pro-duced by the top-secret Chrysalis Project, but he had already possessed the confidence and charisma of a born (or, in his case, manufactured) leader. Even after she and Gary Seven had shut down the Chrysalis Pro-ject, they had kept careful track of Khan and the other superkids, now scattered throughout the world.

Impressed by Khan's obvious brilliance and poten-tial for good, Seven had even made a determined ef-fort to recruit the teenage Khan into their own covert peacekeeping operation, but that bright idea had backfired spectacularly; in the end, Khan proved too ambitious to keep under control, and he had turned against her and Seven, stealing all their information on the Chrysalis Kids in the process. That was three years ago, and Khan had already rounded up several dozen of his supersmart and superstrong siblings, including Joaquin here, and enlisted them in his grandiose campaign to "save" the world by placing it under his complete and total control. Unfortunately, Roberta had the sneaking suspicion that Khan was just warming up. . . .

"What's up with the close shave?" she asked him glibly, stalling for time while she recovered from her shock-induced trip to dreamland. "The last time I saw you, back in eighty-nine, you were sporting a respectable-looking beard. I thought that was mandatory for all male Sikhs?"

Khan nodded, smiling appreciatively. "Very good, Ms. Lincoln. I applaud your cross-cultural erudition." He thoughtfully stroked his smooth and stubble-free chin. "With all due respect to my heroic Sikh ancestors, however, I eventually came to the conclusion that I should not be bound by the traditions of the past. I am a new breed of human being, after all. A new and superior kind of warrior. Thus, on my twenty-first birthday, I shaved off my beard, in recognition of the revolutionary turning point that I, and the others like me, represent in the history of human evolution. Henceforth, I resolved, I would make my own traditions, chart a new path for mankind."

"I see you're still as humble as ever," Roberta observed dryly. As discreetly as possible, she searched her pockets for her servo, but the versatile device eluded her fingers. Had she dropped it back on the gantry, or had Khan and his people confiscated it? "Frankly, I always kind of hoped that your delusions of grandeur were just a phase you were going through, something you'd outgrow eventually." She stopped fishing for the servo and started looking for an escape route; from what she could see, the office had only a single exit. "I guess that was wishful thinking."

Khan scowled, his bogus bonhomie slipping. "Hardly delusions, Ms. Lincoln," he said curtly. "Or have you forgotten how easily I have eluded you and the enigmatic Mr. Seven these past few years, despite the considerable resources at your command?"

True enough, Roberta conceded. Using data stolen from Seven's advanced Beta 5 computer, Khan had even found a way to protect his strongholds against transporter technology, forcing her and Seven to use far more primitive techniques in their periodic attempts to infiltrate Khan's hideouts and headquarters. Just to reach Muroroa, in fact, Roberta had needed to teleport to another island, several miles south of this one, then brave the treacherous currents and coral reefs in an outrigger canoe until she came close enough to the forbidden atoll to jump overboard and scuba-dive the rest of the way, dodging sharks, moray eels, and poisonous jellyfish as she swam to shore not far from the rocket launch pad. A damp wet suit, along with a set of oxygen tanks, were presumably still hidden amidst the sword-shaped leaves of the bushes at the edge of the shore. Sadly, the scuba gear was too far away to do her much good at the moment. *Some South Seas vacation this is turning out to be,* she thought sarcastically.

"Maybe we've been keeping our eyes on you all along," she challenged Khan, then wondered if she had said too much. What if Khan demanded to know the name of her chief informant? "Imagine our disappointment when we found out what you were up to here. Even Seven never thought you'd go this far. . . ."

Khan's face hardened. "Seven has always lacked vision," he said scornfully. "That is why he is content to skulk in the margins of history, when he possesses the means to do so much more. And why I broke with him years ago. The problems of the world require bold, decisive action, not timid, cautious half-measures of the sort you and Seven specialize in."

Roberta didn't back down. "We put out fires. You start them. That's a big difference, as far as I am concerned."

"Fire can be a transforming force, Ms. Lincoln," he stated, "clearing away the rotting debris of the past and making room for new growth." He lifted the carved wooden shark from his desk, crushed it to splinters within his fist, then wiped the dusty residue from his palms. "But enough philosophical debate. Your presence raises crucial questions: Where exactly is Gary Seven at this moment? Can we anticipate his arrival as well, in an attempt to rescue you, or perhaps complete your mission?"

I wish, Roberta thought. In fact, Seven was currently attending a key environmental summit in Rio, while recovering from injuries sustained during the fall of Kabul a few months back. Despite his own superhuman physique, the result of years of selective breeding on a planet light-years away, Seven was in no shape to stage a commando raid on the secluded and well-protected island.

"For someone with a superior brain," she told

Khan, "your math needs work. Seven is in his sixties now; he lets me handle all the house calls."

This was a slight exaggeration, but close enough to the truth that she hoped Khan would buy it. Over the years, she had indeed taken over more and more of the field work, leaving Seven to concentrate on the big picture. *One of these days, we really do need to bring in a new junior operative,* she mused. *Heaven knows I could use some backup right now.*

"So Seven is finally feeling his years, is he?" Khan's voice assumed a magnanimous tone, leading Roberta to suspect that he had taken her protestations at face value. "In a way, this saddens me. In his own fashion, he was a worthy adversary."

A buzzer sounded behind Khan and he strode across the spacious office to answer the intercom on the desk. "Khan here," he declared crisply. "What is our status?"

"We're about ten minutes from launching, sir," a disembodied voice spoke from the intercom. Roberta thought she detected a trace of a Scottish accent, along with the distinctly deferential tone. Her heart sank at the implications of the announcement. She hadn't prevented the launch at all; the Ariane was still ready to deliver its obscene payload into orbit. *I've failed,* she realized.

"Excellent," Khan pronounced, switching off the intercom without waiting for a reply. "I'm happy to say, Ms. Lincoln, that your feeble attempt at sabotage cost us merely half an hour, not nearly enough time to cause us to miss our launch window." Stepping away from the desk, he stared down at her like an adult scolding a wayward child. "You should have remembered that you were dealing with an intelligence deliberately engineered to exceed your own; anticipating sabotage, I had the foresight to install a failsafe advice into the Ariane's guidance systems against any such interference." He smiled condescendingly, pleased by his own remarkable foresight. "My apologies if my countermeasures came as something of, well, a shock to your system."

Very funny, Roberta thought acidly. "Well, as surprises go, it wasn't exactly up there with *The Crying Game.*" She'd be damned if she was going to feed Khan's already gargantuan ego. "But, yeah, I suppose it caught me a little off guard."

Too bad my informant failed to mention Khan's sneaky little safety precaution, she lamented. *Guess that was one secret Khan was keeping under even tighter wraps than usual.* . . .

"Your spirit is admirable," he acknowledged, annoyingly unshaken by Roberta's faint praise, "even if your accomplishments are not." He marched toward the office's only exit. "Bring her," he instructed Joaquin, who grabbed her roughly by the arm and yanked her to her feet. His bruising grip reminded her of Carlos, the hulking guardian of the old Chrysalis Project—and one of the project's earliest genetic experiments. She wondered if Joaquin's muscles had been souped-up with gorilla DNA, too.

Following Khan, Joaquin dragged her out the door. A short flight of steps later, they arrived on the roof of the Mission Control building. The sun was newly risen, Roberta noted, providing her with a panoramic view of the picturesque island and its enclosed lagoon. Rising high above the swaying palm trees, on the opposite side of the tranquil blue waters, the Ariane and its attached launch tower looked incongruous amidst the idyllic South Seas scenery. Observing her gaze, Khan threw out his arms expansively. His pristine white suit reflected the bright morning sunshine. "Welcome, Ms. Lincoln, to Chrysalis Island!"

Roberta refused to concede even the loveliness of the setting. "I thought the whole place belonged to the French," she retorted.

As a matter of fact, as she well knew, the French government had established the Centre d'Experimentation du Pacifique (CEP) on Muroroa back in 1963, as a testing site for atomic weapons, many of which had been exploded underground in artificial caverns carved out of the island's basalt core. Less than three months ago, however, France had suspended its nuclear testing program indefinitely, much to the relief of most of the world. Little did that world know, Roberta mused, that Muroroa was now playing host to something just as nasty—and possibly even more dangerous—than underground nuclear explosions.

And she didn't just mean Khan.

"Our Gallic friends were under enormous international pressure to close this facility," he explained. Roberta recalled seeing news footage of anti-nuke protests on Fiji and the other islands. "Thus, I managed to 'persuade' certain French authorities to let me take it off their hands—discreetly, of course." Roberta could just imagine what kind of "persuasion" Khan had employed. Extortion? Blackmail? Assassination? *It wouldn't be the first time,* she thought; although she and Seven never uncovered definitive proof of Khan's involvement, they had their suspicions regarding a number of recent tragic events, such as the explosive death of that big-name Indian politician last spring.

"Indeed," Khan continued, "this entire complex is perfectly suited to my needs, being equipped with its own electrical generators, desalination plant, airfield, communications center, and so forth, while its location near the equator makes it an ideal site for launching satellites into orbit." He looked out over the sprawling compound, which was guarded on all sides by a high, fully electrified fence. "We have, of course, made key renovations, improving on what the French left behind."

"I can't wait for the guided tour," Roberta said, not entirely sarcastic. With any luck, she would get a chance to scope out Khan's new real estate, before or after she attempted to escape.

A small cluster of people had gathered atop the roof to witness the launch of the rocket. Loudspeakers mounted at the rear of the roof provided a countdown toward the rapidly approaching lift-off: "Launch minus two minutes." Khan toyed with his wristwatch, synchronizing it with the countdown, before strolling across the whitewashed rooftop to join the others. He gestured for Joaquin to bring Roberta along.

"Okay, okay, I'm coming!" she muttered irritably as the thuggish henchman hustled her across the rooftop. Looking away from the distant gantry, Khan's associates eyed her with varying degrees of curiosity, seemingly none too concerned by her status as an unwilling captive.

"Launch minus one minute, thirty seconds."

Khan ignored Roberta's protests as well. "Permit me to introduce a few of the brilliant minds that I have assembled, at great effort and expense, on this island. This is Dr. Liam MacPherson," he began, indicating a lanky, red-haired man in a white lab jacket, "a superlative astrophysicist and the head of launch operations. Doctor, meet Ms. Roberta Lincoln, an uninvited guest at today's event."

MacPherson gave Roberta a cursory examination before turning his attention back to the prepped and pregnant rocket on the launch pad. A compact headset kept him in touch with Mission Control and he stroked his beard, a tuft of coppery bristles, absent-mindedly as he whispered instructions into his mike. Roberta didn't take the snub personally, figuring that MacPherson was naturally preoccupied with the Ariane's imminent departure. "Pleased to meet you, sort of," Roberta murmured, even though the carrot-topped astrophysicist was clearly not listening. "Let's do this again sometime."

"And this," Khan continued, moving onto an exotically beautiful woman strikingly clad in a silk indigo sarong and matching top, "is the most exquisite Ament, one of my wisest and most trusted advisors." Gleaming black pearls, native to the Tuamoto Islands, shimmered upon her earlobes, the nacreous beads as dark and lustrous as her shoulder-length black hair. Cool, amber eyes looked Roberta over silently, conveying an air of haughty amusement. Her lithe, languid body seemed both youthful and timeless.

Roberta disliked her on principle. "Nice pearls," she stated flatly, figuring that if you can't say something nice about a person, you can always compliment their jewelry.

"Thank you," Ament said coolly. Her low, husky voice had a faintly Arabic accent. "They were a gift from Khan."

He nodded, his hands clasped behind his back. "I wrested them myself from the giant black-lipped oysters found only in these islands. Did you know, Ms. Lincoln," he expounded, "that a Polynesian pearl diver can descend up to forty meters in search of treasure? A remarkable feat, for an ordinary human, although, of course, easily within my own abilities."

"Everybody needs a hobby," Roberta said dryly. *A little more pearl diving, a little less geopolitical powermongering,* she reflected, *and the whole world would be a happier place.*

"More like an invigorating diversion," Khan stated by way of clarification. He walked to the edge of the rooftop, the better to observe the rocket on its launch pad. "Not that today requires any stimulation beyond what we are about to witness."

"Launch minus sixty seconds," the loudspeaker announced, calling an end to the introductions. A hush of anticipation fell over the small grouping on the roof. On the launch pad across the turquoise lagoon, the massive metal structure of the gantry retreated from the Ariane, leaving the slender rocket alone upon the launch, pointed up at the sky like a gigantic blue-and-white hypodermic. *An appropriate image,* Roberta thought, given the high-tech poison carried in its payload.

"Launch minus forty-five seconds." Plumes of white steam billowed from the base of the Ariane as its twin booster rockets fired. A deafening roar assaulted Roberta's eardrums, like a dozen jumbo jets taking off at once, and she fought an urge to clamp her hands over her ears, unwilling to show any weakness in front of Khan and his fellow *Übermenschen*. Instead, she crossed her fingers, hoping in vain that something would still go wrong with the launch, that the Ariane would blow up on the launch pad. *I'm sorry, Gary.* She was barely able to hear her own thoughts over the volcanic fury of the unleashed engines, which were straining mightily at the bolts still holding the rocket to the concrete pad. *I tried to stop him.*

"Launch minus thirty seconds." The roar increased as the Ariane's main engines kicked in. Twenty-five tons of liquid hydrogen ignited, sending a rush of superheated gases through the engine nozzles, propelling the massive spacecraft against the pull of gravity.

"Look, Ms. Lincoln!" Khan shouted in her ear, striving to be heard even over the thunderous din. Roberta tried to pull away from him, but Joaquin's heavy hands clamped down on her shoulders, holding her in place. "How fortunate you recovered just in time to behold my greatest triumph to date!"

Lucky me, she thought, unable to look away from the fiery spectacle.

"Launch minus one second . . ." The towering rocket rose from the launch pad, borne aloft by a blazing pillar of fire. Gigantic clouds of steam, produced by the explosive union of the Ariane's red-hot exhaust with a flood of cooling water released in conjunction with the blast-off, swelled outward, hiding the launch site behind a churning, turbulent curtain of vapor. "Lift-off!" the loudspeaker exulted. "We have lift-off!"

Almost against her will, Roberta tipped her head back to follow the rocket's meteoric ascent. She held her breath, still praying that, somehow, someway, the Ariane, along with its malignant cargo, would go the way of the Challenger, spiraling out of control to a catastrophic end. *Please,* she prayed, *let Khan's diabolical plan blow up in his face!*

But nothing of the sort occurred. The lift-off was flawless, with the Ariane's upward trajectory achieving escape velocity within less than a minute. As the rocket disappeared from sight, leaving only a snow-white trail of vapor behind, Liam MacPherson breathed a sigh of relief. Beneath his lab coat, his shoulders slumped as the weight of his worries evaporated in the cool trade winds. Ament led the rest of the onlookers, excepting Roberta, in a round of polite applause.

Khan's flawless profile remained turned to the sky, toward the apex of the vapor trail. Roberta wondered if the Indian prodigy's superior vision had allowed him to follow the rocket's soaring climb longer than she had. "Ah, Lucifer, child of the morning," he declaimed proudly, twisting the Old Testament to his own vainglorious purposes. "How thou art risen!" Lowering his gaze at last, he savored Roberta's crestfallen expression, his dark mahogany eyes gleaming in triumph. "I trust, Ms. Lincoln, that you appreciate the full purpose and potential of my Morning Star, my bringer of light?"

More than I'd like to, Roberta thought unhappily,

knowing that her job had just gotten a lot more difficult. "You stole the technology from us, remember?"
Her voice hardened at the memory. "The day you
raided our office and murdered our computer?"

Images of a younger Khan firing a hail of bullets
into the good old Beta 5 flashed before her mind's
eye. She could still hear the gunshots. . . .

"Technology," he reminded her, holding up a finger
in correction, "that Seven and I personally acquired
from the ageless Dr. Evergreen, and not without considerable effort and hardship. I am as much entitled
to the fruits of that enterprise as your unbearably
self-righteous superior."

Roberta knew what Khan was referring to, even
though she had not taken part in those events. It had
been that ill-fated mission, back in the winter of
1984, that had finally convinced Gary Seven that the
precocious Sikh youth was too reckless (and ruthless)
to be trusted. *Just like his mother,* she thought, recalling the late Dr. Sarina Kaur, founder and driving
force of the Chrysalis Project. Kaur had been utterly
ruthless, too, and fanatical enough to choose death
rather than abandon Chrysalis, which had ultimately
been consumed by a fierce thermonuclear conflagration beneath the deserts of Rajasthan. Roberta
couldn't help wondering if Khan had ever figured out
that she and Seven had been indirectly responsible
for his mother's tragic demise. *Probably not a good time
to bring that up,* she decided.

"Excuse me, sir," MacPherson broke in, "but the
rocket has achieved a low polar orbit. We're ready to
deploy the satellite." He tugged on his beard nervously.
"Perhaps you'd care to join me in Mission Control?"

Khan must be a tough boss, Roberta guessed from the scientist's apprehensive manner. *Even for another superman.* She'd recognized MacPherson's name, of course, from Seven's database on the Chrysalis children. She pretty much knew the entire list by heart.

Khan scowled momentarily, unhappy to be interrupted while fencing verbally with Roberta. Larger aims took precedence, however, and he nodded curtly. "Of course, Doctor, I will be with you shortly." He gave Roberta a parting bow. "We will have to continue our reunion later, Ms. Lincoln. The Bard once wrote that, 'Unbidden guests are often welcomest when they are gone,' but in your case I'm inclined to enjoy your company a while longer." He reached into the pocket of his immaculately pressed white slacks and retrieved a familiar silver instrument.

My servo! Roberta thought, dismayed to see the device in Khan's possession.

"I look forward to chatting with you," he stated, "about the many singular technologies at your superior's disposal; in particular, your miraculous means of teleportation." He deftly rolled the servo between his fingers and across the back of his hand. "I confess that, while I have developed ways to block your ingenious matter-transmission beams, I have not yet succeeded in duplicating them." After tantalizing Roberta with its proximity, he returned the captured servo to his pocket. "Perhaps, with your assistance, I can remedy the situation."

Not if I can help it, Roberta thought fervently. She could barely imagine a worse scenario than Khan Noonien Singh adding teleportation to his arsenal. "You've got the wrong girl," she insisted. "I have no idea how the darn thing works. As far as I'm concerned, it's magic."

This wasn't entirely true; after nearly a quarter-century of broadcasting her atoms around the planet (and elsewhere), she'd learned her way around a transporter coil or two. There was no reason Khan needed to know that, though. With luck, a little old-fashioned sexism would add a veneer of plausibility to her protests. Girls never look under the hood, right?

Khan did not challenge her proclamations of ignorance, but his menacing tone made it clear that she was hardly off the hook. "Perhaps, then, your superior, the ever-manipulative Mr. Seven, will be willing to share his secrets—in exchange for your continued good health."

Stepping away from Roberta, apparently content to let his implied threat linger in her mind, Khan addressed Joaquin: "Put her in one of the holding cells on Level M-2. I will interrogate her later, at my leisure."

Yippee, Roberta thought acidly. *I can hardly wait.*

"But, Your Excellency!" Joaquin blurted, looking chagrined at the prospect of leaving Khan unguarded. His basso profundo voice emanated from somewhere deep within his cavernous chest. The bear's-head belt buckle snarled silently. "Your safety . . ."

"Will not be endangered by your brief absence," Khan assured him. He laid a fraternal hand on the bodyguard's broad shoulder. "My friend, while I appreciate your devotion to duty, I am quite capable of defending myself, especially on my own island." He released Joaquin's shoulder and turned to follow MacPherson. "Go. You shall find me in Mission Control, overseeing the next stage of today's historic accomplishment."

Placated, Khan's looming flunky grunted in assent and took hold of Roberta's arm. "Hey, watch the grip!" she yelped, unable to resist being pulled toward the stairs. "I've still got bruises from the last time you manhandled me!"

Despite her loud objections, plus a great deal of squirming, Roberta paid close attention to her surroundings as Joaquin forcibly escorted her down several flights of stairs, into the lower regions of the former atomic test base. Sealed white doors, labeled in French, hid much from her view, but she took what mental notes she could on the facility's layout and capacities. *A little extra reconnaissance could make all the difference later on,* she reminded herself.

In particular, she kept her eyes peeled for any sign of biological research. According to their best informant, Khan intended to use Muroroa as more than a launch site for his incipient space program; he was also reputedly converting much of the complex into a laboratory capable of advanced biogenetic experimentation. Seven feared that Khan was deliberately trying to re-create the Chrysalis Project in order to duplicate his mother's success at human genetic engineering.

Just what we need, Roberta thought tartly. *A second generation of Chrysalis kids. Like the first batch hasn't been trouble enough....*

Seven's fears, not to mention hers, seemed confirmed when, precisely four floors beneath the sunlit rooftop, they passed what looked like a sturdy metal airlock, bearing the universal symbol for biohazardous material.

GENETIC TESTING AND DEVELOPMENT, read the heavy block letters on the airlock's exterior, printed in both English and Punjabi. AUTHORIZED PERSONNEL ONLY.

Clearly, the signs had been posted after the French cleared out. Roberta couldn't help wondering, and worrying, what sort of genes were being developed on the other side of the sealed metal door. *Nothing warm and fuzzy, I bet.*

The sudden *whoosh* of air escaping from the doorway announced that someone was preparing to exit the bio-lab. Stalling in order to see who it might be, Roberta deliberately tripped over her own feet. "Oops!" she declared, throwing out her free arm in hopes of breaking her fall, but Joaquin halted her clumsy descent by yanking hard on her other arm, nearly dislocating her shoulder. Unlike her stumble, the resulting cry of pain was totally sincere and spontaneous.

"Up," he grunted, easily pulling her back onto her feet with just one hand. Roberta felt like a side of beef hanging on a grumpy, unfeeling meat hook.

"I'm sorry," she stammered, milking the moment for all it was worth. "I guess I'm still a little woozy from that high-voltage hello your boss arranged for me."

A few feet away, the airlock door swung open, disgorging a statuesque Indian woman in a stained white lab coat. Clearly surprised by what she saw, the woman stared at Joaquin and his blond-haired captive with a baffled look on her face. She protectively clutched a three-inch floppy disk to her chest. "What is this?" she murmured. "Who—?"

"An intruder," Joaquin explained gruffly, while Roberta compared the woman's well-made features to the photos in her own memory. Their eyes briefly met, and a shudder ran through Roberta as she saw the horizontal black lines bisecting both of the woman's dark eyes. The inky streaks across her corneas were, Roberta knew, twin legacies of the disastrous chemical disaster in Bhopal, India, many years ago, created when the other woman had squinted to see her way through the clouds of poisonous gas. Seven and Khan were both at Bhopal, Roberta recalled, although they had managed to avoid being scarred in this manner. Numerous survivors, however, had been permanently marked, including one of the Chrysalis children.

There could be no doubt: This was Dr. Phoolan Dhasal, a Nobel Prize-winning biochemist, who, like Khan, was also a product of Sarina Kaur's illicit experiments back in the seventies. Roberta was familiar with Dhasal's work, having once forced herself to wade through the precocious Ph.D.'s groundbreaking paper on the introduction of transgenic exons during late-stage RNA processing. Dhasal had also been one of the youngest contributors to the Human Genome Project, before mysteriously disappearing several months ago; her presence on Muroroa provided the final proof that Khan was up to hard-core genetic hanky-panky here in the South Seas. *I need to report this to Seven, pronto.*

Joaquin did not prolong their chance encounter with Dhasal. Within moments, they had left the entrance to the bio-lab behind, descending even farther into the bowels of Khan's new outpost. By Roberta's calculations, they were well beneath the island's surface, in some sort of sub-sub-basement, far from waving palms and fragrant trade winds.

They finally stopped in front of a door marked DE-TENTION. Joaquin placed his sizable palm against a sensor plate mounted beside the door. A thick steel door slid open with a *whoosh* and they entered a stark white hallway lined on both sides with detention cells, perfect for confining, say, any pushy anti-nuke demonstrators who might have sneaked onto the island during the good old days of atomic testing. *Nice of the French to leave these for Khan,* she thought somewhat less than sincerely.

Bulletproof plastic doors, four inches thick and reinforced with thick metal struts, barred the entrance of each cell. Joaquin tugged open the door of the nearest cell and unceremoniously thrust Roberta inside. "Stay," he ordered redundantly before locking the door back into place. To Roberta's relief, he did not stay to keep her company, but quickly departed, no doubt anxious to resume his post watching over Khan. *Thank my lucky stars,* she thought.

Rubbing her injured shoulder, she took a minute to inspect the latest stop on her Pacific excursion. The accommodations were spartan—a stool, a cot, a toilet—but clean and comfortable as jail cells go. Frankly, she'd been imprisoned in worse places during her two decades-plus as an alien-sponsored secret agent babe. The first Chrysalis, she recalled, had not been equipped with detention facilities at all, so she and Seven had ended up locked in straw-carpeted cages with a menagerie of test animals. This, by contrast, was a definite step up.

Not that she intended to stay all that long. Pressing her face against the transparent plastic door, she checked out the scene beyond her cell. As far as she could tell, she was currently the only prisoner. (But not the first; to her amusement, she noticed a Greenpeace logo carved into the seat of the wooden stool.) There were no flesh-and-blood guards in sight, either, only security cameras mounted opposite every cell door, where no prisoner could reach them. "Hello! Anybody there?"

No answer. *Welcome to solitary confinement,* she thought.

Roberta languished in the cell for half an hour or so. Time enough, she lamented, for MacPherson and his staff to place Khan's so-called Morning Star into a low polar orbit, where it could do the most harm. "No use crying over launched satellites," she muttered, trying to maintain a positive attitude. *Gary and I will just have to keep Khan from ever activating the damn thing, one way or another.*

Only because she was listening for them did Roberta hear the stealthy footprints in the corridor outside her cell. A low hum stirred the air and the unblinking red lights atop the security cameras went dead. Moments later, a solitary figure appeared on the other side of the thick plastic door.

"About time you got here," Roberta said.

CHAPTER TWO

PALACE OF THE GREAT KHAN
CHANDIGARH
THE PUNJAB, INDIA
JULY 10, 1992

"THEY ARE READY FOR YOU, YOUR EXCELLENCY."

Khan checked his reflection in the full-length mirror adorning his private dressing room. Eschewing false modesty, he was pleased by what he saw: a virile and commanding figure, fit of body and proud in demeanor. An expertly wrapped white turban sat atop his brow, while his red Nehru jacket was embroidered with threads of genuine gold. A P226 automatic pistol rested in a holster against his hip. Although still in his early twenties, Khan accurately judged that he carried himself with the confidence and style of a true world leader.

As, indeed, he had been painstakingly created to be.

"Excellent," he told Joaquin, turning his back on

the mirror. His faithful bodyguard stood by the open doorway leading out of Khan's personal quarters. A silver chakram, the traditional weapon of a Sikh warrior, adorned the foyer wall, the razor-sharp edges of the steel ring reflecting the light from the dressing room. Khan basked in the halo the shining circlet bestowed upon him. "Let us not keep our distinguished guests waiting."

Khan stepped past Joaquin into the marble corridor beyond. He strode briskly past polished limestone walls inlaid with jeweled panels bearing stylized depictions of the sacred double helix at the heart of all heredity. Turquoise, malachite, lapis lazuli, carnelian, jasper and other sparkling gemstones represented the various nucleotides arranged on the twisting strands.

Stationed every few meters, Khan's elite guards, composed entirely of genetically engineered specimens of superhumanity, snapped to attention as he approached them. Known as the Exon force, after the crucial two percent of human DNA that actually contains genetic information, they sported metallic silver sashes over their crimson uniforms. "Hail, Khan!" they each trumpeted in succession. Khan acknowledged their tributes with an approving nod, pleased by his soldiers' unquestioning loyalty and devotion to duty. *Someday soon,* he mused, *all mankind will swear allegiance to my superior will.*

The corridor led to an open courtyard, many meters across, awash in sunshine. It was a glorious day in northern India, the sky as blue as Krishna himself, the air warm and dry, yet not nearly as oppressively hot as the scorching days of summer. A spume of crystal-clear water rose from a lotus-shaped fountain in the center of the courtyard, then came cascading into the pool as churning white foam. A cool wind brought a few refreshing drops of spray against Khan's upturned face, as though Nature herself was anointing him in recognition of his growing stature and power.

Armed guards patrolled the high sandstone walls surrounding the fortress, which Khan had modeled, at least aboveground, on Agra's fabled Red Fort, built by the great emperor Akbar over four centuries ago. The towering, reddish-brown fortifications, over thirty meters tall, enclosed a sprawling complex of pavilions, courtyards, pools, and gardens, yet this was only the tip of the iceberg. The true nerve center of Khan's growing empire lay beneath the opulent citadel, hidden from the world's view, not to mention the prying eyes of orbital spy satellites—and whatever other resources Gary Seven might have at his disposal.

"Khan! Khan!" chanted the guards on the ramparts, as they gained sight of him. Unlike his Exon guards, these soldiers were not superhuman like himself, merely ordinary men who had wisely chosen to entrust their futures to him. Khan's heart embraced these hapless, imperfect beings, feeling a distinctly magnanimous sense of noblesse oblige toward these men, and all the world's suffering masses. In the new world he would create, there would be peace and plenty for all.

"Khan! Khan! Khan!" The full-throated chanting swelled in volume, echoing across the length and width of the fortress as Khan marched beneath the

azure heavens, the exultant cries of his followers ringing in his ears. He felt his magnificent destiny upon
him, coursing through his veins with every beat of his
uniquely powerful heart. *Is it not passing brave to be a
king,* he thought, after Marlowe, *and ride in triumph
through Persepolis?*

He quickly left the imperial apartments behind
him and arrived at his destination: a domed sandstone building whose arched entrance was supported
by a pair of imposing stone columns. This was the
fortress's official meeting hall, where Khan now intended to take an important step onto the world
stage. A scarlet banner waved proudly from a flagpole
atop the roof of the building, bearing the image of a
silver crescent moon superimposed upon a bright
golden sun. Khan had chosen the emblem personally.
The sun and the moon together, symbolizing totality,
everything in the world. All that he was fated to rule.

The exquisite Ament, clad in a purple silk sari, met
him beneath the shadow of a festooned archway, then led
him around the corners of the building to a less ostenta-
tious back entrance. "All is in readiness, Lord Khan," she
reported calmly. Her kohl-lined amber eyes held no trace
of apprehension. "Our guests await your arrival."

"Good, good," Khan said approvingly.

Her voice is ever soft, gentle, and low, he observed; *an
excellent thing in a woman.* Among her other distinctions, Ament was one of the few women, superhuman or otherwise, who had proven herself capable of
declining his amorous advances, for which he admired her all the more. Only the most confident and
cool-headed of women could resist a Khan.

Except, of course, for a certain irritating American

blonde, the thought of whom allowed an element of
worry to intrude into his consciousness. "What of my
dear American friends?" he asked, referring to Gary
Seven and his irrepressible handmaiden. Roberta Lincoln's unexplained escape from her cell on Chrysalis
Island remained a frustrating and perplexing mystery;
no one had seen her depart, yet Khan had found her
cell empty when he had finally come to interrogate
her, following the successful launch and deployment
of Morning Star. "Is there any sign of their presence?"

Ament was in charge of internal affairs, including
domestic security and intelligence. "Not even a whisper," she assured him. "The Lincoln woman is report-
edly in Bosnia, attempting to prevent that attack on
the United Nations peacekeeping force." A sly smile
lifted the corners of her lips. "An excellent distraction, Lord, just as you intended."

Khan took a moment to savor the fruits of his own
ingenuity. Providing the would-be ambushers—a
renegade offshoot of the Serbian militia—with funds
and logistical support had required only modest effort on his part, yet it had successfully served to keep
his own enemies occupied while he had more pressing matters to attend to.

"Then all is as it should be," he concluded. Confident now that neither Roberta nor her aged superior
would interfere with today's agenda, he entered the
building, followed by both Ament and Joaquin. The
hubbub of many heated conversations reached his
ears as he rapidly traversed the small backstage area
at the rear of the structure. Khan did not hesitate before striding out into the larger chamber beyond.
Stage fright was for lesser mortals.

A hush fell over the packed auditorium as Khan emerged from behind a velvet curtain. He found himself facing a roomful of high-ranking diplomats and military officers from throughout southern Asia and the rest of the world. Modeled on the General Assembly of the United Nations, albeit on a slightly smaller scale, the meeting hall featured several tiers of seats, accommodating roughly five hundred delegates, many of whom glared at Khan with hostility and suspicion. Engraved placards, fixed to the front of their deluxe leather-covered desks, identified each emissary's nation of origin: Pakistan, Bangladesh, Nepal, Myanmar, Bhutan, Thailand, Cambodia, Vietnam, Malaysia, Singapore, Indonesia, Sri Lanka, and so on.

Scanning the assembled dignitaries, all of whom now waited upon his pleasure, Khan was gratified to see that even the federal government in New Delhi, that stubbornly refused to acknowledge the legitimacy of his reign in northern India, had deigned to send a representative to this conference. Only the so-called governor of Punjab, whose power Khan had already usurped, had chosen to boycott the event. Khan made a mental note to assassinate a state official or two, just to remind the governor who was really in charge in Chandigarh.

Flanked by Joaquin and Ament, he strode to the podium. "Welcome, honored guests," he addressed the conclave. "I am Khan Noonien Singh. I trust I require no introduction." He smiled coldly. "You would not be here if you were not already aware of my influence and ability."

A TelePrompTer, positioned conveniently within

view, remained blank; Khan's superior memory required no assistance. "Behold," he declared, as the heavy velvet curtain behind him drew back to expose an illuminated map of the world. "This is the Earth as we know it, a mere nine years before the dawning of a new millennium. Lamentably, it is a planet still beset by the same grievous ills that have plagued humanity since the beginning of recorded history: war, famine, persecution . . ."

As he spoke, his fingers marched over a smaller, touch-sensitive map installed on the podium. In response, various nations and regions on the larger map changed color, suddenly glowing a vibrant shade of red.

". . . overpopulation, poverty, illiteracy, ethnic cleansing—"

A blood-red tide seemed to wash across the globe as Khan ticked off the evils of the world. He saw some of the delegates squirm uneasily in their seats as their own respective countries acquired a damning crimson hue. *Good,* he thought, savoring his visitors' discomfort. *Let them face the truth of their myriad inadequacies.*

"In short, esteemed guests, the world cries out for a savior, for one powerful sword to slice through the Gordian knot of all the Earth's tangled and intractable woes. I am that sword," Khan declared in his native Punjabi. Electronic earpieces provided the varied delegates with an all-but-simultaneous translation of his words. He resisted an urge to sneer at the naked human frailty that required such measures; he himself spoke over fourteen languages fluently.

"Welcome to the capital of the new world order,

the Great Khanate that even now spreads beyond the walls of this fortress to embrace and envelop all of long-suffering humanity." He tapped decisively upon the miniature map before him, and, upon the larger map, the city of Chandigarh switched from red to imperial purple. Another stroke of his finger, and the entire state of Punjab assumed a purple tint. "Although none of your governments have, as yet, officially recognized my regime, my influence already stretches much farther than the borders of my homeland. As I speak to you now, my followers occupy high posts in most of the governments of Asia, granting me effective control over a quarter of the Earth, from South Asia to the Middle East."

His fingers tapped out new commands with the staccato rhythm of an automatic rifle. A fresh wave of purple radiated outward from the Punjab, rapidly claiming a sizable percentage of the map. The spreading, plum-colored tide was darkest at Chandigarh, where Khan's power was most deeply entrenched, and grew somewhat fainter at the periphery of his domain, where flickering violet tendrils threatened the adjacent territories. Khan paused to give his illustrious audience an opportunity to contemplate the transformed map in silence.

Predictably, it was the delegate from New Delhi who objected first. "This is absurd," he pronounced, rising indignantly from his seat. He was a gaunt, ascetic-looking man who had once served as India's ambassador to the United Nations. "I cannot speak for the rest of the world, Mr. Singh, but the sovereign Republic of India is a democracy, indeed the largest democracy in the world, and I certainly don't recall voting for you." Angry mutterings, outbursts, even a few untranslated profanities, seconded the Indian delegate's sarcastic remarks. "You have no mandate, no legal authority, no diplomatic recognition," he continued. "In fact, despite your grandiose claims, you are nothing more than a common bandit or gang leader, albeit more egotistical than most."

Khan maintained a stern, unmoving expression as he listened to himself being denounced. He had expected a reaction such as this; the old, obsolete ruling powers were bound to squeal like pigs before surrendering their palsied grip on the reins of power. *Their impotent bluster matters not at all,* he knew with absolute certainty. *Destiny and DNA are on my side.*

Casually, almost imperceptibly, he nodded at Joaquin, who nodded back in understanding. Without hesitation, the brawny bodyguard, whom Khan had liberated from an Israeli prison, where the belligerent superman had been serving a life sentence for multiple assaults and homicides, reached for his belt buckle and drew forth the razor-edged throwing knife concealed within the sculpted brass bear's head. Before any of the outraged delegates even realized what Khan's unsmiling myrmidon was up to, Joaquin hurled the blade at the Indian delegate with preternatural force and accuracy.

The knife struck its target between the eyes—in the nasion region, to be precise—and buried itself up to its hilt in the man's skull. The former ambassador died instantly, before he could utter a sound. The impact knocked him backward, where his lifeless head and shoulders flopped onto the desktop of the delegation directly behind him.

Panic erupted in the crowded assembly room as the surviving delegates bolted from their seats and raced for the exits at the back of the auditorium. With the touch of a button, Khan sealed the doors, but the metallic click of the locks was lost amidst the screams and shouts of the terrified dignitaries. Khan watched in amusement as the emissaries and their aides tugged futilely on the door handles, desperate to escape the site of the Indian ambassador's abrupt demise. The Pakistani and Indian delegations, agreeing for once on a common goal, strained together to push open a door that steadfastly refused to budge. Other envoys pounded helplessly on the soundproof doors, crying out for help that was not coming; Khan had insisted that all armed bodyguards remained outside the main assembly hall—for "security reasons."

He let the frenzied diplomats struggle for a moment more, the better to recognize the utter impossibility of escape, before drawing the P226 from its holster and firing a single shot into the air. The blaring report of the gun echoed throughout the auditorium, seizing the attention of the scrambling delegates. Anxious eyes turned away from the exits, back toward the commanding figure before the podium.

"Please return to your seats," Khan instructed loudly, holding the smoking pistol aloft, its muzzle still pointed at the domed ceiling above. He required no microphone to project his voice across the entire chamber. "We have not yet concluded today's business."

His tone, along with the potent visual of the upraised gun, brooked no debate. Hesitantly, and with obvious trepidation, the chastened envoys slunk back to their assigned seats. Tears and/or nervous perspiration streaked the faces of many of the delegates, whose well-coifed hair and elegant attire had been thoroughly disheveled by their frantic, futile rush for safety. Khan waited until his guests' earpieces were back in place before addressing his captive audience.

"I regret what has just transpired," he said, casting a pitiless glance at the Indian ambassador's corpse. "I trust, however, that I have made my point. Those who defy my authority do so at their own peril."

A blank expression upon his face, Joaquin trudged up the steps to the ambassador's body and retrieved his throwing knife, extracting it from the dead man's punctured skull with a single smooth tug on its hilt. He wiped the blade clean with the ambassador's own silk handkerchief and returned the weapon to its hiding place within his belt buckle before descending to the stage. Khan clapped his hands sharply, summoning a team of servitors who swiftly and efficiently removed the ambassador's mortal remains from the premises.

"I remind you," Khan said menacingly, "that I have numerous followers, many of them unknown to you, placed in capitals and corridors of power throughout the world. Every one of them is ready and willing to kill on my command, no matter how highly placed or well-guarded the target." His dark eyes narrowed as he fixed a steely gaze upon the cowed assemblage. "You may depend on this."

He was pleased to note that, while the delegates continued to whisper and murmur amongst themselves, their multilingual mutterings sounded much less defiant than before. A new, and more agreeably tremulous, note could be heard beneath the soft susurrus of distraught and frightened voices. *Excellent,* he thought. *Just as I intended.*

Smiling, he returned his gun to its holster. "I am a reasonable man," he stated. "I understand that full knowledge of my power, if made public too abruptly, might cause unrest and panic. Therefore I am prepared to maintain a relatively low profile until I, and I alone, judge that the time is right to announce the true extent of my domain. Never mistake my deliberate anonymity, however, for any weakness or lack of authority."

To Khan's surprise, one of the surviving delegates rose to challenge him. Khan recognized him as the adopted son of a celebrated American scientist and explorer, now a prominent Calcutta statesman. "You may kill me," the man said. His face was tense and apprehensive, but his voice was steady. A large ruby glittered at the front of his white turban. "You may kill everyone here, but you cannot cut the world's throat. Your gangster tactics will carry little weight with the nations of the world, who have dealt with petty warlords and megalomaniacs before."

Joaquin snarled and reached for his belt buckle, but Khan held up his hand to curb any immediate reprisals. He admired courage, which the outspoken delegate clearly possessed in plenty.

"You are mistaken, sir," Khan said respectfully. "I can, if necessary, cut the entire world's throat." He tapped out a command upon the podium's built-in control panel and the map of the world disappeared from the screen behind him, replaced by a photograph of an artificial satellite in orbit high above the earth.

"Behold Morning Star," he declared, gesturing boldly at the futuristic image on the screen. "Named after Lucifer, the bringer of light, for it is light itself that is my ultimate weapon. Ultraviolet light."

Another press of a switch and the satellite's image was supplanted by a graphic depicting Earth's atmospheric layers. "Many of you are no doubt familiar with the hazardous effects of ultraviolet light, including skin cancer, cataracts, blindness, even genetic damage. Earth's primary defense against UV radiation from the sun is the ozone layer existing in the stratosphere, roughly ten to forty kilometers above the surface of the planet. Sadly, that layer has seen better days."

Live footage of swirling clouds and wind currents, taken from a much higher altitude, appeared on the screen. Much of the photo was colored green, indicating the presence of atmospheric ozone, but there was a much darker region at the center of the image, like a yawning void or cavity. "This is the infamous ozone hole above the Antarctic. First discovered in 1985 by, among others, myself, it is proof of the gradual erosion of the ozone layer caused by rampant use of chlorofluorocarbons."

Khan saw heads nodding throughout his audience. "You may wonder why I am telling you this. After all, the world has been aware of the damaged state of the ozone layer since the eighties, and has even made some small progress toward addressing the problem by legislating against the manufacture and use of CFCs. An admirable example of international cooperation, really, but one that I can undo in a heartbeat.

"The top-secret technology at the heart of my

Morning Star satellite was originally developed by a singular genius who preferred to be anonymous, to repair any holes in the ozone layer. That same technology can also be deployed, however, to tear open new gaps in the ozone layer, of whatever size I desire, wherever I desire—as I shall now demonstrate."

Keying in a password known only to him and no other, Khan initiated a preprogrammed sequence that sent a command to Morning Star, now in orbit above the Antarctic. High above the Earth, and miles away from Chandigarh, the satellite's unique apparatus subtly manipulated the Van Allen radiation belt to create a severe electrical disruption in the stratosphere above the South Pole. A controlled burst of artificial lightning broke apart millions of ozone molecules, causing the pollution-generated ozone hole to expand at an unnaturally accelerated rate. *Thank you, Dr. Evergreen,* Khan thought smugly, recalling the ageless scientist who had created the first ozone-destroying satellite nearly eight years ago. Ever cautious where potentially dangerous technology was concerned, Gary Seven had persuaded Evergreen to destroy that earlier satellite; thankfully, Evergreen's diagrams and data had found their way into Seven's copious computer files, from which Khan had later extracted them. *And to think,* Khan thought, *that Seven would have let this revolutionary weapon molder forgotten in his files, when he could have used it to change the world!* Khan shook his head in disbelief. *Seven always did lack vision.*

On the screen, the yawning gap in the ozone layer grew in size, its amorphous borders spreading outward to consume yet more of the protective vapors.

The sudden surge looked like time-lapse photography, yet Khan knew that the hole's rapid expansion was actually occurring in real time, right before the eyes of the awestruck assembly. "Sim sala bim!" exclaimed the courageous emissary from Calcutta. His fellow delegates looked just as horrified.

As programmed, Morning Star ceased its assault on the ozone layer after exactly five minutes had transpired. A collective sigh of relief rose from the assembled delegates as the hole's growth slowed to a stop.

Khan did not let his guests enjoy any momentary release from anxiety. "At this very moment," he informed them, "the ozone hole above the Antarctic is now twenty percent larger that it was less than five minutes ago." Horrified gasps came from the audience. "Do not be deceived by the relatively modest scale of the projected images. I can assure you that the gap is now as large as the entire continental United States, and as deep as the lofty Himalayas are tall."

He relished the appalled expressions on the faces before him. "Of course, you need not take my word for this. By all means, have your own scientists and meteorologists investigate for themselves, perhaps using the new European Remote Sensing Satellite, launched last year." An unworried smirk conveyed his lack of concern over any independent testing. "They will only confirm what I have already told you.

"Now imagine another vaporous rent, equally vast, appearing in the ozone layer directly above each of your respective nations, exposing your populations, livestock, and crops to lethal levels of ultraviolet radiation. With Morning Star under my exclusive control,

I can easily target individual regions, or, as a final deterrent, destroy Earth's entire ozone layer in a matter of hours. Death, disease, and starvation would soon follow, on a scale not seen on this planet since the extinction of the dinosaurs."

Cutting off the transmission from Morning Star, he subjected his audience to a barrage of swiftly edited, unsettling images: photos of cancerous growths spreading across diseased human flesh, unseeing eyes blinded by filmy cataracts, parched desert plains, dying fish floating atop lifeless seas, the protruding bellies of famished children. Many of the delegates were forced to look away from the unending montage of horrors, while others were riveted to their seats, unable to tear their gaze away from the grotesque and disturbing pictures.

When Khan judged that they had seen enough, he ended the projections, rendering the screen behind him blank for the first time since he had begun speaking.

"Be reassured: I am not a madman. I have no desire to bring about such a doomsday scenario. But know that I can do so, and surely will, if any military attempt is made to depose me." He fixed the assembly with a stern and unyielding stare. "I charge you: make this crystal clear to your superiors. If I fall, the world falls with me."

Having revealed the existence of his most fearsome weapon, Khan chose to conclude his presentation. "The great American novelist Herman Melville once wrote, 'In time of peril, like the needle to the lodestone, obedience, irrespective of rank, generally flies to him best fitted to command.' By virtue of my superior intelligence and vision, no one is better fitted than I to guide struggling humanity past the perils of the present era into a new and glorious tomorrow. I am the future. If you are wise, you—and the governments you represent—will not stand in my way."

He pressed a button on the podium, releasing the locks holding his audience prisoner. "You are dismissed," he told them, declining to open the floor to questions or debate. He answered to no one, and the sooner the so-called leaders of the world recognized this salient fact, the better. He stood silently behind the podium as he watched the shaken delegations file out of the auditorium until only he, Joaquin, and Ament remained.

Ament, ever thoughtful, offered Khan a glass of water. "Was it truly necessary to kill the Indian ambassador?" she asked, now that there were no longer any outsiders within earshot. Ament often positioned herself as Khan's conscience, a role he had no objections to, provided she did not question his decisions in public. Indeed, he welcomed her often critical probings; every king required advisors willing to voice their concerns to their liege.

"I could not risk being perceived as a paper tiger, all show and no real threat," he explained, absolutely confident that he had made the correct decision, "particularly when challenged by someone with, at the very least, a nominal claim to the very land upon which we dwell. The ambassador's death may well prevent additional bloodshed in the days to come, by convincing the world's leaders that I am not to be trifled with."

"If you say so, Lord Khan," Ament stated evenly,

conceding the point. He suspected that she remained not entirely convinced, but he accepted that; ultimately, all that really mattered was that he remained strong and certain enough to do what must be done. *If Ament is reluctant to spill blood,* he mused, *that only makes her counsel more invaluable. I have assassins aplenty; it cannot hurt to have a more forgiving voice at my ear, even if sometimes, as today, that voice must be ignored.*

"Excuse me, Your Excellency."

A trim Nicaraguan man stepped onto the stage. Khan recognized the individual as a member of the Khanate's intelligence corps. "Forgive me for interrupting, but I have important information that I know you have been eager to receive."

"Speak," Khan instructed. *This sounds promising....*

The man smiled cruelly, perhaps anticipating covert action of a sanguinary nature. "We have located the Americans," he said.

CHAPTER THREE

AEGIS FINE BOOKS, LTD.
CHARING CROSS ROAD
LONDON, UNITED KINGDOM
NOVEMBER 5, 1992

IT SOUNDED LIKE A RIOT OUTSIDE. NOISY SHOUTING, along with the smell of burning torches and bonfires, penetrated the cramped, cozy atmosphere of the bookshop, one of several occupying this most biblio-philic of London neighborhoods. Ordinarily, Roberta would be alarmed, but not on the evening of November 5th; she recognized the raucous sound of a typical Guy Fawkes Day celebration.

Through the shop's first-floor window, she saw hordes of costumed revelers marching down Charing Cross Road toward Trafalgar Square. As well as sparklers and torches, the festivants bore aloft life-size papier-mâché effigies of the infamous Guy himself, not to mention various contemporary politicians and celebrities, all destined for the bonfire before the night was out. Roberta spotted three-dimensional caricatures of Fergie and John Major on their way to incineration, bouncing upon the shoulders of their jubilant bearers. A string of firecrackers went off less than a block away, adding to the general tumult.

Sounds like fun, she thought, from her cluttered desk at the rear of the bookshop. A checkered flannel shirt and torn jeans were her concessions to the "grunge" craze emanating from her native Seattle, while a red AIDS ribbon testified to a more tragic sign of the times. Roberta hoped to join the festivities soon, but first she had to take care of some work. In the last week or so, she'd caught wind of a nefarious plot to burn down Windsor Castle sometime later this month. She suspected Khan was behind the scheme, possibly just to keep her and Seven busy while he plotted bigger mischief elsewhere. *Still, I'd better look into it,* she resolved, opening a new (and tightly encrypted) file on her computer screen, then firing off some inquiring e-mails to a number of her most trusted European contacts.

Roberta sighed, contemplating the size of her workload. In recent years, she had taken over handling most of the day-to-day operations and field missions, freeing Seven to concentrate more on the big picture; i.e. the growing threat of Khan and his overambitious supersiblings. She glanced up at the ceiling, figuring that Seven was no doubt hard at work in his "war room" on the second floor. She was glad that she could take some of the load off his aging shoulders, even if it did get a bit overwhelming sometimes. *Don't forget,* she reminded herself, *you've still got to follow up on those new reports from Chandigarh.*

Plus, of course, she also had a new shipment of books to shelve. She wistfully eyed the small cache of fireworks—mostly sparklers and a few Roman candles—waiting atop her desk, and wondered if she would have time to take part in tonight's celebrations. A scented candle, sitting atop her computer monitor, safely away from the fireworks, combatted the musty aroma of the bookstore.

The tinkle of the copper bell alerted her to the arrival of two prospective customers at the shop's front entrance. She quickly replaced her notes on the future castle torching with a more innocuous spreadsheet, then glanced up at her visitors—who turned out to be Prince Charles and Ross Perot.

Or, to be more precise, Guy Fawkes Day merrymakers wearing store-bought plastic masks of the prince and the Texas millionaire. *Not bad likenesses,* Roberta thought, although the second man was considerably taller than the real Perot. *But then, who isn't?* Heavy winter coats protected the impostors from the chill night air outside.

Roberta had spent too much of her life in New York City to be entirely comfortable with the notion of masked strangers entering her store, no matter what night it was. Just to play it safe, she lightly tapped a paperweight upon her desk: a green, translucent pyramid, about the size of three computer diskettes stacked against each other.

The pyramid—in actuality, a remote interface for the artificially intelligent Beta 6 computer upstairs—beeped once and emitted a faint glow as it scanned the newcomers for concealed weapons. She suppressed a sigh of relief as the pyramid beeped a second time, signifying that visitors were unarmed. "Good evening," she said pleasantly, standing up behind her desk. "Can I help you?"

"Yes, please," Prince Charles said from behind his mask. He stepped toward Roberta, leaving his friend to browse the shelves at the front of the store. "I am looking for a book, but I cannot recall the name of the author." His voice held a hint of an Australian accent. "Do you know who wrote *Far Beyond the Stars?*"

Roberta recognized the title as a classic 1950s science-fiction novella. "That would be Benjamin Russell," she volunteered, "but I'm afraid we don't have it in stock." She shrugged her shoulders and gestured toward the overstuffed bookshelves surrounding her. "We mostly carry history, current events, and other nonfiction works."

"I see," the man said amiably, not sounding too disappointed. "Let me write down that name." He removed a small spiral notepad from his coat pocket, then patted himself down, apparently looking for something to write with. "Excuse me," he said after a few seconds of fruitless self-examination, "may I borrow your pen?"

"Certainly," Roberta replied automatically. She reached for her servo, which, among its many other uses, also served as a perfectly functional writing implement, and almost handed it over to the stranger. At the last minute, however, she hesitated, brought up short by a niggle of suspicion at the back of her mind. Holding on tightly to the silver instrument, she peered into the anonymous blue orbs observing her through the cut-out eyeholes of his plastic mask. Was she just being paranoid, or did "Prince Charles" look just a little too eager to get his hands on her pen?

Uncertain, Roberta glanced over at the man's associate, the too-tall Perot. She couldn't help noticing the way he appeared to be lingering by the front door, as if maintaining a furtive lookout. *Maybe he wants to make sure we're not interrupted,* she speculated, feeling a chill run down her spine. *I have a bad feeling about this.*

She drew back her hand, intending to offer Prince Charles a convenient pencil instead, but he must have read her suspicions in her face. With lightning-fast reflexes, he grabbed hold of her wrist and squeezed it with preternatural strength.

Roberta gasped in pain, releasing the servo involuntarily. The bogus Prince caught hold of it with his free hand before it even came close to hitting the floor. Roberta kicked herself for letting her guard down, however briefly. *I should have remembered,* she thought, *that Khan's genetically engineered goons don't need weapons to be dangerous.*

Without releasing Roberta, Prince Charles deposited the captured servo into his coat pocket. *Yet another one for Khan's collection,* Roberta reflected bitterly. She drew meager comfort from the knowledge that Khan wanted her and Seven's technology, especially with regards to teleportation, even more than he wanted them dead. *Which probably explains why he didn't just obliterate the store with a bomb or missile or something.*

Prince Charles nodded at Ross Perot, who locked the front entrance and turned the CLOSED sign toward the outside. Satisfied, Charles let go of Roberta and shoved her down into her seat behind the desk. "Silence," he warned her, closing his fist around an imaginary throat to illustrate what would happen to her if she raised a fuss. "Upstairs," he instructed his masked accomplice. "You take the old man."

Realizing Seven was in immediate danger, Roberta desperately surveyed the disorderly desktop, looking for a weapon to use against the intruders. Her gaze—and hand—fell upon the small pile of fireworks she'd put aside for later that evening. A ten-inch Roman candle, with an exposed wick, bore the useful warning: DO NOT POINT AT OTHER PEOPLE. Hoping there was a good reason for that cautionary note, she snatched up the firework with one hand, her scented candle with the other, aimed the tip of the former directly at her assailant's face, and lit the fuse.

A geyser of white-hot sparks erupted from the end of the Roman candle, only inches away from Prince Charles's face. The enemy agent cried out in pain, the cheap plastic mask bubbling and blackening as he tore the burning disguise from his features. He reeled backward, clutching at his blistered face. Smoke rose from the scorched shoulders of his tweedy overcoat.

"That's for Princess Di!" Roberta quipped, before taking advantage of the imposter's distress to alert Seven via the glowing green pyramid. "Three-six-eight to 194!" she shouted at the pyramid, using her and Seven's respective code numbers. "Condition red, Rubicon scenario. Repeat: Rubicon scenario."

A compliant beep indicated that her warning had been transmitted upstairs. Roberta darted out from behind the desk, only to see the second invader, the one posing as Ross Perot, charge at her from his post by the door. The exaggerated ears and ratlike contours of his disguise reminded Roberta of those trespassing Ferengi she and Seven had chased out of Wall Street a few months before. Somehow, she didn't think this guy was going to be discouraged quite so easily—especially since her Roman candle was already sputtering out.

"American witch!" he snarled, lunging at Roberta. The cramped layout of the store worked to her advantage, though; Perot had to maneuver around the former Prince Charles, who was still flailing about in agony, before he could get within reach of Roberta, giving her time to look around for another weapon. The "New Arrivals" shelf beckoned, and she grabbed for the biggest, heaviest hardcover she could find—a first edition of *Chicago Mobs of the Twenties,* published by Simon & Schuster just that month—and swung it like a club at Perot's head. The massive tome slammed into her attacker's face, cracking the grotesque plastic mask. *Hah!* she thought triumphantly. *Who says hardcovers aren't worth the money?*

The hefty volume would have knocked an ordinary man out cold, but merely staggered Khan's latest supergoon. Not waiting to see how quickly he recovered, she raced up the stairs to the second floor, then ran down a short, carpeted corridor and threw open the door to Seven's office. "Fire up the transporter!" she gasped, only slightly winded by her sprint up the stairway. Defending humanity all around the world definitely provided plenty of exercise. "They're right behind me!"

Gary Seven, a.k.a. Supervisor 194, had already begun the evacuation procedure. He was a tall, lean man whose austere countenance had only grown craggier with age. His once-brown hair was now completely silver, but his icy gray eyes remained as intense and alert as ever. Years of selective breeding on an unnamed planet light-years from Earth had blessed him with impressive longevity; although in his sixties, he looked fifty at most.

"Khan's found us again?" he asked her, swiftly but efficiently stuffing crucial documents into a black attaché case. An immense map of the world was mounted to the wall behind him, with small red pins marking the most recent known locations of all the surviving Children of Chrysalis. The pins were grouped in clusters all over the map; Roberta's gaze briefly gravitated to the mass of pins centered around northern India, Khan's current base of operations.

"Looks like it," she said, slamming the office door and bolting it shut. *That's not going to stop them for long.* She already heard angry footsteps pounding up the stairs. "We've got to vamoose, pronto!"

Seven's office resembled his former headquarters back in New York City, albeit with newer furniture. A silver pen and pencil set on his antique walnut desk activated the futuristic equipment hidden behind a mundane-looking bookcase, which now swung outward to reveal the sealed entrance of their transporter vault. A dauntingly solid steel door, which looked like the entrance to a bank vault or airlock, prevented access to the vault, until Seven manipulated the pen-and-pencil set again, causing the metal door to open automatically, exposing the apparently empty chamber within. Electronic switches and buttons, installed on the inner side of the door, clicked and whirred as Seven activated a preprogrammed escape sequence. A gleaming chrome control wheel rotated 180 degrees.

Roberta held her breath, hoping that there was still time for Seven to get away. *If only this were just a drill,* she thought plaintively, recalling all the times she and Seven had rehearsed this and other scenarios. *And just when I was starting to feel at home in London . . .*

Footsteps racing down the corridor gave way to the sound of fists hammering against the sturdy, reinforced oak door. Irate curses came from right outside, as Khan's superpowered minions tried to force their way into the office. Roberta threw her own weight against the door, lending the deadbolts whatever help she could. "I can't hold them back much longer," she warned Seven. "These guys were literally built for breaking and entering."

"Almost set," Seven assured her. A standing silver frame, holding a color portrait of a sleek black cat, occupied a position of honor on Seven's desk. He carefully added the photo to the vital papers collected in the attaché case, then snapped the case shut. Throwing on a gray tweed jacket over a navy-blue turtleneck sweater, he took the case by its handle and hurried toward the open vault, where, even now, a strangely luminous blue mist was forming, seemingly out of nowhere.

He paused at the threshold of the vault, looking back at his longtime friend and colleague with concern. "Roberta?" he asked, visibly reluctant to leave her in jeopardy.

"Go!" she urged him. The office door trembled against her straining back with each savage blow upon its opposite side. The sound of cracking wood detonated in her ears. "I know what to do." Someone had to stay behind to make sure their extraterrestrial technology didn't fall into Khan's hands. "Your servo," she requested succinctly.

Seven tossed her his own pen, even as, case in hand, he stepped into the swirling azure mist that now appeared to fill the entire vault. She sighed in relief as his rigidly upright figure literally dissolved into the eerily phosphorescent fog. At least one of them was making a clean getaway. . . .

A gloved fist smashed through the door, nearly snagging Roberta's honey-blond tresses. She hurled herself away only seconds before the whole door exploded in a shower of splinters, allowing Khan's two henchmen to invade the office, intent on finishing their sinister mission, at least where Roberta was concerned.

They had both discarded their mutilated masks, but she could tell them apart by the damage she had inflicted on each of them. The Australian, who had suffered fireworks in the face, had blisters and burns on his cheeks, while his partner-in-crime, who looked to be of African descent, had a bloody nose where Roberta had forcibly introduced him to the history of the Prohibition era. She wanted to think that she had actually broken his snoot, but feared that his genetically augmented cartilage was tougher than that.

She glanced longingly at the transporter vault, where the glowing mist was already dissipating, taking Seven with it. Too bad her own escape could not be effected so easily. *No Blue Smoke Express for me,* she lamented, taking aim at the scarred Aussie with her borrowed servo. A pair of delicate antennae sprang from the sides of the slender device. Blue energy crackled briefly between the tips of silver filaments.

A hum filled the air as the invisible tranquilizer beam, set at maximum strength, zapped the Aussie, who tottered uncertainly upon his feet, the murderous expression on his face momentarily supplanted by a look of groggy confusion. Half-lidded eyes struggled to focus, while his jaw dropped open slackly.

The zap should have sent him straight to dreamland, but, to Roberta's dismay, he seemed to be fighting the ray's narcotic effect. Was it his souped-up DNA, she wondered, or simply the stinging pain of his facial burns that gave him the ability to resist the beam? Either way it took a second zap to render the man's limbs as limp as soggy French fries, costing her valuable seconds she could ill afford to lose.

The delay gave the second invader a chance to use his incapacitated companion as a human shield. He shoved the off-balance Australian from behind, propelling the man's sagging body at Roberta, who had to backpedal clumsily to avoid being knocked to the floor by her victim's headlong trajectory. She fired her servo at the hostile African, but the hastily aimed beam missed its target, who tore a jagged plank of wood from the sundered door and hurled it at her like a spear. "You cannot escape!" he shouted furiously, blood still leaking from his nostrils. His accent sounded East African. Kenyan, maybe, or Rwandan. "None can defy the will of Khan!"

Roberta ducked quickly, the timber missile grazing her shoulder as it narrowly missed her head, slamming instead into the pin-infested map on the wall, which fell onto the carpeted floor with a resounding thud. Her servo hummed again, but the African's reflexes were once again better than her aim. He seized

the edges of the polished wooden desktop and effortlessly hoisted it off the floor, shielding himself with
the upturned desk, whose carved legs now menaced
Roberta like the antlers of some freakish, genetically
engineered beast. With a bellicose roar, he rushed at
her, trampling over his own fallen comrade as he
sought to pin Roberta against the nearest wall.

She ran for it. *He's stronger than I am,* she realized,
and faster, too. Even with her servo, the odds were
against her, leaving a rapid getaway her best option.
Firing wildly back over her shoulder, without much
success, she made tracks for the narrow doorway, to
the left of the open vault, which connected the office
to Seven's private living quarters.

Unlike Roberta's own perpetually cluttered
boudoir, across the hall, Seven's room was immaculately clean and tidy, the bed neatly made, all personal
effects securely lodged in the appropriate closet or
drawer. For once, she was grateful for Seven's neat-
freak tendencies, because it meant there was no
chance of tripping over a mislaid shoe, cell phone, or
moon rock, while she dashed for the window at the
rear of the room. *That's the only way out,* she recalled,
diving and rolling across the width of Seven's tightly
tucked sheets before landing on her feet on the other
side of the bed.

She heard the uprooted desk crash to the floor in
the office behind her, as the determined African shed
the unwieldy piece of furniture in order to follow her
through the connecting doorway. Roberta tried to
zap him as he came through the portal, but he moved
too quickly for her, somersaulting into the room with
superhuman speed and agility, then ducking behind a

heavy wooden wardrobe. "Run while you can, inferior sow!" His voice held the strident ring of a true fanatic. "Your time is over!"

Roberta didn't wait for him to turn the wardrobe into a weapon. Hastily resetting the servo, from Tranquilize to Disintegrate, she dissolved the glass straight out of the window frame and started to clamber out onto the fire escape beyond, only to feel a powerful hand clamp hold of her ankle. "Got you!" he grunted. "I told you you couldn't get away!"

Oh yeah? Roberta thought defiantly. Grabbing on to the rusted metal rungs of the fire escape for support, she kicked backward, driving her heel into his chin— hard. It wasn't enough to make him let go entirely, but his grip loosened enough for her to free her foot by sacrificing her boot. Hopping awkwardly, favoring her merely stockinged foot, which froze whenever it came into contact with the icy iron grillework, she scrambled to her feet and edged away from the open window. Looking down at the seldom-used courtyard behind the store, she saw another masked figure, this one impersonating Sting, waiting at the bottom of the rusty steps. *Figures Khan would have all the exits covered,* she thought acidly.

There was nowhere to go but up. Shivering in the frigid November air, she climbed toward the roof, knowing her pursuers were bound to be close behind her. A stray memory, of Julie Andrews and Dick Van Dyke dancing atop the skyline of London, brought a rueful smile to her lips. *I wonder if it's too late to disguise myself as a chimney-sweep?*

When she reached the top of the fire escape, however, she found not Mary Poppins waiting for her, but

Hillary Clinton. Or, rather, a laboratory-bred female assassin wearing a Hillary mask, standing, arms akimbo, upon the flat, black-tar surface of the roof. A maroon leather catsuit showed off the woman's genetically perfect physique. "Surrender at once!" she declared, swinging a pair of weighted nunchucks with what looked like expert skill.

Give me a break, Roberta thought irritably. *The election was over days ago.* Barely remembering to reset the servo to a nonlethal setting, she dropped the bogus First Lady with a single zap, then pulled herself onto the roof.

Despite her easy victory over Hillary, which she figured she was entitled to the way her night had been going, Roberta knew she couldn't afford to relax for a second. Rapid-fire footsteps on the fire escape told her that the bloody-nosed African and/or Sting were on their way up. *Now what?* she asked herself.

Improvising shamelessly, she stepped over Hillary's sprawled body and limped toward the front of the store. From her hard-earned new vantage point, two stories up, she watched a holiday procession make its way down Charing Cross Road, between the rows of ubiquitous bookshops. Costumed marchers brandishing blazing torches escorted a hay-filled cart bearing a papier-mâché replica of the villainous-looking Guy, infamous for attempting to blow up Parliament nearly four centuries ago. Laughing men and women pulled the loaded tumbrel down the street, chanting in unison:

> "Remember, remember,
> Gunpowder, treason and plot,
> I see no reason why Gunpowder Treason,
> Should ever be forgot!"

At the moment, Roberta was less interested in the sacrificial Guy and his notorious scheme, than in the generous layers of straw upon which the dummy rested. She watched anxiously as the procession neared the shop, while glancing frequently over her shoulder at the upper rungs of the fire escape on the other side of the roof. *C'mon, hurry up!* she silently urged the jubilant Londoners pulling the cart along. Firecrackers exploded in the street below, sounding unnervingly like gunshots. *I haven't got all night!*

"There you are!" a familiar voice snarled, as the African sprang from the fire escape onto the roof, only a few yards away. A brick chimney, badly in need of repointing, shielded him from her servo as he called out to Sting and who knew who else, "She's up here! We have her trapped!" He scowled at the sight of Ninja Hillary, snoozing contentedly upon the roof. "You'll pay for assaulting a servant of the Great Khan!"

Not tonight I won't! Kicking off her remaining boot, she balanced precariously at the very edge of the roof, watching the Guy's cart draw ever nearer. The African was unarmed, she knew, but what about Sting and whatever other reinforcements Khan might have sicced on her? *Time to get out of here.*

She glanced down, suddenly flashing on that time she bungee-jumped off a hundred-foot jungle cliff to get away from that hungry allosaurus. This time, there wouldn't be a safety cord.

"Watch out below!" she shouted hoarsely. The cart was as close as it was ever going to get. Stepping backward to get a running start, she launched herself off the top of the building into the empty air above

Charing Cross Road. Adrenaline kept her warm as she arced sharply toward the street below, the chilly night air rushing against her face. Gravity, showing no mercy, speeded her descent.

Oomph! The bales of hay piled high in the cart broke her fall, just as she'd hoped, but the sudden landing still knocked the air out of her. Spitting straw from her lips, she found herself face-to-face with the leering, mustachioed visage of the Guy. "Sorry to drop in unannounced," she told the dummy, after catching her breath. "But don't think this means I'm falling for you."

Her precipitous arrival in the cart unavoidably startled the previously carefree crowd packing the street. The boisterous shouting was cut off in mid-chant, abruptly preempted by startled exclamations and queries. A mob of concerned and curious faces, some masked, some not, peered at Roberta through the slats of the wooden cart, peppering her with questions she couldn't begin to answer.

Besides, she had something more important to do. Rolling onto her back, she aimed the servo at the second floor of Aegis Fine Books, Ltd. and pressed down on the controls. A controlled implosion began inside the bookshop, consuming the entire building as the brick walls tumbled inward, destroying every last trace of Seven's office and the high-tech hardware it concealed. Roberta spared a second to worry about the fate of Khan's various minions, trapped in and about the self-destructing edifice. Would their incredible strength and resilience allow them to survive the building's collapse? She found it hard to care all that much.

A tremendous cloud of dust and debris rose up from the ruins of the bookstore, shrouding the rubble from sight. *Not much of a bonfire,* Roberta appraised, noting the conspicuous lack of soaring flames, but infinitely easier on the neighbors.

Despite its controlled nature, the implosion of the bookshop caused a panic. The interrupted procession broke apart into a flood of fleeing individuals, many of them screaming in fear as everyone raced to put as much distance as possible between themselves and the demolished bookstore. Tumbling out of the cart, whiskers of straw clinging to her jeans and flannel shirt, Roberta joined the chaotic exodus, trusting the crowd and confusion to hide her from any of Khan's agents that might have escaped the explosive demise of Aegis Fine Books.

She let the stampeding horde carry her along, jostling her on all sides as the hysterical throng abandoned the book district. *Fine with me,* she thought; there was a busy Underground station a few blocks away, where she could disappear completely into the sprawling city, prior to making her way to her and Seven's nearest safehouse. A discarded plastic mask, lying atop a trash bin, caught her eye, and she snatched it up as she went by. She fastened it over her face, just to be safe. It was a "Barney" mask, just her luck, but beggars couldn't be choosers. The crowd soon thinned as it dispersed into the various streets and alleys leading away from Charing Cross Road. A safe distance away from the site of the implosion, Roberta paused and looked back the way she'd come, hearing the shrill howl of sirens converging upon her former address.

"Damn," she muttered, finally allowing herself a moment to mourn the passing of the bookshop, and all the precious personal effects and equipment it had contained. *Another secret headquarters up in smoke,* she grieved, shaking her head. It hadn't been easy installing the transporter vault and Beta 6 computer into an ordinary London flat, especially when many of the key components needed to be beamed in from another solar system. She wasn't looking forward to setting up shop somewhere else, all over again. A tear rolled down the face of a plastic purple dinosaur. She liked living in London, darn it, despite the weather and the food. . . .

At Leicester Square, just outside the entrance to the Underground, she saw a holiday bonfire roaring atop a concrete traffic island. Grotesque parodies of Mike Tyson and Camilla Parker-Bowles were going up in smoke as delighted onlookers hooted and hollered in approval. Would a papier-mâché caricature of Khan someday be consigned to the flames, to the cheers of all humanity?

We can only hope, she thought.

CHAPTER FOUR

IT WAS WELL AFTER MIDNIGHT, BUT KHAN WAS NOT at all fatigued. One of the special privileges of being a superior being was that he required very little sleep to function at the height of his abilities; merely two or three hours a night sufficed. This, he believed, was as it should be. He had far too much to accomplish to waste hours of his life in idle slumber.

"Watch yourself, my friend!" he warned Joaquin, as he sparred with his bodyguard in the palace's well-equipped modern gymnasium. Sweat glistened on Khan's muscular chest. He swung his rattan training sword, or soti, at his faithful protector, who defended himself with a marati, a staff of fire-hardened bamboo bearing heavy wooden spheres at both ends. They circled each other on padded mats while honing their skills at gatka, the centuries-old martial art of

Khan's fierce Sikh ancestors. Khan had studied gatka since he was a child, and it remained his preferred form of exercise, especially when his mind was troubled, as it was tonight.

Why have I not heard back from the retrieval squad? he wondered. His agents should have reported the capture of Seven and Roberta Lincoln by now. *Has something gone amiss with the London operation?*

He slashed again at Joaquin, who deftly blocked the attack with his bamboo shaft, then thrust the forward end of the marati at Khan. A solid ironwood sphere came flying at his head, and Khan pivoted on his heel, barely escaping the blow. "A near miss!" he congratulated Joaquin. "Excellent!"

Even as he fought a mock battle against the stolid Israeli strongman, Khan simultaneously listened to Ament's latest report on domestic affairs in the Punjab and elsewhere. The clash of wood upon wood punctuated the trenchant words of his most elegant advisor.

"Inflation remains a problem throughout the country," she informed Khan, standing several paces away from the edge of the training mat, "although there has been a welcome upturn in foreign investment, in part because of the rigorous fiscal policies we have mandated through our proxies in New Delhi. Along those lines, a consortium of Japanese and American investors have applied for permits to build a state-of-the-art auto factory outside Haryana, which would significantly relieve unemployment in that region. The so-called 'official' government is likely to approve the project; we should grant our blessing as well."

Khan trusted Ament's judgment in such matters. "Very well," he agreed. Despite his strenuous exertions, he spoke with no shortness of breath. "Let it be so."

In truth, his mind was elsewhere, and not only because he found the great game of war and conquest rather more compelling than dry economics. How could he concentrate on inflation rates and unemployment figures when this very night his commandos were striking out at his enemies two continents away? *It is almost eight o'clock in London,* he calculated, parrying another lunge from Joaquin with the curved mahogany guard of his sword's hilt. He retaliated by slashing at the bodyguard's head and shoulders with such blinding speed that Joaquin was barely able to defend himself.

"Great Khan! I have news!" An officer of his intelligence force ran into the gym, distracting Khan just as Joaquin jabbed at Khan with one end of his staff. The weighted ironwood sphere slammed into Khan's chest, knocking him off his feet. He landed flat on his back upon the mat, the protective padding only partly blunting the impact of his fall.

"Your Excellency!" Joaquin sounded positively mortified. Dropping the marati where he stood, the stricken bodyguard rushed forward to offer Khan a hand up. Ament chuckled softly as, with Joaquin's oversolicitous assistance, Khan quickly climbed back onto his feet. An ugly purple bruise was already forming where the dense wooden globe had struck him, over his breastbone. "A thousand pardons, sire!" Joaquin stammered. His usually impassive face was uncharacteristically animated. "I did not mean—"

Khan dismissed his servant's apologies with a wave of his hand, just as he ignored Ament's amusement at his expense. He gave his full attention to the newly arrived courier. "Speak," he commanded, speaking in English to keep his urgent inquiries from the ears of the palace's native-born staff of servants and attendants. "What is the word from London?"

The intelligence officer—an Asian woman named Suzette Ling, whom Khan had known as a child at Chrysalis—shuffled uncomfortably. Khan knew at once that the news was bad. "Most of the retrieval team was caught in an explosion at the site of the operation. It is unclear how many survived."

Khan scowled, appalled already at this apparent debacle. "And the targets?"

"The fate of the older American is unknown," Ling reported, "but the woman was clearly seen escaping the structure moments before its collapse." She nervously eyed the rattan sword still gripped in Khan's clenched fist. "Her present whereabouts are also unknown."

The apprehensive officer need not have feared Khan's wrath. A truly superior leader did not waste his fury punishing the messenger. No, Khan reserved his anger and disappointment for the actual wellspring of his present frustration: Gary Seven and his indefatigable Girl Friday.

Damn them! he thought. Seizing the soti with both hands, he snapped the practice sword in half, the sharp report echoing in the open space of the gymnasium. *How long must I put up with their self-righteous interference?* It was all so unnecessary; he had graciously offered Seven and Ms. Lincoln a truce years ago, promising to leave them be provided they did not get in the way of his inevitable rise to power. Yet the insufferable pair had flagrantly trampled on his proffered olive branch, inserting themselves time and again into affairs in which they had no place. The Lincoln woman's recent attempt to sabotage the launching of Morning Star was only the latest in a never-ending series of effronteries committed by Khan's sanctimonious former associates. *Now 'tis the spring, and weeds are shallow-rooted;* he thought, recalling the cogent advice of the Bard. *Suffer them now and they'll overgrow the garden....*

Cold fury gripped his heart. He threw the broken fragments of his sword onto the floor and ground them into splinters beneath his heel. "Will no one rid me of these infernal meddlers?" he snarled venomously.

Puzzlement gave way to anger upon Ament's refined features. "What is this operation you speak of?" An icy tone revealed her displeasure. "Why was I not informed of this?"

"There was no need," Khan stated, his tone softening as he attempted to placate the offended counselor. "Yours is a gracious and nurturing nature, dear lady, best suited to securing the blessings of peace and prosperity for all who dwell within my realm. Do not trouble yourself with the crueler necessities of power." He stared into her striking amber eyes, admiring as always the keen intelligence he found there. "Let me bear that shadow upon my conscience, without burdening yours as well."

Ament appeared unswayed by his flattery. "Such antiquated sexism, disguised as chivalry, hardly becomes a new breed of leader," she said sarcastically. "Furthermore, reckless adventurism of this sort compromises my efforts to procure the very blessings you mention. The World Bank, for instance, whose financial assistance would greatly assist our plans to improve South Asia's infrastructure and economy, frowns on covert military operations conducted on the soil of member nations." Her voice took on a milder tone, sounding more regretful than irate. "You make it too easy for the rest of the world to dismiss you as a terrorist."

"Perhaps," Khan stated skeptically. He accepted Ament's cautious chidings, but only so far. "Yet do not forget that, ultimately, it is the world that must bend to my will, not the other way around." He clapped his hands and a servant ran forward to offer him a towel and a fresh robe. He wiped the perspiration from his body, then let the anonymous menial drape the brocaded silk robe over his shoulders. "Not everything can be accomplished by diplomacy and negotiation, Lady Ament. Sometimes our swords must play the orators for us. That is the way of the world."

Suzette Ling stepped forward. "In fact," she hastened to point out, painfully eager to find a piece of positive news to report, "there is little chance that the mishap in London will be linked to your regime, Great Khan. The British press is already blaming the explosion on the IRA."

Ament released a derisive sigh. "Let us be thankful for small favors," she said wryly. "The less in the headlines, the better."

"You think so?" Khan challenged her. Beneath his

controlled exterior, bitter resentment and frustration churned within his heart, threatening to flood his soul with bile. "In truth, I grow weary of such subterfuge and misdirection, of skulking behind scapegoats and cover stories. I would prefer to fight my battles in the open, to reveal my true nature and destiny to the world."

Once again, Ament counseled caution. "Impatience will be your fatal flaw, Lord Khan, unless you learn to let the future unfold at its own pace. Recall that, for all our genetic superiority, our kind is still vastly outnumbered by those merely human. Better for now to let the world's teeming masses believe that you are one of them; there is no need for them to know otherwise, and knowledge of your true, superhuman nature could well trigger visceral fears on the part of the populace."

Prudence warred with ego as Khan considered her words, which were not without wisdom, he admitted reluctantly. As much as it galled him to lurk behind the scenes of world affairs, scrupulously keeping out of the spotlight, he had to concede that much of mankind would not welcome—more, would react in unreasoning fear to—the advent of a genetically superior ruling class.

Indeed, he reflected, recent events in India provided a sobering cautionary example that lent considerable credence to Ament's arguments. The present government's well-meaning attempts to abolish India's insidious caste system, by such measures as affirmative action for lower-caste and "Untouchable" citizens, had met with violent opposition from upper-caste Hindus who saw their privileged status and lifestyles slipping away. Many thousands of young Brahmans and Kashtriyas had staged marches and demonstrations against the government's policies, some even going so far as to set themselves on fire in protest.

The old order always resists the coming of the new, Khan mused. If India's intractable intercaste conflicts, which were based on entirely artificial distinctions between ordinary men and women, could yield so much fanatical hatred and bloodshed, what destructive passions might be roused by mere humanity's too-sudden discovery that they had been surpassed by their genetic betters? Best, perhaps, to lead the masses toward this realization slowly.

"Your caution is well-founded," he acknowledged, tipping his head at Ament, who accepted his concession with her usual poise and grace. Khan beckoned to Joaquin, summoning the vigilant bodyguard to his side. Servants scurried to clean up after Khan's training session, rescuing stray towels and weapons from the floor of the gym. "Yet be assured that the day will come, when long-suffering humanity has no choice but to turn to us for deliverance, that the name of Khan shall be known and respected throughout the Earth."

"Of course, my lord," Ament agreed readily. She joined Joaquin behind Khan as he exited the gym, toward the waiting world beyond. The sun had yet to rise in Chandigarh, but night would yield to dawn soon enough. "That much is fated."

CHAPTER FIVE

PLEXICORP INC.
SAN FRANCISCO, CALIFORNIA
UNITED STATES
MARCH 15, 1993

IMMORTALITY ON ICE? VISIT THE HEAVENS WITHOUT EVER DYING? Walter Nichols fiddled with the latest cryosatellite designs while trying to come up with the right advertising slogan for his proposed new business venture. The ad campaign had to strike just the right note, he knew; convincing terminally ill people to have themselves frozen and launched into space was going to be a tough sell at first. He was convinced, though, that cryosatellites were sure to be the next big thing, offering hope to the hopeless—and huge potential profits to the first savvy entrepreneur bold enough to get in on the ground floor. A Cure Is Coming? Wake Up to a Healthier Future?

The intercom on his desk buzzed. "Yes?" he asked impatiently, annoyed at the interruption.

"There are some gentlemen here to see you, Dr. Nichols," his secretary, Madeleine, reported from her desk outside his office. Closed Venetian blinds insulated him from the distractions beyond the wood-paneled walls surrounding him, just as his woolly brown cardigan kept him comfortable in the air-conditioned confines of his office.

"Tell them to make an appointment. I'm busy right now." He squinted through his thick glasses at the diagrams spread out atop his walnut desk. Out-of-shape and overworked, Walter's pudgy form leaned over the much-revised blueprints. The cryonic units still need work, he decided; he wasn't entirely satisfied with the primary refrigeration system. Maybe a backup conduction array, diverting more body heat out into space?

To his surprise, the door to his office swung open and three strangers walked in uninvited. In the lead was a clean-cut young man wearing an Air Force uniform; he had the rugged good looks of a hotshot military flyboy. He was flanked by two other men who resembled Secret Service agents, complete with dark suits, shades, earpieces, and stern, unsmiling expressions. Walter wasn't sure, but he thought he spotted suspiciously gun-shaped bulges beneath the men's conservative black jackets. "Wha—who?" he gasped, unsure whether to be irritated or alarmed.

Madeleine appeared in the doorway behind the intruders, looking flustered and confused. "I'm sorry, Dr. Nichols," she stammered, "but they insisted—they're from the government!"

The Air Force officer flashed a piece of ID before Walter's eyes. "Lieutenant Shaun Christopher, United

States Air Force," he identified himself. The ID looked authentic, although Walter wasn't sure he'd recognize a forgery if he saw one. "Are you Dr. Walter Nichols, manager and owner of Plexicorp, Incorporated?"

Walter nodded. He tugged nervously on the collar of his shirt, loosening his tie. All of a sudden, his cozy office felt much too warm.

"My apologies for barging in like this, Dr. Nichols," Lt. Christopher said, "but I'm afraid I have to ask you to come with me."

Walter gulped. His heart raced faster than one of those new Pentium processors everyone was hyping these days. "Right now?"

"Yes, sir."

Madeleine looked on, utterly dumbfounded, as Lt. Christopher and his two taciturn associates escorted Walter out of his office. Unlike his bewildered secretary, however, Walter had the awful suspicion that he knew what this was all about. *Those guys back in '86,* he thought anxiously. *That so-called professor from Edinburgh and his cronies. The ones who gave me the formula.*

Truth to tell, Walter had been dreading a visit like this for close to a decade, ever since two enigmatic strangers had walked into his office one day, claiming to be visitors from Scotland, and bribed him with a revolutionary molecular formula that, after many long hours of experimentation and analysis, had allowed Walter to buy out Plexicorp from its original owners—and send the company's stock soaring toward the stratosphere. *I always knew there was something fishy about that bunch,* he groaned inwardly, castigating himself for his own greed and lack of caution. *Profes-*

sor Scott of Edinburgh, indeed! Who knew where those shady characters actually came from. His stomach churned angrily, and he groped for the bottle of Tums on his desk. *What if the formula was a classified military secret? I could be charged with espionage!*

Without further explanation, Lt. Christopher led Nichols to the helipad on Plexicorp's roof, where, nine years ago, Professor Scott's Asian accomplice had flown away from Plexicorp with a huge sheet of six-inch-thick plastic. Now an unmarked black helicopter waited on the very same pad to spirit Walter off to God knows where. Minutes later, they were in the air, with Walter strapped into one of the rear seats, next to Lt. Christopher.

"Er, what's this all about?" he asked with exaggerated casualness, trying (too hard) to pretend he didn't know.

"I'm afraid I'm not at liberty to discuss that, Doctor," Lt. Christopher answered, politely but firmly. "You'll be fully informed when we reach our final destination."

Which is? Walter wondered anxiously. *Alcatraz? The Pentagon? CIA headquarters?* "I don't suppose you can tell me where we're going."

"Not really, Doctor." A hint of a smile appeared on Lt. Christopher's unlined, twentyish face, as though he were enjoying a private joke. "Officially, it doesn't even exist."

The helicopter took them to a nearby air base, where Walter was hurried onto a waiting jet, which took off with only the hapless engineer and his official escorts as passengers. A short flight later, Walter stepped off the plane onto the tarmac of a narrow runway stretching across a desolate-looking desert valley. The windows of the jet had been blacked out, preventing Walter from viewing any part of their descent, but the arid terrain, along with the brief duration of the flight, led him to suspect that he was now somewhere in the southwest. Nevada maybe, or Arizona.

The sun beat down upon the blacktop, adding to the sticky layer of perspiration soaking through Walter's clothes. A Jeep Cherokee was parked to one side of the runway, along with a driver wearing military fatigues and a holstered handgun. Walter clambered into the back of the Jeep, where Lt. Christopher produced a metal clipboard with a document and ballpoint pen attached. "Please read and sign this," he instructed.

"Um, what is it?" Walter asked, accepting the clipboard. *A written confession?* He tried to read the neatly-typed text before his eyes, but found it hard to concentrate under the circumstances. *I have the right to an attorney!* he all but shrieked inside his mind. *At least I think I do. Are accused traitors entitled to lawyers?*

"Just a standard form," Christopher told him, "stating that you understand that everything you are about to see and hear is classified top-secret by the United States of America, and that revealing any of those secrets to unauthorized individuals constitutes a major felony, punishable by up to life imprisonment."

This explanation did not reassure Walter. "What if I don't sign?" he asked, his mouth so dry he could barely speak.

The Air Force officer gave him a look of wry amusement. "Then we could be sitting here for a very long time, Dr. Nichols."

Since Walter didn't want to spend the rest of his life baking in the hot Nevada (or Arizona) sun, he signed the form, his trembling hand rendering his signature even more illegible than usual. *Maybe they'll take my cooperation into account,* he hoped fervently, *before locking me up and throwing away the key.*

Lt. Christopher folded up the signed document and placed it securely in his jacket pocket. He nodded at the driver, and the Jeep headed toward the rugged granite face of a nearby mountain. Mounted cameras mixed with cacti and flowering yucca plants alongside the unmarked dirt roadway, which the Jeep appeared to have all to itself.

After passing through several security checkpoints, each guarded by soldiers armed with machine guns, they arrived at a large hangar door built directly into the side of the hill. Walter's apprehension grew with each succeeding barrier. He'd never seen security like this before, not even the time he'd toured the Pentagon along with several other Defense Department contractors. "Where the heck are you taking me?" he wondered aloud. His voice sounded so hoarse and strained that he barely recognized it. "Area 51?"

He thought he was joking.

Christopher presented his credentials to an electronic scanner, and the metallic hangar door rolled upward, revealing a paved, well-lighted tunnel leading into the heart of the mountain. Another armed soldier greeted them, and Walter was briskly marched through a confusing maze of interconnected hallways, past numerous sealed doors labeled AUTHORIZED PERSONNEL ONLY. At this point, he was not surprised to see soldiers posted outside each and every door. None of the grim-faced guards made eye contact with Walter. He didn't know if that was a good thing or not.

Walter was half-convinced they had walked all the way back to San Francisco, when Lt. Christopher paused in front of a door that bore, along with the usual warnings regarding admittance, the cryptic designation F-34. "After you," he said, stepping past the latest guard to open the door.

With a nervous glance at the soldier's side arm, Walter sidled past the guard. He found himself in what appeared to be an ordinary conference room, dominated by an oblong steel table, whose narrow end faced the entrance. Three unfamiliar faces regarded Walter from the far end of the table: an older man, who looked to be in his seventies, plus two younger individuals wearing civilian attire. To Walter's slight relief, none of the three looked particularly prosecutorial.

"Ah, Dr. Nichols! How good of you to join us," the elder man said warmly, without any apparent irony. He was a lean, bony, old codger who peered at Walter through a pair of dusty bifocals. A frayed white lab coat was draped over his gaunt frame. "I must tell you how impressed I was by the molecular design of your 'transparent aluminum.' Such a unique and innovative approach to polyelastic bonding! Truly, a genuine conceptual breakthrough."

"Um, thank you," Walter said uncertainly. He'd been expecting hot lights and rubber hoses, not effusive praise. "It just sort of, er, came to me one day."

"You're being too modest," the balding scientist insisted. He came around the table to shake Walter's hand. Despite his age, he had a firm and enthusiastic grip. "Here, let me make some introductions. I'm Dr. Jeffrey Carlson, chief mad scientist around this place. And these," he said, gesturing toward the younger man and woman seated across the table, "are my most invaluable hunchbacks, Jackson Roykirk and Shannon O'Donnell."

"A privilege to meet you, Dr. Nichols," O'Donnell said. She was an attractive, red-haired woman whose raspy voice held a hint of a clipped New England accent. Walter guessed that she was somewhere in her mid-thirties.

"Yes, what Shannon said," Roykirk added somewhat brusquely. A short, unsmiling man with a goatee and receding hairline, he seemed impatient with social pleasantries and not all that interested in meeting Walter, who got the distinct impression that Roykirk was anxious to get back to his work, whatever that might be.

"Shannon is an engineer like yourself," Carlson explained, "not to mention a prospective astronaut on loan from NASA, while Jackson is a positive genius when it comes to cybernetics." Walter wasn't too surprised to find out that Roykirk was a computer geek; he struck Walter as bright but socially challenged.

"And, of course, you've already met Shaun," Carlson added. It took Walter a second to realize that the senior scientist was referring to Lt. Christopher. "Like Shannon, Shaun has a great career ahead of him as an astronaut and space pilot. I fully expect him to be the first man on Saturn someday."

NASA? Saturn? Walter was getting more baffled by the moment. *What does any of this have to do with me?* As much as he was afraid to find out exactly what kind of hot water he was in, the suspense was rapidly becoming even worse. "Um, at the risk of compromising my constitutional right to remain silent, could somebody maybe explain what I'm doing here? And where 'here' is, for that matter?"

Carlson blushed and jokingly slapped himself on the side of the head. "Of course! I'm so sorry, Dr. Nichols." He smiled sheepishly. "Please forgive all the cloak-and-dagger theatrics. We've had some fairly serious security leaks over the years, and I'm afraid it's rendered the Powers That Be understandably paranoid." He exchanged a glance with Shannon O'Donnell that Walter didn't understand, then grinned at Walter with the mischievous look of someone about to spring a surprise party on an unsuspecting acquaintance. "Welcome to the Groom Lake Facility," he said dramatically, "better known to the tabloid writers as Area 51."

Walter's jaw dropped. He'd heard of Area 51, of course, mostly in conjunction with ridiculous UFO stories and conspiracy theories, like the kind you found in bad science-fiction flicks and cheesy cable-TV documentaries. It was supposed to be the U.S. government's top-secret storehouse for captured alien artifacts and entities, but he had never really given the rumors much thought, being much more concerned with the day-to-day operation of his business. Area 51, and its allegedly extraterrestrial secrets, had meant about as much to his life as the Loch Ness Monster and the Abominable Snowman.

Until now, that is.

It was all too much to cope with. His knees went weak and he clutched the table for support. Seeing his distress, Lt. Christopher pulled a chair away from the table and offered Walter a seat. The shaky engineer dropped gratefully into the molded plastic chair. O'Donnell poured Walter a glass of cold water, which he downed in an instant, then asked for more. *This has got to be some kind of joke,* he thought plaintively. *I'm no UFO nut. I never even saw* E.T. . . .

Carlson allowed Walter a minute or two to recover, wandering back to his own seat at the other end of the table. Then he delivered his second bombshell. "How much do you know," he asked, in a conspiratorial tone, "about the so-called Roswell Incident of 1947?"

Walter almost choked on his water. "That's true, too?"

Carlson nodded soberly. "I was there. An alien spacecraft crashed in the desert outside Roswell, New Mexico. Three intelligent, extraterrestrial beings, who called themselves 'Ferengi,' were taken into custody by the United States Army, who assigned me the task of studying them."

He slid a cardboard folder across the table toward Walter, who opened it with more than a little trepidation. Inside were black-and-white photos of three dwarfish creatures with oversize ears and rodentlike features. *This is what genuine aliens look like?* Walter thought in wonder. *Rat people from outer space?* He couldn't believe what he was hearing—and seeing. "Are . . . are they still alive?" he asked uneasily. For all he knew, these "Ferengi" could be only a few doors away!

"I wish I knew," Carlson said, a rueful tone to his voice. "For better or for worse, the aliens escaped

within days of the crash, taking their damaged spacecraft with them." His eyes looked inward for a moment, as though his mind were traveling back in time
to his long-ago close encounter with the aliens. "I've
spent the last forty-six years studying the data we collected during those brief, historic days back in forty-
seven, plus whatever other evidence of alien visita-
tions that the government has located over the last
few decades."

"This is fantastic," Walter admitted, feeling like
he'd somehow been sucked into a Spielberg movie.
"But, I have to ask, what does any of this have to do
with me?"

Carlson glanced at O'Donnell. "Shannon, do you
want to take this one?"

"No problem," the redheaded engineer said. She
glanced quickly over her notes before launching into
her spiel. "Our primary goal here at Project F is to
design and build the prototype for a new generation
of manned spacecraft, incorporating everything we've
learned from the Roswell crash and similar incidents.
Basically, we're trying to reverse-engineer an alien
spaceship, working from photos and records taken in
1947, plus whatever other extraterrestrial artifacts
have fallen into our hands." She paused for a second,
perhaps uncertain of how much to reveal of Area 51's
entire alien inventory. "This is a whole lot trickier
than it sounds, especially since we no longer have the
original Ferengi vessel to study."

She looked Walter squarely in the eye. "That's
where you come in, Doctor. Not only is your transparent aluminum perfect for our purposes, but it actually bears a surprising resemblance to materials ob-

served in the Ferengi spacecraft." She shook her head in amazement, obviously still taken aback by the coincidence. "The Ferengi substance is more sophisticated, naturally, but, believe it or not, it seems to have basically the same molecular matrix."

Walter gulped. *Those guys back in '86,* he recalled. *Professor Scott and the others. They must have been Ferengi in disguise!* "Er, I don't suppose those Roswell aliens were able to take human form?"

Carlson raised a quizzical eyebrow. "Actually, there is reason to believe that at least some of the aliens possessed shape-changing abilities. Why do you ask?"

Walter hesitated before answering. This was the moment of truth: should he come clean about where he got that "molecular matrix" from, or keep on pretending that he had invented transparent aluminum all on his own? *What about my business?* he fretted. *My patents?*

"No reason," he lied. "Just paranoid, I guess." He chuckled loudly, the forced laughter sounding hollow even to his own ears. "I mean, how do I know that you folks aren't aliens?"

"Good point," Carlson conceded amiably. He rolled up his sleeve to reveal a Nicoderm patch just above his elbow. "How many E.T.'s do you know that are trying to quit smoking?"

Walter smiled weakly. *How long can I pull this off,* he worried, *even if I have spent almost a decade studying the layout of those molecules?*

"In fact, Dr. Nichols," Lt. Christopher broke in, "we will be subjecting you to an exhaustive physical examination before you leave this facility, just to make sure that you are one hundred percent human."

I should be, Walter thought. Then a horrible idea occurred to him. *Unless those sneaky Ferengi did something to me when I wasn't looking!* For a second, he almost believed that he'd been injected with alien DNA or something, then he came to his senses. *Calm down,* he told himself urgently. *Don't let your imagination get out of control.*

"Not that we're really worried about that," Shannon O'Donnell reassured him. "We're most interested in your brains, not a blood sample. I'm hoping that, working together, we can refine and improve your formula for transparent aluminum until it's almost as strong and durable as the Ferengi version." She glanced down at her notes, then snapped her fingers as if she had just remembered something else. "We also want to take advantage of your recent research into cryonics."

Walter sat up straight, startled. "How do you know about that?" He hadn't wanted to go public with his new venture until he had all the technical kinks worked out; at best, he was at least a year away from launching his first cryosatellite.

"We have our sources," Lt. Christopher said, feigning a sinister leer. "The important thing is that cryonics is a major part of Project F. Our prototype, the DY-100, is intended to be a sleeper ship, capable of traveling vast distances to the stars while its crew and passengers remain frozen in suspended animation."

"You can see," O'Donnell said, "why we find your cryosatellite concept so intriguing." Carlson said she was an astronaut, Walter recalled; he wondered if she was planning to be one of those frozen space travelers. "We've also been carefully watching that whole

Biosphere experiment in Arizona," she added as an aside.

"So," Carlson inquired cheerfully, "what do you say, Walter? Are you with us?" His enthusiasm and energy were infectious. "We can definitely use a mind as ingenious and imaginative as yours."

Walter had to admit he enjoyed being mistaken for a genius. His whole reputation, not to mention his thriving business, was based on his supposed invention of transparent aluminum. How could he give that up now, especially when he had a chance to be part of history in the making?

Besides, there were bound to be commercial applications to the technology being developed here. Somebody had to keep an eye out for such opportunities, if only for the sake of the average American consumer. . . .

"When you put it like that," he said humbly, "how can I refuse?"

CHAPTER SIX

**PALACE OF THE GREAT KHAN
CHANDIGARH, INDIA
JUNE 14, 1993**

FOR SECURITY REASONS, THE SUMMIT WAS HELD IN A bombproof bunker several levels below the palace. A mirrored ceiling provided the illusion of open space, while also allowing wary bodyguards to view the proceedings from an extra angle. Polished granite walls, inlaid with geometric patterns of red and yellow marble, enclosed a rectangular chamber dominated by a conference-size teak table around which Khan's honored guests were seated. Each attendee had been permitted one armed bodyguard, who stood rigidly behind their respective charges, alert for any sign of danger or betrayal. An unsheathed scimitar that had once belonged to Saladin himself, served as a centerpiece atop the table.

Khan waited until all his guests were in place before entering the chamber. Then he strode to the head of the table, accompanied only by Joaquin and Ament. Golden embroidery glittered on a jacket woven of the finest Gujarati silk. "Welcome," he greeted those present. "I thank you all for accepting my invitation to meet here today."

He took a moment to survey the faces gathered at the table, most of which he had never before witnessed in the flesh. These were his far-flung brothers and sisters, fellow fruits of the Chrysalis Project, whose superior minds and bodies had brought them, despite their relative youth, to positions of prominence throughout the world. They were, he was forced to admit, an extraordinarily diverse lot: a Balkan dictator, a Somalian warlord, a charismatic Peruvian revolutionary, an exiled Chinese superwoman, the self-proclaimed prophet of a millennial cult, and the commander of an American anti-government militia.

They seemed, on the surface, to have little but enhanced DNA in common, but Khan was confident that he could unite his scattered siblings under a single banner. *We owe it to the world,* he believed with all his heart, *to combine our superlative abilities for the betterment of humanity.*

At least some of the attending luminaries seemed anxious to get down to business. "Why have you called us here?" Vasily Hunyadi demanded impatiently. He was a ruddy-faced Romanian, with a drooping mustache and wild, bushy eyebrows, who had lost one eye in the bloody civil wars consuming the former Yugoslavia. Khan was aware that Hunyadi had been accused by U.N. observers of practicing "genetic cleansing" in the areas under his control. "I have a war to fight."

"Yes," agreed Dr. Alberto Gomez, alias "Pachacutec,"

who had raised a rebel army in Peru as part of a decades-long campaign to restore the ancient Incan Empire along Marxist lines. A bristling, salt-and-pepper-colored beard obscured his aquiline features and made him look older than his mere twenty-two years. Despite all his genetic advantages, he appeared to have taken poor care of his body, which looked paunchy and out of shape beneath his ostentatiously proletarian peasant garb. "What is this all about, Khan Singh?"

Khan appreciated their directness. He also desired to cut straight to the heart of the matter. "Over two decades ago, the Chrysalis Project brought forth into the world a new and superior breed of humanity, genetically engineered for the express purpose of leading mankind into a brighter and more glorious future. We are the culmination of that magnificent venture," he informed them, gesturing expansively toward the highly varied personages gathered around the table. "You have all seen the documentation I sent you, establishing irrefutably our unique kinship. Moreover, you must feel in your very bones and blood, as I do, the innate superiority that drives you to make your mark upon the world. You must know, deep down inside, in the biological coding of your chromosomes, that we share a very special destiny, and a duty to see that destiny realized."

He spoke in English, certain that his supremely gifted peers were as fluently multilingual as he. "I am proud to call you my brothers and sisters. Individually, we have each accomplished much. Imagine now what we can do together." His spirit soared upon the exultant wings of his own rhetoric; he saw the future, shining as brightly as the summer sun, radiate outward from this humble bunker to transform the entire planet. "It is within our grasp to reshape history and grant to the world a new golden age, a second renaissance. An era of progress and discovery, of stability and order, unparalleled in human history!"

If he expected applause or affirmation, he was quickly disappointed. "Under whose rule?" asked a stocky African man whose military uniform was adorned with a veritable panoply of gleaming medals and ribbons. Elijah Jugurtha Amin was one of the most powerful warlords battling for control of the famine-stricken nation of Somalia. He eyed Khan with open distrust, his thick arms crossed atop the stout barrel of his chest. "Yours?"

"Sounds suspiciously like a New World Order to me," General Randall "Hawkeye" Morrison drawled dubiously. The only American at the table, the militia leader was clad in khaki-colored military fatigues. Large mirrored sunglasses hid his eyes from the other leaders at the summit. He chewed habitually on a piece of gum as he tipped back in his chair. "Like you might be planning to bulldoze Lady Liberty beneath a load of utopian hogwash."

Standing at Khan's right hand, Joaquin reached for his ursine belt buckle, but Khan discreetly raised a hand to forestall any immediate attempts to punish the American for his defiance. These were not, after all, inferior politicians and government functionaries of the sort who could be easily cowed by an unexpected act of violence; these were his peers, superior beings like himself, who had to be dealt with on an entirely higher level. (Besides, the presence of so many armed bodyguards made any abrupt executions problematic to say the least; Khan had no wish to spark a senseless shoot-out in the bunker of his own palace!)

He remained standing at the head of the table. "In the *Iliad,* the great poet Homer states wisely, 'A multitude of rulers is not a good thing. Let there be one ruler, one king.' " Khan bowed his head with as much humility as he could muster as he presented himself as that ruler. "Naturally, as the prime mover who has brought us all together, I see myself as the head of our alliance, but rest assured," he offered generously, "that each of you will have a voice in the greater Khanate to come. As chief executive and sovereign, I would consider it my responsibility and obligation to advance, to the best of my considerable abilities, our common agenda."

Angry mutterings arose from his assembled guests, but Khan pressed on, raising his voice to be heard above the protests. "Look at the chaotic state of the world today," he exhorted his prospective allies. "War and misery in the Middle East, Africa, and Eastern Europe. Terrorist bombings in New York, England, Italy. Thousands made homeless by flooding in India, Nepal, and the American Midwest. Entire nations breaking apart into anarchy. . . ." Khan shook his head, profoundly offended by the world's disarray. "Can you not see that a single, unified authority is needed to bring order to this tragic state of affairs?"

Hunyadi sneered derisively. "I cannot speak for the rest of the world, but there will be no more conflict in Eastern Europe once we have purified our population, and driven the genetically unfit from our land." His single eye gleamed with cruel anticipation. "Leave that to me."

"Yes," Amin seconded Hunyadi. "There will be peace

in Somaliland, too, but only after I defeat my enemies, including the heinous American occupying forces." Khan recalled that the American president had recently dispatched additional U.S. troops to assist in the United Nations' largely ineffective peacekeeping efforts in Somalia. "Victory is the only peace I crave."

Caustic laughter came from the attractive Chinese woman sitting across the table from Amin. Exiled from her own country after Tiananmen Square, Chen Tiejun had founded a separatist matriarchal colony on a remote island off the coast of New Zealand, attracting like-minded women from all over the world. Her glossy black hair was cut short, rather in the manner of Joan of Arc, and she wore a suit of molded resin body armor with pleated rubber joints. "Just like a man," she ridiculed the Somalian warlord. "Your answer to everything is conquest and oppression. Trademark patriarchal thinking."

"Patience, my brethren," urged a serene, ascetic-looking figure clad in flowing chartreuse robes. The constellation of Orion was tattooed upon his high, pale forehead. "There is no need for strife. All living things will be as one when our transcendent starfathers return to usher in the new millennium."

Gomez snickered and rolled his eyes. "Who invited this lunatic to the meeting. Let me guess, our 'starfathers' come from outer space, yes?"

Brother Arcturus, founder and sole prophet of the Panspermic Church of First Contact, replied with the weary resignation of one who was accustomed to being mocked by an unbelieving world. "As all truly enlightened souls are aware, the evolution of the human race is an eons-old experiment being conducted by higher intelligences originating in the Orion system, who long ago seeded the Earth with their own cosmic DNA." He nodded knowingly in Khan's direction. "I would not be surprised if the so-called Chrysalis Project was all part of the grand design, perhaps initiated by aliens in human guise."

I doubt my mother was from outer space, Khan thought, although he sometimes wondered about Gary Seven. Where *did* all that fantastic technology come from? It was a measure of Khan's rightful self-confidence that he was not intimidated by the prospect of extraterrestrial life; he liked to think that, should he ever meet an alien face-to-face, he would prove its equal or more.

"Utter rot!" Gomez labeled Arcturus's beliefs. "Mindless imbecility of the worst sort, in that it promises salvation from the stars rather than through tireless revolutionary struggle." Gomez had once been a university professor in Lima; his pedantic tone betrayed his academic roots. "Science fiction, it seems, is the new opiate of the masses."

Hawkeye Morrison came to the defense of the genre. "Sure beats all that left-wing Marxist claptrap you trade in," he snapped at Gomez. "Now that's fantasy, all right. Haven't you heard, Señor Professor? Communism is as dead as Elvis."

"Never!" Gomez's voice rang with revolutionary fervor. "The betrayal of the great Bolshevik experiment hardly negates the overriding principles of dialectical materialism. The class struggle is a force as inescapable as gravity, leading inevitably to the rise of a true workers' state." He glared balefully at Morrison, all but spitting out his words. "Your pathetic

Yankee posturings are nothing more than the last feeble bleatings of a morally and socially bankrupt society. We will build the People's Regime atop your own bloated corpse!"

Morrison rose angrily from his seat. "You goddamn commie weasel!" Gomez's bodyguard, an unsmiling mestizo gunman, reacted instantly, drawing a Walther P5 automatic pistol from beneath his woolen alpaca vest.

The militia leader's own bodyguard, a broad-shouldered American bruiser with a crew cut and icy blue eyes, countered by drawing his own gun. All around the table, armed escorts tensed for action, but Morrison did not back down. "Call off your mangy attack dog!" he challenged Gomez, leaning forward with both hands splayed upon the table. "How about you and me take this outside?"

"Typical," Chen Tiejun scoffed in disgust. Her own bodyguard was an amazonian redhead whom Khan suspected was also a product of Chrysalis. "Chest-beating and pissing contests. Classic masculine behavior, reeking of testosterone and gender tyranny." She looked down her classically perfect nose at the quarreling supermen. "Why don't you just compare the caliber of your firearms and get it over with?"

Khan thought he heard Ament snicker quietly behind him.

"Enough of this petty bickering," he declared, determined to restore order to the summit. Pulling out his chair, he made a point of sitting down at the table in a civilized manner. "We should be above politics and personality conflicts; it is manifestly obvious that we are stronger together than divided." He spoke from the heart, hoping to win over the others through the strength and passion of his convictions. "Let us not waste this historic opportunity by pitting our remarkable talents and intellects against each other."

Amin remained unmoved. "Ideology is for fools and weaklings," he stated bluntly. "Only power matters." A glass of ice water sat before him on the table. He handed the glass to his bodyguard, who tested it by taking a sip before giving it back to Amin. "What can you offer me?"

Although the warlord's self-centered attitude irked him, Khan welcomed the opportunity to extol the resources at his command. "Besides a secure power base, and a network of loyal operatives throughout Asia and beyond, I have access to military technology, both offensive and defensive, that exceeds anything else on Earth, including the U.S. Pentagon's newest and most closely guarded toys."

For now, Khan chose only to hint at the formidable arsenal at his command. "Space-based weaponry. Protective force fields. An elite force of genetically engineered warriors and assassins. All this and more I promise you, if you will but swear fealty to me and the noble crusade that I embody."

"Whoa there, Kublai Khan!" Morrison objected, with flagrant disrespect. Glowering at Gomez, the American dropped back into his seat and peered at Khan over the top of his sunglasses. "Not so fast. I'm not above a good, old-fashioned horse trade, exchanging tech for intel and vice versa, but I'm sure as hell not going to be part of any internationalist conspiracy to compromise the God-given sovereignty of the United States, not to mention free men and patriots everywhere." He shook a tobacco-stained finger at Khan. "I haven't raised a militia to fight the federal Beast in D.C. just to hand America over to a foreign prince."

"Free men, you say?" Chen Tiejun drew herself up indignantly. "And what of free women, who are forever oppressed regardless of politics and philosophies?" She symbolically wiped her hands of the whole discussion. "I want no part of any alliance that simply perpetuates the male-centered power structures of the past."

"Then stay on your island, witch," Amin jeered, "and leave the rest of the planet to us." Draining the last of his water, he loudly deposited the glass back onto the table. "I will swear loyalty to no one, Khan Noonien Singh, no matter what technological bribes you offer. I must be dealt with as an equal, or not at all!"

"Ditto!" Morrison exclaimed. He tipped back in his chair and surveyed the ornamented walls of the bunker with an obnoxiously unimpressed air. "Since when does one backward corner of India call the shots in world affairs?" He snorted in derision. "If I won't be bullied by Janet Reno and her storm troopers, let alone the goddamn United Nations, I'm sure as heck not going to take my marching orders from some puffed-up maharajah!"

It required all Khan's superhuman self-control not to smite the insolent American on the spot. Instead he watched and listened in dismay as the meeting degenerated into a babel of bellicose voices shouting to be heard over each other. Old accusations and insults echoed within the bunker as those whom he hoped would be the vanguard of his brave new world instead refought the outworn battles of the past century.

Finally, he could endure it no more. "Silence! Hold

your tongues, all of you!" His fist slammed down upon the teak tabletop with such force that it cracked the sturdy wood, the sharp report momentarily quelling the rancorous hubbub. "Are you all blind?" he raged at the squabbling leaders. "Have you lost your superior vision and mentalities?" He felt like throttling the lot of them with his bare hands. "Is it not obvious that we must speak with one voice, one mind?"

"Not if that voice is yours, Khan," Hunyadi said coldly. He rose from his seat, then headed for the exit. "I have wasted enough time here. Eastern Europe will chart its own course, unswayed by outside interference."

"As will Africa," Amin proclaimed, shoving away from the table. "Stay off my continent, Sikh, and I may let you keep your paltry kingdom in turn."

"This tiny spinning globe scarcely matters in the cosmic scheme," Arcturus said airily. His chartreuse robes rustled softly as he made his way toward the door. "I must prepare my flock for their new life among the stars."

And so it went. One by one, accompanied by their watchful bodyguards, the preeminent progeny of the Chrysalis Project exited the bunker, barely deigning to acknowledge each other as they departed, leaving Khan and his retinue alone in the spacious underground chamber. "Leave me," he instructed Joaquin and Ament, desiring solitude in which to contemplate the wreckage of his vision of unity.

Bitterness ate away at his hopes and ideals. The summit could not have gone worse, he concluded with mordant, mirthless humor, if Gary Seven had dictated the agenda. *What now am I to do?* he pondered, his heroic spirit struggling against despair.

The golden scimitar on the table mocked him with its own illustrious history. Saladin the Great had united the Arab world and led them to victory over the Crusaders. Yet he, Khan, could not even bring together his own kind, designed and conceived in the very same laboratories. *It is as the Old Testament said,* he thought: "A brother offended is harder to be won than a strong city; and their contentions are like the bars of a castle."

Khan felt those metaphorical bars closing in on his dreams. He snatched up the scimitar and hurled it across the bunker, the centuries-old blade striking the farthest wall so hard that it sank deeply into the hardened granite and remained hanging there, embedded like Excalibur in its stone. How dare his supposed peers turn their backs on his long-ordained destiny? How dare they deny the world the balm of his superior leadership?

"Very well," he resolved, clenching his fist before him. He would not permit the base and venal failings of his treacherous kinsmen to subvert the monumental task to which he had been born. The Great Khanate would extend its blessings over all the peoples of the world, even if it meant doing battle against legions of his own kind.

"Let there be war."

CHAPTER SEVEN

Captain's log, stardate 7004.2. First Officer Spock reporting.

While Captain Kirk and the landing party remain on the planet's surface, dealing with the crisis at the Paragon Colony, we are continuing to monitor the Klingon battle cruiser now orbiting Sycorax. Given the potential threat posed by the Klingon vessel, the Enterprise remains on Yellow Alert. . . .

"Mr. Spock!" Ensign Chekov exclaimed from Spock's own science station. The scanner cast a blue light onto the young Russian's startled features. "The Klingon ship is targeting the colony!"

Seated in the captain's chair, Spock swiftly processed the ensign's report and reacted accordingly. "Mr. Sulu," he ordered the ship's helmsman. "An intercept course, with all deliberate speed."

"Yes, sir!" Sulu responded immediately. The image on the viewscreen—the Klingon ship viewed from a prudent distance—tilted as the *Enterprise* zoomed to place itself between the Klingon vessel and the endangered colony.

Spock activated the intercom on the starboard arm of the command chair. "All decks, Condition Red," he stated matter-of-factly. His stoic Vulcan features betrayed no trace of anxiety. "Battle stations."

Alert indicators flashed crimson at key locations around the bridge as they closed on the Klingon vessel, which grew steadily larger on the viewscreen. The D-7 battle cruiser resembled a cross between an old-fashioned submarine and a Romulan bird-of-prey, with its bulbous prow connected to its rear engineering section by a long, tapering neck. A pair of massive wings spread outward from the engineering hull, supporting matching warp nacelles and disruptor cannons.

Spock rapidly considered the situation. The Klingons' hostile actions were not entirely unanticipated; in Spock's experience, Klingons seldom retreated without a fight. The only question was how far Captain Koloth was willing to go in his efforts to strike out at the Paragon Colony. In the past, Koloth had struck Spock as unusually cool-headed for a Klingon, albeit characteristically unscrupulous. Spock hoped that the Klingon commander would choose to forgo a full military confrontation with the *Enterprise,* but acknowledged that the probability of such an outcome was somewhat less than 6.463 percent.

"Lt. Uhura," he addressed the ship's able communications officer. "Hail the Klingon vessel."

The bridge of the *Imperial Klingon Ship Gr'oth* was musky with the scent of impending battle. Koloth leaned forward in his command seat as he contemplated the ugly yellow planet on the main viewer. Crimson lights cast bloody shadows upon the bridge, whose recessed forward area belonged to the captain alone; the bulk of his bridge crew performed their duties on a raised platform behind the command seat. Tactical displays and monitors surrounded the hexagonal viewscreen.

Koloth stroked his goatee thoughtfully. It was regrettable that he would have to destroy the colony below, and all that valuable genetic expertise, but he could not risk letting Paragon's scientific secrets fall into the hands of the Empire's enemies. "Prepare to fire," he ordered curtly. Set at maximum power, the battle cruiser's powerful phase disruptor cannons would make short work of the colony's protective dome.

"Captain!" Lt. K'rad shouted from the auxiliary tactical station, where he had been assigned to keep watch over the *Enterprise*. The silver mesh on his uniform reflected the crimson glow of the bridge lights. "The Earthers' ship is moving to block our cannons!"

Koloth scowled. Captain Kirk and his crew were not making his mission any easier. He had hoped that the photon grenade his first officer, Korax, had planted at Paragon's primary deflector array would be enough to terminate the colony's existence, but sensors indicated that Kirk and the colonists had somehow managed to keep the dome intact despite the sabotage. Now here was the *Enterprise,* complicating matters once again.

"Shall I reposition the ship?" the helmsman, Kinya, asked.

Koloth shook his head. The *Enterprise* would no

doubt simply shift position as well, and Koloth had no desire to spend the rest of his career playing a never-ending game of feint and parry with the Starfleet vessel. *We could be stuck above this wretched planet until Kahless comes back,* he mused sourly.

"We should blow them to atoms," Korax snarled. Koloth's first officer stood, as was proper, at his captain's side. A black eye and a split lip bore testament to Korax's earlier encounter with Paragon's genetically enhanced security guards. "Obliterate *Enterprise,* then those gene-twisting freaks on the planet!"

"All in good time," Koloth counseled, cautiously regarding the *Constitution*-class starship obstructing his view of the planet. He had not risen to his present high command by taking unnecessary risks. A pity, he reflected, that the *Gr'oth* lacked a cloaking device of the sort recently developed by the Romulans; such foolproof camouflage would have allowed him to break this stalemate by striking out at the colony before the *Enterprise* could get in the way. *We must exert more pressure on our so-called allies to share their cloaking technology with the Empire.*

"Captain!" The communications chief, Vlare, called out from his station behind and above the command chair. "The humans are hailing us."

Of course they are, Koloth thought. *Humans would always rather talk than fight.* "On screen," he ordered.

The face of Kirk's Vulcan first officer appeared on the main viewer, confirming Koloth's assumption that Captain Kirk was still on the planet's surface. *"This is First Officer Spock,"* he stated, with an irritating lack of inflection, *"currently in command of the U.S.S.* Enterprise. *We have observed your attempt to target the human*

*colony on Sycorax and urge you strongly to reconsider. We are
prepared to defend the colony if necessary."*

"This is no affair of yours, Vulcan," Koloth retorted.
"The Paragon Colony is not yet a member of the Federation and therefore beyond your jurisdiction. We
have every right to take action against a legitimate
threat to Klingon security." He smirked at the
viewscreen. "For that matter, the colony violates the
Federation's own ridiculously stringent prohibitions
against human genetic engineering. You should thank
us for striving to enforce your laws so forcefully!"

Spock raised a skeptical eyebrow. *"Your sarcasm is
duly noted, Captain,"* he said dryly. *"Nonetheless, the
colony remains under our protection until its future political
affiliation can be determined. I suggest you return to your
own recognized region of space, which does not, at present,
include the planet Sycorax."*

"He's bluffing!" Korax insisted. Sneering, he spit
contemptuously upon the grilled metal floor of the
bridge. "Vulcans have no will for battle."

Koloth was not so sure. He knew, better than most
of his more obstreperous brethren, that a keen intellect and unemotional demeanor did not preclude skill
in warfare. Indeed, in many ways, a cold-blooded
enemy could be the most dangerous of all.

Ultimately, there was only one way to find out if
the Vulcan was bluffing.

"Lock cannons on *Enterprise*," he said, manually
cutting off the communications link between the two
ships. Spock's alien countenance disappeared from
the viewer, and Koloth fixed a predatory gaze upon
the Starfleet warship.

"Fire!"

* * *

Bursts of brilliant green disruptor fire exploded against the *Enterprise*'s raised deflector screens. On the bridge, the concussion rattled the floor, jarring Spock where he sat.

He calmly took firmer hold of the arms of the chair, unperturbed by the attack. It was only logical; placing themselves between the Klingons and their prey necessarily made the *Enterprise* a target. Now the task at hand was simply to survive the conflict without sacrificing the planet below.

"Return fire," he instructed, before the glare of the Klingon's first salvo had fully faded from the viewscreen. At the navigation station, to the right of the helm, Yeoman Martha Landon triggered the already-energized phasers. Beams of sapphire energy shot forth from the underside of the *Enterprise*'s saucer section, converging on the enemy battle cruiser. Spock watched with interest as the phaser energy crackled along the edges of the Klingon ship's deflectors.

The targeting scanner telescoped out from the helm station, permitting Sulu to fully gauge the effects of the phaser strike upon their adversary. "A direct hit on their shields," the Asian crewman reported. "No obvious damage to the cruiser itself."

"Yet," Yeoman Landon added, with a touch more martial zeal than Spock deemed seemly. He made a mental note to recommend her transfer to Security, should they all survive the present conflict.

The Klingons responded by launching another volley of high-intensity disruptor fire. Blazing emerald energy spewed from the cannons mounted on the battle cruiser's wings. The resulting shock wave, stemming from the violent intersection of disruptors and deflectors, rocked the bridge and caused the overhead lights to flicker momentarily. Spock judged the impact perceptibly more damaging than the previous blast.

"Shields down to ninety-two percent," Chekov reported.

Ninety-two-point-eight-five, Spock estimated. "Fire at will, Yeoman Landon," he ordered. A glance at the astrogator revealed that the force of the disruptors had pushed the *Enterprise* a few degrees off mark. "Maintain intercept position, Mr. Sulu," he urged. "We do not wish to provide the Klingons with an angle from which to attack the colony."

"Yes, sir!" the helmsman said, a trace of mordant humor in his voice. "I'll keep us right in the line of fire."

Phasers clashed with disruptors just beyond the boundaries of the planet's atmosphere, barraging the viewscreen with flashes of scintillating blue and green energy. Spock felt the steel-and-plastiform construction of the bridge vibrate beneath the strain of the cataclysmic forces battering the ship's deteriorating shields, each fresh disruptor blast sending a bone-rattling jolt through his entire skeleton. An unexpectedly potent strike caused his jaw to snap shut on his lower lip. He tasted copper on his tongue.

Ignoring any physical distractions, Spock coolly assessed the tactical situation. The warring ships were evenly matched, but the *Enterprise* was handicapped by having to defend the colony as well as itself, thus severely limiting its maneuverability. With evasive action out of the question, the *Enterprise* clearly required some manner of competitive edge. Spock's computerlike mind quickly considered and discarded dozens of possible strategies, both time-tested and untried. It was while reviewing the successful battle tactics of Earth's preunified past that a promising idea occurred to him.

"Yeoman Landon," he requested, rising from the captain's chair, "please step aside." There was no time to explain the intricacies of his stratagem to the young crewmember; it would be faster and more effective to man the weapons controls himself.

Landon promptly surrendered the navigation station, and Spock took her place to the right of the helm. He rapidly reprogrammed the phaser controls to vary the intensity and protonic frequency of the phaser bursts at a significantly accelerated rate, roughly 118.731 times a second. The rapid shifts would, inevitably, lessen the offensive strength of the phasers, but, according to his calculations, might well serve to provide the Klingons with an unwelcome surprise.

He pressed the firing controls, initiating the sequence. On the viewscreen, the incandescent phasers flashed at high speed along an entire spectrum of colors, producing a prismatic strobe effect that left Ensign Chekov blinking in confusion. "What in the name of Mother Russia . . . ?" He scratched his head, a baffled look on his face. "Mr. Spock, are the phasers supposed to be doing that?"

"Affirmative, Ensign," Spock stated, simultaneously adjusting the phaser controls to enhance the strobing. "With their deflectors on full, the Klingons' sensor arrays can only scan along a narrow range of the electromagnetic spectrum. We lack the sheer phaser power to overwhelm their shields, but I theorized that it might be possible to use the phasers to disorient their remaining sensors."

Standing off to one side, Landon watched the light show on the screen with wide, wondering eyes. "Is it working?" she whispered.

One minute, the main viewer had the *Enterprise* directly in its sights. The next, a flashing, kaleidoscopic display of lights and colors usurped the screen, offering Koloth nothing but visual static, with no view at all of the ongoing battle. "Qu'vatlh!" he swore, rising up from his command chair in surprise. "What is happening?"

At the chief tactical station, over Koloth's left shoulder, Lt. Macck frantically worked the sensor controls, trying to restore the image on the screen. "It's not working!" he growled. Frustrated, he hammered the control panel with his fist. "The processors can't make sense of the EM readings!"

"Targeting sensors inoperative," the gunman, Krevorr, reported from the weapons station. "We've lost our lock on *Enterprise!*"

"Navigational sensors, too!" Kinya called out. "We're flying blind!"

Koloth suddenly felt as though he were being nibbled to death by tribbles. His fists clenched angrily as he glared with icy fury at the malfunctioning main viewer. The flashing pyrotechnics, devoid of usable data, made his head hurt. "Compensate!" he ordered his crew. How could he fight a battle when he couldn't even see his enemy? "Compensate, for Kahless's sake!"

* * *

"Mr. Spock!" Chief Engineer Scott's voice exclaimed over the bridge's intercom system. *"What the devil are ye doing to me poor phaser banks?"*

Still seated at the navigation station, Spock opened a line to Engineering. "My apologies, Mr. Scott, but there was no time to inform you of my intentions." He observed the strobing phasers on the viewscreen, while signaling Sulu to reposition the *Enterprise* with regards to the Klingon vessel. "Although unorthodox, I believe my present use of the main phaser arrays will not exceed their operational capacities, provided our encounter with the Klingons is not too protracted."

"If you say so, Mr. Spock." The canny engineer sounded skeptical. *"Just don't be making a habit of this, mind you. Phaser settings were never meant to go spinning like pinwheels!"*

"Your point is well taken, Mr. Scott." Spock's gaze never left the viewscreen, where fierce green disruptor blasts could be seen blazing across empty space, missing the *Enterprise* entirely; it certainly seemed as though the enemy battle cruiser was now firing blind. "Spock out."

"It's working!" Yeoman Landon exclaimed, looking over Spock's shoulder at the viewscreen before them. "You've knocked out their sensors."

"In fact," he corrected her, "their sensors are not so much knocked out as overstimulated."

"A brilliant move, Mr. Spock!" Chekov enthused. The emotive young Russian looked up from the RVS scanner to congratulate his commander. "Wherever did you get the idea?"

Spock took little note of the ensign's fulsome praise. "From one of Earth's own global conflicts," he divulged. "Your second World War, to be exact." He targeted the Klingon ship with a reverse tractor beam, giving the bedeviled battle cruiser a solid push so that, in theory, the Klingons would not even be certain of their own position. "Allied forces defending the Suez Canal from German Luftwaffe bombers fit ordinary searchlights with tin reflectors, then engineered the lights so that they would spin rapidly, projecting 'cartwheels of light' into the night sky that effectively dazzled the German pilots, rendering them unable to keep the canal in their bombsights. The ploy was successful, and the canal kept safe." *Much as Sycorax is now,* he observed. "I merely adapted the same technique to modern technology."

"I see," Chekov said, grinning. "World War Two, you say? Sounds like a Russian's idea to me."

Spock arched an eyebrow, bemused by the ensign's atavistic nationalism. "In fact, the strategy is credited to one Jasper Maskelyne, a British stage magician."

Chekov frowned, eyeing Spock dubiously. "Are you quite sure it wasn't Maskelynovich?"

An explosion buffeted the *Gr'oth,* causing the bridge to tremble like a frightened targ. Sparks flared from the tactical console, singeing Macck, who angrily snuffed out the flames with his bare hands. Only a few strides away, Koloth's heart sank; a veteran of numerous battles, he knew the impact of a photon torpedo when he felt one.

"Shields down to eighty-six percent!" K'rad reported from the auxiliary station. Warning lights flashed on his control panel, and he pounded on the recalcitrant instruments as though they were drums.

His swarthy face a veritable portrait of unchecked rage, Korax grabbed his captain by the shoulder. "We are under attack!" he growled, displaying an impressive grasp of the obvious. Spittle flew from his lips as he shouted into the captain's face. "We must retaliate!"

Koloth struck Korax hard across the face with the back of his hand, reasserting his authority. "No!" he decreed forcefully. "I am not about to waste any more of our firepower by shooting blindly in the dark." He sneered at Korax in disdain. "Only a fool throws spears at shadows."

The intemperate first officer wisely withdrew his hand from Koloth's person. Crimson droplets fell from Korax's freshly bloodied nose and lips. Inwardly, Koloth felt relieved that Korax had backed off so readily; the last thing he needed right now was a challenge from his second-in-command. He had other problems to deal with, like a mission rapidly going to Gre'thor.

The useless visual clutter on the main viewer taunted him, and Koloth paced back and forth across the bridge, exasperated and irate. "Will someone fix that cursed viewer!" he cried out bitterly. "Am I surrounded by incompetents?" He felt his icy demeanor and self-control melting away. Was it just the fire in his blood, or was the bridge getting uncomfortably warm?

"Captain!" K'rad shouted. "I have it!"

Sparing his captain the tiresome technical details, K'rad stabbed at the backup sensor controls. Koloth's hopes surged as the headache-inducing flashes gave way to a clearer, sharper view . . . of churning yellow clouds!

"No!" Koloth gasped as the truth hit home with the force of a disruptor blast. No wonder the bridge felt so oppressively hot; they were plunging into the planet's acidic atmosphere. "Reverse course!" he yelled hoarsely, as Sycorax's gravity seized his ship, causing the floor of the bridge to slope downward precipitously. Koloth grabbed on to the nearest support beam to keep from falling face-forward. Reacting less quickly, Korax tumbled head over heels into the base of the main viewer.

"Climb!" Koloth hollered. He could feel the sweltering heat of their descent all the way through their tattered shields. He heard the wrenching sound of inertial dampers being pushed beyond their limits. Black, acrid smoke erupted from half a dozen consoles as warning alarms blared throughout the bridge. "Climb!"

"Mr. Spock," Chekov called out. "The Klingon vessel is escaping the planet's atmosphere."

"Understood," Spock said, acknowledging the report. "Their status?"

Chekov peered into the scanner, even as, on the viewscreen, the globular prow of the battle cruiser emerged from the murky depths of Sycorax's turbulent atmosphere, followed by its extended neck and once-menacing aft wings. The outer hull of the vessel was visibly scorched, while plasma leaked from its ravaged impulse engines and disruptor cannons.

"Their shields are shredded!" Chekov announced jubilantly. "Less than forty-three percent operative, with holes you could fly a shuttlecraft through!"

"That should not be necessary, Ensign." Spock gave the navigator's post back to Landon and returned to the captain's chair. The injured battle cruiser lurched awkwardly across the screen. Spock was gratified to note extensive damage along the entire length of the ship. Its running lights flickered uncertainly while phosphorescent vapor jetted from the emergency vents, as well as from the reactor cooling system below its engineering hull. Even the bolognium shielding on the warp nacelles was scarred and dented.

"Shall I take offensive action, Mr. Spock?" Landon asked, her fingers poised over the weapons controls.

"Phasers at maximum," he instructed, unwilling to give Koloth and his crew a chance to recover from their recent reversals in fortune. "Target their sensor arrays and shield emitters, taking care not to hit their warp engines." His fingers were steepled pensively beneath his chin as he contemplated the besieged battle cruiser. "We want to give the Klingons the opportunity to escape."

"Yes, sir," Landon said, sounding a trifle disappointed. Beams of azure energy assailed the Klingon vessel, slicing through its already battered hull. The last vestiges of its shields flickered impotently along its charred metal skin.

"Do you really think the Klingons will withdraw?" Sulu asked Spock, looking away from the targeting scanner. "I didn't think 'retreat' was in their vocabulary."

"I believe the precise term is 'HeD,'" Spock informed the helmsman. The guttural syllable felt singularly out of place on his Vulcan tongue. "And, unless I am severely mistaken, Captain Koloth is too pragmatic a commander to sacrifice his ship to no good purpose."

"As a matter of fact," Lt. Uhura reported, a touch of amusement in her voice, "he's hailing you now, sir."

"Onscreen," Spock requested, while signaling Landon to halt her phaser assault on the Klingon ship.

Koloth's overly familiar visage appeared on the viewscreen. Spock noted that the usually urbane commander was looking rather less than his best. Koloth's widow's peak of black hair was in disarray, while his silver-and-black military uniform was rumpled and stained with soot. Peering past Koloth's disheveled head and shoulders, Spock thought the Klingons' bridge seemed even smokier and more dimly lit than it had before. Flames licked the surface of the visible control consoles. He heard groans and coughing in the background.

"Spock here," he stated flatly. As a Vulcan, he felt no need to gloat over the Klingons' sorry state. "How can I help you, Captain?"

"You could never have been born," Koloth answered wearily. A mirthless smile tweaked the corners of his lips. "Be that as it may, I applaud your ingenuity, Vulcan. Please extend my compliments to Captain Kirk on his excellent choice of first officer." His sardonic manner faded as his face took on a graver expression. When he spoke again, there was no trace of mocking humor in his voice; he was deadly serious. "But do not be mistaken: this matter is not over. Be warned that the Klingon Empire will never tolerate any alliance between the Federation and the Paragon Colony."

The transmission ceased abruptly, as though Koloth felt that he had said all that was needed. Spock watched thoughtfully as the wounded battle cruiser warped out of sight, leaving only subspace ripples behind.

"Contact the captain," he instructed Uhura. "Inform him that the Klingons have departed—for now."

CHAPTER EIGHT

WHEN THE BLAST OF WAR BLOWS IN OUR EARS, KHAN thought, seeking inspiration in the immortal words of the Bard, *then imitate the actions of the tiger.* Seething with justifiable fury, he descended the marble steps of his palace, too impatient to wait for an elevator. *Stiffen the sinews, summon up the blood, disguise fair nature with hard-favored rage; then lend the eye a terrible aspect....*

The control room for the Morning Star satellite was hidden in the lowest level of the palace, below even the bombproof bunker that had just hosted the ill-fated summit meeting. Khan had designed the underground chamber to survive anything short of a nuclear attack, and perhaps even that; should his entire fortress be reduced to ashes, he would still be able to retaliate with the destructive power of the satellite.

He had hoped never to use Morning Star's ozone-destroying capabilities, but that was before his fellow supermen revolted against him. *They brought this on themselves,* he thought bitterly. Anger flooded his veins like a drug. *They must learn that defying me carries a heavy price.*

A pair of Exon warriors, armed with automatic rifles, guarded the door of the control room. They saluted and stepped aside as Khan approached the dense titanium door, which was merely the second line of defense standing between the satellite controls and any unauthorized trespasser. He keyed today's ten-digit code number into the touchpad to the right of the door and, with a *whoosh* of released air, the titanium barrier slid out of his way.

Khan strode decisively into the chamber beyond, where two of his most trusted security officers, Suzette Ling and Vishwa Patil, manned the outer booth, carefully monitoring both the satellite and the space surrounding it. They rose in attention at Khan's entrance, but he dismissed such formalities with a wave of his hand. "What is the status of Morning Star?" he demanded without preamble, as the massive door slid shut behind him. "Is the satellite in any danger?"

"All is well, Your Excellency," Ling reported promptly. Glowing radar screens cast a green glow upon one side of her face. A matte-black phone built into the console provided her with a hotline to notify Khan if anything was amiss. "Morning Star remains fully operational, nor is there any indication that it is under attack."

The orbiting satellite was monitored twenty-four hours a day, both from Chandigarh and Muroroa, lest any of Khan's many enemies attempt to put Morning Star out of commission. Although Morning Star was equipped with a force field generator, to shield it against both particle beams and Gary Seven's insidious transporter device, the satellite's best defense remained under Khan's constant vigilance; he had made it known that, should any foreign satellite, missile, or spacecraft even come within ten kilometers of Morning Star, he would immediately launch a preemptive strike against the aggressor, burning a nation-size hole in the ozone layer directly above any country rash enough to threaten his ultimate weapon.

"Good," he said, gratified that he still had the upper hand where Morning Star was concerned. "Continue your watchfulness; these are perilous times." With the woeful collapse of the summit only an hour ago, his list of enemies had just grown accordingly. Who knew when Vasily Hunyadi, Hawkeye Morrison, or one of the other rebellious supertraitors might grow bold enough to move against him? All the more reason to strike quickly, he resolved. As the Bard also wisely wrote: "Delays have dangerous ends."

A second titanium door, even more impregnable than the first, stood between these monitoring stations and Morning Star's actual firing controls. Only one other person besides Khan knew the sixteen-digit numerical sequence required to gain entry to the inner chamber. He used his body to shield the touchpad from the view of the two security officers as he expertly keyed in the entire sequence from memory. It was not that he mistrusted Ling and Patil, but some privileges, like the ability to activate Morning Star, were best kept in the fewest possible hands.

The secondary door admitted him, and he stepped inside the control booth. A single molded plastic chair faced a state-of-the-art ergonomic control panel, dominated by a large red button beneath a transparent sheet of unbreakable plastic. An illuminated map of the world stretched above the control panel, the shifting national borders constantly updated by an artificially intelligent computer program attuned to the ever-changing fortunes of war and politics. A blinking green dot tracked Morning Star's location as the satellite orbited continuously above the planet.

Khan took his seat and rested his hands on the controls. Without hesitation, even as the door automatically closed behind him, he swiftly entered the final twenty-digit command code into the computer.

"Command authorization approved," the computer greeted him in Punjabi. High-powered cybernetic hardware hummed and clattered. *"Please select target."*

He stared balefully at the illuminated map. Which of the treacherous supermen should be the first to feel his wrath? Amin? Gomez? Arcturus?

Hunyadi, he decided after only a moment's consideration. Geographically, the one-eyed Romanian war criminal possessed the largest power base at present; in addition, he had been the first attendee to walk out on Khan's summit, spurring the others to do the same. *Let him then serve as an example.*

Khan's dark gaze zeroed in on the territory currently controlled by the Serbian government, including key areas of Bosnia-Herzegovina. The nebulous borders flickered visibly before his eyes, reflecting the most recent developments in the ongoing Balkan conflict. Khan fed the appropriate coordinates into the targeting computer and watched with satisfaction as, on the glowing map, the Serbian possessions acquired a damning crimson hue.

"Target selected," the computer confirmed. Symbolized by the flashing red dot, Morning Star began moving into position above Serbia. *"Please stipulate operational parameters."*

It was in Khan's power to choose the precise degree to which the ozone layer was devoured above Hunyadi's domain, to heighten or temper the corrosive effect as he so desired. Today, frustrated by the collapse of his planned global alliance, he was not in a merciful frame of mind.

He typed 100%. He smiled coldly, recalling that it was now almost summer in Eastern Europe. Let them feel the full force of the sun. Perhaps a sudden outbreak of blindness, cancer, and starvation would be enough to chasten the arrogant Romanian—and put the fear of Khan into the rest of his insubordinate siblings.

"Parameters selected," the computer announced. *"Arming satellite."*

On the screen, the once-green dot changed to a cautionary shade of yellow, indicating that the satellite was in standby mode. Khan tracked the flashing amber marker with his eyes, as Morning Star, propelled by its powerful directional jets, maneuvered into place, one thousand kilometers above the Earth. *Soon,* Khan thought with vengeful anticipation. *Very soon.*

Finally, in less than thirty minutes, Morning Star came to rest above its target. *"Satellite in position,"* the computer informed him, as the blinking yellow dot turned the same brilliant shade of red as the designated area on the global map. *"All systems armed and ready."*

On the control panel, the clear plastic shield slid away, exposing the oversize red button. This was the final firing mechanism, which would signal Morning Star to begin its deadly work. His right hand drifted inexorably toward the waiting button.

"Lord Khan," a concerned voice interrupted. "What do you think you are doing?"

Khan spun around in the chair to find Ament standing in the open doorway. Although startled, he was not surprised to find the graceful Egyptian woman here; Ament was the only other person, besides himself, to whom Khan had entrusted the command codes for Morning Star, in the event that he was killed or incapacitated during a sneak attack. Her cool temperament, thoughtful manner, and incorruptible conscience made her the ideal custodian of the satellite's apocalyptic power during any such emergency. He knew he could trust Ament to wield this most awesome of weapons wisely.

At the moment, however, he might have preferred a touch more privacy. "Your tread is admirably light, Lady Ament," he said wryly. "I did not hear you approach."

She stepped fully into the control booth, letting the door slide completely shut; this discussion was not for the ears of Patil or Ling. "I ask again, my lord: What are you doing?"

"Showing my insolent siblings that I am not to be disrespected in my own palace," he said. "You were there, my lady. You saw how they defied me." His face hardened at the memory, still fresh enough to stoke his ire anew. "They must learn that they reject my authority at their own peril."

"Indeed, Lord Khan," she agreed readily, "but would you inflict untold misery upon countless innocents, merely to punish their leaders?" Her amber eyes found the luminous map, noting the telltale red stain spreading over Serbia. "It is not Hunyadi who will suffer the most, but the hapless men, women, and children under his rule."

Khan winced inwardly at this undeniable truth, but remained committed to the course he had chosen. "Such are the cruel realities of war," he observed reluctantly. "It is unfortunate, but sometimes innocents must be sacrificed in pursuit of a larger goal."

"Perhaps," she admitted, "but can you not find a more precise, more surgical means of striking out at Hunyadi and the others? A scalpel rather than a flamethrower?" She shook her head mournfully, a pensive frown upon her ruby lips. "Morning Star is a weapon of mass destruction, best employed as a last resort or deterrent." She nodded at the map above their heads. "I fear also, my lord, that reckless use of Morning Star might invite an armed response from the great powers of the world, who, at present, are resigned to letting us be. Once you actually deploy the satellite, it becomes less of a deterrent and more of a threat requiring immediate action."

Khan leaned back against the molded support of his chair, compelled, against his inclinations, to consider the merits of Ament's argument. His wrath was great, and he was in no mood to be second-guessed thus, yet he could not deny that her counsel held, as ever, a substantial measure of wisdom.

It would be enormously satisfying to press that red button, to inflict vengeance of Biblical proportions upon his enemy with but the tap of his finger. Hunyadi and his seditious peers deserved no less. However, as Ament suggested, perhaps a truly superior ruler would rise above such a temptation, no matter how justifiable, and pursue other options before resorting to something as vast and terrible as Morning Star.

The red button waited, as did the satellite hovering over Eastern Europe.

"Curse you, woman," Khan said finally. He pressed the Cancel command on the control panel. The plastic sheath slid back over the fateful red button, shielding it from his touch. On the map, the blinking crimson dot turned green once more, then resumed its original orbit.

"Targeting sequence terminated," the computer stated. *"Aborting procedure."*

"You have chosen wisely," Ament said.

Have I? Khan wondered dourly. His thwarted rage festered inside him like a loathsome parasite gnawing upon his entrails. "Hunyadi shall pay," he promised darkly, more to himself than to her.

"Of course, Lord Khan." She pressed a rectangular button next to the exit, opening the door to the outer chamber.

"They shall all pay, and dearly."

"As you wish, my lord." She lingered in the doorway, as if reluctant to leave Khan alone in the control room, lest he revert to his original intention.

Fear not, he thought wearily. With a heavy sigh, he rose from the plastic chair to follow his sagacious, if sometimes inconvenient, advisor out of the control room. Ling and Patil did not look up from their monitors, curbing whatever curiosity they might have felt about what had just transpired in the inner chamber. Khan did not consider informing them.

Hunyadi will pay, he vowed once again.

But not today.

CHAPTER NINE

PRIMITIVE AS IT WAS, GARY SEVEN HAD TO ADMIT that Earth was a beautiful planet.

He stood upon a winding hillside trail, looking out over the rolling farmland below. His elevation offered him a panoramic view of the quiet Scottish island, with its verdant glens, clear running streams, and fathomless lochs. Purple heather was ankle-deep in the brush beside the dirt path, competing with the brown and green mountain grasses. Many yards below, at the bottom of the trail, a barking dog herded a flock of recalcitrant sheep, while, in the distance, Seven glimpsed the rooftops of the nearest village, a tiny fishing community bearing the unlikely name of Blackwaterfoot, which he had always thought sounded like something badly translated from Andorian.

He rested his weight upon a gnarled hazelwood walking stick, contemplating the exotic locale where he had so improbably ended up. The isle, along with the rest of Earth, bore little resemblance to the distant world where he had been born and reared: a highly advanced, cosmopolitan planet, populated by representatives of every known (and unknown) intelligent species. Now he could barely remember the last time he saw a Horta, and he still occasionally missed the tangy taste of hot plomeek soup, despite Roberta's best efforts to replicate the recipe from his description.

Have I truly lived on Earth for over a quarter of a century? he pondered. The thought boggled his mind, yet he had few regrets. Earth—and humanity—were well worth the years he had spent striving to assure their survival. At times he had been tempted to head back to more civilized quarters of the galaxy, delegating affairs on Earth to able lieutenants such as Roberta, but the situation here had always been too precarious, too fraught with potential catastrophe, to risk trying to supervise things from hundreds of light-years away. How could he leave Earth, the planet of his ancestors, with the likes of Khan still running amok.

"Tuppence for your thoughts?"

Seven pivoted slowly upon his cane to see Roberta trudging up the hill toward him. Several paces behind her, a wisp of white smoke rose from the chimney of the refurbished stone farmhouse that now served as their new headquarters; following the London fiasco, he and Roberta had decided to stay away from major population centers, thereby endangering fewer civilians by their presence. After all, they had reasoned, when you have a transporter, you can set up shop almost anywhere.

"Simply enjoying the afternoon, and the view," he replied, not entirely honestly. Why spoil Roberta's mood with his own dour ruminations? He leaned upon his cane as she joined him at the crest of the hill, puffing slightly from the climb.

"It is gorgeous here," she agreed, smiling as her gaze swept over the scenery below. Not for nothing had the Isle of Arran been described as "Scotland in miniature," with all manner of picturesque terrain, including marshes and mountains, rocky cliffs and cozy beaches, crammed onto one small island, only twenty-five miles long and ten miles across. Looking north, one could see a ring of standing stones rising like petrified fingers from the boggy, peat-covered surface of a lonely moor. The ancient megaliths, which dated back to the Neolithic period, reminded Seven of how far Homo sapiens had come in the last few millennia—and how far they still had to go.

"Remember the first time we visited these islands?" Roberta watched a kestrel circle beneath the cloudy blue sky, on the lookout for an unsuspecting hare. "Back in seventy-three?"

Seven nodded, letting his memory drift forward to a time considerably more recent than the Stone Age. They had been investigating, on behalf of an old friend, the mysterious disappearance of a Scottish policeman on a nearby island, which had proved to be home to a bloodthirsty pagan cult. "A rather unsettling excursion, as I recall."

"I'll say." Roberta shuddered, no doubt recalling

how close she had come to being burned alive inside a gigantic wicker effigy. Seven himself had been severely disillusioned to discover human sacrifice still being practiced in the late twentieth century. "Who would have ever guessed," she added, "that we'd wind up living only a few islands away?"

Seven noticed a sheaf of papers caught beneath Roberta's arm, in the crook of her bushy fleece sweater. "What do you have there?" he asked.

She handed the documents over to Seven. "Today's *New York Times,* hot off the Beta 6," she explained, "plus the usual updates on various global hot spots."

He glanced at the front page of the *Times.* "PLO and Israel Accept Each Other After 3 Decades of Relentless Strife," read the banner headline across the top of the page, reporting on substantial progress in the ongoing Mideast peace talks. Seven was encouraged by the news, but feared that achieving true peace in that troubled region would prove easier said than done. Lower on the page, a less hopeful headline informed him that "U.S. Troops Fire on Somalis; Death Toll May Reach 100."

A long way to go, indeed, he thought, acutely aware that the situation in Somalia was being exacerbated by the megalomaniacal ambitions of one of Khan's supersiblings. *With luck,* he thought, *Amin will be taken out of the picture by either the Americans or one of his fellow warlords.*

"Any other highlights?" he asked, flipping through the newspaper. The bulk of the coverage seemed to concern the peace talks in Washington, but he knew that Roberta had other, equally reliable sources of information.

She shrugged. "Yeltsin is threatening to dissolve the Russian Parliament. Saddam is playing games with the U.N. inspectors again." She paused, searching her memory for any other relevant tidbits. "Oh, NASA is on schedule to fix the Hubble space telescope in December. That's okay now, right?"

"I believe so," he stated. Back in 1990, he and Roberta had sabotaged the ambitious astronomical project by covertly shaving seven hundred thousands of an inch off the Hubble's primary mirror, rendering the $1.5 million dollar space eye effectively nearsighted. Such tampering had been necessary to prevent unprepared human astronomers from observing the passage of a Vulcan trading fleet through the Lambda Sector; in Seven's judgment, Earth was not yet ready for that sort of first contact. Fortunately, the Vulcan caravan had since warped beyond the range of the Hubble, so he saw no harm in allowing NASA to correct the telescope's vision.

"What about Khan?" he asked.

Roberta's face grew more somber. "Ominously quiet, at the moment." The red-winged falcon continued to circle above their heads, awaiting prey. "Our spies suggest that he's regrouping after the total failure of his big superman summit in June. He's had some dealings with Morrison's militia in the States, exchanging info and technology, but mostly he seems to be gearing up to defend himself from all the other would-be Napoleons out there. Things are particularly frosty between Khan and Hunyadi, who are wrangling over Turkestan. Hunyadi's people assassinated a couple of Khan's most highly placed pawns in the local government earlier this week; this morning,

Khan retaliated by taking out an entire Serbian intelligence cell." Lines of worry deepened around her eyes and mouth. "I wouldn't be surprised if that particular cold war gets real hot real soon."

Sadly, Seven had no reason to doubt Roberta's dire reading of events. Almost twenty years after he destroyed Sarina Kaur's underground laboratory in Rajasthan, it seemed that her Chrysalis Project was still casting a long shadow over world affairs. *Like Landru on his world,* Seven thought. There were times, in his darker moments, when he almost wished that he had let the budding children of Chrysalis be incinerated along with their creator. But, no, that had never truly been an option; he could not have condemned blameless innocents to death for crimes they might someday commit, even if that meant dealing with Khan and his ilk two decades later.

I mustn't lose hope, he thought. Perhaps Earth could still escape the sort of eugenic madness that had corrupted so many other civilizations. Thankfully, many of Khan's more unstable peers had already self-destructed, like that would-be messiah in Texas. Others, such as Alberto Gomez, were being neutralized in a reasonably discreet manner; thanks to some undercover assistance by Roberta, the Peruvian government had finally captured the brilliant revolutionary leader less than a month ago, promising the return of something resembling normalcy to that war-torn nation. Seven had been relieved to see Gomez behind bars at last, unable to turn his superlative mind to future acts of violent insurrection. *One terrorist mastermind down,* he thought, gratefully striking "Pachacutec" from his mental to-do list.

But that still left Khan and Hunyadi and the rest, along with their respective throngs of superhuman followers. Seven stared at the pastoral peace and beauty of Arran, and wondered how long such serenity could survive in a world overrun by indomitable conquerors whose grandiose ambitions were encoded in their very genes. Sometimes he feared that, despite his best efforts to protect mankind's infinite potential, the human race would ultimately destroy themselves anyway, spurred on by the perilous feuding of Khan and his kin.

Good thing I have a backup plan, he thought. *Just in case.*

CHAPTER TEN

AJORRA CAVES
MAHARASHTRA STATE
CENTRAL INDIA
SEPTEMBER 30, 1993

CHISELED OUT OF THE GRANITE HILLSIDE BY GENERA-
tions of ancient monks and artisans, the enormous
cave-temple took Khan's breath away. Larger even
than the Parthenon in Greece, the towering edifice
rose toward the night sky, its venerable exterior generously adorned with intricately carved friezes depicting picturesque scenes from Hindu folklore and
mythology. Epic battles, royal weddings, and acrobati-
cally amorous couples, all lovingly sculpted in elaborate detail, proliferated upon the walls of the temple,
being all the more impressive when one realized that
the entire structure, including its rampant decoration, had all been hewn from the same solid piece of
rock, carved from the top down rather than built up
from the bottom.

"Magnificent!" Khan pronounced. Even in nocturnal darkness, its myriad surfaces illuminated only by the flashlights of Khan and his entourage, the temple presented almost too much visual detail to take in all at once. *Hard to imagine,* he thought, *that such an astounding work of art and engineering was created by ordinary, primitive humans.*

Unsurprisingly, Joaquin was too concerned with Khan's personal safety to appreciate the splendor before his eyes. "I don't like this," he muttered gruffly, the cool white beam of his flashlight searching for hidden snipers. "It's too quiet."

By day, and during the peak season, the temple was a major tourist attraction. It was now nearly 3:45 in the morning, at the tail end of the annual monsoon, however, and Khan and his party appeared to have the place to themselves. They were gathered on the rocky plain outside the temple's main gate, with a clear view of the spacious courtyard beyond. The helicopter that had brought them here rested several paces behind them on a blacktop parking lot usually reserved for tour buses. Although the rain had mercifully abated for a time, swollen clouds promised another downpour before morning.

"That was the intention," Khan reminded Joaquin, referring to the silent and deserted setting. "Our contact desired privacy, as you recall."

"This is too private," the bodyguard insisted. He was always unhappy when Khan ventured beyond the safety of his fortress in Chandigarh. "It could be a trap."

Khan did not share his protector's fears. "We have taken the necessary precautions," he observed, gesturing toward the team of armed Exon warriors accompanying them. He, too, was prepared for combat, his P226 automatic resting securely against his hip. "Besides, I have always meant to visit this site." He swept the beam of his flashlight over the intricate carvings climbing the walls of the temple gate or gopuram. "Spectacular, is it not? A tribute to human achievement and artistry."

Someday, he reflected, *after I have won my wars of conquest, I shall be a great patron of the arts and sciences. Under my benevolent sponsorship and protection, there shall be an intellectual renaissance unrivaled since the Medicis ruled Italy.*

He looked forward to that day.

Joaquin remained unmoved by the temple's grandeur. "We should not have come here," he argued once more. "Now is a bad time. There is too much trouble in the air."

This much is true, Khan conceded regretfully. Nineteen ninety-three had been a bloody year on the Indian subcontinent, marked by months of religious strife and rioting. Thousands of Muslims had been killed by militant Hindu mobs, sparking retaliation both in India and abroad. Indeed, there had been almost a dozen bombings in nearby Bombay alone. *All the more reason,* he thought, *for me to cement my control over the entire region.* Panic-tinged memories, of being chased through the streets of Delhi by an anti-Sikh mob, in the harrowing days following the assassination of Indira Gandhi, flashed unwillingly before his mind's eye. It saddened him that senseless sectarian violence still tore at the delicate social fabric of his homeland. *I will put a stop to such madness,* he vowed, *even if I must conquer the entire world to do so.*

"I do not dismiss your fears lightly, my friend," he assured Joaquin, placing his hand upon the bodyguard's brawny shoulder, "but I cannot let apprehension alone dictate my actions. Great victories sometimes require great risks, and I believe the prize we seek tonight fully warrants whatever hazards we tempt by coming here."

Joaquin seemed to realize he could not dissuade Khan. "As you wish, Your Excellency." He turned toward the Exon soldier nearest the temple, who was scanning the imposing structure with a handheld mechanism of Khan's own design. "Well?" Joaquin demanded of the trooper. "What do you read?"

The soldier kept his eyes on the scanning device. "I am detecting only a single individual within the temple." He double-checked the readings, just to be safe. "The granite is very thick in places, I'm afraid, so the results are not one hundred percent certain."

"An acceptable risk," Khan declared quickly, before Joaquin could raise any further objections. "Post your guards outside every exit. Make sure no one leaves or enters while you and I are inside." His dark eyes narrowed as he stared at the forbidding stone walls of the deserted temple. "We shall enter alone, as arranged."

The anxious bodyguard would undoubtedly have preferred Khan to be accompanied by a full security detail, but Joaquin held his tongue, maintaining a stony silence as he and Khan walked beneath the temple gate, leaving the armed troopers behind. An autumn wind whistled through the upper towers of the sculpted sanctuary like the mournful notes of the shehnai, a Hindustani instrument not unlike an oboe. Thunder sounded somewhere in the distance.

Khan did not look back.

The gateway led to an open courtyard, whose basalt tiles had been worn smooth by the passage, over the centuries, of myriad pilgrims. A central worship hall provided access to the three-story shrine beyond, whose pyramidal design was meant to mimic Mount Meru, the Himalayan home of the gods. Smaller shrines flanked the granite pyramid, known as the shikara, beneath which the top-secret rendezvous was scheduled to take place. *Let us hope,* Khan thought, *that this trip is worth my while.*

A flicker of trepidation passed through Khan as they stepped into the cavernous entrance of the worship hall, but he dismissed it as unworthy of his exalted station. Nonetheless, he remained alert for any hint of ambush, keeping one hand on the grip of his pistol as he followed the beam of his flashlight deeper into man-made caverns hollowed out of the living rock twelve centuries before. The incandescent beam fell upon striking tempera murals, painted, many generations ago, on the dry surface of plastered cow dung. Although the murals' once-brilliant colors, including cinnabar-red and lapis lazuli-blue, had necessarily faded over the centuries, the frequently erotic artwork retained much of its original power. Khan admired the cavorting gods, demons, and lovers painted on the tunnel walls, even as he remained on guard against treachery.

Finally, they came to the location described in the coded communications leading up to this meeting: a somber shrine, or chaitya, deep in the heart of the immense pyramid. Parallel rows of ornate stone columns supported a high, rib-vaulted ceiling, with a dancing stone Shiva presiding over the chamber from an altar at the rear of the sanctum. Elaborate bas-reliefs, depicting various episodes from the life of Shiva, ran around the cornice bridging the thick granite columns.

Much decoration, in other words, but no glimpse of the emissary Khan had arranged to meet here. He briefly turned the beam of the flash upon his own wristwatch. It was exactly 3:50 A.M. He was a few minutes early.

"Show yourself!" he demanded, unwilling to wait upon the other man's convenience. His impatient voice echoed within the artificial cavern. "My time is valuable. Do not waste it."

"Very well, Khan Singh," a raspy voice whispered from the shadows. Khan turned his flashlight toward the voice and saw a skeletal figure step out from behind one of the timeworn columns. "Far be it from me to try the patience of such as yourself."

The speaker, whose voice held a Russian accent, looked more dead than alive. His gaunt face was pale, bloodless, and emaciated, like that of a concentration camp victim. Rheumy, bloodshot eyes examined Khan from the depths of sunken, discolored sockets. He trembled in the coolness of the cave, despite his double-breasted, steel-gray greatcoat, of the sort formerly favored by the KGB. Khan heard the Russian's lungs wheeze painfully with every breath, and guessed that the man was dying. Used to the physical perfection of his closest associates, he found the stranger's decrepit state disturbing.

How long had the Russian been standing there in pitch blackness? "Where is your own light?" Khan asked, puzzled by the man's behavior.

"Here," the haggard Russian answered, removing a compact flashlight from a coat pocket and flicking it on, so that the light shone in Khan's face, forcing him to blink and look away. "I was merely accustoming myself to the dark. Not a bad idea, you must admit, given that it is in unending darkness that we must all ultimately spend eternity."

Khan had little interest in the man's morbid musings. "Do you have what you promised?" he asked impatiently, stepping forward to push the other man's flashlight away from his face. "Show me what you have."

He had come to Ajorra in search of knowledge; specifically, technical know-how relating to advanced genetic engineering. Despite the assiduous efforts of Phoolan Dhasal, her team at Chrysalis Island had not yet been able to duplicate Sarina Kaur's success at cloning multiple copies of a single fertilized human egg, a key step in the application of genetic engineering on a large scale. Conventional wisdom had it that such an egg could only be cloned twice before expiring, yet somehow his mother had developed a technique for producing dozens of identical copies of a single egg, thus increasing the odds of successful hybridization later on. Alas, that secret appeared to have died with her, consumed by the cataclysm that had destroyed the original Chrysalis Project nearly two decades ago.

Until a few weeks ago, that is, when Khan had been contacted by the man before him, who claimed to have classified scientific information from a top-secret genetic research project conducted by the Russian military some years before the collapse of the

Soviet Union. The Russian, whom Khan knew only by the code name "Strigoi," had offered him the information in exchange for political asylum and a generous pension, boons Khan was perfectly willing to bestow upon the expatriate Russian, provided that the data was all that it had been professed to be.

Now that he had met Strigoi face to skull-like face, and seen the sorry state of the Russian's health, he could not help wondering why the infirm man was even bothering to make provisions for a future that could not possibly amount to very much time at all. His code name, a Russian synonym for "vampire," seemed bleakly appropriate, given how much the man resembled a walking corpse.

I suppose, Khan observed philosophically, *even the dying and the diseased cling to whatever meager prospects they might possess.* He liked to think that, when his own time finally came, ninety or a hundred years from now, Khan Noonien Singh would not go gently into that good night. *I will fight on, pitting my strength and intelligence against the universe, until my dying breath. . . .*

How then could he blame this wretched specimen for trying to make the best of whatever time remained to him? "Well?" he demanded again, aware that Joaquin was anxious for Khan to conclude this meeting and return to the protection of the guards waiting outside. "What is the matter? Give me the data."

Instead of handing over any sort of folder or disk, the Russian casually looked around the lavishly ornamented shrine. "A fascinating place, don't you think?" His flashlight beam, which wavered in the man's trembling grip, rose to find an exquisite bas-relief depicting Shiva at war against an army of demons. The god was sculpted with four arms, bearing a fire, a horn, a drum, and a trident, respectively. A garland of skulls was strung about the deity's neck. "They say that over 200,000 tons of rock were cut away from the hillside to shape this temple and its surrounding walls. Can you imagine the dedication, the commitment, required to undertake such a feat?"

Khan got the distinct impression that Strigoi was stalling. Eyeing the man suspiciously, keeping him caught in the glare of his flashlight, Khan noticed that the Russian seemed to be fumbling with something in the left pocket of his heavy greatcoat. *A weapon?* he speculated. *Or perhaps a computer disk bearing the data I seek?*

He did not wait for the overly discursive Russian to get around to the business at hand. Moving with the speed and ferocity of a Bengal tiger, Khan shoved Strigoi against the nearest column, then held the man in place with a single hand around his throat while handing over his flashlight to Joaquin so that his other hand was freed to search the man's pocket. The Russian's neck felt so dry and brittle that Khan had to make an effort not to crush it by squeezing too hard. "Enough delays," he snarled at his prisoner. His fingers closed on a small plastic object in the pocket of the coat. "Let us see what you have here."

To his surprise, the confiscated item turned out to be a miniaturized walkie-talkie of some sort. Had the Russian been transmitting their meeting to parties unknown? Khan held the incriminating device up to his mouth and pressed the Speak button. "This is Khan Noonien Singh," he said angrily. "Who is this?"

"Good evening, Khan, or should I say good morning?" He recognized the heavily accented voice of Vasily Hunyadi. "I am gratified to hear that you are indeed there in person, just as I hoped." Khan could easily visualize the sardonic amusement in the Balkan dictator's sole remaining eye. "I am so sorry to hear about the tragic earthquake in your country."

Earthquake? "What do you mean?" Khan barked into the transmitter, while continuing to pin Strigoi to the wall with his left hand. Adrenaline flooded his system as he sensed the jaws of a trap closing on him. "Explain yourself!"

"Interj," Khan," Hunyadi said, bidding him farewell in Romanian. The transmission broke off at the other end, so that only static came from the plastic communicator. Khan crushed the useless device within his fist, intending to do the same to the captive Russian if he was not immediately forthcoming with answers.

Then the first tremor struck.

A deafening roar arose from the earth beneath his feet. The floor of the ancient temple shuddered violently, almost throwing Khan off-balance. Dust and debris rained down from the ceiling, followed by heavier chunks of solid granite. Releasing his grip on the Russian's throat, Khan watched in alarm as the massive columns tottered unsteadily, threatening to topple entirely—and bring the entire shrine down upon their heads.

His usually stolid face alight with panic, Joaquin tried to call out a warning, but his words were lost in the clamor of the quake. The jarring vibrations shook the flashlight loose from his grip. The dislodged electric torch hit the ground hard, then rolled across the quaking floor, causing the light to race erratically across the chamber, adding to the nightmarish chaos. "What have you done?" Khan shouted over the din, more furious than frightened by Hunyadi's apparent perfidy. "What is this?"

Crouching on the floor, unable to stand atop the shaking ground, the Russian laughed hoarsely. "The darkness I spoke of, Khan Singh." Stirred-up dust aggravated his already failing lungs, forcing him to cough convulsively between every other syllable. "It has been decided that you should join me there, rather sooner than you may have expected!"

There is no classified Soviet data, Khan realized with dreadful certainty. Struggling to stay upright, he clasped a hand over his mouth and nostrils, trying to keep out the dust and powdered stone. *This entire exercise has been a suicide mission, aimed directly at my life. Small wonder Hunyadi chose a terminal man as his stalking-horse!* But how had Hunyadi managed to trigger an earthquake at will? *Time enough to discover that later,* he counseled himself pragmatically, *should I survive.*

Despite the peril to his own safety, Khan was tempted to slay the deceitful Russian with his bare hands. *At least let me take my assassin with me,* he thought, but a falling fragment took that option out of his hands, striking Strigoi in the head, flattening his skull. Khan saw that, ironically, the man was killed by a sculpted frieze bearing the image of Shiva, the destroyer, crushing the demon Ravana beneath his toe.

Khan feared that he and Joaquin, too, would soon

go the way of Ravana. Shards of broken granite bounced off his back and shoulders, bruising him to the bone. Khan turned toward his faithful servitor only to see an outcropping of solid rock rear up from the floor beneath Joaquin's feet, knocking the ponderous bodyguard to the ground. The breath knocked out of him, unable to shield himself from the falling rubble, Joaquin was struck by heavy lumps of shattered stone. He flailed uselessly against the bombardment for a heartbeat, then fell alarmingly still.

"My friend!" Khan cried out. Keeping his head low, he stumbled across the swaying floor to Joaquin's side. Throwing aside the jagged rocks that threatened to bury the unconscious bodyguard, he grabbed hold of Joaquin beneath his arms in hopes of dragging him to safety.

But where? Khan looked about desperately for shelter, his eyes straining to penetrate the dust and murk. Perhaps between two of the sturdy columns? He staggered across the rubble-strewn floor toward the nearest pillars, only to hear a tremendous cracking noise directly in front of him. To his horror, he saw one of the teetering columns break free from its moorings and topple toward him. Hundreds of kilos of solid stone came crashing at his head.

Only his superhuman reflexes saved both him and Joaquin from instant death. Dropping the insensate bodyguard back onto the ground, Khan threw up his arms with lightning speed and caught the falling pillar before it smashed his skull. A grunt escaped his lips as he absorbed the impact of the gigantic column. The awesome weight pressed down upon his arms, back, and knees, but, bracing his boots against the rocky floor, he managed to keep the pillar aloft, at roughly a forty-five-degree angle to the floor, its killing weight suspended only centimeters above his head.

Mercifully, the tremors had begun to subside, although great hunks of debris continued to fall from the earthquake-weakened walls and ceiling. In a curious twist of fate, the column that had almost killed Khan now served to shelter him and Joaquin from the plummeting rubble, at the expense of his straining muscles, which already ached from holding the uprooted pillar. Rocky detritus fell on both sides of the column, burying Khan up to his ribs in crumbling heaps of stone. Would he and his loyal servant soon be interred alive, along with the already smothered remains of the Russian traitor?

"Help me!" he shouted, still bearing the entire weight of the leaning column. "Guards! Anyone!" The hollowed-out chaitya was now almost completely filled with debris; there was no place to throw the immense pillar even if he wanted to risk bringing more rubble down on top of him. The bouncing flashlight shattered beneath the falling stonework, casting Khan into total darkness. "Help me! We require assistance!" The ear-splitting roar of the earthquake faded away with the tremors, so that Khan heard only his own voice and the unnerving sound of loose granite settling all around him. One good aftershock, he feared, might bury them completely. "Someone help us, I command you!"

No answer came. *I should save my breath,* he realized, unsure how much oxygen remained within the collapsed cave-temple. Forcing himself to concentrate, despite the back-breaking weight of the mammoth column, he called upon time-tested yoga techniques to control his breathing. An appropriate response, he acknowledged wryly, given that, traditionally, Shiva himself was credited with introducing yoga to mankind. Despite his Sikh ancestry, Khan was not a religious man, but right now he gladly welcomed whatever divine assistance might be available. *If not for me,* he bargained, *then for the injured Joaquin, who fell in my service.*

Controlled breathing did little, however, to relieve the constant weight of the huge pillar pressing down on him. Agonizing exertion contorted his features. Every muscle in his body cried out in anguish. Sweat soaked his dust-covered garments and his teeth were clenched tighter than a vise. He felt like Atlas, condemned to bear the weight of the world for all eternity, or perhaps Samson, in reverse, using every ounce of his preternatural strength to raise up the pillars of a temple instead of pulling them down.

Eons of unceasing torment seemed to pass. In the utter blackness, unable to peer at his watch, Khan had no surefire way of reckoning time. *How long have we been trapped here?* he wondered, thanking his exemplary genetic heritage that claustrophobia was for lesser mortals. *How much longer must I endure?* Even his remarkable strength had its limits; Khan knew he could not support the ponderous column forever. Would he have to choose between being crushed to death or buried alive? And which fate would he choose for Joaquin?

"Joaquin? My friend?" Khan grunted through clenched teeth. The battered servant remained unconscious at Khan's feet, oblivious to his master's attempts to rouse him. Although the toppled column shielded the downed bodyguard from falling debris, Khan feared for the other man's life. Joaquin's breathing was labored and hoarse, his windpipe partially clotted by powdered stone. Racking coughs and incoherent groans rose from the unresponsive figure, the pitiful noises tearing at Khan's heart. He knew that, superhuman stamina notwithstanding, Joaquin needed prompt medical assistance, yet it was all Khan could do just to keep the colossal pillar from squashing them both. *Fear not, my friend,* he vowed silently. *I shall not abandon you while strength remains in my arms.*

Hunger and thirst added to Khan's suffering. His lips were dry and cracked, tasting only the muddy trickles of sweat streaming down his face. From the angry rumbling of his stomach, reminiscent of the earthquake itself, he guessed that several hours had passed since his last meal, a small repast of minced lamb and yogurt consumed en route to the temple. *Damn you, Hunyadi,* he cursed silently. As he strained and sweated beneath the toppled column, which inched ever closer to his skull with each passing hour, his churning mind occupied itself devising fiendishly ingenious ways to torture the nefarious, one-eyed Romanian. *I must survive,* he resolved, exhausted but undefeated, *if only to wreak terrible vengeance upon Hunyadi.*

He heard the drilling first, before any light reached him. Just when he thought that he could not support the column any longer, as his pain-racked arms surrendered millimeter after millimeter to the pillar's ex-

cruciating, slow-motion descent, the sound of a
power drill cutting through rock reached his ears. For
a moment, he worried that he was imagining the
noise, that his weary mind and body had succumbed
to an auditory hallucination, but the drilling noise
grew louder and he realized that a rescue team was on
its way at last.

"In here!" he shouted, risking a further cave-in.
"Hurry!" It would be the bitterest irony, he thought,
if his strength gave out only minutes before his res-
cuers reached him. He breathed in deeply, marshaling
all that remained of his superior vigor and endurance.
No, he thought defiantly, *I shall not falter at the very
brink of our salvation.* Straining to the utmost, he
pushed upward, actually succeeding in lifting the column a few centimeters higher. "Here!" he hissed
through clenched teeth. "Quickly!"

"Your Excellency!" an excited voice yelled over the
noisy reverberation of the drill. Khan heard the rattle
of small rocks rolling toward the ground, then an incandescent shaft of light invaded the darkness. After
uncounted hours lost in blackness, the glare seemed
blindingly bright, but Khan welcomed the eye-
watering blaze, knowing it to be the harbinger of his
imminent release. "Hold on, Your Excellency!" a
straining Exon warrior shouted through a gap in the
piled debris; Khan guessed that the rescue squad had
tunneled down from the central worship hall above.
"We are working as fast as we can!"

Excellent, Khan thought, proud of the able supermen he had recruited to serve him. *How could I have
ever doubted them?* A superior human being can accomplish anything, as long as the will remains strong.

He shouldered his burden gladly, content now to wait patiently for his inevitable liberation. *You see, Hunyadi, you could not defeat me. The greater leader always prevails. . . .*

It took several more minutes, working with admirable care, to clear a path to Khan's place of imprisonment. Soldiers rushed forward to lift the column higher, allowing Khan to gratefully slide out from beneath the nearly unbearable load. For the first time in who knew how many hours, the weight of the pillar did not oppress him. He could barely lower his arms, though, which were stiff and numb from their labors. "See to Joaquin," he ordered, determined that the bludgeoned bodyguard be treated as soon as possible. "Be careful; I do not know the extent of his injuries."

While a team of engineers worked diligently to buttress the suspended column, along with the rest of the quake-ravaged shrine, an attentive doctor knelt beside Joaquin's supine form, checking the unconscious man's vital signs. "Multiple fractures of the rib cage, pelvis, and extremities," the physician reported after a quick examination, "but his spine appears intact. There's no indication of paralysis, although he's suffering from shock and internal trauma." The doctor glanced up at Khan, looking both relieved and impressed. "Given how many hours you were trapped here, I'm amazed he's not in worse shape."

"Joaquin is of hardy stock," Khan understated, grateful for the genetic genius that had endowed them both with more than ordinary recuperative powers. Even still, he knew they were lucky to have been rescued when they were. *I could not have lasted another hour.*

As he watched over Joaquin, a paramedic bandaged Khan's chafed and bleeding palms. Cool water was provided to soothe his parched throat, but he refused to leave the collapsed chaitya until he saw Joaquin carefully carried out on a stretcher. Although the bodyguard remained dead to the world, his agonized groans and whimpers mercifully subsided as powerful painkillers, administered by the well-equipped doctor, took effect.

Another stretcher was offered to Khan, but he preferred to exit the temple upon his own two legs, no matter how sore and fatigued they were. The remaining medics and rescue workers settled for escorting him back to the surface. They draped an army blanket over his shoulders, which Khan wore as proudly as an ermine cloak.

Ament met him beneath the arched doorway of the gopuram with a cup of hot *chai*. That she had been able to travel all the way here from Chandigarh, almost twelve hundred kilometers away, provided some indication of just how long he had been entombed within the wrecked temple. So, too, did the sunlight filtering through the cloudy, rain-swept sky. The rain blowing against his face felt cool and refreshing after his long, grueling internment within the temple. *The dawn has risen,* he observed triumphantly, consigning the darkness of the last several hours to the past. *A new day begins....*

"I am relieved to find you well, Lord Khan," Ament greeted him. His fingers were still too cramped to grip the cup, so she held the rim of the cup up to his lips for him to sip. The hot tea tasted sweet and invigorating. "Joaquin's misfortune saddens me, but I am sure that, with time, he will recover."

Although Khan's body had yet to recover from its ordeal, his mind was already thinking ahead. "The quake," he croaked hoarsely to Ament. "Somehow Hunyadi caused it."

Ament looked unsurprised. "Details are fuzzy, but we suspect that someone exploded some kind of concussive device at the bottom of a nearby reservoir. In theory, sufficient force, added to the pressure of the water in the reservoir, could have overloaded an underlying thrust fault, triggering seismic activity nearby." She wiped the caked-on dust from his face with a clean towel. "There is still much to be investigated, of course."

No need, he thought venomously. Anger burned inside him like a funeral pyre. *I know who is responsible.*

Shortly, from the passenger seat of his private helicopter, Khan had an opportunity to witness the full extent of the disaster. A heavy rain was falling, but Khan could still make out the flattened remains of numerous small villages, many of which had been almost completely destroyed by the earthquake. Traditional stone-and-mud buildings had collapsed upon themselves, no doubt crushing the sleeping inhabitants within. Elevated water tanks had crashed to earth, their spilled contents adding to the muddy chaos enveloping the countryside, the pouring rain making rescue efforts all the more difficult. Khan looked on the devastation with mounting shock and anger. Often, all that remained of once-prosperous villages were a few thatch huts, which, ironically, came through the quake in better shape than the more expensive clay and timber structures. The earth itself was ruptured in places, with jagged scarps of fractured bedrock jutting from the ground beside open chasms and fissures. *The very land is wounded,* Khan discerned, *as much as the pitiable wretches who dwelled upon it.*

Seated behind him, Ament provided Khan with informed commentary on the tragic scene beneath them. "Preliminary reports suggest that over twenty villages have been largely obliterated, rendering an estimated 130,000 people homeless. To make matters worse, the quake struck at exactly 3:53 A.M., when most of the residents were asleep in their homes. Fatality rates remain unclear, but the final death toll may climb as high as 30,000 victims."

Khan struggled to grasp the enormity of the catastrophe. *An entire population bombed out of existence,* he marveled with growing fury, *and all Hunyadi's fault.* He clenched his fists, ignoring the pain to his raw and bandaged palms. The helicopter passed above a ruined brick schoolhouse, now nothing more than a heap of collapsed masonry, and Khan's desire for vengeance against the ruthless Romanian superman took on new dimension and urgency. Hunyadi had not only tried to eliminate Khan, he had also callously butchered thousands of innocent souls whom Khan considered under his protection.

A twinge of guilt reminded Khan that he had once contemplated a similar atrocity, deploying Morning Star against the population of Bosnia. But that had been in a moment of anger, ultimately superceded by Ament's appeal to his conscience. Hunyadi had shown no such restraint.

Justice demanded that Hunyadi pay for his crimes against Khan's people, and Khan could think of no one better than himself to carry out a mandatory sentence of death. *"Fiat justitia et ruant coeli,"* he murmured solemnly, as the harsh rain splattered against the transparent canopy of the 'copter.

Let justice be done though the heavens fall.

CHAPTER ELEVEN

"NO THANKS, I'M EXPECTING SOMEONE."

Roberta sighed wearily as yet another amorous lounge lizard cruised away from her table, after offering to keep her company. *Here I am trying to keep a low profile,* she thought, *and suddenly I'm more popular than Heidi Fleiss.*

It wasn't like she hadn't chosen the darkest, most shadowy corner of the lounge in which to wait for her rendezvous. From where she was sitting, at the rear of the stuffy, smoke-filled lounge, she could barely see the stage, where low-wattage country star Sonny Clemonds was performing his novelty hit, "Don't Send Me No E-Mail Unless You're a Female," to a mostly oblivious and/or intoxicated audience. Judging from the way Sonny kept slurring his lyrics, she wasn't sure he was all that sober either.

Oh well, she reflected philosophically, taking a sip from a very watered-down cocktail, *I guess I can't complain too much if I'm still a wolf magnet at age forty-four.* She methodically scanned the lounge, keeping a watchful eye for any sign of genetically engineered superassassins. Nothing like a life on the lam to keep you in shape.

She glanced at her watch, wondering what was keeping her contact. Bored, and momentarily confident that Khan's goons were nowhere to be seen, she flipped open a newspaper she had picked up on her way to the lounge. A front-page headline caught her attention: "Human Genome Project Sets Out to Map DNA." Roberta groaned aloud as she skimmed the article about the ambitious attempt, beginning today, to map and sequence the entire structure of human DNA. She and Seven had known this particular endeavor was in the works, of course, but it still came as a shock to see it spelled out in black-and-white on page one of the paper, especially after all the obsessive secrecy concerning the true origins of Khan and his ilk.

Here we go again, she thought. She prayed that this new project would yield more positive results, like cures for various genetic diseases and disorders, than Sarina Kaur's late and unlamented Chrysalis Project. *We can always hope,* she reassured herself. *Seven says that humanity can learn from its mistakes, no matter how slow and painful the process.*

"Helen?"

A familiar voice snapped Roberta out of her mournful reverie. She looked up to see Shannon O'Donnell, her favorite future astronaut, peering down at her through the lounge's dim lighting. "Sorry to keep you waiting, but something came up at the lab, and I couldn't exactly explain that I had a more urgent appointment." She brushed a lock of auburn hair away from her eyes. "As far as the top brass know, I'm just here in Vegas for a little R&R."

"No problem," Roberta said. She glanced around quickly, to make certain no one was listening to them, then lowered her voice. "So how's life at Area 51?"

Shannon slid into the seat across from Roberta. "The design for the impulse engine is still giving us problems. The power yield ratios are steeper than I'd like; we're burning up way too much deuterium in order to get the sort of power output we need to approach lightspeed." She leaned across the table toward Roberta. "Perhaps you might be able to shed some light on the problem?"

"Perhaps," Roberta allowed. Recovering her handbag from the floor between her feet, she removed a manila envelope from the bag and scooted it across the table to Shannon. "You may find some useful ideas here."

The younger woman couldn't resist taking an immediate peek at the contents of the envelope. Despite the lounge's murky ambience, she opened the envelope and drew out several pages of diagrams and equations. Her chestnut eyes widened as she perused the papers. "Of course," she murmured to herself, with obvious excitement. "I would have never thought of that!" Hastily sliding the documents back into the envelope, she gazed at Roberta with a mixture of awe and gratitude. "Thank you so much, Helen! I can tell already—this is going to save us months, maybe years, of development!"

Roberta winced inwardly, feeling a twinge of guilt every time Shannon addressed her as "Helen." The young NASA engineer was putting her career—and her security clearance—on the line every time she met Roberta like this, yet the older woman still used the alias "Helen Swanson" whenever she dealt with Shannon. It was unavoidable, though; the fewer people who knew about Roberta Lincoln, and her connection to Gary Seven, the better.

"I wish I could take credit for the dazzling scientific insights," she joked, "but I'm just the go-between, you know."

"So you keep telling me," Shannon said skeptically. She looked like she didn't entirely believe it.

Roberta had first met Shannon O'Donnell seven years ago, when the older woman had teleported into Area 51 to recover a few items of twenty-third century technology that the *Enterprise* crew had accidentally left behind during their 1986 whale-napping expedition. Shannon had impressed Roberta at the time, and, in the weeks and months that followed, Roberta had, cautiously and discreetly at first, cultivated Shannon as a useful ally inside Area 51. With Seven's blessing and encouragement, "Helen" had been feeding Shannon occasional tips on starship engineering for years now, while keeping the extraterrestrial origins of the info a secret even from the eager young aerospace worker.

"Dr. Carlson is still the only person at Groom Lake who knows about our special arrangement?" Roberta asked, determined to keep Seven's covert assistance to the DY-100 project on a strictly need-to-know basis.

"Absolutely," Shannon insisted. A regretful look

passed over her face. "I wish there was some way to bring Shaun—Lieutenant Christopher—in on the secret, but . . . no, that's not possible." She shook her head sadly. "He'd feel honor-bound to report it. He's a straight arrow that way. Just like his dad."

Roberta recalled that Lieutenant Christopher's father was a decorated Air Force pilot who had once been involved in a minor UFO incident. Roberta herself had later rescued Captain John Christopher from an obsessed alien hunter, little knowing that his then-unborn son would someday be an integral part of one of Seven's side operations. *Forget Kevin Bacon,* she thought. *We're all just six degrees of separation from Mr. Spock!*

"I think for now it's best that this remain our little secret," she said, having difficulty imagining any circumstances in which it would be a good thing to let another person in on this operation. Khan's spies were everywhere.

A waiter swung by to take Shannon's order, and Roberta took advantage of the occasion to order another mimosa for herself as well. *After all,* she thought, *I'm not exactly driving home.*

Shannon carefully tucked the folded envelope into her own handbag, then leaned back to wait for her cocktail. A flutter of applause greeted another Sonny Clemonds ditty. "I don't suppose you're going to tell me, at last, where all this astounding technical know-how is coming from?" She smiled ruefully. "I ask you every time, and you never spill a bean."

Memories of Reykjavik flashed through her brain. "Er, that's not entirely true," she said cryptically. "But trust me, it's better this way."

"But what do you get out of it?" Shannon pressed her,

the anonymous nature of her benefactor clearly weighing on her mind. She lowered her voice to an urgent hush. "Why are you going to all this trouble to help the U.S. government build a top-secret sleeper ship?"

Roberta squirmed uncomfortably in her seat. How could she tell the idealistic young woman that the DY-100 was Gary Seven's backup plan, just in case World War III proved unavoidable? If necessary, the high-tech starship could serve as a futuristic ark, capable of ferrying a handful of human survivors to a brand-new beginning on another world. Roberta prayed it wouldn't come to that, but there was no way to be sure, especially in a world containing Khan Noonien Singh, i.e., the Tyrant Formerly Known as Noon.

"Believe me," Roberta told Shannon. "You don't want to know."

CHAPTER TWELVE

THIS MUST BE WHAT SPACE TRAVEL IS LIKE, KHAN mused as his submarine cruised far beneath the waves. Cocooned within a hull of high-yield steel, in an artificial bubble of air, he traveled in near-silence through the icy depths of an environment utterly inimical to human life—much as he would be on a voyage to the stars. *Someday,* he thought, *after I have subdued the Earth and brought peace to its suffering billions, perhaps I should aspire to conquer space as well. In my old age, possibly, like Tennyson's Ulysses, setting forth on one last heroic adventure "beyond the utmost bound of human thought."* The notion pleased him, and a private smile lifted the corners of his lips. It would be a fitting end. . . .

But that was many long decades from now. First, he had more brutal business to attend to; specifically, the immediate destruction of Vasily Hunyadi and his faithless superhuman lieutenants.

He stood within the control room of the *SGK Kaur* as the nuclear submarine, the first in an intended fleet, cruised toward the entrance of the Adriatic Sea. Reliable intelligence had placed Hunyadi and his top cadre at a base in the Bosnian city of Dubrovnik, so Khan meant to sail close enough to the city to launch a Tomahawk missile, purchased at great expense on the black market, at his enemy's lair. Armed with a conventional high-explosive warhead, the missile would reduce the heavily guarded building to ashes before Hunyadi even knew he was under attack.

The element of surprise was crucial to his strategy. Although the effective range of the Tomahawk was over fifteen hundred kilometers, meaning that Khan could have conceivably launched the missile from anywhere in the Mediterranean, Hunyadi's headquarters was guarded by bootlegged Patriot missiles, of the sort used in the Gulf War to intercept attacking SCUD missiles. By slipping into the Adriatic, and firing the Tomahawk only a few hundred kilometers from Dubrovnik, Khan hoped to give Hunyadi's forces little or no time to react to the launch; the Tomahawk would strike its target before a single Patriot could be deployed against it.

At least that was the plan. With NATO currently enforcing a no-fly zone over Bosnia, an attack by submarine had struck Khan as the ideal way to get his revenge on Hunyadi without having to fight his way through contested airspace or war-torn terrain. Even Ament, who customarily frowned on military "adventurism," had agreed that an underwater approach offered the least chance of exposure and/or open confrontation; it was, in her words, "admirably low-profile."

For himself, Khan worried less about avoiding public censure and more about taking Hunyadi by surprise, although he granted that there were definite diplomatic advantages to avoiding the United Nations peacekeeping forces patrolling the region. Ament had originally urged Khan to let the U.N., with the military support of NATO, deal with Hunyadi along with several other Balkan war criminals, but Khan had little faith in the abilities of lesser men to mete out justice to the likes of Hunyadi. Besides, he had a personal grudge to settle with the Romanian superman. *The souls of thousands of murdered countrymen cry out for vengeance,* he thought resolutely, *and all because Hunyadi sought my life.*

Like a bad marksman, the Romanian had missed his target, but killed countless others in the attempt. By contrast, Khan planned a surgical strike on Hunyadi that minimized the risk to innocent civilians. *There you see the fundamental difference between us,* he reflected, *and why only I was truly born to rule wisely over mankind.*

"Lord Khan." The commander of the *Kaur,* Captain William Hapka, approached Khan on the raised platform overlooking the rest of the control room. Two cylindrical periscopes, one optical, one electronic, rose like bolted metal pillars from the center of the pedestal. Behind the platform, at the rear of the control room, a team of junior officers charted the sub's progress on tracing paper stretched over the plotting table. "We are nearing the Strait of Otranto."

"Excellent," Khan commended the captain. The *Kaur* had made good time since departing Bombay almost four days ago. Their route had taken them up the Red Sea and through the Suez Canal undetected. Now, as they headed straight for the mouth of the Adriatic, between the shores of Italy and Albania, Khan already tasted the heady wine of revenge. Only hours remained before the sub came within range of Dubrovnik.

The hushed atmosphere of the control room, where noise was habitually kept to a minimum, provided little indication of the focused attention and efficiency of the crew. From his vantage point on the periscope pedestal, Khan could survey the sub's busy nerve center. Highly trained personnel, in matching aquamarine uniforms, manned computerized control consoles situated around and ahead of the central platform. The consoles faced away from the pedestal, so that Khan and the captain could effectively look over the shoulders of the seamen as they worked side by side, at navigation, helm, or weapons control. Closed-circuit television screens watched over the engine room, reactor compartment, sonar shack, and other vital compartments. Illuminated gauges and displays cast colored shadows on alert, determined faces representing a wide variety of races and ethnicities. Elbow room was at a premium, but Khan was impressed by how efficiently the crew functioned despite the cramped conditions.

Just as well that Joaquin could not accompany me, Khan thought. It felt distinctly odd, but also strangely liberating, not to have the huge bodyguard shadowing him as usual; still recovering from injuries sustained in September's horrendous earthquake, Joaquin had been in no condition to embark on this voyage—or to prevent Khan from doing so.

Every one of his advisors had counseled Khan against personally joining the sub's mission, but he had overruled them all. *I am not one to sit by idly while others fight my battles,* he reiterated in his mind, *nor to miss my flagship's baptism of fire.*

One of a kind, the Ship of the Great Khanate *Kaur* was a state-of-the-art nuclear submarine, roughly modeled on the U.S. Navy's *Los Angeles*-class vessels, but with a few special design features of Khan's own devising. Costing over forty billion rupees to construct, the ship was only the beginning of what he envisioned as a war fleet to rival that of the United States or Russia. The *Kaur,* named after Khan's martyred mother, was a swift and silent undersea predator, as Hunyadi would soon discover.

Khan noticed a stirring of activity below. A message was transmitted from the sonar room, one compartment away, to the Officer of the Deck, who promptly delivered the news to Captain Hapka. The grilled-metal platform rattled slightly beneath his tread. "Passive sonar detects the presence of mines dead ahead, sir."

"I see," Hapka said. Khan took a step backward to allow Hapka to deal with the matter. Although all aboard had sworn to live or die by Khan's command, he did not wish to undermine the captain's authority unless absolutely necessary. "Can we go around them?" Hapka asked.

"No, sir," the OOD reported. He was a burly, tattooed sailor from Marseille, who had resigned from the French navy to protest the 1985 bombing of a Greenpeace vessel, the *Rainbow Warrior,* by French intelligence agents. A name badge on his lapel identified him as Lt. Guillaume Cassel. "The mines are blocking the choke point."

Hapka stroked his beard as he considered his options. Silver crescents glittered on his collar, while his breast pocket bore an impressive collection of polished medals and decorations. Although not a product of genetic engineering, the captain had already achieved a distinguished reputation as a submariner before joining Khan's private navy, having served with distinction in the Falklands war. That was many years ago, and Hapka's rust-colored whiskers were now streaked with silver, yet Khan knew he was fortunate to have such an experienced seaman in command of his flagship.

"Well, we've come too far to turn back now." The captain did not let the threat of mines deter him. "Initiate a phased-energy sweep. Full-strength. Ninety degree dispersal." He turned toward Khan, as the OOD verbally passed along the captain's orders to the weapons officer in charge of the *Kaur*'s forward lasers. "It seems, Your Excellency," Hapka told Khan coolly, "that we have been given the opportunity to see how your new laser system works in the field."

"I have great faith in both the technology and your crew, Captain," Khan replied confidently. Originally trained as an engineer, he had personally devised the sub's unique defense system, which employed a bank of high-intensity, phased-energy lasers to sweep the sea in front of the *Kaur* clear of any physical obstacles, man-made or otherwise. The system had performed magnificently in staged trials off the coast of Bombay, but had yet to be tested in actual combat. "May we observe the operation more closely?"

"Of course, sir." Hapka nimbly led Khan down a short flight of metal steps to the ground floor of the control room. Turning sideways, they squeezed past the various crewmen at their posts until they stood right behind the junior officer seated in front of the laser controls. If the weapons officer, a young Filipino woman, was troubled by her superiors' scrutiny, she concealed her nerves admirably, keeping her gaze fixed intently on a mounted display screen as she manipulated a series of knobs and switches by hand. "Any contacts, Lieutenant Bataeo?"

"Not yet, sir," the youthful sailor reported crisply. Her jet-black hair had been closely cropped. "Commencing second sweep now."

A bright white line swept back and forth across the faint green glow of the screen, like a windshield wiper working diligently to clear away spattered raindrops. Khan had little trouble visualizing the reality represented by the display; in his mind's eye, he saw an incandescent sapphire beam cutting through the Stygian darkness outside the ship, carving out a swath of safety many meters ahead of the *Kaur*'s rounded prow. *Like a flaming sword,* he thought proudly, *blazing brightly beneath the sea.*

"There!" Bataeo blurted, pointing at the screen where a circular blip briefly flared along the length of the sweeping phosphorescent line. A low-pitched electronic beep accompanied the blip. "Contact!"

A heartbeat later, a shock wave rocked the control room, forcing Khan to grab on to the handle of an overhead chart cabinet to steady himself. A mine, he understood at once, detonated by the laser. In theory, the explosion had occurred at a safe distance, far

enough ahead of them so that the sub itself would
not be damaged; nevertheless, Khan spent a few apprehensive seconds reviewing the calculations in his
head. *We should be in little danger,* he thought, *unless
these mines pack considerably more firepower than the conventional models.*

He heard the young lieutenant gulp involuntarily as
the shock wave passed over them, leaving them
shaken but unscathed. "Is that it?" Khan asked mockingly. He grinned wolfishly at the captain. A loose
lock of hair fell across his eyes, and he brushed it
away from his face; he had eschewed a turban in def-
erence to the submarine's low ceilings. "Our foes will
have to do better than that if they hope to halt our
advance."

He had no doubt that Hunyadi's forces had strewn
the strait with mines, in a vain attempt to eliminate
their vulnerability to sea attacks. But they had woe-
fully underestimated both Khan's resolves and his resources. *A fatal mistake,* he prophesied.

"Again! the exuberant weapons officer called out.
Khan glanced at the screen in time to glimpse a second white blip fade away, like a meteor burning out of
existence. "We got another one!"

This time Khan did not grab on to the cabinet
handle for support. Instead, anticipating the shock
wave, he spread his legs apart, bracing himself against
the jolt, which caused the floor of the sub to roll beneath his feet as though the submarine were being
tossed about atop a stormy sea and not cruising unseen over two hundred meters below the waves. Dangling cords and cables swung wildly back and forth.
The deep-sea turbulence reminded him of the life-

shattering tremors that had shaken Maharashtra over four months ago, adding fuel to the righteous fury smoldering in his chest. His fists clenched at his sides, he rocked in sync with the tempest-tossed sub, determined never to be thrown off-balance again by Hunyadi's treacherous machinations.

As before, the disturbance generated by the mine's explosive death throes subsided in a matter of seconds, having failed to put an end to the *Kaur*'s journey of vengeance. Khan felt justifiably proud of his ship's stellar performance. "I believe, Captain, that the lasers have passed the test with flying colors."

"So it seems, sir," Hapka admitted. A worried expression belied his grudging endorsement of the laser defense system. His gaze darted upward, as if anticipating an attack from above. A low ceiling, equipped with white fluorescent lights, blocked his view of the thick steel hull above the control room, all that protected them from the pressure of two hundred meters of icy seawater. "Those mines were noisy buggers, though."

Khan understood the captain's concern. Destroying the mines, however necessary to their mission, had inevitably compromised the *Kaur*'s stealthy passage through the strait. Who knew what hostile ears might have registered the twin detonations, and thus inferred the presence of an intruder in their waters? A sub's greatest asset was its silence, and the *Kaur* had just been forced to ring an underwater doorbell—twice. *So much for the element of surprise,* Khan thought ruefully. He could only pray that word would not reach Hunyadi before the *Kaur* came within firing range of Dubrovnik.

To his credit, Captain Hapka did not suggest turning back and aborting the mission. Just as well; Khan
would have sacked him instantly had he done so. "We
should be on guard against an enemy vessel," Khan
commented.

"Always, sir." Hapka turned and issued fresh instructions to the OOD. "Change course heading by
two-oh-five degrees, and take us down another fifty
meters." Khan understood that the captain was taking evasive action to throw off any hostile parties
that might have detected the clamor of the exploding
mines. "Return to our original course and bearing
once we've put a kilometer or two between us and
those firecrackers back there."

Cassel repeated the captain's orders to the diving
officer, who instructed the sailors actually manning
the helm controls. Khan felt the floor tilt beneath his
feet as the sub descended at roughly a ten-degree
angle. If fortune was with them, the maneuver would
allow the *Kaur* to continue its voyage unchallenged,
even if the zigzag cost them a little extra time. Khan
resolved to remain patient. He had waited four
months to strike back at Hunyadi. Another hour or
so would make little difference.

Or so he hoped. A sudden, loud ringing noise, like
the sonorous peal of an enormous bell, echoed within
the control room, dashing all such expectations.
Khan did not need the captain's help to know what
the ringing meant: the *Kaur* had been located by another vessel's sonar.

An intercom crackled to life, bearing urgent mes-
sages from the sonar room. *"We have contact! Underwater, bearing straight toward us, speed thirty knots . . ."*

There was a momentary pause as the *Kaur's* computers attempted to identify the approaching vessel from its sonar profile. On the TV screen monitoring the sonar shack, a headphone-wearing crewman listened to the approaching signal with a look of acute concentration, identifying its source just as quickly as the computers. "An *Akula*-class attack sub, closing fast!"

"Battle stations!" Hapka reacted. He bounded back up onto the periscope pedestal, snatched a handheld speaker from its cradle, and repeated the order into the intercom. Khan hurried after him, taking the steps two or three at a time. "Recharge lasers!"

Khan cursed beneath his breath. Obviously, they had not left the site of their minesweeping activities fast enough; the twin detonations must have attracted the *Akula,* which Hunyadi had surely acquired from his allies within the Russian navy. *It seems we must battle our way to Bosnia after all,* he realized. He assumed a commanding posture, his hands clasped behind his back, his jaw set defiantly. *So be it.*

Rotund chimes reverberated through the control room, loudly testifying that the hostile sub was still "pinging" the *Kaur* with its sonar. Tinted red emergency lights began flashing inside protective metal cages. Despite the *Kaur's* considerable firepower, Khan felt uncomfortably exposed and vulnerable.

"Sonar to Conn, enemy is flooding torpedo tubes." Preparing to attack, in other words. *"Opening torpedo doors!"*

Hapka spit out orders faster than water gushing through a perforated bulkhead. "Begin targeting, snapshot mode. Lasers for defense. Torpedoes for attack." Grave concern deepened the creases of the captain's weathered features. He glared along the bearing of the attacking sub. "Flood the tubes—and get me those solutions, pronto!"

Khan instantly grasped the captain's strategy, to use the lasers against any oncoming torpedoes while targeting the *Akula* itself with *Kaur*'s own torpedoes. Shrewd tactics, he judged approvingly, especially since the *Kaur* had at least one very special torpedo in its arsenal.

"Two torpedoes launched and running!" the sonar room warned, then began a continuing report on the projectiles' speed, bearing, and range. At the same time, Khan knew, a linked computer system transmitted all the sonar data on the approaching torpedoes to the targeting circuits of the laser defense system. *"Torpedoes have acquired!"* the intercom blared, meaning that the enemy torpedoes had successfully locked onto the *Kaur*. *"Repeat: torps have acquired!"*

"Lasers?" Hapka asked fiercely, glancing at the weapons control station to his right. Khan drew comfort from the knowledge that, even underwater, a beam of light traveled faster than a jet-propelled torpedo.

"Taking a snapshot!" Bataeo called out. Targeting was a tricky business, especially with three swiftly moving objects involved. Ideally, there would be time to check and recheck all the relevant computations before firing; while under attack, however, the best the computers could do was take a quick "snapshot" of the situation and hope for the best. "Torpedoes acquired, sir!"

"Lasers, fire!" Hapka ordered, and Khan visualized twin sapphire beams coursing outward to intersect with the deadly torpedoes. He caught himself holding his breath, then willed himself to relax as much as was superhumanly possible. Would his glorious career end here, beneath the unforgiving sea? If so, Khan vowed to meet his fate bravely, regretting only that Hunyadi and his minions did not perish before him.

Another underwater shock wave buffeted the *Kaur,* the explosion feeling much closer than before. The submarine yawed sharply starboard, throwing Khan against the massive steel column of the electronic, high-tech search periscope. His red silk tunic caught on a metal bolt, tearing the fabric and scratching the skin underneath. Khan ignored the pain, worrying instead about any injury to the sub itself. Had one of the torpedoes struck the ship, or merely exploded dangerously nearby?

"Torpedo One—destroyed!" Bataeo reported with a grin. Perspiration gleamed on her bright, attractive features. Her jubilant tone evaporated a heartbeat later as she stared at her screen with a look of dismay. "Target Two—still closing!"

No! Khan thought. The lasers had stopped one torpedo, but missed the other. "Brace for impact!" Captain Hapka shouted, only seconds before the guided warhead smashed into the *Kaur.*

The platform pitched sharply and Khan wrapped his arms around the lowered periscope, holding on for dear life. Undersea thunder roared in his ears, along with the clanging of battered metal. The overhead lights sputtered, so that, for a few unnerving moments, the control room was lit solely by the glowing, multicolored displays and control panels embedded in the walls, like exotic, bioluminescent fish shining in the waters of a darkened aquarium. Khan glanced over at Hapka; to his shock and chagrin, he saw the captain's body lying sprawled upon the matte-blue floor of the pedestal. His bloody brow matched a crimson smear on the casing of the adjacent periscope. Khan guessed that Hapka had cracked his head against the attack periscope during the impact.

With no time to ascertain the extent of the captain's injuries, Khan immediately took command. "Call a medic for Captain Hapka," he instructed the deck officer brusquely; Cassel was doubtless a competent sailor, but, at this critical juncture, Khan preferred to trust his destiny to no one save himself. "I am taking charge of this vessel."

The OOD gulped visibly, but, wisely, did not challenge Khan's decision. "As you command, Your Excellency." Drawn features and an anxious tone betrayed the Frenchman's uneasiness.

Khan was worried, too, even though the *Kaur* could conceivably survive a single torpedo strike. Its dense double hull, modeled on that of a Russian *Typhoon*-class supersub, had also been reinforced with a unique, impact-absorbing alloy found only in one remote and isolated African kingdom. Khan had gone to great lengths to obtain this alloy for his flagship, which might have been the reason he and the rest of the *Kaur*'s human inhabitants were still alive.

But for how much longer? Khan couldn't even begin to guess what sort of damage had been done to the submarine's vital systems and functions. *I fear the worst,* he thought.

"Lasers down!" Bataeo exclaimed, and Khan realized they had lost their first and best defense. "That second torp totaled the whole array!"

Emergency power kicked in, bringing maybe eighty percent of the control room's lights back on. Khan spotted signs of damage amongst both the crew and the equipment. Warning lights flashed on nearly every console, while bruises, cuts, and minor burns scarred the faces of the anxious-looking sailors. Steam jetted from a ruptured pipe, hissing like an incensed cobra, until one of the crewman, stretching his arm to reach the ceiling, closed a valve manually. Sparks erupted from short-circuited control panels, until quenched by the hasty application of a fire extinguisher. A smoky haze contaminated the enclosed atmosphere of the control room, which smelled of cold sweat and apprehension. Khan heard men and women coughing at their stations.

Khan watched grimly, his face as immobile as a plaster death mask, as two sailors helped a fallen comrade back up onto his seat among the navigation consoles. The man's leg appeared to have been injured in his tumble; Khan could not tell right away whether the limb was broken or merely sprained. In any event, the man did not request to be relieved from his duty, but instead returned to his post, grimacing in pain as he tried to bring the ship's computerized global positioning system back online. A trickle of blood leaked from beneath the man's pants leg onto the scuffed metal floor of the control room.

Brave souls, Khan thought, pride swelling within his chest. He could ask no better of his soldiers, and prayed only that he had not led them all to a watery death. "Now would I give a thousand furlongs of sea," he murmured after the Bard, "for an acre of barren ground."

Their foe gave them little time to nurse their wounds or assess their status. *"Torpedo in the water!"* the intercom announced from the sonar room. Bursts of static broke into the warning, rendering key data inaudible. *"Bearing zzzt!-zero-zzzt! Speed forty knots. Range zzzt! thousand and closing—"*

Khan hoped the targeting computers were getting the full story. "Helm! Hard to port!" he ordered forcefully. With the lasers disabled, evading the torpedo was their only hope. He stepped over the captain's prone and bleeding form to shout directly at the weapons control team. "Deploy countermeasures!"

"Yes, sir!" an alert Norwegian seaman acknowledged, as the *Kaur* jettisoned a pair of decoys via the ship's ejector tubes. Khan heard them wailing loudly outside the *Kaur*. With luck, the noisemakers would confuse the torpedo, luring it away from the sub.

Cassel spared a moment to address Khan. "Your Excellency, you should go!" he urged. Khan could hear echoes of Joaquin's worried voice in the Frenchman's plea, and understood the man's concern; it was unlikely that the *Kaur* could weather another direct hit, but there might still be time for Khan to escape the beleaguered sub, if he moved swiftly enough. "It is not safe for you here. The danger is too great!"

"No!" Khan roared. His very soul rebelled at the idea of fleeing from a battle before a single shot had been fired back at their foe. *We must destroy the* Akula *utterly,* he realized, *before they can attack us again.* "Do we have a targeting solution plotted?" he asked Bataeo intently. "For our torpedoes?"

Seated at her console, the young weapons officer nodded. "Yes, sire. A good snapshot, at least." Her fingers stabbed emphatically at her control panel. "Feeding the data to the torpedoes now."

Then we still have a chance, Khan thought. "Fire at will," he commanded, then paused for an instant as he debated playing his trump card. *Better now than never,* he decided. "Tube Four."

He exchanged a glance with Cassel, who clearly understood the significance of Khan's choice. "The Shkval?"

"Exactly," Khan confirmed. "Nothing else is faster."

An ordinary torpedo could travel at best 130 kilometers per hour, but the Shkval, an experimental torpedo developed by the Russians in the late seventies, and improved upon since, could reach a top speed of 100 meters per second; it operated on the principle of supercavitation, which reduced hydrodynamic drag by enclosing the torpedo within a self-generated bubble of water vapor and gas. Khan had paid a pretty penny to obtain a single Shkval for his sub. *Hunyadi is not the only superman with connections in the former Soviet Union,* he reflected somberly.

"Torpedo launched!" Bataeo reported. The boom of the Shkval's ferocious exit from the tube resounded through the control room, momentarily drowning out the constant pinging of the *Akula*'s sonar.

Khan nodded in satisfaction. Only the Shkval, he reasoned, could turn the tide of the battle, by striking out at the *Akula* before the Russian sub could even begin to defend itself or retaliate. No submersible craft yet devised could move fast enough to evade the rocket-powered, supercavitating, ultrahigh-speed torpedo—assuming the Shkval performed as advertised.

He held his breath, knowing the answer would not be long in coming. *Either we succeed now, or almost certainly perish.*

"Hostile torpedo veering away from us," the sonar room reported, reminding Khan that a third enemy torpedo was still in the water. *"It's going after the decoys!"*

Khan smiled. Perhaps fortune was on his side, after all. A sudden shock wave, mild compared to the impact of the second torpedo against the *Kaur's* outer hull, suggested that the oncoming torpedo had destroyed one or more of the noisy decoys rather than his submarine. *A miss!* Khan thought triumphantly. Now it was up to the Shkval to ensure that the *Akula* did not have another chance to fire at the *Kaur.*

"Closing, closing," Bataeo reported on the Skhval's progress, struggling to keep up with the torpedo's murderous velocity. She sounded like an auctioneer calling out bids at a rapid-fire pace. "Got her!"

The pinging of the enemy's sonar halted abruptly, leaving only fading echoes behind. Khan heard instead, muffled but unmistakable, the sound of forged steel being torn asunder. *"She's breaking up!"* the sonar room announced excitedly. Khan could hear the unseen sailor's relief, even over the intercom. *"Target is destroyed. Repeat: target is destroyed!"*

So falls another foe! Khan savored the intoxicating nectar of victory. *Come not between the dragon and his wrath!* He basked in the adulation of the crew, who gazed up at him with gratitude and admiration upon their sweaty, smoke-smudged faces. He marched confidently to the forward edge of the periscope platform and gave the apprehensive OOD a hearty slap on the back. "Helm, continue course to Dubrovnik."

He spoke loudly and clearly, so that the entire control room could hear him. "Let us send the butcher Hunyadi our compliments."

Cheers and laughter greeted his jest. Trusting that the crew's morale had been restored, and that the crisis had been averted, he felt at ease enough to see to Captain Hapka. The ship's medic, a Dr. Hoyt, had already responded to Khan's summons, and was even now kneeling beside the injured captain, who remained unconscious on the floor of the pedestal. Hoyt shone a light into Hapka's eyes, checking the dilation of his pupils.

"Well, Doctor," Khan addressed the physician. "How fares the captain?"

"A severe concussion," Hoyt reported, "possibly a hairline fracture to the left parietal bone." Khan noted that the doctor himself had not escaped the battle unscathed; his right hand was swathed in bandages and he seemed to be missing a tooth or two. "I do not think his injury is life-threatening, but I should get him to the infirmary."

"Of course," Khan agreed. He was reluctant to lose any of the control room personnel while the *Kaur* remained in hostile waters, so he instructed the OOD to summon a pair of sailors to assist Hoyt in transporting Hapka. "What other casualties do we have, Doctor?"

Hoyt bandaged the captain's bleeding skull as he replied to Khan's query. "Three enlisted men were killed by an exploding bulkhead in the turbine room, and another sailor was badly burned by a fire in the galley." The doctor's uniform smelled of grease and smoke. "Thankfully, there's no trace of any radiation leakage from the reactor." He shook his head dolefully at the very thought. "It could have been much worse, Your Excellency."

"This is so," Khan affirmed. He regretted the loss of any lives under his command, but knew that his sovereign duty to avenge the murdered villagers of Maharashtra, and end Hunyadi's overweening ambitions, justified whatever sacrifices were required. *Such are the fortunes of war,* he reflected, while resolving to see to it that the widows and children of the deceased crewmen were well taken care of, once today's bloody business was concluded.

Khan found himself anxious to complete his mission and return to India. Glancing up at the TV screens mounted around the control room, he watched the crew battle to contain leaks and small fires all over the ship. To his relief, he spotted no fatal damage to the *Kaur*'s VLS missile tubes. "How soon can we launch the missile?" he asked aloud.

"Approaching launch point," a navigation officer called out, keeping an eye on the automated plotting board. A GPS-based target plan had already been entered into the missile's guidance system; the *Kaur* merely needed to reach the preprogrammed launch location to ensure an accurate strike. "Estimated time till launch point: ten minutes, sixteen seconds."

All the better, Khan thought, anticipation setting his blood pounding. At long last, the hour of vengeance was almost at hand. "Take us up, Helm," he commanded eagerly. The *Kaur* needed to ascend to periscope depth before releasing the Tomahawk, plus slow to a near stop. "Reduce speed to one-third."

But before the diving officer could relay Khan's orders to the two men controlling the ship's diving planes and rudder, a sudden explosion rocked the entire submarine. The periscope platform lurched starboard, throwing Khan hard against the safety rail, bruising his ribs. Blue-hot sparks flared from control panels, forcing their operators to leap backward or risk electrocution. Sundered metal shrieked in protest in the crawlspace beneath the control room, and the periscopes rattled within their housings. Helmsmen, buckled securely into their seats, wrestled with their control wheels, fighting (and failing) to keep the *Kaur* on an even keel. "What havoc is this?" Khan gasped in confusion. His eyes feverishly searched the shaking compartment, seeking an explanation. *Another attack sub?*

His Gallic countenance as pale as a raw oyster, the OOD supplied an answer. "A mine, Your Excellency!" He glanced down from the pedestal at the floor below, a look of bitter realization on his face. "It must have been hiding on the seabed, waiting for us to pass over it!"

Khan cursed himself for failing to think three-dimensionally. He had vaguely known of the existence of such mobile mines, capable of launching themselves from the ocean floor when they detected an enemy submarine above, but had worried only about the mines floating directly in his path. *Would Captain Hapka have been caught so unawares?* he wondered, in a rare moment of self-doubt. *Only the unforgiving spirits of the sea may ever know. . . .*

"Your Excellency! Lord Khan!" the OOD shouted over the shrill, hysterical keening of emergency klaxons. Warning lights flashed at every station, but

Khan was proud to see that not one seaman had deserted his post. The OOD staggered across the pedestal, cradling a bleeding arm, until his face was only centimeters away from Khan's. "You must flee, sire!" he said in an urgent hush, coughing from the greasy black smoke pervading the control room. "This ship will not see the sun again!"

Flee? Khan shook his head violently, whitened knuckles holding fast to the safety rail, which crumpled beneath his powerful grip. His distraught brown eyes took in the heartrending site of the doomed sailors valiantly staying at their posts amidst the wreckage of the control room. How could he abandon such people, such loyalty?

"No, no," he murmured. The OOD tugged on Khan's upper arm, trying to pull him toward the steps at the rear of the platform, but Khan angrily yanked his arm free. "Unhand me!" he shouted, his face contorted by rage and despair. He shoved the OOD aside, his unchecked strength sending the Frenchman flying, so that he slammed backward into the lowered optical periscope several paces away. *Where has my victory gone?* Khan stormed inwardly, certain vengeance snatched without warning from his grasp. *What must I do now?*

With laudable persistence, the cast-off OOD shrugged off his brutal collision with the periscope and limped back across the platform toward Khan. "Lord Khan," he insisted, anguished, idealistic eyes beseeching his chosen commander. "The world needs you!"

His heartfelt plea gave Khan pause, cooling to some slight degree the volcanic emotions surging within his chest. Part of Khan wanted nothing more than to go down with his ship, yet another, more calculating segment of his soul argued against that fatal temptation, reminding him that he had a responsibility to the greater realm beyond the ruptured walls of this dying sub. Perhaps there was no better way to honor the sacrifice of these gallant men and women than by ensuring that they did not die in vain. *I must survive to continue the fight,* he realized, *for the sake of all humanity.*

"Very well," he relented, the taste of the words bitter upon his tongue. He let the limping crewman escort him down from the platform toward the exit aft of the plotting area. The floor was tilted sharply to starboard, making walking difficult. Severed cords and conduits dangled from the ceiling like hanging vines, which brushed against Khan as he stumbled across the askew flooring, amidst the lurid scarlet glow of the blinking emergency beacons. The sights and sounds triggered an unwelcome flashback to another frantic exodus, almost twenty years ago, when, as a four-year-old child, he had been forcibly evacuated (by Gary Seven's transporter?) from the underground headquarters of the Chrysalis Project only minutes before the entire subterranean complex, along with his visionary mother, had been destroyed in a blaze of thermonuclear fire. *I have accomplished so much since that night,* he thought ruefully, galled beyond all measure that he had been reduced to a fleeing refugee once more.

"Make way! Make way!" the OOD hollered as he and Khan shouldered their way through a clot of desperate sailors struggling to keep the *Kaur* alive and habitable for as long as humanly possible. Khan had to step over a discarded fire extinguisher, rolling noisily across the floor, to reach the compartment beyond, where the forward escape trunk rose like the base of a bolted steel redwood, a meter-and-a-half in diameter. The trunk offered Khan a means of swift egress from the sub, provided he moved quickly enough.

"Hurry, Your Excellency!" Cassel pleaded, while Khan rapidly donned the wet suit and breathing hood contained in one of the compartment's closets. A warning sticker alerted him to the fact that the hoods were only safe at depths of 180 meters or less; Khan recalled that the *Kaur* had been cruising at roughly 200 meters below when the mine struck. *An ordinary man would never survive an ascent from this depth,* he realized, *but I am no ordinary man....*

He heard gushing water flooding the mess area one level below, along with the agonized shouts and curses of dying men and women. *Yet more lives senselessly snuffed out by Hunyadi,* Khan thought furiously, adding the crew of the *Kaur* to the debt to which he would someday hold the Romanian pretender accountable. With Cassel's help, he placed the hood, a watertight hybrid of life jacket and breathing apparatus, over his head. "Your sacrifice and courage will not be forgotten," he promised the intrepid Frenchman. "And have no doubt, your death will surely be avenged!"

"I believe you, sire," the OOD said, opening the hatch at the bottom of the escape trunk. Khan clambered inside the dense steel drum, built to withstand the full pressure of the invading sea, and filled the hood's air reservoirs from a nozzle inside the trunk. Then, bidding the mortally wounded ship farewell, he flooded the chamber and waited for the trunk's upper hatch to open, releasing him into the frigid waters outside. Although he knew that, ultimately, he was doing the right thing, leaving the *SGK Kaur* and its heroic crew behind, he could not help feeling that he was abandoning his mother for a second time.

The hatch slid open and Khan rocketed toward the surface of the Adriatic, hundreds of meters above. The insulated wet suit provided him with some protection from the icy cold of the depths; his superhuman endurance protected him even more. He breathed slowly and steadily within the hood, so as to avoid getting the bends, while the ghastly sound of the *Kaur*'s final implosion followed him all the way up to where he broke through the waves, to find himself bobbing beneath a cold winter sky, many miles from the safety of the Italian shore.

How? he wondered, shivering amidst the spray and the sea. *How had such a glorious mission gone so tragically and catastrophically awry?* With an epic swim ahead of him, of so arduous and Herculean a nature that only a superior human specimen could even dream of setting foot on land once more, Khan somehow sensed the subtly manipulative hand of Gary Seven at work. *But how does that American know my every move?*

CHAPTER THIRTEEN

THE FIRE WAS BEGINNING TO DIE OUT, SO GARY Seven tossed another log onto the smoldering timbers, then settled back into his chair to enjoy the invigorating warmth radiating from the fireplace. The cheery blaze helped to dispel the cold Scottish weather creeping in through the roughhewn stone walls of the restored farmhouse. *The trick to maintaining a fire,* he reflected, his pensive gaze captured by the dancing orange flames, *is to keep the flames going without burning the whole house down.*

His aging bones rested comfortably within the plush embrace of an upholstered Queen Anne armchair as he sipped slowly from a cup of hot peppermint tea. A velvet dressing gown was belted against the cold; felt-lined slippers protected his feet. Walnut bookshelves lined the walls of the cozy den while a framed portrait of Isis rested prominently upon the mantel of the red brick fireplace. The elegant black cat posed regally within the photo, a glittering silver collar draped around her neck. "I wish you were here, doll," he whispered nostalgically. If nothing else, Isis would have enjoyed curling up in front of the fire.

A sheaf of dossiers, on everything from the Middle Eastern peace talks to the aftermath of the recent L.A. earthquake, rested on his lap, demanding his attention, but he found it difficult to concentrate on the stapled, neatly typed reports while impatiently awaiting word of the brewing confrontation in the Adriatic. *Has Khan's sub encountered Hunyadi's defenses yet?* he wondered. *And who, if anyone, has prevailed?*

He looked up expectantly at the sound of footsteps rushing briskly down the stairs from the second floor, where their primary offices resided. A moment later, the door to the den swung open, admitting Roberta, who hurried into the room clutching a fistful of crumpled faxes. "You have news?" he asked, leaning forward in his chair.

"Yep," Roberta confirmed; he heard excitment in her voice. "I still have to corroborate some of the details, but it looks like a total washout for both sides. Khan's shiny new submarine was completely destroyed, but not before taking out at least one of Hunyadi's secondhand Russian hunter-killers." Her blue-green eyes searched Seven's face, waiting for his reaction. "That's good, right?"

Seven nodded solemnly. "As good as can be expected," he acknowledged, "under such unenviable circumstances." He sincerely regretted the loss of life aboard the two subs, but took solace from the knowledge that both Khan and Hunyadi had been significantly weakened by their fruitless undersea engagement. Fully equipped nuclear submarines were neither cheap nor readily available; both would-be conquerors would be a while recovering from this costly imbroglio. And at least the subs' awesome firepower had been turned on each other, rather than defenseless innocents.

It's a dangerous game I've embarked upon, Seven thought soberly, *playing Khan and his rival supermen against each other. But how else to minimize their potentially catastrophic impact on world affairs?* That was why he had, through a complex and meticulously indirect series of go-betweens, deliberately alerted Hunyadi to Khan's intentions to attack Bosnia via the Adriatic, thereby guaranteeing a naval confrontation between the two supermen—with exactly the results he had intended.

"So far, so good," he informed Roberta. In a best-case scenario, the internecine competition between Chrysalis's most megalomaniacal progeny would prevent any single superman (or superwoman) from completely warping the course of human history.

In the worst case . . . well, Seven didn't want to consider that dismaying prospect just now.

He placed the empty teacup on the varnished cherry end table next to his chair. "How public has this gone?" he asked intently, worried about the effect that news of the undersea battle might have on various precarious political situations around the world. "What sort of exposure are we looking at?"

"Minimal," Roberta assured him. A wool tartan sweater, argyle sweatpants, and fluffy pink slippers ensured that she was adequately fortified against chilly drafts. "The nice thing about submarine warfare is that it takes place largely out of sight." Pulling a burgundy wing chair up in front of the fire, she sat down beside Seven. "I suspect that the major superpowers have an inkling of what happened under the Adriatic, but nobody seems to be in a hurry to alert the media.

"Besides," she added with a smirk, "the entire global news apparatus is too busy covering Tonya and Nancy to notice a little thing like a eugenics war." Her brow wrinkled as she made a show of searching her memory, only partly in jest. "I can't remember, were either of them conceived at Chrysalis?"

Seven had more pressing matters to worry about than a pair of feuding ice skaters, no matter how genetically gifted they might be. But he was glad to hear that, as of the moment, the fatal undersea conflict had escaped the world's view. "Let's keep our eyes out for any potential news leaks," he advised Roberta; if at all possible, he hoped to keep the existence of the Chrysalis-bred supermen from becoming common knowledge, for fear of igniting full-scale genetic warfare and panic, of the sort that had destroyed entire civilizations on Alba IV or Trasker Prime. *Time enough,* he resolved, *for future generations to uncover the true nature of this era's conflicts.*

"What about Khan?" he inquired. Of all the man-made prodigies currently contending for power, the charismatic Sikh superman held the most potential to change the world, for better or for worse. He was fundamentally saner than the rest of Chrysalis's wild crop, thus all the more dangerous. "We know he intended to oversee the attack personally. Do we know if he survived the battle?"

Seven knew he would mourn Khan's death, remembering the brilliant and courageous youth he had tried to take under his wing. But he also admitted, if only to himself, that he would be undeniably relieved if Khan had perished beneath the waves. He glanced upward instinctively, knowing that somewhere high above them Morning Star still orbited, tempting Khan with the ability to completely destroy Earth's ozone layer. To date, Seven had been unable to devise a foolproof way to disarm or destroy the threatening satellite, at least not without alerting Khan to their mole within his organization. That was an ace in the hole he'd just as soon hang onto right now. . . .

"Our spy in Chandigarh reports that a rescue operation is under way," Roberta replied, "which suggests that they have some reasonable expectation of finding Khan alive. I believe that the *Kaur* may have managed to get out some sort of coded transmission before taking its final plunge, alerting the folks back home that Khan had abandoned ship." She shuddered, perhaps imagining the freezing temperatures of the Adriatic this time of year. "Do you really think that anybody, even Khan, could survive being lost at sea, in hostile waters, no less?"

Seven recalled the ease with which Khan singlehandedly outfought a squadron of heavily armed Russian soldiers back in 1986, during his daring raid on Red Square. "I think we would be foolish to underestimate him," he told Roberta, the gravity of his tone divulging the extent of concern. "Until we learn otherwise, we should assume that Khan is still a major factor in our calculations. Possibly *the* major factor."

It occurred to him that, with Khan missing and out of touch, temporarily at least, now might be the perfect time to have their mole try to sabotage Morning Star once and for all, but in such a way as to make Khan believe it was still operational. *Definitely something to think about,* Seven decided, *but was it too dangerous?* He didn't want to expose their spy too early.

A blazing log cracked loudly in the fireplace, making a sound like a gunshot. A handful of glowing orange embers jumped free of the fire, landing on the scorched hearthstone in front of the fireplace. His sixty-five-year-old bones creaking somewhat, Seven lurched out of his chair and walked a couple of paces over to the hearth, where he coolly stamped out the fiery embers. While he was up, he took the opportunity to toss another log onto the fire, then prodded it into place with a nearby iron poker. The newly fed flames rose up vigorously, throwing off a welcome blast of heat, but stayed obligingly within the brick-lined confines of the fireplace.

So far, Seven thought, *the fire is not burning out of control. But for how much longer?*

CHAPTER FOURTEEN

**PALACE OF THE GREAT KHAN
CHANDIGARH, INDIA
APRIL 21, 1994**

THE SOUNDS OF ANGRY SHOUTS AND CHANTING, coming from outside the fortress walls, intruded upon the sanctity of the royal garden, where Khan was attempting to pose for his official portrait. Cries of "Down with Khan! Where is Khan?" reached his ears despite his best efforts to tune them out. *Ungrateful curs!* he thought indignantly. *Who are they to judge me?*

"Please, Your Excellency!" the painter, an artistically gifted German whom Khan had rescued from a career of painting tawdry paperback covers in New York, pleaded with his distracted subject. "Try not to scowl so!"

"My apologies, Herr Vogellieder," Khan replied. Taking a deep breath to calm his fraying nerves, he rearranged his features into a more serene and inspirational expression, lifting his chin in order to better look into the glorious future he envisioned for the world, quite apart from the petty vexations of the present. *Patience,* he counseled himself, albeit with effort. *Rome was not built in a day, and even Caesar sometimes had to put up with the fickle mob.*

A golden turban rested upon his brow, shielding his superlative brain from the mounting heat of the morning sun. Although it was not even noon, the temperature in the garden already felt like it was climbing toward forty degrees Celsius; Khan's meteorologists were predicting an unusually hot summer this year, and so far their projections were looking right on the money. Khan glanced longingly at the tempting shade of the leafy mango trees sprouting in the lush outdoor garden, which was nestled amidst his private apartments at the rear of the palace; alas, the painter preferred direct sunlight for his labors.

At least Joaquin was able to take advantage of the dusky coolness offered by the verdant trees. The bodyguard watched Khan pose from the comfort of a wrought-iron bench situated in the shadow of a fruit-laden bough. Having largely recovered from the grievous injuries he had sustained during September's earthquake, Joaquin had wasted no time resuming his duties as Khan's personal guardian. Khan valued Joaquin's loyalty more than ever, especially with the discontented howls of the rabble ringing in his ears at this very moment.

"Open your eyes, Khan! Khan, go home!"

For this official portrait, intended for the palace's formal banquet hall, Khan had chosen to pay respect to his Sikh ancestry by wearing the traditional karra, or silver bracelet, on his right wrist, as well as a kirpan, or dagger, on his belt. Although he had donned the kirpan for ceremonial reasons, he now wished he could use the curved silver blade to slice the unworthy throats of the protestors.

Khan's mood darkened further as Ament emerged from the marble portico connecting the garden to the interior apartments. Lately, it seemed as though he and his once-trusted advisor seldom saw eye-to-eye anymore, particularly regarding foreign affairs. He found himself increasingly reluctant to share the details of his war strategies with her.

"Pardon me, Lord Khan," she spoke, thoughtfully staying out of Vogellieder's line of sight. "I am sorry to interrupt your sitting, but I fear that more pressing matters demand your attention." She glanced in the direction of the shouting mob. "As you may have gathered," she added dryly.

Khan was tempted to dismiss her out of hand. How dare she presume to tell him where his priorities lie? But cooler instincts prevailed and he rose reluctantly from the simple white cane chair he had chosen for the portrait. "Very well," he assented, turning to address the busy artist. "That will be all for now, Herr Vogellieder. I will summon you when I am ready to pose again."

"Yes, Your Excellency," the German complied, adding a few last strokes to his canvas before commencing to pack up his brushes and oils. "Thank you, Your Excellency."

Ament strolled across the garden to inspect the unfinished portrait. "An excellent likeness," she commented. "He captures you at your best."

Khan could not help but hear an implied criticism

in her observation, as though he had not always lived up to that standard in her eyes. He bristled inwardly, but refused to be baited into a discussion of his personal failings.

"Well?" he demanded brusquely. "What is so important that you thought it necessary to disturb me?"

She cocked her head toward the sound of irate men and women venting their displeasure just outside the fortress. "I would have thought that would be self-evident."

"That?" he said scornfully. He walked over to a waist-high sheshamwood table where a pitcher of iced *chai* had been laid out for his refreshment. He poured himself a glass and calmly took a sip before speaking again. "What have I to fear from the senseless yowls of a malcontented minority?"

Ament followed him over to the carved wooden table. She did not ask for a glass of her own and he did not offer one. "This is not the first such demonstration," she persisted, "nor is it likely to be the last." She spoke in Hindi to avoid being overheard by the departing painter. "Your popularity is slipping among the general populace. Inflation and unemployment are rising throughout the Punjab, as well as the rest of India and Pakistan, yet the common people fear that you no longer hear their cries, that you are preoccupied with other matters."

"I am fighting to save the entire planet!" Khan protested vehemently. The spicy taste of the tea turned to bile in his throat. He downed the last of the *chai* in a single gulp, then placed the empty cup back down upon the table. "You know that as well as I."

Ament declined to let the matter drop. "Perhaps,

my lord, but the people neither know nor care about your secret wars against Hunyadi, Gary Seven, and the rest. They feel only the effects of your neglect." She shook her head reproachfully, reminding Khan of a disapproving headmistress. "The loss of the *Kaur* alone cost us millions that might have been spent instead on new schools, hospitals, and industries. And then there's the rocket base in the South Pacific, and Dr. Dhasal's genetic experiments. . . ."

"Enough!" Khan exploded, throwing up his hand to staunch the hectoring flow of words. He glared at her balefully. "I will not be lectured to like an errant schoolboy." His voice turned cold and dismissive. "You forget your place."

A look of disappointment, and even sadness, passed briefly over the Egyptian woman's immaculate features. For the first time, he thought he saw a hint of hurt in her striking amber eyes, although she quickly regained her customary sangfroid. "There was a time," she reminded him pointedly, "that you welcomed my dissent."

That was before I went to war against my brothers, Khan brooded unhappily. Before the dream of a unified planet, enjoying a golden age of peace and prosperity under the enlightened rule of a single ruler, was held hostage by clashing ambitions of those who should have been his allies. *Before my lofty plans for humanity devolved into an endless game of strike and counterstrike, of espionage, sabotage, and assassination.*

He found he had less use for a flesh-and-blood conscience these days, or perhaps that was simply a luxury he could no longer afford. "Leave me," he told her curtly. "I am not in the giving vein today."

"As you wish." Ament exited the garden as gracefully as she had entered it, leaving him alone with Joaquin and the uncompleted painting. Khan stared bleakly into the reflective waters of a lotus-shaped lily pond as he wondered when exactly his destiny took such a darker turn. The strident chants of the demonstrators taunted him, filling him with dissatisfaction and resentment.

Fools! Peasants! Inferiors! Khan yanked the turban from his crown in frustration and hurled the wad of golden silk across the garden with all his strength. *Can they not see that I have the best interests of them all at heart? They should be thankful that I see them as anything more than useful cannon fodder!*

Alerted to Khan's obvious distress, Joaquin rose from his bench and limped over to the lily pond. "Shall I have the palace guard disperse the protesters, Your Excellency?" He glowered murderously in the direction of the clamoring horde, at those who dared to challenge the will of his lord and master. "Just give me the word and they will be taken care of."

Khan suspected that Joaquin had a fairly permanent solution in mind. "No, my friend," he said. "Let them have their say—for now." A rueful smile conveyed a measure of hard-won patience and restraint. *Why risk a riot or a massacre?* Khan remembered Tiananmen Square, and had little desire to sully his own reign with such a bloodbath, at least for as long as the remorseless tide of history allowed. *Not that Hunyadi or some of the others are likely to show similar forbearance,* he thought venomously. *It would almost serve the croaking masses right to let them experience the tyranny of a truly ruthless superdictator.*

"But, Your Excellency—!" Joaquin sounded as though he could not believe his ears. "They defy you at your very door! We must make an example of them!"

Khan shook his head. "Others would simply take their place," he predicted bitterly. "There are too many inferior, irrational people in the world. Too many primitive minds, keeping humanity mired in barbarism, thanks to their unmitigated ignorance and prejudices."

He gloomily considered the sorry state of the world. War and portents of war everywhere he looked. NATO launching air strikes against Serbian forces in Bosnia. North Korea threatening to employ nuclear weapons against its rival to the south. Tribal warfare erupting in Rwanda after the assassination of its embattled president only five days ago. Massacres and terrorism in the Middle East. A violent peasant uprising in Mexico. Paramilitary death squads in Haiti. Civil war in nearby Afghanistan.

A wave of despair threatened to overwhelm him. How could one man, even such a man as he, eradicate all the chaos and savagery at large in the world today? There was too much turmoil, too many unengineered humans barely one step removed from a tribe of yammering apes. The continually impeded pace of his march to glory frustrated him beyond endurance, yet what was he to do in the face of never-ending opposition from man and superman alike? The unruly crowd outside represented only an insignificant portion of the many millions of fractious, close-minded primitives he had yet to bring under his benevolent control. *Executing a mere handful would accomplish nothing,* he reflected morosely; *I would have to exterminate billions to crush such resistance completely.*

"Excuse me, my lord."

Khan stirred from his doleful reverie to see a minor palace functionary standing a respectful distance away. *Now what?* Khan thought impatiently, displeased at being disturbed once more. "Yes?" he inquired crossly.

The servant, an assistant chamberlain named Atal, blanched at Khan's ill-tempered tone. "A thousand pardons, Lord Khan, but there is a stranger who desires an audience with Your Excellency." He watched Khan's face apprehensively, fearful of incurring his master's wrath. "He says he knew your mother."

My mother? Khan regarded the messenger with greater interest. "A stranger, you say?"

"Yes, Your Excellency. An Englishman, I believe."

Now more intrigued than irritated, Khan desired to know more. "Bring him to me," he instructed.

"Your Excellency . . . ?" Joaquin sounded a cautionary note.

"Fear not, my friend," Khan assured him. "Our visitor could not have come this far without being thoroughly searched by our security forces." He confidently admired the high sandstone walls surrounding the garden. "You are my last line of defense, but hardly my only one."

"If you say so, Your Excellency." Joaquin's hand hovered over the gleaming brass hilt of his belt-buckle knife nonetheless. He positioned himself in front of Khan even as the attendant left to fetch the unnamed stranger.

Khan doubted that the assassin existed who could

overcome both him and Joaquin single-handedly. After all, Khan, too, was armed, with his ceremonial kirpan, so it was only natural that curiosity exceeded caution in his soul. *An associate of my mother?* he wondered in astonishment. *After all these years?* Sarina Kaur's former colleagues had scattered throughout the world after the fall of the Chrysalis Project. Some had died, some had disappeared into new identities, while still others had been placed under lifetime observation or house arrest by their respective governments. Khan had made intermittent attempts to recruit some of the surviving scientists to assist Phoolan Dhasal in her lab on Chrysalis Island, but had ultimately concluded that the effort required more trouble than it was worth. The leftover geneticists were merely ordinary humans, after all; deprived of his mother's visionary genius, it was unlikely that they could offer any skills or insights beyond that which Dhasal and her staff already possessed.

And yet, here was a purported compatriot of his mother showing up at Khan's doorstep almost two decades after the first Chrysalis's thermonuclear destruction. A mysterious Englishman, no less. Khan felt his pulse quicken with excitement. *Who knows what new possibilities this unanticipated guest may bring?* he thought hopefully, feeling his spirits lift from the dreadful malaise that had engulfed him. Did not the poet Homer teach, "All strangers and beggars are from Zeus" . . . ?

He waited long minutes until Atal returned with their visitor. At first glance, the anonymous caller proved a disappointment; Khan frowned at the sight of a short, dumpy, older man, whose disheveled and unhealthy appearance inspired little confidence. Bald and overweight, with sagging jowls and the flushed complexion of a heavy drinker, the pear-shaped stranger looked to be maybe seventy years old, and well past his prime. His ruddy face was slick with sweat, and perspiration soaked through the front of his button-down denim shirt as well as beneath the armpits of his rumpled khaki bush jacket. His shabby safari garb, reminiscent of the bygone days of the British Raj, made him look like a one-time Great White Hunter gone very badly to seed.

"Good morning, Mr. Khan," he said, obsequiously clutching a dented pith helmet to his chest. He shambled across the garden toward Khan, wheezing with exertion. "Thank you so much for receiving me."

"Lord Khan," Joaquin corrected him sternly.

"Yes, yes, of course," the man stammered nervously. "Lord Khan, naturally." His breath smelled of tobacco and gin. "I don't suppose you remember me, Lord Khan?" He peered up at Khan hopefully, grimacing awkwardly like a man having his driver's license photo taken. "Dr. Donald Archibald Williams? Late of the Chrysalis Project?"

Khan probed his encyclopedic memory. He had been only four years old when his mother died, but he thought he vaguely recognized the debilitated Englishman from his early childhood at Chrysalis. Scouring backward through the veil of time, he dimly remembered seeing Williams in the company of his mother, looking only marginally younger and healthier than he did today. Khan found it hard to imagine that so pitiful a specimen of mortal man could have played any part in the creation of a new and superior breed of humanity, yet his fragmentary recollections appeared to confirm that his visitor was telling the truth, at least in part.

"Quite late, I assume," Khan said coolly. *To think that my mother perished at Chrysalis, yet this cringing wretch survived!* He took an immediate dislike to Williams, but strove to hear the man out, for hospitality's sake if no other. "How can I help you, Doctor?"

"Well, you see," Williams began, wheezing strenuously. A fit of wet, violent coughing derailed his explanation, and he dabbed at his sweaty brow with a well-worn handkerchief. "Perhaps," he suggested plaintively, after the coughing subsided, "if I could sit down somewhere, out of the sun?"

Khan nodded at Joaquin, who obediently assisted the feeble visitor over to the iron bench beneath the mango trees. Williams dropped gratefully onto the bench, his chest heaving. "Yes, that's much better," he gasped, clearly exhausted by his short walk across the garden. "Many thanks."

Placing his pith helmet down beside him on the bench, Williams began rooting around in the front pockets of his bush jacket. Joaquin tensed, just in case the palsied Englishman had somehow managed to smuggle a weapon past the palace's assiduous screening process. He relaxed only slightly when Williams produced a packet of cigarettes and a lighter instead. "Do you mind if I smoke, Your Lordship?" he asked, apparently anxious to inflict more damage on his already-blighted lungs.

"Yes," Khan stated unequivocally. He was starting to question whether this decrepit Westerner was worth his time. He gazed down imperiously at his seated visitor. "Please get to the point, Dr. Williams."

The wheezing fossil sheepishly put away his cigarettes. "Whatever you say, Lord Khan." He looked up at Khan through watery, bloodshot eyes. "As I started to explain before, I worked closely with your mother back at the old Chrysalis Project, at our underground facility in Rajasthan." He vainly searched Khan's stony face for any trace of sympathy or softheartedness. "She was quite a remarkable woman, Your Lordship. A brilliant mind coupled with a positively indomitable will and sense of purpose. There would have been no Chrysalis Project without her, Your Lordship."

"So I have always understood," Khan stated flatly. His visitor's fulsome praise of his mother did little to assuage his growing impatience; did this man have nothing to offer him except nostalgic reminiscences of bygone days? "Go on, Doctor."

Williams seemed to realize that he was trying Khan's patience. "Yes, right," he said hastily. A nervous tremor shook his dilapidated frame. "Anyway, after everything went to hell in seventy-four, I thought it best to drop out of sight for a while. By then, the authorities had somehow twigged on to what we'd been up to at Chrysalis, and a number of my colleagues ended up in custody, or else disappeared entirely. I suspect that some of them got drafted into one covert government project or another, and that others were simply 'retired' permanently, if you get my drift."

The geriatric caller ran a finger across his throat to clarify his meaning. "Me, I've been lying low ever since, keeping body and soul together by selling my scientific expertise under the table, as it were."

Khan wondered, without too much interest, what manner of dubious enterprises Williams had been involved with. He had heard rumors of recent illegal cloning experiments, involving everything from human embryos to the Shroud of Turin. Whatever sort of illicit research the seedy Englishman might have been engaged in, Khan felt certain that it had been highly disreputable.

"Recently, however, through no real fault of my own, mind you, I've found myself in a bit of hot water with respect to a couple of my more, er, unforgiving clients." Williams paused, clearly reluctant to elaborate, then jumped ahead in his narrative. "Consequently, a change of scenery seemed to be in order, and it occurred to me to look you up." He fixed a calculating gaze on Khan, providing a glimmer of a wily mind within his wasted shell. "I must admit, I've followed your career with some interest, Lord Khan. Your mother would be quite proud of the heights to which you've risen, I assure you. It's a pity she didn't live to see you fulfill the tremendous potential she crafted for you."

My destiny will be complete when the world is mine, Khan thought, *and not a moment before.* He noted that the sun had risen significantly since he had first sat down to pose for Herr Vogellieder; the morning was swiftly passing away. "Permit me to save us all precious time by cutting to the core of your purpose here today," he said disdainfully. "Having incurred the wrath of unspecified third parties, whose activities I suspect are of questionable legality, you have come here seeking my patronage and protection, trading solely on your long-ago affiliation with my deceased mother." He did not bother to blunt the sarcastic edge of his tone. "Isn't that correct, Dr. Williams?"

"Yes—I mean, no, Your Lordship!" Flustered and distraught, Williams heaved his sloppy bulk back onto his feet, clutching his chest as he did so. An angry blue vein throbbed wildly on his right temple. "That is, yes, I would certainly appreciate your hospitality and financial assistance at this difficult period, but, no, Your Lordship, I have not come here empty-handed, with no other claim besides the legitimate fact of my past service to your mother." He grabbed onto Khan's sleeve, as if fearful that Khan was about to turn his back on him. "I have far more to offer you than that!"

Khan was skeptical, but still willing to be convinced. "Explain," he commanded, pulling his arm free of the man's cloying grip. "Quickly."

A sly expression crossed Williams's florid countenance. "Have you ever heard of necrotizing fasciitis?" he asked with an unsavory grin.

Khan thought the term somewhat familiar, but he had been trained as an engineer, not a biologist. "Some manner of bacteria, correct?"

"A flesh-eating bacteria," Williams said with positively ghoulish gusto, "capable of devouring living tissue at a frightening, and invariably fatal, rate. Specifically, it's a strain of antibiotic-resistant streptococcus." He leaned toward Khan, lowering his voice to a conspiratorial whisper. "Before she died, your mother developed an unusually potent strain of the flesh-eating bacteria. She also made sure that you, and the rest of the Chrysalis children, possessed a genetic immunity to all forms of streptococcus."

Khan stared at Williams in shock, torn between horror and morbid curiosity. This was the first he had heard of any such genetically engineered bacteria. "But why would my mother do such a thing?"

"Why, it was all part of her master plan, Your Lordship!" Williams chuckled evilly, growing bolder now that he had clearly captured Khan's attention. "To clear the world of its surplus population when you and the other children were ready to take over. The plan, which only a very few of us knew, was to wait until you came of age, then unleash the bacteria all over the planet."

Khan took hold of the Englishman's grimy collar. "Is this true?" he demanded, uncertain what he should think or feel about this startling revelation. Germ warfare—against all of humanity? The very idea was horrific, and yet . . . wasn't it only less than half an hour ago, right here in this tranquil garden, that he had despaired of ever bringing peace to the world's warring billions? Hadn't he lamented aloud to Joaquin that there were too many ignorant, inferior people in the world? *Is it even possible to cleanse the world the way Williams is describing?* With a single hand, he lifted the pudgy scientist off the ground, so that Williams's feet dangled several centimeters in the air. "If you are lying to me," he snarled at the Englishman, leaving the precise nature of his threat to the older man's imagination.

"I swear it! Cross my heart!" Williams flailed helplessly in Khan's grip, choking on his twisted collar. Saliva sprayed from his contorted lips. Frantic, blood-rimmed eyes bulged from their sockets. "Dr. Kaur—your mother!—she had already acquired the missiles from the Russians, equipped with experimental bio-warheads to disperse the bacteria!" His portly body trembled like an overripe fruit before the monsoon. "It's all true, I tell you!"

The extremity of his fear lent credibility to his panicky assertions. *They say the tongues of dying men,* Khan thought, after Richard the Second, *enforce attention like deep harmony.* Rather than pressing Williams quite that far, he released the man's collar, dropping the terrified relic back onto the terra-cotta walkway. "What became of the bacteria?" he asked coldly.

Shaking and plastered with sweat, his body doubled over so that his hands rested on his quivering knees, Williams struggled to catch his breath. "It can be yours, Your Lordship!" he gasped. "I pinched the recipe—the exact genetic sequence—right before Chrysalis blew up!"

Khan could readily imagine Williams's actions that fateful night, pocketing the precious formula as he scrambled for safety, leaving Sarina Kaur to perish with her dream. "In other words, you stole my mother's secrets, then abandoned her!"

"No, Your Lordship, it wasn't like that at all, I swear!" He clutched his throat, massaging his brutalized windpipe, while the pulsing vein on his temple threatened to explode. "There was no way I could have saved your mother. She was determined to stay on at Chrysalis until the bitter end!" Panic elevated the timbre of his voice. "I was just trying to preserve the fruits of her genius!"

"And your own craven skin," Khan accused. *I was*

only a child, he thought guiltily. *I had no choice but to leave my mother behind when Chrysalis was evacuated.* But what was Williams's excuse for deserting Sarina Kaur at her moment of greatest need?

Khan's hand fell upon the hilt of his silver kirpan. He was sorely tempted to execute Williams on the spot, in long-delayed payment for his cowardice twenty years ago. The Englishman must have spotted the deadly intent in Khan's eyes, for he dropped onto his knees and raised his clasped hands in supplication. "It wasn't my fault," he pleaded, wringing his hands together fearfully. "It was Seven and that damn blonde! They're the ones who got your mother killed!"

"What?" Khan hissed, feeling his blood turn to ice. "What did you say?"

"It was two American spies," Williams insisted, letting loose a torrent of shrill explication. "A man named Gary Seven and this blonde chippie who called herself Veronica Neary. They infiltrated Chrysalis right there at the end. We never found out who exactly they were working for, but Seven somehow managed to activate Chrysalis's emergency self-destruct procedure. The whole place went up in a mushroom cloud, taking your mother with it." Williams's red-veined eyes were wild with fear, and his shallow, labored breaths came so rapidly that Khan suspected he might have to summon a medic. "There was nothing I could have done, Your Lordship! I swear it upon my life!"

The Englishman's meaningless oaths meant little to Khan, yet he knew with utter certainty that Williams had spoken the truth. In the back of his mind, he had always suspected that Gary Seven and his pert amanuensis had played some part in the destruction of Chrysalis. Why else would Seven have tracked Khan and the other superchildren so meticulously? At times, Khan even thought he recalled being spirited away from Chrysalis by the swirling blue energy of Seven's matter-transporter device, even though the passage of decades had left the memory maddeningly elusive and unreliable.

It was one thing, however, to suspect Seven and the ubiquitous Ms. Lincoln of complicity in his mother's death; it was quite another thing to have those dire suspicions confirmed at long last. *You should never have let me live,* he silently admonished Seven, *let alone tried to convert me to your cause.* His fists clenched so tightly that his manicured nails dug into his palms, Khan contemplated with growing fury all the manifold ways in which Seven had attempted to twist Khan's destiny to his own design. *No more,* he vowed. *You and your perfidious henchwoman will regret that you ever set foot in India.*

"Please, Your Lordship! Have mercy!" Down on his knees, Williams continued to beg for his life. Sweat streamed down his abject face like pus from an open sore. "I meant no harm! I only came here because I knew you could protect me!"

Khan reached down and effortlessly pulled the groveling scientist back onto his feet. In light of what he had just revealed about Seven, the Englishman's own crimes no longer seemed of much consequence. Khan had weightier matters on his mind, namely a son's rightful vengeance—and his mother's last legacy.

"Tell me more about this flesh-eating bacteria," he commanded.

CHAPTER FIFTEEN

FORT COCHISE
SOUTHEAST ARIZONA
UNITED STATES
AUGUST 16, 1994

THE TIGHT SECURITY REMINDED ROBERTA OF AREA
51, or East Berlin back during the bad old days of the
Cold War.

Barbed wire and timber watchtowers barricaded
the outer perimeter of the militia headquarters.
Goons in paramilitary uniforms patrolled the grounds
with fierce-looking guard dogs that resembled a cross
between a Doberman and a pit bull. (*A doberpit?* she
wondered.) From the outside, the compound resembled a prison or concentration camp more than the
voluntary residence of dozens of self-styled patriots.

Roberta gazed at the camp through the tinted windows of the black Humvee carrying her toward the
fort. Sitting in the backseat, behind the driver, she
did her best to conceal her apprehension as the vehi-

cle pulled up to the front gate, where an Uzi-toting guard manned a lowered steel barrier. *Remember,* she reminded herself, *you're thrilled and excited to be here.*

"So this is it, huh?" she asked.

"Uh-huh," the driver, who called himself "Butch," confirmed laconically. Not exactly the talkative sort, he had resisted all of Roberta's sporadic attempts to make small talk since picking her up at the Tucson airport a few hours back. She wondered if he was this uncommunicative all the time, or only with nosy new arrivals?

The Humvee braked in front of the horizontal crossbar and Butch rolled down the window to talk to the khaki-clad guard standing watch over the gate. "Freeman Butch Connors, returning from a pick-up in Tucson," he informed the sentry in clipped, military tones. Unlike the surrounding guards, Butch was clad in civilian garb, the better to blend in outside the camp.

"Password?"

"Ruby Ridge," Butch responded.

Only partly satisfied, the guard peered in through the window at Roberta, scowling at the sight of the unfamiliar woman. "Passenger?"

"A potential new recruit," Butch explained. "Here to meet with the General."

The guard nodded, but continued to eye Roberta with suspicion. "Please step out of the car, ma'am," he said sternly, a Colt Commando assault rifle slung over his shoulder. His breath frosted the air outside the window.

Not wanting to make waves, Roberta did as the guard asked. Her legs were stiff from the long ride from the airport, but it felt good to get out of the car. Looking back the way she'd come, she saw a lonely desert road stretching through an arid landscape distinguished by sun-bleached cattle skulls and PRIVATE PROPERTY signs. Tumbleweeds rolled along dried-up riverbeds, past reddish-orange rock formations jutting up from the earth. Scattered cacti and yucca plants hinted at a trace of moisture somewhere beneath the arid soil. Not much of a vacation spot, she decided.

"Name?" the gatekeeper demanded, brandishing a pen and a clipboard.

"Roberta Landers," she lied. The guard dutifully jotted down the name on his sign-in sheet.

It was a cold, clear morning in Arizona, and Roberta hugged herself in hopes of hanging onto some of the warmth trapped inside her fringed leather jacket. A flannel shirt, Levi's, and cowboy boots completed her outfit, which seemed appropriate to her present assignment. Slightly jet-lagged from the red-eye flight from Spokane, where "Bobbie Landers" supposedly lived, she would have killed for a cup of hot espresso, but suspected that there wasn't a convenient Starbucks anywhere in the vicinity.

"Please raise your arms." The guard frisked Roberta, a bit more intimately than she thought was strictly necessary, then waved a wand-shaped metal detector under her arms and along the outline of her body. The wand beeped once, forcing her to extract her servo from her pocket in order to appease the guard. He gave the apparent fountain pen a cursory inspection, while she pretended to be unconcerned. *What if he wants to confiscate it?* she worried. The disguised device was more than just a weapon; it was her lifeline back to Gary Seven and the Isle of Arran.

A second guard, walking what looked like a mean-tempered doberpit, circled the Humvee. Straining at its leash, the dog sniffed around the vehicle, then padded over to snuffle warily at Roberta's ankles. Its slobbering jaws drooled over the toes of her snake-skin boots, while she waited anxiously to see if the first guard would be taken in by the servo's innocent contours.

"All right, ma'am." The guard returned the all-purpose device, and Roberta repressed a sigh of relief. He nodded at Butch, who had remained behind the wheel of the Humvee. "You can take her in."

Grateful to have passed the security screening, she climbed back into the car. The steel barrier raised in front of them, and Butch drove her past the fort's outer defenses. A large wooden sign, reading KEEP OUT! TRESPASSERS WILL BE SHOT ON SIGHT! did little to calm her nerves.

Fort Cochise, headquarters of the "Army of Eternal Vigilance," was built on the site of a defunct mining town, abandoned in the early thirties when its precious gold and silver deposits ran dry. Many of the original adobe buildings were still standing, converted into dormitories and storage areas. Roberta spotted the crumbling facade of the old town jail, complete with bars over its windows. *Let's hope I manage to stay out of there,* she thought.

Butch parked the Humvee just past the barbed wire fence, then led her across the grounds of the compound. Uniformed men and women, wearing various shades of khaki and cammo gear, went diligently about their business, repairing fortifications, patching up weathered adobe, or transporting heavy crates of food, medicine, and ammunition from one building to another. Roberta couldn't help noticing that every one of the fort's adult inhabitants appeared to be heavily armed, with shotguns, pistols, or both. Even a group of women stringing up laundry to dry had handguns holstered to their hips.

A sudden burst of automatic gunfire startled Roberta. Raising her hand to shield her eyes from the sun, she spotted several militia members practicing at a firing range set up on the western side of the compound. Round after round of unleashed firepower blew apart cardboard cutouts of Janet Reno, Hillary Clinton, and the Secretary-General of the United Nations.

Yikes! Roberta thought, gulping at the sight. A former flower child and self-described "hippie chick," she felt more than a little out of place. *I'm a long way from Woodstock,* she realized. *Geographically, chronologically, and psychologically.*

The whole camp, in fact, seemed to be on a war footing, gearing up for some big siege or battle that might break out at any moment. Unfortunately, as Roberta knew before she even got on the plane in Spokane, the enemy these people were preparing against was their very own government—and anyone else they perceived as part of a nebulously defined global conspiracy. Even worse, Fort Cochise was not unique in that respect; similar camps and private armies had sprung up throughout America over the last decade or so. *But only one militia is run by a genetically engineered superman,* Roberta recalled, trying to look on the bright side.

Ironically, given all his anti-government rhetoric, General Morrison's personal offices turned out to be housed in the refurbished shell of the town's long-dead post office. More men, equipped with automatic rifles and doberpits, guarded the entrance of the building, where Roberta endured another round of passwords, searches, and overly invasive inspections before being handed off to a rangy, grim-looking soldier, who finally led her into the presence of the AEV's supreme commander.

Hawkeye Morrison rose from behind his desk as Roberta entered the room, escorted by her intimidating new baby-sitter. She recognized the notorious militia leader, and one-time Chrysalis kid, from various right-wing periodicals, not to mention her and Seven's own surveillance photos. "Welcome to Fort Cochise," he greeted her cordially, his jaw working on a piece of chewing gum as he spoke. Tan-and-olive army fatigues clothed his stocky, alpha-male physique. A holstered Glock pistol rested on his hip.

"Please, call me Bobbie," she insisted, seeing her own face reflected in the General's silver mirrored shades. Confident that her alias would do the same, she surveyed Morrison's office with open curiosity.

An authentic Revolutionary War-era flag, bearing the defiant motto "Don't Tread on Me," hung on the stucco wall behind Morrison's desk, while a framed news photo immortalized the choking smoke and flames of the Waco disaster. On the wall to her right, a mounted world map, dotted with numerous brightly colored pins, bore an eerie resemblance to a similar map currently residing in Gary Seven's office in Scotland. *Looks like he's keeping track of his superpow-*

ered siblings, Roberta deduced, *but as potential allies or enemies?*

Thankfully, Jugurtha, Pachacutec, and many of the lesser supermen had self-destructed by now, or else were bogged down in bloody civil wars throughout Africa, South America, etc. But she was worried about the growing size of General Morrison's militia, which seemed to be gaining converts by leaps and bounds.

"It's such an honor to finally meet you!" she burbled energetically. There were no windows in the room, probably as a concession to Morrison's paranoia, but she heard the sound of mechanical air filters humming away in order to get the office adequately ventilated. "You're a genuine American hero."

Morrison accepted her praise with a show of humility. "I'm just an old-fashioned patriot, determined to protect our freedom to the best of our abilities." He sat back down behind the desk, which struck Roberta as frighteningly tidy and well-ordered, as opposed to the "creative" clutter of her own desk back at the farmhouse. "Please take a seat," he offered, gesturing toward a plain wooden chair resting on the Navajo carpet in front of the desk.

She plopped down into the chair. Her current escort, whose sun-baked, leathery face appeared locked in a permanent scowl, remained standing, stiffly watching over her from behind. Only a scary glint in his eyes, hinting at fanaticism and pent-up violence, provided evidence that the man was actually alive and not carved from an immobile block of wood. The monosyllabic Butch, who had been dismissed from duty after turning Roberta over to this would-be storm trooper, was starting to seem positively bubbly by comparison.

"Don't let Freeman Porter make you uncomfortable," Morrison said, referring to her taciturn shadow. "He's here strictly for my own protection." He offered Roberta a stick of spearmint gum, which she politely declined. "Given the insidious forces arrayed against our cause, I can't afford to take any unnecessary chances."

"Of course not!" she agreed readily. "The Beast will stop at nothing to stamp out the last flickers of individual liberty." Righteous indignation, or a reasonable facsimile thereof, added heat to her fervent declaration. "That's why I contacted you via your Web site, to join your all-important crusade against godless collectivism."

"So I understand," Morrison said. "I was impressed by the passionate eloquence of your letter, as well as by your own fledgling efforts in the struggle." He gave his PC's monitor a half-turn, so that Roberta could glimpse the screen as well, then quickly keyed a familiar URL into his Web browser.

A headline composed of animated flames appeared at the top of the screen, against a red-white-and-blue background. *The Unblinking Eye* read the burning block letters, above columns of densely-spaced type. Smaller headlines, over various front-page stories, hyped such startling revelations as FEMA: THE SECRET GOVERNMENT and BAR CODES: MARK OF THE BEAST?

"Your online newsletter is one of the best I've seen," Morrison congratulated her. "You appear to have a first-rate grasp of the fundamental issues at stake in these perilous times."

"Thanks," Roberta said. To be honest, she was perversely proud of the *Eye,* which she had started up a few months back to cement her cover. Although the text was a ridiculous mishmash of urban legends and half-baked conspiracy theories, most of them lifted from other "patriotic" Web sites, she thought she had captured just the right tone of belligerent paranoia. "It's just so obvious that you can't trust the so-called 'legitimate' news media to tell you what's really going on in this country. I felt I had to warn people about what our government was up to."

Morrison nodded approvingly. "It's not only Washington, D.C., we have to worry about. The Feds are just one tentacle of a greater Beast, a secret New World Order ruled by an elite group of genetic supermen. I know this for a fact, because I've stared the enemy in the face—and in the mirror."

He removed his mirrored sunglasses to look Roberta directly in the eye. Oversize red orbs, like the eyes of a hunting bird, stared into hers, and she abruptly realized that "Hawkeye" was more than just a colorful nickname; it was the unvarnished truth.

"Let me tell you something that few people know, that I share only with my own trusted brothers- and sisters-in-arms. I'm a bit more than human myself, the product of the same unholy conspiracy that give birth to the Beast." His crimson eyes blinked like a bird's, complete with separate nictitating membranes. "Among other things, I've got a touch of raptor DNA in me, giving me extraordinary eyesight."

Roberta gasped out loud, feigning surprise. "You?" She stared at him with wide-eyed confusion. "But how—I don't understand. . . ."

"It's very simple," he explained. "To my mind, my duty as an American takes precedence over the dictates of my tainted DNA, therefore I've vowed to defend humanity against my own kind." He brought his fist down hard upon the desktop, rattling the neatly arranged trays of pens and paper. "Someone has to stand up for the common man, and that fight is starting here at Fort Cochise, named after the valiant Apache warrior who fought to preserve his way of life from federal troops." Deeply felt emotion thickened his voice. "He defied the Beast for eleven years. I intend to win that battle, no matter the cost."

That's exactly what scares me, Roberta thought, recalling why she had decided to infiltrate the AEV in the first place. Crazed, right-wing militias, packed with trigger-happy gun nuts and conspiracy theorists, were dangerous enough, but a militia headed by a genetically engineered *Übermensch* . . . ? That was something she wanted to keep a very close eye on, especially given the rapid growth of Morrison's private army. She had already tried planting an undercover operative inside the AEV, only to have her agent die in a mysterious "car wreck" several weeks ago. *If nothing else,* she thought, feeling a pang of guilt over the spy's death, *I owe it to her to make sure the AEV doesn't claim any more victims.*

"Ohmigod," she exclaimed, giving Morrison the reaction he expected. "I always knew there was a conspiracy at work, eating away at our freedom, but I never guessed how truly diabolical the threat really was!" Roberta figured she deserved an Oscar for her performance. *Eat your heart out, Meryl Streep.* "You must let me stay and do what I can to help the cause!"

The really ironic thing was, Morrison was right in a way. Genetically engineered supermen were out to take over the world, unbeknownst to ninety-nine percent of the general public. Khan, in particular, would like nothing better than to establish a New World Order with himself on top. Unfortunately, Roberta feared that Morrison's agenda of violent resistance was primarily driven by acute paranoia and his own inflated sense of manifest destiny. *The U.N. and Bill Clinton aren't the problem,* she thought; *it's super-charged loose cannons like Khan and Morrison.*

Avian eyes looked her over speculatively. "Let me be straight with you." Pulling out a drawer beneath his desk, he removed a bulging file folder held shut by thick rubber bands. He dropped the file onto the desktop, where it landed with a muffled thud. "We've had you checked out thoroughly; otherwise you wouldn't be here."

Roberta recalled all the hours she, Seven, and the Beta 6 had spent painstakingly constructing Bobbie Landers's phony existence, complete with birth certificate, Social Security number, past addresses, employment history, academic records, magazine subscriptions, deceased ex-husbands, and so on. *Guess it all paid off,* she thought, *although I'm probably never going get off some of those crazier mailing lists!*

"Trust me," she promised mendaciously. Years of undercover missions, as everything from a nun to a trapeze artist, had taught her how to lie convincingly. "I've got nothing to hide."

Morrison sliced through the rubber bands with an eagle-headed silver letter opener and spread open Roberta's file. He began flipping through the enclosed documents faster than Evelyn Wood, perhaps to demonstrate his superhuman powers of comprehension. "Your résumé checks out," he observed, "and you seem reasonably fit for a woman your age."

Ouch! Roberta thought. *I'm only forty-five!*

"Nevertheless, besides your undeniable commitment, I'm not entirely sure what else you bring to the party." He looked up from the file's contents, regarding Roberta with a sympathetic but skeptical expression. "We have a difficult struggle ahead, against the toughest of foes, and I wonder if you're exactly army material."

"I see," Roberta said frostily. She rose from her chair, as if preparing to exit with as much matronly dignity as she could muster. Then, without warning, she jabbed her elbow into the six-pack abs of the hulking bodyguard standing behind her. He doubled over, and she grabbed onto his ears until he shrieked with pain.

She let him suffer for a second, then released his ears, just to give him a chance to retaliate. His leathery face red with rage, he lunged for her with both hands. Roberta was ready for him. One deft jujitsu move later, Porter was flat on his back on top of Morrison's desk, crushing Roberta's file beneath his expertly redirected weight. A quick karate chop to the appropriate pressure point effectively ended the uneven skirmish; Roberta stepped back from the desk, wiping her hands of any unpleasantness.

"Well?" she asked Morrison, arching an eyebrow.

The militia leader's jaw dropped in mid-chew. His startled gaze swung between Roberta and the poleaxed guard and back again. "Lord have mercy!" he exclaimed, then let loose an enormous belly laugh and slapped the desktop in a burst of boisterous enthusiasm.

"Welcome to the AEV, Freewoman Landers!"

CHAPTER SIXTEEN

"THE SERBIAN PEOPLE HAVE NOTHING TO APOLOGIZE for!" Vasily Hunyadi roared defiantly, pounding his fist upon the black marble podium of the Grand Assembly Hall. Over two thousand hostile faces, representing nearly every nation of the world, as well as some eight hundred members of the international press, stared down at him from behind their green leather-covered desks. Seated in alphabetical order, from Albania to Zimbabwe, the gathered delegates seriously outnumbered the one-eyed Romanian dictator, but he was not intimidated by the throng of naysayers, even though he knew that the vast majority of his audience considered him a war criminal. "We have only acted to reclaim our rightful territories, and to ensure the genetic purity of our population."

He had come to Geneva to address this plenary session of the United Nations to demonstrate to all the world that he was not afraid of defying public opinion and international censure in pursuit of a Greater Serbia. Many of his more timorous advisors had counseled against this appearance, fearing for his safety away from his well-defended strongholds in Serbia and Bosnia-Herzegovina, but he trusted that the European headquarters of the U.N. provided a secure enough venue for his bold repudiation of the outside world's self-righteous charges and accusations. Not even Khan, he had reasoned, would dare to strike at a grand assembly of the United Nations (although, just be to safe, his spies were carefully watching all of Khan's known operatives in Europe). *The only thing I have to fear,* Hunyadi mused, *is any weakening of my own iron resolve.*

Which meant that he feared nothing at all.

"Send your NATO warplanes!" he thundered from the podium, clad in a severe gray suit reminiscent of the Soviet era. His bushy black eyebrows and drooping mustache were animated by the fervor of his delivery. "Drop your smart bombs! Enact your petty economic sanctions!" He visualized himself on CNN, addressing the entire planet. "We shall not be deterred. My stouthearted forces and I will not refrain from driving our enemies from the Balkans by any means necessary!"

There was a momentary delay while the U.N.'s simultaneous interpreters translated his Russian into Arabic, Chinese, English, French, and Spanish, then a cacophony of angry muttering and catcalls greeted his brazenly unapologetic oration. Hunyadi smiled thinly beneath his hirsute upper lip. *Let them jabber like the unevolved apes they are,* he thought contemptuously, pausing to let the scandalized delegates voice their impotent objections. *A superior will always triumphs over the clucking of the weak and foolish.*

Above and behind him, mounted on the sloping, bronze-plated wall of the spacious Assembly Hall, the circular emblem of the United Nations lent its imprimatur to the proceedings. Hunyadi was preparing to speak again, to aggressively warn the U.N.'s member nations against any further interference in the affairs of Eastern Europe, when a peculiar odor reached his superhumanly acute nostrils. *What is that smell?* he wondered irritably, wrinkling his nose in disgust. *It stinks like a dead rat.*

He appeared to be the first to notice the stench, but, within moments, he saw puzzled delegates and journalists sniffing and looking around in confusion. A hideous possibility entered his mind, sending an icy chill down his spine, and he looked up in dismay at the ventilation grilles meant to provide fresh air to the crowded Assembly Hall. He did not see any noxious vapors entering the chamber via the vents, but that did not mean that there was nothing there.

The first symptoms struck before he had a chance to escape. Hunyadi suddenly experienced trouble breathing, as though a heavy weight had been dropped upon his chest. Mucus streamed from his nose, sliming his bristly mustache. His head started pounding and his single eye burned, tearing up beyond control. He tried to speak, to call for help, but his tongue was numb, his speech slurred. Chills racked his body. His teeth chattered. His throat ached.

Nor was he alone in his distress. Through a watery
eye, he saw many members of his audience succumbing to the same unexpected affliction. Distinguished
diplomats and their aides panicked and bolted from
their desks, coughing and vomiting uncontrollably.
Pandemonium broke out amidst the entire august assembly, producing a babel of terrified voices in over a
dozen different languages. Stricken delegates fell to
the floor, a bloody froth appearing at the corners of
their mouth. Too late, Hunyadi recognized the telltale signs of a weapon he himself had considered
using on occasion.

Sarin, he realized in horror. *Nerve gas!*

"The Palais des Nations became the home of the
U.N. in Geneva in 1946 and it is now the busiest office of the United Nations outside New York City in
America. The room you are currently standing in is
known as the Salle des Pas Perdus, and is the main
foyer of the Grand Assembly Hall. The elegant decor
features fine marble from all around the world, while
the floor is made from imported pink marble from
Finland."

The English-speaking tour guide paused to let the
group admire the palatial lobby. Claire Raymond, a
thirty-five-year-old homemaker from Secaucus,
looked around in respectful awe at the high ceiling
and looming marble columns, as well as the lofty bay
windows looking out on nearby Lake Geneva. Clear,
crisp sunlight filtered through the high windows, the
better to show off the luster of all the polished stone.
In the distance, she could even see the snow-capped
peak of Mont Blanc.

It's a shame Donald and the boys can't be here, she thought wistfully. Unfortunately, her husband was tied up in an important meeting this afternoon, while their two sons, Tommy and Eddie, had been too busy in school to tag along on their father's business trip. Claire made a mental note to pick up some nice postcards after the tour was over.

The friendly guide called their attention to a pair of immense bronze doors. "Behind these doors, masterfully decorated in Renaissance style, is the Grand Assembly Hall, where delegates from around the world meet to discuss issues of international importance." A pair of bored guards in matching blue uniforms stood outside the brass doors, and the guide shrugged his shoulders apologetically. "I'm afraid that, for security reasons, the Hall is not open to the public while the Assembly is in session, but perhaps you'll be able to come back and see it another day."

Murmurs of disappointment rose from the rest of the tour group, but Claire couldn't blame the U.N. for taking no chances, especially given all the trouble in the world today. She had been favorably impressed by the tight security at the Palais; just to enter the building she'd had to go through a metal detector and let a guard inspect the contents of her handbag. A bit time-consuming, to be sure, but better safe than sorry.

Just as the guide was getting ready to lead them on to the next stage of the tour, a horrible caterwauling, like an entire mob of people being tortured, came through the huge double doors leading to the Assembly Hall. Claire heard ear-piercing screams of terror, only slightly muffled by the thick brass gates. *Oh my*

God! she thought, suddenly aware that something dreadful was happening. *What's going on?*

The twin guards looked at each other in alarm, but before they could do anything to investigate, the massive doors burst open, spilling forth a flood of well-dressed men and women running for their lives. They pushed and clawed at each other in their headlong rush out of the assembly chamber. Plastic headphones still dangled around some of the delegates' necks, and their hands were clamped protectively over their mouths and noses.

Thinking fast, Claire threw herself up against a soaring bay window in order to avoid being trampled by the riotous stampede. Her hands clasped over her mouth in extreme fear, her back pressed tightly against the towering sheet of glass, she watched the nightmarish scene unfold before her eyes.

Many of the fleeing people, she noticed, seemed to be suffering from some sort of ghastly sickness or seizure. Foaming at the mouth, or throwing up violently, they collapsed onto the pink granite floor and began twitching spasmodically, unable to help themselves or even avoid being stepped on by the panicked diplomats running behind them, trying desperately to outrun whatever unspeakable evil had attacked the assembly. A white-haired African gentleman, his face streaked with tears, dropped onto his hands and knees only a few feet away from Claire. He reached toward her piteously, crying out for help in a language she didn't recognize, and she was shocked to see that the pupils of his eyes had contracted until they were nothing more than tiny dots. Flecks of pinkish foam dribbled from his cracked and bleeding lips. His tongue looked swollen and inflamed.

Tentatively, she eased away from the wall, cautiously extending her arm toward the fallen man. Just as her outstretched fingers came within inches of his, however, a shrieking tide of fear-crazed tourists and U.N. attendees crashed over him, dragging him under. Choking back screams, Claire backed away once more, unable to do anything to keep the elderly stranger from being trampled to death. Yet more terrified people rushed past her, their eyes and noses streaming, their tortured bodies shaking and jerking convulsively.

This is insane! she despaired, battling hysteria. Scared almost out of her wits, she wanted to get away, but feared getting caught, and perhaps seriously injured, in the middle of the frenzied exodus. And what if the maddened horde was contagious? *I don't understand!* she thought. *What's causing this?*

Her frightened gaze swept the foyer, searching feverishly for some kind of explanation. Through sheer happenstance, she spotted something odd. Across the floor, on the other side of the Salle des Pas Perdus, a man wearing a surgical mask emerged from an inconspicuous side door labeled, in English and French, KEEP OUT! MAINTENANCE PERSONNEL ONLY. Unlike everyone else in sight, including Claire, the masked man, who was dressed in a grease-stained olive jumpsuit, like a janitor or maintenance worker, did not appear shocked or appalled by the bizarre disaster engulfing the U.N. Instead, he looked on coolly while holding on to an innocuous-looking tin lunch box, which he opened in an unhurried and deliberate manner. Carefully keeping clear of the scrambling people, he produced a small hypodermic syringe, like diabetics used, and expertly injected himself in the forearm. *Insulin,* Claire wondered, *or an antidote?*

She felt a sudden conviction that the nameless stranger, with his protective gauze mask, was somehow responsible for the mysterious pestilence sweeping through the Palais des Nations. The man's next actions, however, were more puzzling than incriminating. Reaching again into the open lunch box, he pulled out an ordinary cardboard juice box, just like the ones she packed in her little boys' lunch bags. *Huh?* she thought, bewildered; she couldn't imagine the masked man was feeling thirsty.

Rather than raise the miniature box to his lips, which were covered by the gauze mask anyway, he purposely dropped the box onto the granite floor, then, with obvious premeditation, stomped on it with the heel of his boot. A greasy, yellowish fluid, roughly the color of beer, spurted out onto the pristine polished floors, whose stones, she reminded herself irrelevantly, had been shipped all the way from Finland. *I don't think that's apple juice,* she thought, an overwhelming sense of dread clutching at her heart.

A smell, like paint thinner or worse, reached her even over the nauseating reek of spilled blood and vomit. Something tightened in her chest and she started gasping for breath. *Is it just me,* she wondered, *or is it really hot and stuffy in here?* She tugged at the collar of her souvenir "I ♥ SWITZERLAND" T-shirt, suddenly feeling feverish and light-headed. A painful throbbing started behind her eyes and, queasy and disoriented as she was, it took a second or two to realize that, oh dear God, whatever had sickened all those other people had gotten to her as well.

I'm not going to get away, she understood in a moment of blinding clarity. Strength oozed from her legs and she slid to the floor, landing in a sitting position at the base of the window. Her nose began to run, but she could barely raise her arm to wipe it with her sleeve. Her limbs twitched erratically. *I'm going to die.*

Knowing there was no escape, she stopped worrying about herself. Instead she grieved for her husband and sons, who were bound to take her death hard. *I'm sorry,* she told them sadly. *I didn't mean for this to happen. I was going to send you postcards.*

The pain behind her eyes grew and grew, like the mother of all migraines, exceeding even the agony it took to breathe with paralyzed lungs that could hardly move. As her vision faded, and the sunlit foyer was lost to the shadows encroaching on her sight, she remembered, bizarrely, the wacky get-rich-quick scheme that had brought Donald to Geneva in the first place, something about securing European funding for this cockamamie new business venture that involved freezing dead people and rocketing them into outer space for safekeeping, just in case someone figures out how to bring them back to life later on. *Cryo-something,* she recalled, trying to dredge up the right word. *Cryo-satellites, that was it.*

To be honest, she'd thought it was a pretty goofy idea, but Donald had taken it more seriously. *Wouldn't it be funny,* she thought, as the lobby grew darker and stuffier, *if something like that actually happened to me? Imagine waking up in outer space hundreds of years from now!*

The pain in her head exploded and everything went as black as the void.

What a ridiculous notion . . . !

* * *

Hunyadi leaned helplessly upon the black marble podium, unable to support his own weight anymore. The view from his single eye had dimmed dramatically, and there was a curious yellow tint to what he did see as he clung to the podium, determined to die on his feet if possible. A lesser man would have already succumbed to the ravages of the nerve gas, but Vasily Hunyadi had the strength and endurance of five ordinary mortals.

Even so, he knew his end was upon him. Agony squeezed his skull like a vise, and his dying breaths were shallow and labored. *Damn you, Khan!* he cursed, convinced that the wily Sikh had somehow engineered this atrocity, despite all their efforts to watch out for his agents. *Bravo, Khan. I salute you, you Indian bastard!*

Through the oppressive yellow haze, he looked out upon a vast auditorium now inhabited by only the dead and those soon to join them. Rows of empty desks, strangely unpeopled, mocked the self-confidence and bravado that had lured him to Geneva. *So much for sending a message to the world!* he thought bitterly, spitting a mouthful of bloody foam onto the floor of the stage. A message had been sent, to be sure, but not the one Hunyadi had intended.

Slumping against the podium, he watched as a faithful aide tried to perform mouth-to-mouth resuscitation on the lifeless form of the Brazilian ambassador, only to inhale even more of the fatal fumes herself. Hunyadi admired the aide's loyalty even as he questioned her intelligence. He gazed dispassionately as she crumpled to the floor, coughing and puking furiously. Her limbs spasmed fitfully, then fell still.

Hunyadi had seen much death in his time, and caused even more, yet he faced his own imminent demise with growing trepidation and regret. He had dreamed of so much more, of becoming the undisputed ruler of the Balkans, then triumphantly carrying his banner across the length and breadth of Europe and beyond, but now those magnificent ambitions had evaporated into the air like the toxic vapors poisoning his lungs. He had lost, leaving another to reign supreme over mankind.

Who would conquer the world now?

CHAPTER SEVENTEEN

FORT COCHISE
SOUTHEAST ARIZONA
UNITED STATES
AUGUST 29, 1994

NOT EXACTLY MY MOST GLAMOROUS UNDERCOVER assignment, Roberta thought as she knelt beside a cranky air cleaner, unscrewing its perforated steel housing in order to get at the burnt-out capacitor inside. The omnipresent air cleaners, which were installed all over the militia compound, were forever breaking down, necessitating never-ending repairs and maintenance. As a dedicated new recruit to the Army of Eternal Vigilance, "Bobbie Landers" was naturally expected to pitch in and do her part to keep the atmosphere of Fort Cochise safe from dust, dander, and surprise government gas attacks.

General Morrison, she had discovered, was positively obsessed with poison gas. Although this particular air cleaning device was located in the women's barracks, a hangarlike structure with whitewashed adobe walls and a corrugated tin roof, the steady hum of the filters could be heard inside every enclosed region of the compound, including the underground bomb shelters the AEV had fashioned out of the ghost town's old gold and silver mines. *Just another symptom of Morrison's rampant paranoia,* she wondered, *or does he know something I don't?*

Screwdriver in hand, wearing a secondhand set of faded army fatigues, she strained and sweated to open up the balky mechanism while her overactive mind chewed over what she had learned about the militia so far. She had spent close to two weeks here now, working and drilling alongside the rest of Morrison's private army, yet she remained uncertain of just how great a threat the AEV posed to world peace. *Am I wasting my time?* she fretted. A campful of trigger-happy nutballs was nobody's idea of a good thing, but did Morrison's superhuman leadership abilities make the AEV intrinsically more dangerous than any of the numerous other right-wing survivalist outfits playing war games in the backwoods of America?

My gut tells me yes, she thought, resolving to stick it out at least a little longer. Over the years, she learned to trust her instincts as much, if not more, than the case studies and mission profiles churned out by the Beta 6. *Morrison is a menace, I'm sure of it.*

"Speak of the devil," she whispered as, out of the corner of her eye, she saw the general approaching on one of his frequent surprise inspections of the camp's defenses. Morrison regularly toured the premises, his raptor's eyes searching for chinks in his citadel's armor; after all, you never knew when those infamous black helicopters might come diving out of the sky, commencing the Beast's much-anticipated assault on Fort Cochise.

The general was accompanied by his second-in-command, Freeman Clayton Porter, whom Roberta had so effectively ambushed on her very first day at the fort. The taciturn lieutenant, who had apparently worked as a rancher before joining Morrison's army, still held a grudge against Roberta, so she tried to stay out of his way.

"I want the entire camp on a heightened state of alert," Morrison told Porter. Roberta noted that, like a hawk, Morrison had to turn his entire head to look in any given direction, suggesting that his peripheral vision might be as weak as his avian eyesight was acute. "Now is when we are most vulnerable; we must expect swift and forceful retaliation for our Geneva operation."

Retaliation? Geneva? Roberta's ears perked up, even as she appeared to be deeply engrossed in her battle with the malfunctioning air cleaner. A set of phony Walkmans made it look as though she were listening to music as she worked, an illusion she reinforced by bobbing her head in time to an imaginary pop song; in fact, the plastic headset actually enhanced her hearing, making it easier to eavesdrop on Morrison and Porter from several feet away. *What's he talking about?* she worried, not liking the sound of this. *Retaliation for what?*

"Yes, sir," Porter replied. "I've doubled the guards on the watchtowers and set up searchlights to scan the skies after it gets dark." His body language was stiff, his manner characteristically intense; Roberta had never seen the man relax. "Nobody's going to catch us with our pants down, General. You can count on that."

"Good," Morrison said. His jaws methodically worked his chewing gum as he ran a white glove over the weapons locker positioned at the end of the first row of empty bunks; this late in the morning, the female barracks was empty except for Roberta. "What about that force field gadget we got from our friend in Chandigarh? Have our tech boys got that up and running?"

"We think so, sir, although it's hard to tell if it's genuinely doing anything." Porter lowered his voice and looked around cautiously before answering; thanks to the audio amplifiers in her Walkman, however, Roberta could still hear him loud and clear. "Do you really believe that the government truly possesses some kind of matter-transporter device? That sounds awful sci-fi to me."

Morrison snapped his gum as he spoke, the sharp cracking noise sounding like a gunshot to Roberta's ears. "Do not underestimate the resources of the Beast," he warned. "If the redoubtable Mr. Singh says that our enemies can teleport into our very midst, then we would be reckless not to take him at his word, particularly when he also claims to have provided us with a means to block any such transmission." He paused in his inspection long enough to look sternly at Porter. "I assume our technicians have thoroughly inspected the field generator and concluded that it doesn't serve any other ulterior purpose?"

"That's true," Porter conceded reluctantly. "It

doesn't appear to be a bomb or listening device or anything like that." He scratched his head worriedly, as if he didn't even like thinking about the mystery machine. "As far as we can tell, it's just emitting a strange sort of energy that none of our people have ever seen before."

Roberta couldn't believe what she was hearing. *Khan had shared his anti-transporter force field technology with Morrison?* She had suspected that there had been dealings between Khan and the superhuman militia leader, but she would have never expected Khan to give one of his rivals an extra defense against her and Gary Seven. *This makes my mission a whole lot more complicated,* she realized, swallowing hard, *especially if I can't just 'port out of here if things get hairy.*

She was tempted to pull out her servo and check for the force field right away. That might be a little too conspicuous, though, with Morrison and Porter gabbing only a few rows of bunks away. Better to play it cool, she decided, and scope out the situation when she had a bit more privacy.

"I don't know, sir," Porter said, shaking his head. His creased, humorless face looked even scowlier than usual. "I don't trust that crafty Indian, General."

For once, Roberta agreed with him. What was Khan up to here?

"Neither do I, Freeman Porter," Morrison stated. "But for now our interests appear to coincide. Don't forget: all he asked in exchange for the force field generator was that we stage the Geneva operation on one particular day." His silvered sunglasses reflected the empty barracks, which was built on the foundation of a demolished frontier dance hall. "If sometimes we have to make a deal with the devil to strike back at the Beast—well, war is a dirty business. There will be time to wrangle with Khan Noonien Singh later on, after we've taken down the rest of the New World Order."

"If you say so, sir." Porter looked unconvinced. He gave Roberta a dirty look as he and Morrison's inspection carried them right past the khaki-clad repairwoman, who scrambled to her feet and saluted diligently as the general went by. Morrison saluted back distractedly, scarcely glancing in Roberta's direction.

So Khan was in cahoots with Morrison on this mysterious Geneva operation? Roberta would have appreciated this info more if she'd had any idea at all what the general was referring to. *Something big has happened,* she gathered, *but what?*

A yard or so beyond Roberta, the general resumed his hushed discussion with Porter. "Phase One, Geneva, is a success," he pronounced. "Are you and Connors ready for Phase Two?"

"Yes, sir," Porter answered. "We already have our passports and plane tickets."

"And your 'refreshments'?"

Roberta caught an ironic tone to Morrison's query, but its significance went over her head. *Refreshments?*

"Packed and ready, sir."

"Don't forget to pack the antidote as well," Morrison cautioned him.

Porter cracked a rare smile, as if the very idea was laughable. "Not likely, sir!"

"Excellent!" Morrison said, slapping Porter on the back. "We've struck a major blow against the New

World Order today, but Geneva is only the beginning. The malignant forces of collectivism threaten human freedom as never before. Liberty will never truly be safe until we have rid the entire planet of our enemies, once and for all."

Their impromptu stroll finally took them beyond the range of Roberta's artificially enhanced hearing, leaving her frustrated and feeling badly out of touch with what was going on in the outside world. No surprise, considering that Morrison tightly controlled the flow of news into the compound. She and the other rank-and-file members of the militia were completely cut off from the rest of the planet: no TV, no radio, no newspapers, no Webzines, nothing. The mainstream media were just the mouthpieces of the Beast, right? So why risk contaminating the troops with corrupt government propaganda? Even e-mail was suspect; as far as Roberta knew, the only computer in the compound with a working connection to the Internet was the one in Morrison's personal office.

I need to find out what happened in Geneva, she realized. As soon as the two men left the barracks, she pulled out her servo and tried to contact Seven. In theory, he was keeping a close eye on the ongoing nuclear showdown between North and South Korea, but he would surely be able to update her on what was going on in Europe as well.

No such luck. Just as she feared, she was unable to send a transmission out of the compound. *That darn force field,* she realized; apparently, it was indeed fully operational.

That left her only one option: that computer in

Morrison's office. *Now's my chance,* she thought, while the general was out making his rounds.

Hastily screwing the top of the air cleaner shut again, she scrambled to her feet, wiped the dust from the knees of her khaki trousers, and headed off in the opposite direction from the route Morrison and Porter were taking. She knew she had to move quickly, before the general finished his inspection.

Fortunately, the remodeled post office was not far from the women's barracks. Beneath a cloudless Arizona sky, she walked at a brisk but unsuspicious pace across the dusty grounds of the busy camp. Target practice and boot camp training shared the repopulated ghost town with more domestic chores; Roberta's mouth watered as she smelled barbecued spare ribs cooking over by the communal mess hall, while one of her fellow "Freewomen" was hanging laundry out to dry on a line stretched between two freshly plastered adobe buildings. There wasn't much variety in the dangling garments, which came exclusively in varying shades of olive, tan, and khaki. Roberta found herself pining for the garish colors and fashions of her bygone hippie days.

Two rifle-toting guards, standing watch over the entrance to Morrison's headquarters, posed a major obstacle to her plans. She briefly considered zapping them both with a tranquilizer beam, but that would pretty much blow her cover, especially in broad daylight. Too many people, including the guards on the watchtowers, were likely to notice.

What I really need is a good distraction, she decided. Glancing around furtively, she again noticed the paramilitary laundry hanging on the line. "Perfect," she whispered, setting her servo on Burn. An invisible beam zipped across the courtyard, igniting the dangling clothing, which burst immediately into flame, clothesline and all.

Roberta didn't need to sound the alarm herself. Several passing militia members, including the startled woman collecting the laundry, did that for her. "Help! Fire!" the cry went up, drawing the immediate attention of everyone within earshot. "Help!"

As hoped, the two watchmen guarding the old post office ran to help put out the fire, which Roberta hoped would be chalked up to spontaneous khaki combustion. Taking advantage of their momentary absence, she sprinted for the front door of the squat adobe building and silently darted inside. A quick zap from her servo shut down the interior security cameras.

Closing the door quickly behind her, she made a beeline for Morrison's office. The inner door was locked, but that presented little problem to her servo, which also served as a high-tech skeleton key. Another zap and she quietly entered the general's private sanctum. The droning hum of a working air cleaner sounded like a swarm of bees thanks to the sonic amplifiers in her headphones, but she kept the bogus Walkman on in order to keep an augmented ear out for the sound of Morrison's return.

Thankfully, Morrison had a fast modem—and a sufficiently hackable operating system. Plopping herself down behind the much too orderly desk, Roberta searched the Web for news of the notorious Geneva operation, whatever that might be.

She didn't have to search very hard. Although the

official news outlets were playing it cautious, acknowledging only unconfirmed "rumors" of some sort of disaster and/or terrorist attack at the United Nations offices in Geneva, Switzerland, the rest of the Internet was abuzz with horrific first- and secondhand reports of people dropping like flies during a special assembly at the Palais des Nations. A few survivors even mentioned a peculiar smell in the air right before the catastrophe—and speculated ominously about nerve gas.

Ohmigod, she thought, feeling sick to her stomach. She suddenly understood, with chilling certitude, that Morrison's paranoia regarding poison gas was simply a psychological projection of his own monstrous agenda. Looking around the tidy office, trying in vain to understand how anyone could conceive of such an inhuman crime, let alone implement it, her gaze fell upon Morrison's desk calendar, on which today's date been circled in red with a thick magic marker. A date, she recalled, which had apparently been specified by Khan.

But why? she thought, racing to make sense of it all. Morrison's motives, although insane, were pretty obvious; in the general's warped worldview, the United Nations was synonymous with the many-tentacled Beast he blamed for Waco and other purported assaults on individual liberty. But where did Khan fit into this picture? Khan was ruthless, but he wasn't crazy; why would he help Morrison carry out this unprovoked attack on the United Nations?

Roberta was baffled at first, but the blurry picture came crystal-clear when she noticed just who the U.N. was hosting at the time of the massacre: Vasily

Hunyadi, now believed to be one of the many fatalities claimed by the deadly incident. *Of course,* she comprehended at last. *That's why Khan persuaded Morrison to stage the attack today. He was using one superman to take out another.*

Just like Seven was trying to do, but with a lot more innocent casualties. Even now that she had figured out Khan's part in today's atrocity, she was still shocked to realize that Khan had willingly sacrificed hundreds of blameless bystanders just to eliminate a single enemy. *He's getting more and more dangerous,* she thought sadly, finding it hard to reconcile Morrison's cold-blooded co-conspirator with the charismatic child she had rescued from Chrysalis twenty years ago.

A glance at her watch reminded Roberta that time was running short. Even with a small fire to distract him, Morrison was bound to be returning to his office soon. *Forget Phase One for a second,* she urged herself, as horrible as the disaster in Geneva sounded. That was over and done with, leaving an even more important question still to be answered: *What the heck is Phase Two?*

Flipping through the upright desk calendar revealed another date circled in red: November 14. A handwritten notation on the page listed a specific time as well: 8:23 GMT. "Okay, that gives me when," she muttered, although the significance of the time and date escaped her. The "GMT," short for Greenwich Mean Time, gave her a clue as to where. Now she just had to uncover the what.

Morrison's anal-retentive tendencies came to her rescue once she used the servo to open the locked file drawer beneath the desktop, where she discovered, neatly and meticulously labeled, a hanging folder tagged OPERATION: APPLEJACK, PHASE TWO. *Thank the Aegis for genetically engineered neat freaks!* she thought in relief. *I might just get to the bottom of this, after all.*

Inside the folder she found, much to her surprise, a newspaper clipping concerning the beginning of passenger service, on November 14, of the recently opened undersea tunnel linking England and France. A yellow Post-it note, affixed to the article, contained Morrison's own scribbled annotations:

Step One: Unite U.K. + Continent
Step Two: Complete European Union
Step Three: One-World Gov't.

Uh-oh, Roberta thought, her heart sinking. It seemed all too clear that Morrison saw the opening of the Chunnel (as the brand-new tunnel was popularly known) as a vital first step in the establishment of the New World Order he so feared. She tried to imagine the consequences of releasing poison gas into the Chunnel once it was in full operation, then shuddered as the nightmarish scenario played out in her mind. Hundreds, maybe thousands, of innocent commuters and tourists might be killed, even as a triumph of international cooperation was turned into a disaster site.

In an instant, all the time she'd spent worming her way into the AEV seemed more than worthwhile. Reacting quickly, she fired off an emergency e-mail to Gary Seven, telling him everything she knew about Phase Two, including concise physical descriptions of both Porter and Butch Connors, whom she assumed would be carrying out the attack on the Chunnel. She then efficiently erased the note from Morrison's hard drive and software, along with any evidence of her prior Web surfing.

And none too soon. Just as she was finishing up, the sonic amplifiers in her headphones picked up the sound of Morrison's irate voice booming right outside the adobe walls of the former post office. "A fire!" he bellowed in angry disbelief. "How does a load of soggy laundry catch fire?"

Time to get out of here, she thought, *but how?* From the sound of it, she definitely wasn't leaving the way she came in, and, thanks to Morrison's handy-dandy new force field generator, she wouldn't be catching the Blue Smoke Express either. *There's got to be another way out,* she thought fervently, her blue-green eyes searching every nook and cranny of the sturdy and windowless office. *Morrison is too paranoid not to have some kind of emergency escape route!*

Her servo scanned the sun-dried brick walls around her, trying and failing to locate a secret passage. Roberta heard footsteps in the hall outside, along with the sound of Morrison and Porter heatedly discussing the mystery of the flaming laundry. She didn't need the headphones to know that they were heading straight for the office.

Buying time, she used the servo to fuse the doorknob, locking the two men out. The door was a substantial one, constructed of dense oak, but she knew that it wouldn't keep out the superstrong general for long. On a hunch, she scanned beneath the genuine Navajo rug covering the floor.

Eureka! The servo detected a hollow passageway beneath the carpet. *Yes!* Roberta thought. The fused doorknob rattled in its socket and she heard an incensed voice on the other side of the oak timbers. "What in thunder—?" Morrison pounded on the door with his fist. "Is anyone in there? Open up, dammit!"

Yanking the colorful Native American rug aside, Roberta discovered an old-fashioned trapdoor with a flat metal ring for a handle. She wondered briefly if it dated back to the town's mining days, then pulled open the trapdoor with both hands. Well-oiled hinges made nary a squeak.

"Let me in, you trespassing spy!" The oaken door shook in its frame as Morrison vented his volcanic displeasure. "You can't get away!"

I beg to differ, Roberta thought. Beneath the trapdoor, a rusted metal ladder led straight down into a beckoning black pit. Shining a bright beam of light from her servo into the abyss, she glimpsed the rocky floor of a shadowy tunnel about twenty yards below. *The old mines,* she guessed at once, now providing refuge rather than riches.

A gun went off outside as either Morrison or Porter fired blindly into the office. High-caliber ammunition slammed into the wall behind Morrison's desk, shattering the glass sheet protecting the Waco photo and ripping the antique Revolutionary War banner to shreds. "Don't Tread on Me" abruptly became "Fire at Will" and a ricocheting shot struck the monitor of the general's computer, which exploded in a shower of sparks and plastic shards.

Her head ducked low for fear of shrapnel, Roberta

decided that she had definitely outworn her welcome. She hurriedly clambered down the ladder, tugging the door of the trapdoor shut above her. There was no way to put the rug back into place, so it was going to be pretty obvious how she'd escaped, but hopefully she'd be able to find a way out of the mines, and maybe even back up into the camp, before anyone noticed that "Bobbie Landers" had gone missing. Knowing Morrison, he was probably going to blame the CIA or the ATF anyway.

The important thing was that she had gotten the word out to Seven. Now it was up to him to see that the Chunnel didn't suffer the same ghastly fate as the Palais des Nations. She had plenty of faith in Seven's ability to save the day, but there was still one more thing that worried her more than anything else.

What else was Khan up to these days?

CHAPTER EIGHTEEN

"You may bring in the subject now."

Dr. Phoolan Dhasal waited patiently as her assistants wheeled the test subject into the hermetically sealed experimental chamber. Fluorescent lights shined down on the scientists and their subject. Strapped onto a gurney, the specimen squirmed against its restraints, appearing highly agitated.

"Stop! You can't do this!" Brother Arcturus cried out. Electronic sensors, affixed to his skull, limbs, and torso, monitored his vital signs, which, at the moment, included a significantly elevated heart rate. "I demand you release me!"

Dhasal briefly wondered if she should have had the specimen sedated, but, no, that would cloud the results of today's experiment. Better to observe the subject in a natural, undrugged state, even if his hysterical vocalizations bordered on the distracting.

"Please!" the specimen begged. Stripped of his customary chartreuse robes, his epidermis completely shaved of body hair, the captured cult leader was recognizable only by the astrological tattoo upon his forehead. "Do not do this, my sister! The stars forbid it!"

Standing next to Dhasal, wearing an identical yellow hazmat suit, Donald Williams flinched visibly. "Can't we put a gag on him or something?" he asked squeamishly.

"No," Dhasal stated flatly. "It may be necessary to interrogate him regarding his symptoms, if any." She inspected a tray of medical instruments resting on a wheeled metal cart; among the apparatus was a compact electronic excruciator, to be used if the subject refused to cooperate. "A verbal description of his subjective experience could be extremely illuminating."

At her instruction, the assistants elevated the gurney until the subject was at an eighty-degree angle to the floor. Dhasal checked the restraints to make sure they were secure; given the subject's genetically enhanced strength, she did not wish to take any unnecessary chances.

"Please, for the love of our celestial starfathers, release me!" Arcturus's arms were strapped to his sides, and his shaved head held in place by a reinforced leather band across his throat. His brilliant sapphire eyes glowed with an unattractive mixture of fright and religious fervor. "I must prepare the way."

Dhasal ignored the specimen's superstitious rantings. Satisfied that Arcturus was adequately restrained, she gave the assistants permission to leave the test chamber via the attached airlock, leaving her and Williams alone with the subject. Sterile white walls cut them off from the rest of Chrysalis's advanced biomedical research facility. She sealed the hood of her Neoprene hazmat suit and activated its self-contained breathing apparatus, while directing Williams to do the same.

Of course, she could have observed the experiment from behind the transparent glass window of the observation gallery overlooking the test chamber, but she preferred a more hands-on approach. She wanted to examine at close range the effects of the flesh-eating bacteria on a specimen of genetically engineered humanity.

Following the mass suicide of his followers, Brother Arcturus had conveniently fallen into the hands of Khan's agents, who arranged to have the disgraced cult leader secretly transported to Muroroa. Dhasal was grateful for the opportunity to study a genuine product of the first Chrysalis Project without having to sacrifice one of her own people.

"Are you ready, Doctor?" she asked Williams. A microphone in her hood allowed her to address the other scientist, despite the multiple layers of rubber and plastic separating them.

Williams nodded hesitantly. Seen through the clear plastic faceplate of his hood, the Englishman's ruddy face was nervous and slick with perspiration. His bloodshot eyes gazed uncertainly at the subject on the gurney. "All right," he muttered finally. "Let's get this over with."

Dhasal chose to overlook his lack of scientific enthusiasm and objectivity; the man was merely human, after all. She was slightly more embarrassed by the subject's undignified behavior; a biologically superior being should have met his fate with more equanimity.

Raising her hand, she signaled the technicians on the other side of the glass window to release the bacteria into the closed environment of the test chamber. A low hissing sound, coming from vents in the ceiling, confirmed that the experiment had commenced.

She and Williams had labored strenuously over the last several months, to the regrettable neglect of Dhasal's other projects, to improve and refine the genetically engineered strain of strep-A developed by Sarina Kaur many years ago. Producing an airborne version of the bacteria had been particularly challenging, but preliminary tests on a wide variety of nonhuman test animals had been extremely encouraging, yielding an over eighty-five percent mortality rate.

The sudden hissing alarmed the test subject, who struggled fruitlessly against his bonds with renewed fervor. "What is that?" he demanded anxiously. "What's happening?"

"Quiet," she instructed, using the excruciator to discipline the specimen. The ingenious device, invented by Khan himself, punished the nervous system without inflicting any lasting damage. "Don't force me to have your larynx removed."

The excruciator caught the subject's attention. He shrieked once, his agonized cry echoing off the stark white wall, before falling silent as requested. Dhasal glanced at the gauges monitoring his vital signs; his heart rate and respiration were still faster than normal, but perhaps that wasn't entirely a bad thing if it meant that the specimen would absorb the bacteria into his system even more quickly.

Her eyes narrowing, so that only the opaque band across her cornea was visible, she examined Arcturus for any sign of the carnivorous microorganism taking effect. According to Williams, all of the children conceived at the original Chrysalis had been expressly endowed with a genetic immunity to all forms of streptococcus, including this particularly virulent strain, but Dhasal did not intend to accept that premise as a given until tested. With luck, Arcturus would settle the matter—one way or another.

Half an hour passed, then a full hour. Ninety minutes after the bacteria was introduced into the chamber, the specimen continued to display no obvious signs of infection. "Shouldn't he have reacted by now?" Williams asked hopefully, refilling his oxygen tank from a nozzle built into the wall. His face showed the strain of their unbroken vigil over the specimen.

"Perhaps," she admitted. All of their earlier test subjects had succumbed to the bacteria's ravages within minutes of inhalation. "Are you experiencing any discomfort?" she asked Arcturus, who rested pale-faced and trembling upon the angled gurney. "Nausea? Fever? Muscular aches?"

"Of course," the specimen whimpered. "I'm cold and hungry." His hairless body shivered pitifully. "My mortal receptacle requires rest."

Despite the subject's childish complaints, Dhasal did not believe that Arcturus was exhibiting any of the early symptoms of necrotizing fasciitis. A glance at the vital signs monitors confirmed that he was neither feverish nor in shock. His blood pressure, although elevated, was well within normal parameters for a genetically engineered superman. *Fascinating,* she thought. *In theory, an ordinary human would already be dead.*

"Watch him," she instructed Williams curtly, as she walked across the floor and keyed a top-secret security code into the touchpad of an inset videophone. A secure satellite link instantly connected her with Chandigarh, half a world away, where she knew Khan was eagerly awaiting the results of the test.

His noble visage appeared on the miniature video screen. "Well, Doctor," he inquired courteously. "How fares your experiment?"

She plugged her microphone into the console so that she could communicate with Khan in private. "The results exceed my expectations," she reported. "Although I still wish to perform a few more tests, all evidence suggests that those of our elite genetic makeup are indeed immune to the carnivorous form of strep-A, along with all other strains of the bacteria."

"Excellent!" Khan declared. "It seems the unsavory Dr. Williams did not mislead us after all; my mother's brilliant creation truly provides a means of separating the wheat from the chaff, so to speak."

"As you say, Lord Khan." Dhasal did not concern herself with the practical implications of her discovery; she was happy simply to have pleased her leader. "The late Dr. Kaur was clearly an exceptional woman."

A calculating look came over Khan's face. "Speaking of Dr. Williams, would you say that his usefulness is at an end?"

Her gaze shifted from the video screen to the imperfect human in his protective plastic suit. Williams paced nervously from one end of the chamber to another, while keeping an absurdly safe distance from the helpless superman strapped to the gurney. "Is that Khan?" he asked her fretfully, peering over her shoulder. His florid features and portly contours exemplified all that was weak and fallible in ordinary humanity. "What are you telling him?"

"Yes, my lord," she answered, confident that Williams could not eavesdrop on their conversation. "He was initially helpful in reconstructing your mother's bacteria from the original genetic sequence, but we have moved far beyond those early stages now. I do not believe that he has anything more to contribute."

"I see," Khan said, stroking his chin contemplatively. "I do not trust a man who would trade such a lethal secret for his own security, nor one who has already abandoned Chrysalis once." A hard edge entered his voice. "You know what to do, Doctor."

The dark streaks of Dhasal's eyes focused on the unsuspecting Englishman. "Yes, Lord Khan. I understand." Her cool, analytical gaze shifted from Williams to the nearby instrument tray before returning to the screen. "What of the bacteria?"

"I want more of it," he declared without hesitation. "I want you to devote all your resources, every vat and test tube, to producing the bacteria in large quantities, enough to consume the world if necessary." Khan's dark eyes were cold and implacable. "You should also continue your laudable efforts to improve the destructive capacity of the strain."

She did not bother to wonder why Khan desired

carnivorous strep-A in such quantity; that did not fall under her purview. Yet she worried about the toll such an ambitious enterprise might take on other promising fields of research, such as her ongoing attempt to re-create Sarina Kaur's unprecedented success at cloning genetically engineered human eggs. "Excuse me, my lord," she said respectfully, "but our work with this particular organism, as remarkable as it is, has already delayed progress on various other fronts. What of, for example, our goal of surpassing the original Chrysalis Project by designing a new generation of superior beings?"

"That must wait," Khan stated, unswayed by her concerns. "We are at war, Doctor, and war dictates its own priorities. For now, I want you and your able staff to concentrate entirely on the mass production and refinement of the flesh-eating bacteria." His commanding tone brooked no further discussion. "I will also be in touch with Dr. MacPherson about installing sophisticated bio-warheads on his suborbital rockets."

"As you command." She would regret placing her other projects on the back burner, but trusted that Khan knew best. "I will instruct my staff accordingly."

Khan nodded in approval. "One more thing, Doctor. As we have previously discussed, it is important that awareness of this bacteria remain on a strictly need-to-know basis. You and your people are not to discuss this topic with any unauthorized individuals, including certain members of my executive staff."

"Understood," she acknowledged. Khan had already made it clear to her that Ament, his chief domestic advisor, was not to be informed of Dhasal's research into necrotizing fasciitis. Fortunately, Muroroa's distance from Chandigarh made it easier to keep the secret away from Ament's attention. *And soon,* Dhasal thought, *there will be one less person familiar with what we have wrought here.*

No doubt occupied with other pressing matters, Khan bid her farewell and ended the transmission. Unhooking her mike from the communications console, she turned to confront an increasingly restive Dr. Williams. "Well?" the flustered Englishman inquired anxiously. "What did he say?"

"He is satisfied with our results," she told him honestly. Walking over to the equipment cart, she lifted a scalpel from the tray on top of the cart. Her thick butyl-rubber gloves made it difficult to handle the delicate instrument, but she succeeded in getting a firm grip on its handle.

"Thank God!" Williams exclaimed, his overheated breath momentarily fogging part of his faceplate. "Does that mean this wretched experiment is over?"

"Almost," she answered, crossing the floor toward Williams. Hanging on the gurney, Brother Arcturus stared bleakly into space, perhaps hoping to catch a glimpse of his imaginary alien forebears. Sensors continued to register his heartbeat, which had finally slowed to a less frenetic tempo. More and more, it appeared that the specimen had been completely unaffected by breathing in the airborne bacteria. *Most intriguing,* she thought.

Williams fumed within his encapsulated yellow suit. "Well, it's about bloody time!" He tapped an orange rubber boot against the floor restlessly. "I can't wait to get out of this miserable suit. I'm positively suffocating in here."

"Permit me to assist you," Dhasal said calmly. Her face devoid of emotion, she stepped forward and methodically slashed William's hazmat suit with her scalpel. The razorsharp blade sliced easily through the protective layers of Neoprene, carving out deep gashes across the front of the suit, breaking the skin beneath, so that tiny red droplets of blood flew from the edge of the blade as it came clear, sprinkling like rain upon the pristine linoleum floor.

"Oh my God!" Williams gasped, shocked and surprised by Dhasal's unexpected attack. His gloved fingers frantically probed the gaps in his suit, confirming the awful truth that his airtight protection had been compromised. "What have you done?"

"Finished the test." Dhasal stepped backward, raising the scalpel defensively, in the event that Williams reacted violently. A rapid glance upward at the observation gallery revealed a row of startled faces staring down at the unforeseen drama playing out in the test chamber. "Do not be alarmed," she informed her staff via microphone. "Everything is under control and proceeding as it should."

"What!" Williams lunged toward her awkwardly, reaching out with his black rubber gloves, but, reacting with quantitatively faster reflexes, she retreated behind the equipment cart, keeping the stainless steel wagon safely between them. "You streak-eyed witch, you've killed me!"

Dhasal suspected that she could easily evade or overpower the decrepit old man even if she wasn't blessed with superior DNA. As it was, his pathetic lunge turned out to be the last gasp of his fading physical reserves. She watched with interest as the infection took hold.

Sweating profusely, Williams fumbled clumsily with the seal of his hood, finally succeeding in ripping the gear from his head. "It's so hot!" he gasped, clutching his throat while reeling unsteadily. "I can't breathe." He staggered across the floor, grabbing onto the metal cart for support, but the wheeled conveyance slid out from beneath him, causing him to topple forward, almost losing his balance entirely. His grasping fingers dislodged the instrument tray, causing it to tip over onto the floor, landing with an enormous clang. Scalpels, syringes, stethoscope, and excruciator spilled onto the blood-stained tiles, adding to the clatter. "Water!" he pleaded, doubled over in agony. His red-rimmed eyes bulged from their watery sockets. "I need water!"

Fever and dehydration, Dhasal noted with clinical dispassion. *Interesting.*

His symptoms developed at a vastly accelerated rate, exceeding even the characteristically rapid progression of necrotizing fasciitis. He dropped to the floor, unable to stand, and rolled over onto his back. His black-gloved hands groped uselessly in the air above him. A purplish rash appeared on his face and throat, which also began to swell grotesquely.

Astounding, Dhasal thought, impressed with the speed of the attacking pathogen. Ordinarily, such advanced symptoms would take three to four days to develop.

Blisters broke out upon Williams's flesh, leaking a foul black fluid. The same dark effluvia oozed from the gashes in the dying man's chest. Dhasal regretted that there wasn't time to strip the shredded hazmat suit from Williams's body entirely, the better to observe the progress of the infection elsewhere on his anatomy, but consoled herself with the thought of performing a full postmortem on the Englishman later on.

As a survivor of Bhopal, and a researcher of biological warfare, she had a strong stomach. Even still, as the voracious bacteria attacked Williams from within, she grew highly appreciative of the plastic faceplate sparing her from the stench of living tissue necrotizing before her very eyes.

"Celestial starfathers!" Arcturus shrieked from the gurney, distracting Dhasal, who had almost forgotten that the earlier specimen was still present. The hairless superman strained futilely against his bonds, horror-struck eyes locked on the writhing form of the infected scientist. "What malignant, terrestrial blasphemy is this?"

"Quiet!" she shushed him impatiently. "You and I are perfectly safe." If not for the undoubtedly nauseating odors emanating from the rotting tissue, in fact, she would have discarded her own hood by now, so confident was she that the modified strep-A posed zero threat to her and her kind. *Yet one way,* she reflected, *in which we surpass the common herd of humanity.*

The end came quickly, if probably not speedily enough from Donald Williams's perspective. Much of his swollen, mottled flesh died before he did, turning a pale necrotic blue, but toxic shock finally stopped his heart only minutes after his exposure to the contaminated air. Dhasal made a mental note to check the exact duration later.

It had all happened so fast, she marveled. *Almost too fast to observe properly.* Thankfully, the chamber was fully equipped with video cameras, so she would be able to review the entire process at her leisure, preferably in slow motion.

Energized by the highly satisfying results of the experiment, she promptly moved onto the next stage. "Flush the atmosphere in the test chamber," she ordered the onlooking technicians, dictating instructions into the microphone at a rapid clip. "I want complete bloodwork and X rays on both specimens, followed by immediate dissection and analysis of Dr. Williams's remains."

A blood-curdling howl emerged from Brother Arcturus as his questionable sanity snapped completely, but Phoolan Dhasal was in too good of a mood to care. She looked forward to updating Khan on the outcome of the experiment.

CHAPTER NINETEEN

WAITING JUST PAST THE AUTOMATED ENTRANCE gates, on the international concourse, Gary Seven could only hope that today would indeed mark General Morrison's Waterloo.

The impressive new terminal sported a high glass ceiling and walls. Four full levels offered convenient electronic signboards, cozy departure lounges, a cafeteria, information counter, newsstand, shops, telephones, and even a *bureau de change* for exchanging pounds for francs and vice versa. A palpable aura of excitement suffused the crowded terminal on this, the Eurotunnel's first real day of operation. Although the Chunnel had officially opened several months earlier, at a gala event attended by both Queen Elizabeth and French President Mitterrand, commercial train service from London to Paris had not actually begun until today. TV news crews were on hand to broadcast the event, just as General Morrison no doubt intended. The eyes of the world were on Waterloo Station; it was Seven's job to make sure they weren't forced to witness a massacre.

Frankly, he would have preferred the terminal to be not quite so spacious; it was going to be hard enough to spot Porter or Connors in this mob scene. To play it safe, he was keeping careful watch over the front entrance, hoping to spot either of the militiamen before they disappeared into the swarm of eager passengers waiting for the 8:23 departure for Paris. *If he gets past me here,* he admitted grimly, *I'll have a devil of a time locating him before he can release the nerve gas.*

The mainstream media had done a pretty good job of covering up what had really happened in Geneva two months ago, but a careful analysis of the unofficial reports had convinced Seven that sarin gas had been the weapon of choice in that attack. That was definitely cause for concern; the barbaric concoction was over twenty times more deadly than cyanide gas, and easily transportable in liquid form. "Could be worse," he murmured quietly to himself; at least humanity hadn't invented biogenic weapons yet.

Wearing a conservative gray suit, he scoured the faces of the new arrivals making their way through the security and passport controls. The screening process appeared relatively well-managed, but hardly equipped to catch a seemingly ordinary American smuggling a small quantity of nerve gas. Fortunately for him, however, it was fairly easy to identify the Americans in the line, almost all of whom wore some variation of the standard uniform of a U.S. tourist traveling abroad: baseball cap, souvenir T-shirt, jeans, and sneakers.

By these criteria, he had successfully isolated several likely prospects, but, regrettably, none of them had matched the photos of Clayton Porter and Butch Connors with which the Beta 6 had managed to provide him. He frowned pensively, worried that his target had already slipped by him in the crush of new arrivals.

He was also concerned that one of the men may have targeted the Paris station as well. Suppose Morrison wanted to strike at both ends of the Chunnel simultaneously? Even Seven couldn't be in two places at once, at least not without seriously warping the space-time continuum.

He glanced apprehensively at his wristwatch. It was already 7:55 A.M. Sunlight shone through the smudge-free glass walls and ceiling as the concourse rapidly filled with travelers. "Excuse me, sir," a helpful voice accosted him, distracting him from his all-important surveillance of the terminal's entrance. A youthful Eurostar employee, wearing a navy-blue uniform accented by a yellow scarf and tie, stepped between Seven and the front gate. "Can I help you?"

"No, thank you," Seven replied, trying to remain casual while maintaining his lookout for the American terrorists. His worried expression, he feared, had attracted the young woman. "I'm just waiting for a friend."

"If you'd like, we can have them paged," the overly solicitous railways worker volunteered. Seven found himself longing for less attentive customer service.

"No thanks," he insisted. Was that another baseball cap coming through the gate? He tried to peer past the chirpy young Brit, but the woman's shoulder got in the way. "I'll be fine," he declared, as firmly as he could without attracting the attention of station security.

"Very well, sir." His unwanted helper finally seemed to get the message. "Thank you for riding Eurostar."

She moved on to another lost-looking customer, but Seven could not spare a moment to breathe a sigh of relief. What had happened to that red baseball cap? A large Pakistani family was now making its way through the gate, and Seven looked around the terminal anxiously, terrified that his quarry had evaded him while his attention was elsewhere. What if Porter or Connors had already entered the terminal?

Wait! Seven spied the cap in question bobbling along above the heads of the crowd, just a few yards beyond where Seven was now standing. Seen from behind, the cap's wearer fitted Roberta's general description of Porter: a tall, rangy man with a somewhat military bearing. Unfortunately, Seven could not manage to get a glimpse of the man's face.

The alien-raised supervisor had only a moment to decide whether to continue his stakeout or take off after the suspect. If he gambled wrong, and pursued the wrong man while the real terrorist proceeded unobstructed, the consequences would be dire. The lives of hundreds of travelers, journalists, and Eurostar employees depended on him. *I have to take a chance,* he realized, *and hope for the best.*

He looked again at his watch. It was 8:06. If the attack was indeed scheduled for 8:23, and the militiamen had yet to arrive at the terminal, then they were

calling it pretty close. Seven guessed that the real terrorists would be more cautious than that. *If I were responsible for this operation, I would already be here.*

His decision made, although not without some
trepidation, he hurried after the tall man in the red
cap. The servo in his pocket had mercifully made it
past the metal detectors, and he fingered it in anticipation as he followed the other man (Porter?) deeper
into the terminal. *Now what?* he pondered. Would the
terrorist actually board the waiting train, or would he
release the nerve gas inside the crowded terminal,
now temptingly packed with humanity?

Seven predicted the latter. According to his research, the passenger cars on Eurostar's deluxe high-
speed bullet trains carried only forty-plus travelers
apiece and, for purposes of safety, had sealed fire
doors between the individual cars. Morrison's assassin
could more easily achieve maximum carnage by deploying the sarin in the comparatively wide-open
spaces of the cathedral-like terminal.

A public-address system announced, in English and
French, that the 8:23 train would be leaving in ten minutes. The announcement caught the attention of the
baseball-capped stranger, who turned to look up at one
of the electronic signboards, finally giving Seven a
glimpse of his profile. A very human surge of relief went
through the gaunt, gray-haired older man as he gladly
recognized the leathery, tight-lipped features of "Freeman" Clayton Porter, late of Arizona's ignominious Fort
Cochise.

Thank the Aegis! Seven thought with feeling. *I made
the right choice, after all.*

All doubt removed as to the suspect's identity, he endeavored to get closer to the roaming militiaman. The milling throng, now heading for the escalators that would take them up to the loading platform, impeded his progress, but Seven steadily shouldered his way toward Porter, who had paused in the middle of the wide concourse, showing little interest in boarding the train. Seven kept the other man in his sights, grateful that they were both relatively tall.

It was now 8:19.

Porter wore a checked wool hunting jacket unzipped to reveal a buttoned-down flannel shirt. Reaching into the front pocket of the coat, he drew out a small package that Seven recognized as a miniature juice box, of the sort American children packed in their school lunch boxes. Squinting his eyes to read the label on the box, Seven saw a photo of a succulent red apple.

What name had Roberta said was written on that file in Morrison's office? Operation . . . Applejack? In liquid form, he recalled, sarin was a greasy fluid roughly the color of beer—or apple juice.

Between the sun shining down through the glass ceiling, and the accumulated body heat of several hundred unsuspecting men, women, and children, the temperature within the terminal was uncomfortably toasty, yet Seven severely doubted that Porter was worried about dehydration. He watched in alarm as Porter, looking about furtively, dropped the juice box onto the floor, then raised his foot to stomp on the tiny cardboard container. Grasping his intention, Seven immediately visualized the so-called "juice" spurting all over the station floor.

Once released, the liquid sarin would quickly evaporate into the atmosphere. . . .

"Excuse me!" Shoving a slow-moving Englishman out of his way, Seven charged across the concourse at top speed. Sinews strengthened by generations of selective breeding propelled the sixty-five-year-old secret agent toward Porter in the split-second that the other man's leather-soled cowboy boot hovered only inches above the malignant juice box. "Coming through!"

The toe of his own shoe collided with the box before the boot came down. "Careful!" he warned helpfully, kicking the carton out from beneath Porter and sending it sliding across the smooth tile floor. Seven watched with a certain amount of unease as the neatly-packaged container of sarin spun away from both of them, ricocheting through a maze of rushing feet. "You almost stepped on that."

"What the hell—?" Porter glared at Seven furiously, the veins of his neck standing out like a Cardassian's. Seven met the outraged man's gaze with a steely look of his own, one that left no doubt that he knew exactly what Porter had been up to. The thwarted militiaman quailed before the icy authority of Seven's regard; his Adam's apple bobbing, Porter turned and made tracks away from the aging extraterrestrial operative.

Seven fully intended to go after him, but first he had a more important chore to deal with. Even his hard-earned self-possession was rattled a little by the sight of the unclaimed juice box being kicked back and forth across the floor of the terminal by the heedless traffic of dozens of migrating railway customers. So far the carton's air-tight lining did not appear to have been perforated, but Seven knew that it was, at most, only a matter of minutes before someone trampled on the fragile cardboard container, spraying liquid sarin into the unprotected air.

There would be no way to evacuate the terminal fast enough; people would start dying almost immediately.

He did not waste time chasing after the footloose box. Instead, drawing his servo from his pocket, he carefully drew a bead on the moving object, trying to anticipate its every bounce and ricochet. It was a tricky proposition, particularly with all the dashing tourists moving in and out of the way; a shiver of anxiety tickled his spine as he waited, with bated breath and tightly-clamped impatience, for his shot.

Then . . . there it was! The shifting sea of legs parted momentarily, granting him a straight shot at the juice box at the very moment that it temporarily skidded to a halt. Seven fired his servo, disintegrating the carton (and its virulent contents) down to their constituent atoms.

This was one time, he mused, *when an apple a day wasn't in anyone's best interests.*

So much for that threat. Now to deal with Porter.

Looking about hurriedly, he spied the fleeing terrorist on one of the many escalators rising up to Platform 23, where the morning train was preparing to depart. Lighted departure screens informed passengers which escalator to take to reach the coach containing their reserved seats. Surmising that Porter was intent on catching the train, Seven scurried onto the same escalator, racing uphill several steps at a time.

He couldn't afford to let Porter get away, not while there was still a chance that the fanatical militia member might have another lethal juice box on his person.

The escalator carried him swiftly up to the boarding platform, where he was happy to see that the train had not yet pulled out of the station. The sleek modern streamliner, painted white with a yellow tip, looked uncomfortably like a missile. Coach numbers and destinations were indicated by highly-legible liquid-crystal displays located alongside the power-operated plug doors. Peering down the length of the platform, which looked to be nearly a half-kilometer long, Seven saw Porter dart into a nearby coach.

Seven followed after him. He had reserved a seat on the train, of course, to guarantee access into the terminal, but had hoped to intercept Porter before he boarded the train. Seven wondered briefly if the militiaman had even planned on taking the train as well, or were they both making this up as they went along?

The coach's interior was surprisingly plush and roomy, like the imperial carriage on Deneb IV. Reclining seats, with plenty of leg room, faced fold-out tables covered by spotless white tablecloths. Most of today's inaugural travelers had already taken their seats by now, clearing the corridor between the seats except for a few late arrivals, a conductor checking tickets, and, at the far end of the spacious coach, the escaping Porter.

Another bilingual boarding announcement warned that the train would be departing momentarily. Automated plug doors slid sideways, then pulled in to seal the coach. *All's aboard that's going aboard,* Seven thought wryly. *Looks like I'm definitely taking a train ride today.*

Glancing back over his shoulder, Porter saw Seven pursuing him. Their eyes met across the length of the passenger car, and Porter redoubled his efforts to avoid capture, rushing toward the closed glass door leading to the next car. Seven hurried down the carriage after him, only to be delayed by the sharply-dressed Eurostar conductor. "Excuse me, sir. Can I help you find your seat?"

Ulcer-inducing memories of the excessively helpful station employee flashed through Seven's mind. Resolved not to go through the whole routine again, he reached into the interior of his gray tweed jacket and drew out an unusually intimidating piece of ID, thoughtfully manufactured by the Beta 6 prior to the mission. "Interpol," he said curtly, flashing the bogus ID in the conductor's face.

"Yes, sir!" the ticket taker said with a gulp, hastily stepping aside to let Seven pass. Keeping the absconding militiaman in his view, Seven saw Porter enter the open vestibule between this coach and the next, then pull open another glass door to gain access to the adjacent car.

The train started moving, and Seven reached instinctively for the closest seatback to steady himself. He needn't have bothered; the streamliner's acceleration was so smooth and gradual that you could barely tell that the train was moving at all, aside from the excited mutterings of the seated passengers and the sight of the boarding platform rushing past the windows. The gentle purr of the high-speed electric engines reminded him of Isis, and he couldn't help remembering how much he missed her company. *I could sure use your help today, doll,* he thought.

Entering the connecting vestibule himself, Seven noted the presence of the recessed yellow fire doors, currently withdrawn and inactive; he guessed that the safety doors would not slide into place until the train actually entered the Chunnel, roughly an hour from now, but was glad to know that there was a means of further sealing off the individual coaches just in case Porter had more sarin to disperse.

Quickly but carefully, he crossed the open vestibule. A slight but perceptible rise in the floor over the bogie almost tripped him up, but he managed to hold on to his balance, making it into the next car, where Porter was already halfway down the corridor, en route to the next set of glass doors. A look of panic came over the man's sun-creased face as he spotted Seven gaining behind him. *Good thing he doesn't have a gun,* the older man reflected, confident that the security at Waterloo Station had been competent enough to keep anyone from entering the terminal with a firearm; otherwise, Porter looked as though he might have started firing wildly at Seven, heedless of whoever might be in the way.

"Out of the way! Interpol!" Seven shouted, brandishing his phony ID to clear his way through the center of the carriage, past startled passengers wrestling bags to and from overhead luggage racks. There were, he recalled, at least sixteen coaches and two bar cars between the missile-nosed power cars at both ends of the train; Seven hoped he wouldn't have to chase Porter through every one of them. Despite his superior conditioning, he was starting to feel winded from the chase. *I'm getting too old for this,* he realized.

Roughly shoving an elderly tourist aside, Porter

raced out of the coach only a few paces ahead of
Seven, who clutched his ready servo in his free hand.
Porter lunged across the second vestibule, but Seven
moved even faster. The servo hummed and the fire
doors slammed shut in front of Porter, trapping him
in the vestibule with Seven. "Give it up, Porter," he
warned, resetting the servo to Tranquilize. "It's over."

Spinning around to confront Seven, his back to the
closed yellow door, Porter glared at his relentless pur-
suer. "Who are you?" he demanded, spittle spraying
angrily from his lips. "How do you know my name?"
His hand burrowed energetically into the pockets of
his red-and-black hunting jacket, removing, just as
Seven had feared, another box of counterfeit apple
juice. "Stay back!" he threatened, drawing back his
arm to hurl the snack-size carton at Seven. "I won't
surrender to the Beast!"

Seven sighed wearily. When was the human race
going to grow out of this sort of corrosive paranoia?
With the fire doors sealed, Porter's threat to unleash
the nerve gas carried little weight; Seven had pru-
dently injected himself with the antidote, pralidoxine
chloride, before transporting out of Scotland this
morning.

"The only Beast is unchecked human aggression,"
he replied, not that he seriously expected Porter to
listen to him. The servo hummed once and an unfo-
cused glaze replaced the homicidal zeal in the terrorist's eyes. A goofy grin transformed his surly features,
rendering him almost unrecognizable. He slumped
back against the door to the next car, his menacingly
poised arm drooping harmlessly to his side. "I'll take
that, if you don't mind," Seven murmured, easily pry-

ing the juice carton from Porter's pliant fingers. He tucked the captured box carefully into the pocket of his gray jacket.

Porter was tottering somewhat precariously above the bogie connecting the two cars, so, grunting with effort, Seven threaded his arm beneath the tranquilized man's shoulders and began guiding him back toward the stabler footing of the adjacent coach. A click of the servo's controls caused the activated fire doors to slide back into their recessed hiding places, so that only a single glass door stood between them and the waiting passenger area. To Seven's slight surprise, someone else opened the door and he found himself face-to-face with a bewildered-looking British couple. "Er, is this the way to the bar car?" the male pensioner asked, looking askance at the sagging, bleary-eyed Porter.

"I'm afraid so," Seven admitted glibly, struggling to keep the tranquilized terrorist upright. "As my friend has obviously already discovered."

The couple *tsk*ed disapprovingly at the apparently inebriated American ("And so early in the morning, too!" the scandalized older woman declared), but obligingly allowed Seven to slide past them with his slack-limbed charge. A vacant lavatory caught his eye, and, with an apologetic shrug, he deftly shoved Porter into the tiny rest room, then squeezed in after him and pulled the door shut.

It was a tight fit, but Seven welcomed the privacy. He dropped Porter onto the waiting toilet and raised his servo to his lips. In a moment, he intended to teleport both he and Porter back to Scotland, where he could make arrangements to turn the captured terrorist over to Roberta's contacts in the FBI; first, however, there was one more matter to look into.

What about Paris? he worried. Porter's crony, Connors, remained unaccounted for, and Seven feared that another sarin-wielding maniac had targeted the other end of the rail line, four hundred and seventy-six kilometers away.

Which is why he had taken care to have a very special operative posted at the Eurostar terminal in Paris' Gare du Nord. "Seven to Guinan," he whispered urgently into the servo's receiver. "Please report."

"Guinan to Seven, chill out." His tense frame relaxed significantly at the sound of the El-Aurian woman's amused voice emanating from the tip of his servo. *"Everything's tres cool at this end. Paris is not burning."*

That was just what he wanted to hear. "And the terrorist? Connors?"

"Sleeping it off, and ready for pick-up," she assured him.

Seven allowed himself a bemused smile. He didn't impose on Guinan often, but he knew that he could always count on her when he did. And, over the years, the unflappable alien had tipped him and Roberta off to any number of brewing situations; she was one of his best informants on this planet, not to mention a few others. "Thanks again, Guinan."

"Just remember: you owe me one, Seven." He could readily imagine her mischievous expression. *"Au revoir, toots."*

"Till next time," Seven replied. Ending the transmission, he promptly sent a signal to transporter controls in Scotland, requesting an immediate extraction for both him and Porter. A tingly blue mist began to fill the tiny lavatory, even as an inquisitive knock rattled the door of the rest room.

"Excuse me, sir?" a worried voice asked. "Are you quite all right in there?"

Seven wondered how long the conductor would wait before forcing his way into the empty rest room.

CHAPTER TWENTY

"GET A MOVE ON! THE BEAST IS ON ITS WAY!"

Rifle-toting militiamen herded dozens of confused and sleepy-eyed people toward the bomb shelters beneath the fort. It was three o'clock in the morning, Arizona time, but the entire camp had been roused in expectation of an imminent attack by the shock troops of the New World Order. Men, women, and children, in varying stages of undress, grabbed onto their guns and lined up to enter the underground shelter via a descending concrete ramp. "This is it!" a wild-eyed freedom fighter exclaimed, sounding more enthusiastic than apprehensive. "We're making our stand!"

Of the assembled horde, only "Bobbie Landers" had a glimmer of what was really going on. *Seven squashed*

Operation Applejack, she guessed, *and now Morrison is panicking.* She had been afraid of something like this, which was the main reason she had stayed on at Fort Cochise for the last few months, in hopes of preventing another bloody showdown like Waco or Ruby Ridge. With a campful of heavily armed fanatics anticipating an apocalyptic confrontation with a diabolical foe, all the ingredients were present for a truly godawful tragedy.

Not if I can help it, she thought earnestly. Unlike many of the groggy people around her, who had been yanked from their cots in the wee hours of the morning, Roberta had only been feigning sleep when the alarm came; knowing what was going down in London this morning, she had been ready for anything. Besides the de rigueur personal firearm—in her case, a loaded blue-steel shotgun that she clutched close to her chest—she also had her servo tucked into the pocket of the flimsy nylon windbreaker she wore over her stylish, khaki-colored pajamas. A pair of buckskin moccasins completed her ensemble, which she hoped would get her through whatever the morning had in store.

Fifty feet beneath the renovated ghost town above, the primary bomb shelter was a huge concrete structure the size of a football field. A large-screen television monitor occupied the entire north wall of the bunker, while a patriotic mural, painted by an artistically inclined member of the militia, ran along the remaining three walls, depicting key moments in the never-ending battle for Liberty, from Lexington and Concord to the Fall of the Berlin Wall. Roberta shuddered involuntarily at that last image, remembering when and where she was when the Wall came down. *That was when Khan really started getting out of control,* she recalled.

"Keep moving, people!" The crowd pouring into the shelter pushed Roberta to the far end of the chamber, not far from the colossal television screen. Claustrophobia threatened as her elbow room swiftly evaporated, leaving her packed in tightly with too many people and even more guns. The hubbub of hushed and excited voices blended with the tearful cries of confused infants and children, over the omnipresent hum of powerful, industrial-strength air cleaners. Roberta was disturbed to see, standing only inches away from her, a cammo-clad young mother balancing a swaddled baby on one shoulder and a gleaming Remington hunting rifle on the other. *Yikes!* she thought, taken aback even after her eye-opening stint at Fort Cochise. *Hope she doesn't try to burp the wrong one!*

So many bodies crammed into even so generous a space rapidly raised the temperature to a sweltering level, forcing Roberta to unzip her jacket in search of relief. *Whatever Morrison is up to,* she thought, fanning herself with her hand, *I wish he'd get on with it.* She stood on her tiptoes, searching the faces of the throng for the hawk-eyed militia leader, but could not see the general anywhere. *I wonder where he is?*

Instead, one of Morrison's meaner-looking lieutenants, a beefy ex-cop named Dunbar, seemed to be in charge. Rumor around the base was that Dunbar had been kicked off the LAPD for excessive brutality—which was really saying something these days! Roberta found it ominous that the thuggish enforcer was taking the lead in this morning's sudden mobilization, presumably with Morrison's offstage blessing.

"All right, people!" Dunbar shouted to get the crowd's attention. He stood on top of a horizontal weapons locker in the northwest corner of the bunker, just to the side of the blank television screen. His light brown hair had been cut short, army-style, while his broad shoulders hinted at a past as a linebacker. He clutched the grip of a Beretta automatic pistol in his one hand while holding up a megaphone with the other. "Quiet down! The general has something to say!"

The noisy chatter subsided, aside from a few crying babies, as all eyes turned toward the back of the bunker where Dunbar was standing. The overhead lights dimmed, revealing the bright white glow of the blank screen. Static crackled, and the televised image of General Randall "Hawkeye" Morrison appeared before the hushed assemblage.

Larger than life, Morrison was seated behind his desk, looking like a president addressing the nation. Old Glory, replacing the antique flag shredded during Roberta's raid on the office two months ago, was stretched on the wall behind his head and shoulders. His silver mirror shades reflected the blinking red light of the video camera while simultaneously sparing his audience the sight of his freakish avian eyes.

"My fellow free men and women," he began solemnly, barely audible at first, until an unseen technician adjusted the volume. "It is my unfortunate duty to inform you that our final stand against the rapacious appetite of the Beast has already begun. Early this morning, at approximately zero-one-hundred-thirty, Mountain Standard Time, Freemen Clayton Porter and Butch Connors, acting on my orders, attempted to strike a heroic blow against the one-world state by attacking both ends of the so-called Euro-tunnel between London and Paris."

A few enthusiastic whoops and cheers rose up from some of the slower members of the audience, who clearly failed to pick up on the general's doleful tone. Roberta herself held her breath, hoping that Seven had dealt with the threat just as effectively as she expected. The rest of the crowd waited tensely to hear what Morrison said next, holding on tightly to their guns and offspring.

"I have no doubt that Freemen Porter and Connors strove to carry out their duty to the best of their abilities. The Army of Eternal Vigilance is honored by their commitment and courage. However, as each passing hour brings no word of success overseas, nor any fresh communications with our valiant soldiers abroad, I must reluctantly conclude that the mission has failed and that our security has been compromised."

Gasps greeted Morrison's dire pronouncement, followed by muttered curses and sobs. Next to Roberta, the rifle-packing young mother bit down on her trembling lower lip, a single teardrop leaking from the corner of her eye. "Don't worry," she whispered hoarsely to her child, her moist eyes agleam with maternal fervor. "Mommy won't let the Beast put his Mark on you."

Roberta didn't know whether to be touched or terrified. *Maybe a little bit of both,* she thought.

"Alerted to our intentions and military capabilities," Morrison continued, "the enemy will surely

counterattack, probably before the sun rises. Knowing our resolve, they will have no choice but to obliterate us utterly, lest the last, lingering spark of our
fearless resistance ignite an inferno that will ultimately consume them."

"Let them come!" someone yelled defiantly, waving
his rifle above his head. Others seconded his strident
call to battle, flaunting their own weapons. "We're
ready for them."

Oh my! Roberta thought in alarm, suddenly feeling
as though she were literally standing in the middle of
a powder keg on the verge of exploding. For a second,
she almost forgot that, chances were, there were no
evil black helicopters zooming toward Fort Cochise
at this very moment; the threat was all in Morrison's
deluded mind—and in the minds of those who followed him blindly.

Not that it really matters, she realized. The situation
was dangerous and volatile enough even without the
added complication of a real-life United Nations
strike force. Her mind raced through scenario after
scenario, trying to figure out the best way to defuse
the crisis—and keep the AEV from destroying itself,
and possibly many others, in a blaze of gunfire.

Reacting to the belligerent war cries of his army,
Morrison shook his head mournfully. "As much as my
heart tells me to go on fighting, even against overwhelming odds, my head tells me that we do not
stand a chance against the full fury of the Beast. Our
adversary has had many generations to marshal its satanic forces, whereas we, for all our valor, are not yet
ready to win this war."

What's this? Roberta thought, feeling an unexpected

flicker of hope. *Was the general finally coming to his senses, more or less?* She crossed her fingers, praying that maybe Morrison would instruct his soldiers to stand down and disperse. All around her, the gathered recruits looked puzzled and uneasy about the defeatist direction in which their leader seemed to be heading. *Tough luck,* Roberta consoled them, both silently and sarcastically. *No revolution today.*

Or so she hoped.

"But there is still a way," Morrison declared, with a maniacal intensity that chilled Roberta's blood, extinguishing her short-lived hopes of a peaceful resolution, "that will send a message to our enemy and inspiration to our allies. Over two thousand years ago, on a mountaintop in ancient Palestine, another band of freedom fighters stood opposed to the New World Order of their day, the fearsome Roman Empire. They were the Zealots and their mountain fortress was called Masada."

No! Roberta thought, realizing in horror where Morrison was going with this. *He can't be serious!*

"When the voracious Roman legions finally overran the mountain," Morrison declaimed, his voice quaking with emotion, "they discovered that every one of the fortress's defenders, over one thousand unconquerable souls, had taken their own lives rather than live as slaves to the Empire. Two millennia later, Masada is still remembered as an undying symbol of freedom and courage. Today, Fort Cochise will enter history as well."

There's a difference, you bird-brained maniac! Roberta thought angrily, tempted to blow a hole in the screen with her servo before Morrison could utter another manic-depressive word. The ancient Zealots really were fighting an all-powerful empire out to conquer the world. Morrison wanted to sacrifice his troops to spite a global conspiracy that existed only in his fevered imagination.

She looked around worriedly at the faces surrounding her. Were Morrison's people buying into this? She saw a few heads nodding in agreement, but more expressions of shock and betrayal. People turned to their neighbors in confusion, searching for confirmation of their own doubts. A murmur of dissent, subdued, even surreptitious at first, quickly grew in anger and intensity. "The general's lost it!" a middle-aged man near Roberta said, outraged indignation in his voice. His waxed handlebar mustache quivered with emotion; he wore a flak jacket over his khaki T-shirt and boxer shorts.

"Damn straight!" an auburn-haired woman in an ankle-length nightshirt chimed in. She looked to Roberta for support. "Do you believe this, honey?"

"Nope," Roberta said honestly.

"I don't know," the woman with the infant said. To Roberta's dismay, the tearful young mother looked genuinely undecided. "I don't want anybody to put a computer chip in my baby's brain." She rocked the child gently as she spoke. "Maybe he'd be better off dead. . . ."

"Don't you believe it, sweetie!" the other woman admonished her passionately. "If you want to keep your youngster safe from the Beast, then praise the Lord and pass the ammunition." She raised her voice so the whole room could hear her. "We won't go down without a fight!"

Dozens of other voices echoed her sentiments. Atop the green, army-surplus weapons locker, Freeman Dunbar shifted his weight uneasily, perhaps sensing the mood of the crowd turning against his leader. "That's enough!" he bellowed into the megaphone. "Everybody, quiet down and listen to the general!"

He raised his Beretta in a menacing manner.

Big mistake.

Within a heartbeat, a veritable militia of muzzles turned toward the arrogant ex-cop. It dawned on Roberta that, if you were trying to organize a mass suicide, there were probably easier crews to control than a concrete bunker packed with trigger-happy gun nuts. *For all his superpowered smarts,* she thought, *I think Morrison misread his own corps.* She checked out the stubborn disposition of the crowd. *These people aren't just going to lay down and die. They'd rather reenact the Alamo than Masada.*

If Morrison was aware of the brewing insurrection in the bomb shelter, he gave no sign of it. "I do not ask this sacrifice of you lightly," he said from the screen, raising his hand to salute his soldiers, "but know that America—and the world—will never forget what we do here today."

He raised a remote control from his desk and clicked a button, causing two things to happen almost simultaneously. The screen went blank and, several yards behind Roberta, a heavy iron door slammed down, trapping them all inside the bunker. *Uh-oh,* Roberta thought. *This doesn't look good.*

The shocked militia reacted with an outpouring of fear and anger. An ugly mob stormed the front of the shelter, dragging Dunbar down from atop the weapons locker and threatening him with bloody murder if he didn't open the door immediately. "I can't!" he protested helplessly, already sporting a black eye and busted lip. "Only the general can!"

At the rear of the bunker, other distraught militia members attacked the iron door directly, pounding on it with their fists and the butts of their rifles. "Let us out!" they pleaded with anyone who might be listening on the other side of the adamantine steel barrier, but neither their cries nor their blows had any effect on the unbudging iron. "Please, for God's sake, get us out of here!"

Despite all the noisy tumult, a peculiar silence troubled Roberta. It took her a second to realize what was missing: for the first time in weeks, she wasn't hearing the steady drone of the fort's ubiquitous air cleaners. *Ohmigod,* she thought. *No wonder Morrison had us all herded into this shelter. He wants to asphyxiate us!* She kicked herself mentally for underestimating Morrison, and for not seeing this coming. *How else do you exterminate an entire campful of heavily armed men and women?*

For a moment, she feared that the insane general planned to take them all out with the same nerve gas he used in Geneva. Roberta sniffed the air nervously, but did not detect any sort of chemical odor. Nor were her eyes or throat burning in any way. Perhaps, she prayed, after several tense seconds passed, Morrison wasn't willing to inflict that nasty a fate upon his own people. *No, he's just going to suffocate us instead,* she guessed indignantly. *What a sweetheart!*

Was she just imagining it, or was the air in the

crowded bunker already growing thin? In any event, she knew that, without any sort of ventilation, the bunker would turn into an airless deathtrap in no time at all, especially with so many lungs to support. "The situation is officially out of control," she murmured, her sotto voce observation going unheard amidst the general chaos. "Time to play my trump card."

Gladly dropping her shotgun onto the floor (after making sure the safety mechanism was fully engaged), she pulled her servo from her pocket. A crackle of blue energy flickered as its twin antennae sprang outward. Roberta adjusted the collar ring on the servo's midsection, setting it to just the right frequency, then fired off a single short signal.

Boom!

In actuality, stuck as she was in a soundproof bomb shelter with a throng of loudly rampaging hostages, she couldn't really hear the explosive charge as it went off, elsewhere in the labyrinthine mines beneath the old ghost town, but she could readily imagine it blowing apart the electronic innards of Morrison's imported force field generator.

It had taken her literally weeks of snooping, but she had finally discovered the hidden location of the high-tech, transporter-foiling device that General Morrison had horse-traded for with Khan. It had required even further late-night skulking to discreetly rig the generator to explode when she gave the right signal.

Now to see if all her prior efforts had truly paid off. "Three-six-eight to 194," she whispered urgently into the servo, hoping she could once again contact

Seven. There was a seven-hour time difference between Arizona and the U.K., so hopefully Seven
would have finished his business in the Chunnel by
now. "Three-six-eight to 194, please come in."

"One-nine-four to 368," his familiar voice replied.
Roberta breathed a sigh of relief. *"Good to hear from
you again."*

"Right back at you," she told him sincerely. "Everything go okay over there?"

"The threat has been averted," he assured her, confirming Morrison's worst expectations. *"What is your status?"*

Roberta figured she could pump him for the full
scoop on his Chunnel mission later on, after she dealt
with the present crisis. "I need an emergency point-
to-point transport," she stated, zapping him the necessary coordinates. "But, first, there's something else
we have to do. . . ."

All around her, frantic people were rapidly approaching the breaking point. Sobs, screams, vocifer-
ous prayers, and angry recriminations bounced off
the concrete walls of the bunker, scraping at the fraz-
zled nerves of Roberta and everyone else trapped inside the overcrowded shelter. She heard fights breaking out between Morrison's steadfast supporters and
those who felt betrayed by their onetime leader. Nobody had started shooting yet, but she figured it was
only a matter of time.

An emotionally charged situation. Overwrought
people. Too many guns. Roberta knew a potential
bloodbath when she saw one, so she explained to
Seven exactly what was required.

Within seconds, a distinctive blue mist began to
permeate the stuffy atmosphere of the bunker. The

phosphorescent azure haze swiftly engulfed the interior of the shelter, like a heavy fog rolling in from some strange radioactive sea. The unnatural phenomenon momentarily hushed the crowd, that, unlike Roberta, did not recognize the static tingle of the mist against their skin. Unavoidably, however, it quickly became a fresh source of anxiety and alarm.

"We're being gassed!" a horrified militiaman shouted, understandably if inaccurately.

"Nobody fire their weapon!" someone else shouted in a panic. "You could set the whole place off!"

Roberta regretted giving the frightened crowd one more thing to be scared of, but saw no way around it. The transporter fog was providing a needed function, which would increase everyone's safety in the long run. *Just hang on, folks!* she urged her freaked-out neighbors silently. *This won't hurt a bit, I promise!*

Fortunately, for the trapped hostages' peace of mind, the eerie blue mist disappeared as quickly as it had arrived, leaving behind a bunker full of confused and disoriented people. "What in Sam Hill . . . ?" muttered the older woman in the nightdress.

"Transport accomplished," Seven declared via the servo.

"Great," Roberta said, feeling a whole lot safer all of a sudden. And none too soon; she found herself on the verge of gasping, taking deep, gulping breaths to secure ever smaller quantities of oxygen. Scanning the people around her, she saw many of the bunker's other prisoners were breathing hard as well, some of them looking more than a little faint, particularly the ones she knew to be heavy smokers. *The air's already getting pretty thin in here,* she realized. *I'm running out of time—and oxygen.*

Unfortunately, her whispered conversation with Seven caught the ear of the anguished young mother beside her. "Hey!" she shouted harshly, eyeing Roberta with jittery suspicion. "What are you doing?" Hugging her baby with one arm, she swung up the barrel of her Remington until the muzzle was pointed directly at Roberta's head. "Over here!" the militia madonna shrieked loud enough for the whole bunker to hear. "I've caught a spy or something! She's talking to someone on her pen!"

Roberta instantly felt like Veronica Cartwright at the end of the 70's version of *Invasion of the Body Snatchers,* exposed and surrounded by pod people. A small arsenal of guns turned toward her, backed up by a sea of hostile, paranoid faces. "Put down that gadget, lady!" growled a surly-looking individual in full combat gear. Roberta recognized him as one of the militia members who was beating up Dunbar only a few minutes ago. "Hand it over or I'll shoot, I swear it!"

That he was utterly serious she had no doubt; nevertheless, Roberta held on to the servo, blithely ignoring all the impatient firearms aimed at her tinted, honey-blond scalp. "Okay, Seven," she told him. "Get me out of here."

"That's it, lady!" the life-size G.I. Joe snarled. "I warned you!" He pulled the trigger of his Ruger Mini-14 assault rifle, at the same time that several other militia members, including the stressed-out woman with the baby, tugged on their triggers as well.

The crossfire would have killed most of the shooters, let alone Roberta, had not Seven already 'ported away every speck of gunpowder in a five-mile radius. *Now that's what I call gun control!* Roberta thought as she listened to half a dozen rifles and pistols click impotently around her, while their dumbfounded owners stared at their weapons in frustrated bewilderment.

She didn't stick around long enough to explain. A discrete column of swirling blue plasma enveloped her, much to the amazement of the flabbergasted onlookers. "What—?" the baby's horror-stricken mother gasped, backing away from the roiling pillar of smoke as though it were toxic waste. "Who the hell are you?"

Ordinarily, Roberta avoided 'porting in front of witnesses, but there was no time to find a more private spot. She was already starting to feel light-headed from lack of oxygen. She would have to count on the confusion, not to mention the AEV's serious lack of credibility, to protect her anonymity this time around. ("But, Your Honor," she imagined a diehard militia member telling the authorities, "she disappeared into thin air, probably onto a top-secret UFO piloted by the CIA!")

It wouldn't be the first time one of her exploits ended up in the pages of the *Weekly World News.*

She waved good-bye to her fellow freedom fighters as the fog evaporated, carrying her away from the bunker. This trip on the Blue Smoke Express was even faster than most, though, as she quickly rematerialized right outside the huge iron door.

The sun was still hours from rising, but a full moon gave Roberta enough light to see by. A surprised gila monster skittered away from the entrance to the shelter, while a hoot owl watched her from the rusted remains of an abandoned ore car. She looked around hastily for some sort of emergency release switch, then realized that, in theory, the barricade had surely been intended to keep an attacking force out of the bunker, making it unlikely that it could easily be opened from outside; presumably Morrison had over-rode whatever locking mechanism existed on the inside of the shelter.

Fine, she thought tenaciously. *We'll just have to do this the hard way.* Setting her servo on Disintegrate, she blasted out a couple of airholes near the top of the iron gate, safely above the heads of the crowd on the other side. *There. That buys us some much-needed breathing room, in more ways than one.*

She considered leaving the entire militia trapped in the bunker while she dealt with Morrison, then decided not to chance it. What if, in a worst-case scenario, something happened to her before she could return to liberate the captives? That would leave them buried alive, at the mercy of hunger and dehydration, not to mention any other nasty surprises the general might have up his khaki-colored sleeve.

Morrison would have to wait, while she took the time to laboriously carve an exit-size hole out of the dense steel door. "Stay back!" she warned the hostages, hoping they could hear her through the newly created airholes; if nothing else, she was counting on the glow of disintegrating metal to alert the bunker's unwilling inhabitants to back away from her impromptu demolition project. "I'll have you out in a minute or two!"

The invisible beam cut through the six-inch metal like Lorena Bobbit's cutlery sliced through her husband's, er, servo. *Wonder what the hot tabloid story is now?* Roberta thought, looking forward to a little mindless TV-watching after several months of compulsory media deprivation. Within minutes, she finished the makeshift exit. "Watch out below!" she hollered as a roughly six foot by ten foot rectangle of iron toppled over onto the floor of the bunker.

Thankfully, no one appeared to have been squashed, although it was hard to tell as a panicky stream of escaping militia members came flooding out of the breached shelter. Roberta wisely jumped to one side to avoid the pell-mell exodus, although she was relieved to see that the woman with the baby was among those making the disorderly flight to safety. She wondered briefly how many, if any, true believers would feel obliged to stay behind in the bunker, awaiting further crazed instructions from their general.

They'll be waiting a long time, if I have anything to say about it, Roberta vowed. With the AEV's mass "suicide" put on hold permanently, dealing with Morrison was next on her agenda. As his nearly fatal stunt in the bunker proved, the superhuman militia leader was far too dangerous to remain at large. Now that his private army was in disarray, Roberta fully intended to take the general into custody until she and Seven could arrange to turn him over to the proper authorities. With luck, some of his disillusioned followers could be persuaded to testify against him. *Stockpiling weapons is one thing,* she thought, ticking off the charges that could be brought against Morrison. *Trying to suffocate dozens of people is something else indeed.*

Not to mention whatever evidence Seven might be able to amass regarding all that nerve gas unpleasantness . . . !

Doberpits barked and howled indignantly as scores of former militia members abandoned Fort Cochise. Roberta heard the roar of multiple automotive engines as every truck, Jeep, bus, and recreational vehicle in the camp's motor pool gunned into life and headed for the front gate, unmanned and unguarded for the first time since Roberta's arrival back at the middle of August. She glanced up at the looming watchtowers and saw they were unoccupied as well, their searchlights dark, their gun placements deserted. She guessed that the once-bustling compound would be a ghost town again before dawn.

Spurred on by their close brush with asphyxiation, none of the fleeing refugees accosted or even noticed Roberta as she determinedly made her way toward the old adobe post office that served as Morrison's headquarters. *Was he still sitting behind his desk,* she wondered, *and what was he thinking now that his lunatic ambition to re-create Masada had gone down the tubes?* He had to know that his plans had gone awry somehow; there was no way he could escape the chaotic sounds of his army defecting en masse. Even now, Roberta could hear raised voices arguing as people fought over the last few provisions and vehicles, making her gladder than ever that Seven had turned all of Fort Cochise into a gunpowder-free zone. *Things are just a little too intense right now,* she observed, noting that many of the vamoosing militia types were still hanging onto their various pistols and rifles anyway. An enforced cease-fire and cooling-off period was definitely a good idea.

Making a mental note to report Morrison's key lieutenants to the FBI later on, Roberta climbed the steps to the closed front door of the old post office, past an antique hitching post. No light escaped around the edges of the oak door, making her question whether the general was still at home. She worried that Morrison might have already fled the compound, or, worse, disappeared into the maze of mining shafts underneath the ghost town. No way could she find him down there.

"Here's hoping he stayed put," she whispered. The door was locked, but her servo hummed it open easily. Not quite as soft-footed as Isis had always been, she tiptoed down an empty hallway toward Morrison's private office at the rear of the building She used the servo as a penlight, letting a narrow beam of white light guide her way through the darkened post office. A sturdy metal door had replaced the wooden timbers Morrison had smashed through after Roberta locked him out during her previous stint of breaking and entering. She placed her ear against the door, but heard only silence beyond; it was looking more and more as if the hawk-eyed general had already flown the coop.

Trying the knob, she found the office door unlocked. Holding her breath, she shoved it open and peered inside. No moonlight penetrated the windowless chamber, forcing Roberta to rely on the light from her servo. The incandescent beam found an empty chair behind Morrison's neatly ordered desk, then slid down to reveal that his Navajo rug had been shoved aside, exposing the open trapdoor beneath. "Damn," Roberta muttered.

Just for a moment, she wished that she hadn't wasted precious time freeing the fruitcakes trapped in the bunker. But what else was she supposed to do? Leave all those terrified people (and their children!) locked underground indefinitely? She had done the right thing, she knew, even if it meant that she and Seven would have to track down Morrison all over again.

Maybe the lonely office held some clue as to the general's future whereabouts? Holding the servo before her, she stepped warily into the unlit room, with an eye toward raiding Morrison's files and hard drive. *Assuming he hasn't shredded or trashed them all,* she thought.

A karate chop slashed down against her arm, shattering her wrist and sending her servo flying out of her fingers. A shadowy figure darted out from where it had been hiding, up against the wall to the left of the doorway, and grabbed onto the collar of Roberta's windbreaker, yanking her roughly to one side.

"Did you really think I wouldn't hear you sneaking up on me?" Morrison snarled into her ear. His hot breath carried the spearminty scent of his chewing gum. "My ears are almost as good as my eyes, which means they hear a helluva lot better than any average grunt's."

Wincing in pain, clutching her fractured wrist, Roberta could not put up a fight as Morrison dragged her farther into the room, then shoved her brutally into the wooden chair in front of his desk. Her eyes desperately sought out her servo, rolling across the floor a couple of yards away, but Morrison snatched it up before she could even think of retrieving it. "I'll hang on to this little doohickey," he told her sneeringly. "You stay right where you are."

I don't have much in the way of options, she thought, biting down on her lip to keep from whimpering. Unarmed and injured, with stomach-churning waves of agony coursing up her arm, she doubted she could outrun a genetically engineered superman with enhanced night vision. Shock and nausea battered against her ability to concentrate, making it hard even to keep an eye on Morrison as he sat down behind his desk, clasping his hands atop the desktop like a high school principal preparing to lecture a misbehaving student.

Although keeping the overhead lights dark, he clicked on a bendable halogen reading lamp atop his desk. His mirrored sunglasses were tucked neatly into the breast pocket of his short-sleeved khaki shirt, so that he gazed at Roberta with the enlarged red eyes of a bird of prey.

"Freewoman Landers," he addressed her, "if that's your real name. So you're our resident snake-in-the-grass. I wish I'd caught on earlier, before you had a chance to sabotage all of our noble plans and aspirations." He leaned toward her, like a raptor stalking fresh game. "Who are you working for? Who sent you here? The FBI? FEMA? The Illuminati?"

Don't be ridiculous, Roberta thought. She tried to grin feistily, but ended up grimacing instead. *Seven and I shut down the Illuminati years ago.*

Morrison held up her captured servo to the glow from the lamp. Its silver casing shimmered in the light. "Impressive ordnance," he remarked, rolling the slender instrument between his meaty fingers, while his jaws masticated an unseen wad of gum. Stubble peppered his jowls, making him a good deal more disheveled than usual. "My security cameras caught you using it before."

He tapped the keyboard of his computer, rousing it from powersave mode. The monitor lit up, and he rotated it around so that Roberta could glimpse the screen, where she saw a videotaped image of herself utilizing the servo to slice through the bunker door like an acetylene torch. Roberta thought she looked faintly ridiculous in her nylon jacket and khaki pajamas.

"At one time I would have loved to know who your supplier is," Morrison said, winking at her with his nictitating membranes. "But that was before you spoiled everything, casting this nation's last hope for freedom into the abyss."

"That's one way of looking at it, I guess," Roberta said, spitting out the words between razor-sharp pulses of pain. She was hurting too much to try to talk sense to this lunatic. "A crazy, what-planet-are-you-on kind of way."

Morrison glowered at her, unhappy at having his delusions punctured. "Crazy?" he asked fiercely, an edge of genuine madness in his voice. Standing up suddenly behind his desk, knocking his chair onto its back, he reached for the Glock holstered at his hip and, with preternatural speed, drew his weapon faster than any legendary gunfighter who ever rode the West. "I'll show you crazy!"

He aimed the gun at Roberta and pulled the trigger repeatedly. Nothing happened, of course, Seven's transporter having emptied all of Morrison's firearms of gunpowder, too. "You see!" the general exclaimed, hurling the useless Glock away in disgust. "Who else but the Beast could have devised such a diabolical means to strip free men of the constitutional right to bear arms?

His irate query put Roberta at something of a loss; explaining the extraterrestrial origins of the transporter was not likely to calm Morrison down. *Best just to keep my mouth shut,* she reasoned, *especially since I'm in no shape for a debate.*

Turned out it was a rhetorical question anyway. "I'll tell you what kind of planet I'm on, Ms. Landers. It's a planet that, thanks to you, will soon fall under the absolute dominion of a soulless, all-powerful, world government controlled by the likes of Khan Noonien Singh." Avian eyes the size of silver dollars regarded Roberta mercilessly. "I don't know about you, little lady, but that's not something that I'm looking forward to."

For once, Roberta was forced to agree.

Morrison fiddled with the servo, finding the adjustable collar ring. "So how do you fire this gizmo?" he asked, applying his augmented intellect to the task of mastering the alien instrument's controls. He fired experimentally at the screen of his computer, switching settings randomly until an invisible beam burned right through the monitor, causing a gout of white-hot sparks to gush from the screen. "Whoa there!" the general laughed joylessly. "Now I'm getting the hang of it."

I always knew that thing was too darn user-friendly, Roberta thought, cradling her splintered arm. She figured Morrison would be using her for target practice next.

He looked like he was thinking about it, but then he looked upward with a start. "Wait!" he exclaimed, his hawk's eyes searching the stuccoed ceiling. "Do you hear that?"

Roberta didn't hear anything, not even the howl of a coyote. "Hear what?" she asked.

"Don't lie to me! There it is again!" He craned his head back, staring at the ceiling fearfully. His jaw dropped open, revealing a mass of green chewing gum stuck to the inside of his cheek. "It's the copters!" he declared with paranoid certainty. "The black helicopters! They're coming for me at last!"

"There are no helicopters," Roberta whispered, chilled to the bone by the sight of pure, naked insanity. A teardrop welled at the corner of her eye, and it struck her, with heartbreaking force, that twenty years ago little Randy Morrison had been one of the precocious superkids she'd rescued from Chrysalis. "There's nothing there."

Morrison was beyond hearing her. "Hear that? They're getting closer." His head rotated back and forth, from right to left to right again, like an agitated bird. "But I won't be captured, not by them! There'll be no show trial, no kangaroo court, no goddamn propaganda victory for the New World Order!"

He turned the tip of the servo toward his own head.

"No!" Roberta blurted. "Wait! Don't do it!"

Hawklike eyes stared past her, gazing into limbo. "Tell the world I never surrendered."

The servo hummed, and one more ghost joined the phantoms haunting the deserted mining camp. Roberta looked away, feeling sick to her stomach. *He was such a bright kid, I'll bet,* she thought forlornly, remembering an underground day-care center full of budding supergeniuses.

How in the world did we end up here?

CHAPTER TWENTY-ONE

PALACE OF THE GREAT KHAN
CHANDIGARH
MARCH 17, 1995

KHAN STOOD UPON THE RAMPARTS OF HIS FORTRESS, looking out on the city below. He did not like what he saw.

Designed by a Swiss architect merely forty years ago, Chandigarh enjoyed a deserved reputation as India's most modern and well-organized city. Wide, leafy boulevards met at tidy right angles, according to a sensible grid pattern that neatly divided the city into discrete zones and sectors. Open lawns and parks provided welcome oases of green amidst steel-and-concrete buildings of modernist design. In contrast to, say, the sprawling disorder of Old Delhi, Chandigarh conveyed an impression of cleanliness and control, which was one of the reasons Khan had chosen the city as his capital.

Now, however, parts of Chandigarh, namely the

sector dominated by Khan's fortress, were beginning to resemble an armed camp. Roadblocks and checkpoints, manned by Khan's own soldiers, obstructed the spacious avenues leading to the palace. As a precaution against car bombs, the nearest streets had been closed to unauthorized auto traffic. Snipers prowled the parapets atop the fortress' high sandstone walls, alert to the possibility of attack. Thirty meters below, in the once-public plaza outside the main gate, a team of army engineers were digging a trench along the base of the fortress, then rigging the moat with mines and motion detectors.

This is not the brave new world I envisioned, Khan brooded morosely. The ugly fortifications threw a melancholy pall over his soul, darkening his spirit despite the crisp blue sky overhead. He had hoped to create an orderly utopia in which even the lowliest of his subjects could walk the streets in safety at any hour of the day or night; instead, he found himself barricaded inside his own palace grounds, increasingly cut off from the humanity he had desired to rule.

"Your Excellency," Joaquin entreated, uncomfortable in such an exposed setting, "you should come down from here. It is not safe."

Khan leaned out over the battlements, resting his palms against the sculpted ocher crenellations. Summer was still a month away, and the stonework felt cool beneath his touch. In the distance, he saw a handful of families touring the city's famed Rock Gardens; he envied their simple, carefree lives. "Is that what it has come to, my old friend? I am no longer safe upon the walls of my own citadel?"

The stalwart bodyguard could not lie to him. "There have been death threats, Your Excellency. And plots against your life, both from here and abroad." He divided his uneasy surveillance between the city streets and the skies, as if anticipating an assassin's bullet or an aerial assault, respectively.

The worst part was, Khan knew Joaquin's fears were not unfounded. The more Khan attempted to ensure the security of his domain, by showing zero tolerance for any subversive elements at work, be they religious fanatics, malcontented students, or disgruntled academics, the more bitter the opposition to his reign seemed to become. *Fools!* he railed against them in the sacrosanct privacy of his mind. *Ungrateful troglodytes!* Did his unappreciative subjects not realize that their seditious rumblings, their irksome demonstrations and work stoppages, but played into the hands of his enemies? He did not relish playing the heavy-handed tyrant, but in these perilous times he could ill afford to show any sign of weakness.

"Please, Your Excellency," Joaquin pleaded, stepping hopefully toward the watchtower wherein the nearest convenient stairwell was located. Fully recovered from the injuries he had sustained at Ajorra, the bodyguard no longer showed any evidence of a limp. "Let us return to the safety of your private apartments. Or one of the enclosed gardens, if you prefer."

Khan shook his head. He was not yet ready to abandon the relative freedom of the open ramparts. He spent too much of his life locked away these days, strategizing against his enemies, obsessively devising ruthless moves and countermoves to protect his embattled regime from a world that seemed increasingly arrayed against him. Hunyadi was dead, along with Morrison and Amin, but he still had Gary Seven to contend with, not to mention the increasingly restive attentions of the planet's so-called "legitimate" superpowers. *There is too much stubborn opposition in the world,* he lamented sourly, *crossing me at every turn.*

"Lord Khan!" an unhappy voice accosted him. Khan turned away from his view of the city to behold, to his surprise and dismay, the Lady Ament striding toward him across the rampart. A glossy sable cloak, drawn shut against the chill March air, concealed her exquisite figure, but nothing hid the marked displeasure upon her refined and elegant features. "I must speak with you at once."

Keen to the hostile tone in her voice, Joaquin instinctively stepped between Khan and the approaching female. Khan appreciated the impulse, but he was not a man to shy away from a confrontation, no matter with whom. Whatever had incurred the superwoman's ire, he was inclined to deal with the matter without delay.

"Good afternoon, Lady Ament," he said evenly, stepping out from behind the looming bodyguard. He smoothed down the silver sash across his chest, which he had donned in solidarity with his loyal Exon warriors. "What brings you up onto these lofty fortifications?"

"Not the view," she said dryly. Her amber eyes were alight and full of purpose. The wind blew a strand of her lustrous black hair across her face, which she deftly batted away. "I was reviewing our yearly expenditures when I happened upon a rather distressing purchase, hidden away in a fund designated for medical research and development." Glancing about to make certain that none of the patrolling snipers and guardsmen were within earshot, she lowered her voice so that only Khan and his ever-present shadow could hear. "Perhaps you can explain, my lord, why Dr. Dhasal has seen fit to acquire over two hundred working bio-warheads from the former Soviet Union?"

Khan's face hardened. "That is a security matter," he said coldly.

"Which you chose to keep from me," Ament deduced, her icy tone conveying exactly what she thought of being so excluded. "Yes, I understand that much." Moving beyond her own bruised feelings, she grilled Khan in the manner of a prosecuting attorney. "What I do not comprehend is why you are transforming Chrysalis Island from a genetic research facility into an incubator and launch pad for full-scale biological warfare?"

"We have many enemies," Khan stated vaguely. He had always known that someday he and Ament would have this debate, but, now that the time for unvarnished truth had arrived, he found he had little taste for the discussion.

"Two hundred warheads, my lord?" she pressed. "What possible use could there be for such an arsenal? And for a mutated strain of flesh-eating bacteria?"

Her last riposte caught Khan by surprise. "How do you know of that?" he asked in a low voice, his dark brows descending like lightning bolts hurled down from Olympus.

Ament raised her own brows archly. "I am not without my own resources," she said without apology. She
threw back the right half of her cloak, revealing a collection of folded newspapers tucked beneath the
crook of her arm. Her amber eyes locked on Khan, she
handed the papers over to him; he accepted them warily. "These were among my first clues," she explained.

He unfolded the documents, which proved to be
the front pages of various London tabloids, dated
June of 1994, many months ago. "Eaten Alive!"
screamed the large block letters upon the first paper,
while a second tabloid bore the even more lurid headline: "Killer bug ate my face!" Khan quickly flipped
through the rest of the clippings, all of which concerned a sudden outbreak of necrotizing fasciitis in
the British Isles. He recalled that Dr. Dhasal had indeed conducted some field tests with the recon-
structed bacteria around that time, simply to ensure
that the original recipe lived up to the late Dr.
Williams's grisly promises. His understanding was
that the pathogen had been much improved upon
since then.

"Tabloid sensationalism," he said dismissively,
thrusting the yellowing scandal sheets back at
Ament. "What has this to do with me?"

Ament smiled at him sadly. "Do not dissemble,
Lord Khan. It is unworthy of you." She neatly folded
the damning papers and replaced them beneath her
arm. "These were but the tip of the iceberg. More evidence is there if one cares to look for it. I know all
about this new form of streptococcus, and of Dr.
Dhasal's mandate, at your own instruction, to culti-
vate the bacteria in mass quantities. But why, my

and unknowable. *There is no art,* he reflected, after Macbeth, *to find the mind's construction in the face.*

Finally, she spoke, choosing her words carefully. "I will never cease from speaking my conscience," she informed him, "nor from hoping to dissuade you from this dreadful enterprise you seem intent upon embarking, but you need not question my allegiance." Her words held both a promise and a warning. "I will be with you until the end."

Very well, Khan thought, his doubts about her fidelity not entirely laid to rest. He turned once more to look upon the chaste, cosmopolitan promise of Chandigarh, sullied only by the base, imperfect beings infesting the city with their perversity and ingratitude. He tried to imagine the roomy boulevards and avenues swept clean of useless human flotsam. *'Tis a consummation devoutly to be wished.*

"Until the end," he echoed.

CHAPTER TWENTY-TWO

THE TUAMOTO ISLANDS HAVE LONG BEEN KNOWN as "The Dangerous Archipelago," due to its sudden storms, shifting currents, and hidden reefs. Since Khan had taken possession of Muroroa, that particular atoll had become more deadly still, guarded day and night by a squadron of his finest Exon warriors. Radar and antiaircraft batteries searched the sky above the island, enforcing a strict no-fly zone, while armed speedboats, equipped with searchlights and heavy artillery, circled Muroroa ceaselessly, watching out for unauthorized vessels and chasing away any hapless pleasure crafts that happened to sail too close to the forbidden atoll.

Only a single channel passed through the verdant ring of the island to the inner lagoon, and this crucial inlet was kept under constant watch, both above and below the waves. Once, three years ago, Roberta Lincoln had managed to invade the island by using scuba gear to swim unnoticed through the passage, but security had been tightened considerably since then; now underwater cameras observed every shark, squid, and jellyfish that made its way from the sea to the lagoon and back again. The stringent surveillance had yielded the desired results: since that previous incursion, on the occasion of Morning Star's launch, no unwelcome stranger had set foot on Chrysalis Island.

Until tonight.

A large brown manta ray swam toward the lagoon, gliding over the floor of the channel like a giant aquatic bat. The ray attracted little attention from those watching the live feed from the submerged spy-eyes; the Polynesian waters were home to a diverse assortment of marine life, so the sight of a prowling devilfish was not uncommon.

Its winglike pectoral fins flapped gently as the manta cruised through the channel without incident, then made its way beneath the turquoise surface of the lagoon until, surprisingly, it rendezvoused with a black-tipped reef shark, two bottle-nosed dolphins, and another sizable ray. Upon the manta's arrival, the eclectic coterie of sea creatures deliberately beached themselves upon the sandy shore, where a strange, undinal transformation took place.

The manta rose upon a pair of slender legs and handily shed its glistening wings and torso, which, upon careful inspection, could be seen to be a painted rubber facsimile of a real giant ray. A handsome Chinese woman emerged from the counterfeit devilfish, then watched in silence as four other women discarded their finned disguises, which they then slid back into the briny water lapping at the beach. Like the first woman, their faces had been painted with overlapping shades of black and green, the better to blend in with both their camouflaged commando gear and the shadowy jungle flora at the edge of the shallow beach.

Gifted with exceptional night vision, Chen Tiejun did not require night-vision goggles to take a quick head count. She was glad to see that all of Team Artemis was accounted for. *Good,* she thought solemnly. It was far too early in the mission to start losing amazons.

The exiled superwoman rapidly surveyed their situation and surroundings. As planned, it was a clear, moonless night, throwing a comforting blanket of darkness over this narrow strip of sand. The air was warm, maybe twenty-five degrees Celsius, and mercifully free of humidity. Typhoon season was months away, she recalled. Little did Khan's minions know that another kind of storm was creeping up on Muroroa.

Despite the blackness of the night, the beach was still too exposed for her tastes. At her signal, the team slipped stealthily into the concealing jungle brush, leaving their aquatic disguises hidden beneath the opaque surface of the lagoon. A battery-powered blower erased their bootprints from the sand.

Chen crouched amidst rustling fronds and ferns, listening intently for the sound of Khan's sentries on the move. A balmy tropical fragrance pervaded the atmosphere, tantalizing her senses. A shame she wasn't here on vacation; it seemed like a beautiful night. The swaying palms and mangroves struck her as exotic compared to the rugged forests of her own island colony of Penthesilea, four thousand kilometers away.

While her team inspected and assembled their weapons, she took a minute to remove a compact communications device, about the size of the latest cellular phones, from the pocket of her trousers. She flipped open the lid of the device and keyed in a top-secret number. *Now a word from our sponsor,* she thought wryly, checking in with the enigmatic instigator of tonight's covert action. "Artemis to Butler," she whispered in English. "Repeat: Artemis to Butler."

A blond-haired American woman in her mid-forties, whom Chen knew only as "Caroline Butler," appeared on the communicator's miniature viewscreen. *"Copy that, Artemis,"* the older woman answered. Her blue-green eyes held many worries, belying the forced cheer in her voice. *"Where are you?"*

According to the American, the communicator utilized a signal that could not be traced or detected by any earthly means. "We have successfully reached the inner shore of the lagoon," Chen reported. She could spy the lights of the Centre d'Experimentation du Pacifique, roughly half a kilometer away, up a sloping hillside carpeted with dense vegetation. "What is your latest intel regarding the first and secondary targets?"

"All systems are go," Butler assured her. *"According to a very reliable source, Khan's stockpile of carnivorous bacteria is being stored in an airtight isolation chamber in the main biological testing area, two levels down. You should have no problem finding it; just look for the stuff they're being extra careful with."*

Chen shook her head, amazed that even Khan could have spawned such a lethal abomination, threatening the lives of billions of innocent women and, somewhat less importantly, their men. She would not have believed it had not Butler presented her with irrefutable evidence of Khan's genocidal intentions. "It will be ashes by dawn," she promised. The contents of her backpack would guarantee that, if nothing else. "What of the secondary target?"

"That's good, too," Butler said. *"By all reports, Dr. Dhasal is working late in her labs, as usual. With luck, you should be able to snatch her without too much trouble."*

Chen was tempted to laugh at the American woman's unfounded optimism. She knew from experience that there was no such thing as a trouble-free military mission. Amazons would die here tonight, but her two-pronged mission, to destroy the malignant bacteria and deprive Khan of his foremost biological sorceress, more than justified any sacrifice.

"You may count on us," she said confidently. "My misguided sister will no longer serve Khan after this night, even if I must destroy her myself."

"Er, let's hope it doesn't come to that," Butler gulped. *"Still, whatever happens, I want to thank you for taking on this assignment. It really is a matter of life and death—for the whole crazy planet. At this point, Khan is only weeks away from being able to launch his bio-warheads, filled with enough mutated strep-A to eat the flesh off just about everybody."* She shuddered at the thought. *"I'm sorry I'm not there with you."*

Chen doubted the other woman would be much use in combat anyway, being both middle-aged and the product of routine, random genetics. "You need not apologize. As we both know, there is at least one very good reason why you cannot take part in this raid. And why, ultimately, this is a task that only I and my amazons can accomplish."

"*I know,*" Butler admitted. "*That's why I came to you in the first place.*" Chen glimpsed roughhewn stone walls behind the American's head and shoulders. "*Good luck!*"

"Wish the world luck. If we fail, it will need it." She saw that her commandos were armed and ready. "Artemis out."

She inspected her troops, now lurking among the sword-shaped pandanus leaves and coconut-laden palm trees. Zenobia, Shirin, Rani, and Nina. All were superwomen, born of Chrysalis, and veterans of dozens of daring raids and rescue missions waged against the oppressive forces of patriarchy and misogyny. "Remember," she softly reminded them all. "We must not be overconfident. Our foes tonight, Khan's Exon warriors, are as superhuman as we. They will not be conquered as easily as most men."

She nodded at the lighted complex atop the hill, once the nerve center of France's blasphemous nuclear assaults on Mother Earth and now host to an even more heinous obscenity. "There is our target, just as the American described." She tugged on the straps of her backpack, making sure her special cargo was resting snugly against her back, then conducted a quick inventory of her weapons: a 9mm Beretta pistol (with silencer), a K-Bar fighting knife, multiple grenades and smoke bombs, flare gun, and, last but not least, her trained, conditioned, and genetically perfect body.

"Go!" she whispered.

Zenobia, who years before had served as Chen's bodyguard at Khan's disastrous superhuman summit in Chandigarh, took point, leading them uphill, zigzagging here and there to take full advantage of the scattered stands of palms. Her bright red hair had been dyed raven-black in the interests of stealth. The others followed closely, with Shirin watching their rear. She was an Afghan refugee who had traded her stifling burqa for a Kevlar vest and combat gear.

It was a steep climb that only became more so as they went on, reminding Chen of some of the more arduous obstacle courses back on Penthesilea. The abundant foliage, although providing valuable cover, was also a chore to force their way through. Thorns and twigs, branches and brambles, tugged at their uniforms and skin, scratching against their faces. Lizards and caterpillars scurried across their path, sometimes dropping onto the backs of their necks.

They had been lucky so far. Chen knew that they couldn't avoid detection forever. At some point they would need to fight their way into the fetid bowels of the Centre. She glanced back over her shoulder. From this height, she could easily see the towering rocket gantry rising from the forest on the other side of the lagoon. An Ariane 5 rocket, intended to deliver Goddess knows what unholy payload into the pristine heavens, rested upon the launch pad, held securely by the gantry's mechanical embrace. A sly smirk appeared upon Chen's face, knowing what was to come.

A sudden explosion rocked the ground beneath her, and she threw herself face-first onto the leafy hillside. A blast of heat scorched her shoulders and the acrid smell of smoke and burning flesh assaulted her nostrils. Risking a peek, she raised her head slightly to look for the source of the explosion; to her dismay, she saw a billowing column of black smoke rising from farther up on the hillside, where Zenobia had crept only seconds before.

A mine? A hidden tripwire? Chen offered a brief prayer for her sister's departed spirit, knowing that the formerly flame-haired amazon had somehow fallen victim to the island's defenses. Orange flames licked the leaves of a nearby pandanus shrub, threatening to set the surrounding underbrush afire.

Besides claiming the life of their comrade, the detonation also cost them the advantages of surprise and subterfuge. Within seconds, alarms sounded from the building above. Lights flicked on in every window of the Centre, and Chen heard excited voices and the sound of boots pounding on pavement. Their cover, she concluded, had well and truly been blown.

"Amazons, attack!" she cried out, rising rapidly to her feet. Her surviving sisters-in-arms rose from the jungle brush like mythical soldiers sprung from the strewn teeth of an unequivocally female dragon. They held their weapons at the ready, charging up the smoking hillside at superhuman speed. Before drawing her own Beretta, Chen first took hold of the flare gun hanging from her belt. Without hesitation, she pointed the gun at the sky above the lagoon and fired a single flare that exploded phosphorescently above the shimmering waters, signaling the second wave of the invasion. "Now, my sisters," she whispered to the all-female army waiting offshore. "Now!"

Team Hecuba struck first, as proven by the gigantic fireball that suddenly roared from the base of the rocket gantry, across the lagoon. The colossal explosion, caused by a 60mm mortar fired from the surrounding jungle, ignited the Ariane itself, turning the gigantic launch vehicle into an inverted Roman candle, consuming itself from the bottom up.

The Ariane's fiery demise marked the beginning of the amazons' full-scale assault on Chrysalis Island. Hang-gliding warriors, launched from speedboats hidden behind the neighboring islands, came soaring over the island in droves, their pitch-black nylon wings all but invisible against the vacant sky. They strafed the ground with machine-gun fire while hurling grenades at the antiaircraft emplacements below. Fireballs blossomed amongst the tropical greenery, all intended to draw Khan's soldiers away from the Centre.

Its moorings melted by the ferocious heat of the self-destructing Ariane rocket, the massive gantry toppled to earth with a thunderous crash that could be heard all the way across the island. Savoring the apocalyptic destruction, Chen followed the remainder of her team toward their ultimate destination: Phoolan Dhasal's biological shop of horrors. Masculine voices, barking orders in Punjabi, sounded from the top of the hill and she yanked a grenade from the bandolier across her chest. "Heads down!" she shouted to her comrades as she lobbed the grenade at the willing guardians of Khan's vile contagion.

An ear-pounding blast of fire and smoke cleared her way, all but knocking at Dhasal's door.

A dynamic computer model charted the spread of the flesh-eating bacteria, based on its estimated communicability, available vectors, geographic deployment, resistance to antibiotics, etc. According to the most recent projections, it would take approximately 79.32 days to infect the entire human race, excepting those conceived at Chrysalis, of course.

Phoolan Dhasal looked up from the full-color computer display, giving her tired eyes a break. She had been putting in long hours the last several weeks, as the launch date for the epidemic drew near. Khan wanted daily updates on the status of their preparations, and she had endeavored not to disappoint him.

She sat alone before the computer. A double layer of transparent glass and plastic separated her from the isolation chamber on the other side of the window, where industrial-size fermentation vats capable of holding several hundred kilograms of cultured streptococcus-A rested safely within an airtight environment. Mechanical arms, currently at rest, gave her the option of extracting and manipulating minute samples from each vat, for the purpose of testing virulence and communicability. *Idle waldoes are the devil's playthings,* she thought wryly, although it was hard to imagine how the articulated metal arms could cook up anything more diabolical than what they had already helped to concoct.

Dhasal rubbed her eyes. A bowl of half-eaten curry sat on the gleaming white counter next to her keyboard. Frankly, she was getting bored with necrotizing fasciitis and was looking forward to the advent of the plague just so she could get back to work on some other promising lines of inquiry. She had been making significant progress, as she recalled, in cloning transgenic organisms before Khan ordered that the entire resources of the Centre be devoted to the refinement and mass production of strep-A.

Soon, she promised herself. Once the epidemic

began, thinning the planet's excess population as Khan desired, she would have all the time in the world to pursue more interesting experiments. There had been some intriguing work done recently with regards to synthetic glands and enzymes. . . .

The computer model blinked once, demanding her attention. With a sigh, she forced herself to examine the revised epidemiological projections, looking for ways to tweak the program to produce an even more efficient result. There was very little that could be done with the pathogen itself at this late date, so she concentrated on the probable dissemination patterns, trying to figure out the ideal targets for each of their available bio-warheads. *Perhaps we're concentrating too much on North America,* she speculated, *and neglecting Africa and the Middle East?*

Downing a spoonful of lukewarm curry, she adjusted the distribution parameters, then leaned back in her chair to observe the results. Before the model finished its work, however, a tremendous roar penetrated the walls of the bio-laboratory, sounding like a bomb going off somewhere outside. Dhasal looked up in alarm as warning klaxons went off suddenly, hurting her ears.

Sabotage? An accident? Against her will, memories of Bhopal descended upon her and she recalled the sirens blaring as the toxic white fumes, released from the ramshackle pesticide factory on the outskirts of the city, chased her down the midnight streets, burning her lungs, scarring her eyes. . . .

Enough! she thought, forcibly squashing an attack of post-traumatic jitters. Bhopal was over a decade ago; she had a far more immediate crisis to cope with.

She stabbed at the intercom button next to her computer console. "Dhasal to Security," she snapped insistently, feeling a desperate need for more information. "What was that noise? What is happening?"

"We are under attack, Doctor!" an agitated voice announced shrilly. She barely recognized the heavily accented tones of Geir Jonsson, the Centre's deputy chief of security. "Madwomen with guns and grenades, they're attacking the entire island!"

Explosions and gunfire crackled noisily in the background, along with angry curses and screams. It sounded as though hell itself had broken loose on Muroroa. Dhasal rolled her chair back from the intercom speaker instinctively, repelled by the unmistakable din of warfare. Her heart, still trapped in Bhopal, pounded wildly in her chest, but, through sheer concentration and force of will, she somehow managed to keep from trembling.

Think! she commanded her powerful mind. She had learned all she needed to know. The first explosion had been no accident; they were definitely under attack, although she was unsure by whom. It all seemed so unreal; Dhasal had attended, as required, periodic security briefings, but she'd never truly expected to face an armed invasion of her laboratories. *I am a scientist,* she thought angrily. *Not a soldier. Why can't I be left alone to do my work?*

An Exon soldier, recognizable by his silver sash and beret, leaped from behind the trunk of an ancient palm tree, an M60 machine-gun in hand. A burst of gunfire, flaring red in the nocturnal shadows, winged Shirin, who dropped from sight even as Chen's

Beretta put a bullet between the eyes of her attacker. Crouching low to present a smaller target, the Chinese superwoman raced to the side of her fallen comrade, whom she found sprawled on her back atop a bed of crushed green leaves. A spreading puddle of blood looked black in the dim light.

Kevlar had protected the Afghan woman's chest and midsection, but her right arm and thigh had been blasted apart. She was bleeding so profusely that Chen would have rated Shirin's chances for survival low even if they weren't in the middle of a firefight.

She glanced up at the sky. Through intersecting branches, she saw dive-bombing amazons being cut down by antiaircraft fire from below. Although the high-flying female warriors had initially seized the offensive, Muroroa's defenders had soon gone into action as well, belatedly attempting to even the score. Now murdered amazons crashed like falling stars into the leafy trees and waiting lagoon. Chen could only hope that a significant proportion of her forces made it to earth intact, to engage in further combat with Khan's ground forces.

The busier they keep them, she recognized pragmatically, *the better the odds for our mission.* Still, it wounded her to see the spirits of so many sisters extinguished in a single night. *Khan must pay for making this necessary,* she vowed, the weight of her laden backpack suddenly feeling all the heavier.

"Go," Shirin urged her through gritted teeth. Chen knew she had no choice; more lives than theirs depended on the success of their mission. She pressed the hilt of her K-Bar knife into the palm of Shirin's working left arm, so that the injured woman could defend herself—or take her own life if need be.

"Be brave and strong as a lioness." With an unsoldierly lump in her throat, Chen tore herself away from the dying amazon's side, catching up with Rani and Nina, who were in the process of cutting through the razor-wire fence around the Centre. Dead Exon soldiers, or pieces thereof, littered the earth around them. Rani, a former cat burglar with a talent for breaking and entering, efficiently sliced away at the metal links with a diamond-edged wire cutter while Nina, a Polish bodybuilder with tight black braids, provided cover with continuous fire from her M4 carbine.

"Almost through," Rani grunted, snapping apart one last link of razor-wire. She kicked out a triangular section big enough to duck through by bending low enough. "Watch your head," she warned, sliding past the severed links without a snag. In theory, there was a locked back entrance to the Centre approximately fifty paces from this section of the fence; Rani hurried ahead to prepare the way.

The hellish cacophony of war filled the warm night air: bombs, bullets, shouts, crashes, and screams. Heavy artillery rocked the island, perhaps directed at the fleet of speedboats attacking Khan's gunships beyond the barrier reef. Flocks of terns and petrels took to the skies in panic, adding to the confusion, while flying foxes glided madly from tree to tree, seeking refuge from the noise, fire, and general chaos. Chen smelled cordite and napalm on the breeze, overpowering the perfumed fragrance of the jungle, and longed for the peace and quiet of her own island, thousands of kilometers to the west. She wondered if she would ever see Penthesilea again.

"After you!" Nina shouted over the din, nodding toward the gap in the fence. A heartbeat later, a burst of automatic weapons fire threw the muscular amazon back against the fence, where the barbed razor-wire held her bullet-riddled body erect even after her spirit was driven from her flesh. Chen spotted a flash of silver in the wilderness below and fired back with her Beretta, never knowing if she had avenged her sister's death.

Diving through the hole in the fence, she rolled back onto her feet and sprinted for that promised back entrance. A whiff of plastic explosive, smelling strangely like marzipan, told her that Rani was already preparing to blow the door off its hinges. Despite the grievous losses they had already sustained, Chen grinned savagely as she closed in on her objective. *I'm coming for you, Dhasal,* she thought triumphantly. *For you and your Goddess-cursed bug!*

A red light went off above the entrance of the control room. Dhasal knew what that meant. The invaders had penetrated the Centre itself and were now at large somewhere in this very building. Fortunately, Dhasal recalled, there was a contingency for such a scenario. Conquering her nerves, she methodically keyed in the necessary instructions, then nodded in approval as air vents opened in the isolation chamber beyond the glass. Powerful pumps, built into the walls, thrummed to life even as the valves on the pressurized fermentation vats all opened automatically, allowing the airborne bacteria within to escape, not only into the isolation chamber but into the Centre's main ventilation system.

I may not be a soldier, she thought, *but I'm not without a weapon of my own....*

* * *

A cool draft, accompanied by the hiss of air being forcibly expelled into the corridor, elicited a mirthless laugh from Chen Tiejun. Just as the American woman predicted: Dhasal or one of her lab-jacketed minions was pumping the killer germ into the building's air supply in a last-ditch attempt to slay any invaders in their tracks.

A clever idea, Chen admitted, *against almost any other foe.* She and Rani, however, sprinted down the infected hallways with impunity; unlike every other commando force on Earth, Chen and her amazons were immune to the voracious bacteria, as required by Khan's own genocidal design. *It is well that the American woman did not join us after all,* she reflected grimly. *Her merely human skin would already be rotting on her bones.*

With Khan's security forces engaged elsewhere on the island, at the ruined rocket base and in the murky jungle, the two surviving members of Team Artemis encountered little resistance as they stalked through the multistory research complex. Terrified scientists and technicians cowered in their labs and cubicles, hoping to avoid the invaders long enough to come through the attack alive. Chen let them hide; she was after bigger game.

"Help me!" a male voice called out to her as they took a shortcut through a storeroom packed full of wire cages containing experimental test animals of various sizes and species. Pausing momentarily, Chen was amused to see Brother Arcturus, late of the Panspermic Church of First Contact, locked in a cage of his own, alongside the squawking chimpanzees and squeaking lab rats. She felt a sudden stab of sympathy—for the chimps and rats. "Please," he begged her, grasping the bars of his cage. Straw carpeted the floor of his cell, and his hairless, revoltingly masculine body looked pale and undernourished. Only the astronomical tattoo upon his forehead retained any color or vitality. "You have to help me!"

"I'm busy," she snapped curtly. "Ask your starfathers instead." Picking up her pace once more, she left the caged superman behind. Bestial barks and growls drowned out his plaintive cries as she exited the storeroom. *I might have heeded his pleas more seriously,* she thought, gaining on the racing amazon ahead of her, *if he had paid more homage to his star*mothers *instead.*

Rani quickly located the stairwell their American partner had informed them of; if Butler was correct, Dhasal's main laboratories were two levels below the ground floor. The door to the stairway had shut automatically when the building went into emergency lockdown mode, but this presented little challenge to Rani, who enthusiastically blew the lock apart with her high-caliber Desert Eagle pistol. Both women wore rubber-soled boots to protect them from the sort of high-voltage booby traps Butler said had tripped her up before, on a spying mission three years ago.

Galloping down the stairs, guns drawn and ready, they came to a heavy metal door marked with the universal symbol for biohazardous material. *Looks like the right place,* Chen thought jubilantly. *We made it!*

Thank the Goddess they had stopped Khan before he had a chance to launch his plague missiles . . . !

* * *

In the control room outside the isolation chamber, Dhasal had finally succeeded in contacting Khan in Chandigarh. His noble features glared from the screen of her computer, only a slight visual stutter betraying the long-distance nature of the transmission. There was, she knew from long experience, over a fifteen-hour time difference between Muroroa and India, so this hellish night was already late afternoon where Khan was.

"You know what you must do, Doctor," he told Dhasal. Only the smoldering anger in his eyes and the vibrant timbre of his voice hinted at his reaction to the attack on the island—and by their own kind, no less! With the failure of the pathogen to strike down the intruders, Dhasal had belatedly realized the true nature of the invaders. *"There is no other recourse."*

Her face went pale. "Are you quite certain, Lord Khan?" she asked tremulously, daunted by the awesome responsibility suddenly thrust upon her. "The target selections have not been finalized. I wanted to run more projections, take into account seasonal migration patterns and the demographic availability of medical infrastructures—"

"No matter," Khan interrupted her, before she could babble further. *"The warheads are loaded, the missiles are ready, even earlier than we originally planned. Fine-tuning our target list is a luxury that has just been stolen from us."* His image flickered alarmingly, and she feared for their connection. *"We must not waste time polishing the cannonball, Doctor, when the enemy is at our very door."*

"But the rockets—the missiles—are more Mac-Pherson's province than mine," she protested. To her infinite frustration, the Scottish launch supervisor was away from Muroroa at this time of crisis; in fact, he was with Khan in Chandigarh, presenting a long-term plan for space exploration following Khan's total conquest of Earth. As she recalled, he had high hopes for salvaging all of NASA's bases and facilities after the plague destroyed America. . . . *How dare he leave me here,* she thought bitterly, *to cope with this invasion on my own?*

"You must be strong, Phoolan," Khan admonished her. *"Our enemies have forced our hand, so we must strike as swiftly and unexpectedly as they."* A burst of static momentarily rendered his words inaudible. *"—must launch the missiles immediately."*

His steadfast resolution inspired her. "Yes, my lord. I understand." His image flickered once more, then disappeared completely; Dhasal guessed that the satellite dish on the Centre's roof had been destroyed by enemy fire. She tried jitteringly to restore the connection, but to no avail. She was on her own.

Never mind, she told herself. Khan's orders were clear. She activated the speaker on her intercom. "Dhasal to Mission Control. Prepare to launch missiles."

REMOTE TESTING CONTROLS said the sign on the metal door. AUTHORIZED PERSONNEL ONLY.

Slamming her shoulder against the door, Chen smashed her way into the control room. She was the only member of Team Artemis left; concealed lasers, hidden in the ceiling just past the biohazard warning, had taken out Rani before either of them had recognized the danger. Only quick shooting on Chen's part, even as the surprised cat burglar slumped lifelessly to the floor, had saved the amazon leader from a similar fate.

"Don't move!" she snarled at Phoolan Dhasal, brandishing the smoking muzzle of her Beretta. The Indian biochemist was instantly recognizable by the opaque streaks across her brown eyes. Wearing a knee-length white lab coat, she was backed up against a blinking wall of computer banks, clutching a soiled fork as her only weapon. The control room smelled of fear and curry.

"Drop the fork," Chen instructed, her Beretta aimed precisely between the scientist's scarred eyes. Dhasal complied, and the utensil landed with a clatter onto the floor. "Dr. Phoolan Dhasal," Chen charged, "you are a traitor to womankind and my prisoner." She nodded at the gleaming steel cylinders on the other side of the clear glass window. "Is that your witches' brew?"

"Merely a representative sampling," Dhasal replied. Her voice had a fatalistic tone, as if it no longer mattered what she did or said. "The bulk of our output has already been loaded into exactly 235 bio-warheads, aimed at every continent except Antarctica." She raised her chin defiantly, meeting Chen's scornful gaze with her own bisected stare. "You are too late, amazon."

What? Chen thought, fear clutching at her heart. "But I thought you were not yet ready!"

"You were misinformed," Dhasal said coolly. "Safe in their silos, the missiles are being fueled as we speak." Her gaze drifted to the monitor of a nearby computer, where Chen now saw that a digital countdown was rapidly ticking down to completion. 00:09:38 read the flashing red numerals on the screen. *Less than ten minutes to go . . .*

"You may kill me if you wish," Dhasal gloated, tempting Chen mightily, "but the will of the Great Khan cannot be thwarted. You will live to see the common herd of humanity perish, in approximately three days by my calculations."

Goddess, no! Chen reacted in horror. She knew there was no way her warriors could seize control of the missile silos in under ten minutes. That left her with only one option available.

"Good-bye, sister." With only the barest twinge of regret, she shot Dhasal twice in the head. She had never killed a woman before, least of all in cold blood, but these were extraordinary circumstances; she could not keep an eye on Dhasal and still do what needed to be done.

Kicking the door shut behind her, then jamming a rolling office chair up against the door to further ensure that she was not disturbed, she hastily shed her bulging backpack and removed its fearsome contents: a portable nuclear device of Chen's own invention. Utilizing top-secret cold fusion technology, the suitcase nuke would produce a ten kiloton explosion, more than enough to destroy the missiles before they launched—and sterilize the entire island.

Pressing a single button, she started the high-speed arming sequence, then glanced up at the digital display on Dhasal's computer. 00:08:52.

It was going to be close. . . .

Twenty-one years ago, she recalled, somewhere beneath the sands of India's great Thar Desert, the first Chrysalis Project had been consumed by a purifying thermonuclear conflagration. Now, it seemed, history was about to repeat itself.

She thought of Shirin, possibly still alive in the tangled jungle outside, as well as all the other amazons fighting valiantly all over the island. With the fate of mortal womankind at stake, Chen had thrown her entire army into the fray; after tonight, only a handful of amazons would survive to remember those lost on Chrysalis Island.

The suitcase bomb hummed to life, a subatomic chain reaction racing the countdown to the release of the plague missiles. Exhausted, Chen Tiejun rested her weight against a white concrete wall, not far from the body of Phoolan Dhasal, whose disaster-streaked eyes now stared glassily into the void. Chen's greatest regret was that Khan himself was not present to be incinerated with the rest of them.

Let us hope, she thought, *that our American partner deals with him.*

The nuke beat the missiles with three minutes to spare.

CHAPTER TWENTY-THREE

CALIFORNIAN TOMATO PUREE—MADE WITH GENETI-cally modified tomatoes!

Gary Seven contemplated the label on the can with bittersweet amusement. According to Roberta, who had acquired the canned vegetables on one of her transporter-assisted jaunts around the globe, these new "Flavr Savr™" tomatoes had already gone on sale in the United States and England. *A revolutionary new technology reduced to hucksterism in less than a generation,* he reflected, amazed at how commonplace genetic engineering was becoming, in marked contrast to the days when the Chrysalis Project performed their recklessly ambitious experiments in darkest secrecy. Plump, extravagantly red tomatoes posed like a still-life painting on the aluminum can's brightly colored packaging, beneath a garish yellow banner proudly proclaiming their unnatural pedigree. Would that all products of genetic resequencing could be so reassuringly banal!

Sighing, he placed the brightly packed aluminum upon his desktop and glanced out the window of the farmhouse. It was a cold and foggy day outside; a good day, in other words, for staying indoors and getting some thinking done. He was worried about the situation in Chechnya, not to mention the faltering Mideast peace process. . . .

Roberta entered his office bearing printouts of today's newspapers. "Extray! Extray!" she hawked with an exaggerated Bronx accent. "Get your red-hot headlines here!"

"Any more fallout," he asked, "from the nuclear blast at Muroroa?"

"No pun intended?" she replied, quickly rifling through the thick stack of printouts. Blue-green eyes scanned the headlines. "Seriously, French President Chirac is still taking plenty of flak for, quote, 'resuming nuclear testing in the South Pacific,' end quote." She shook her head in disbelief. "I'm still amazed that we managed to get the French government to go along with that cover story."

"Better than admitting that they leased their facilities to a genetically engineered terrorist who almost destroyed the world." A somber tone entered Seven's voice as he recalled the enormous sacrifice made by Chen Tiejun and her amazons. "We should have never let matters get that far."

"It's not like we had a lot of choice," Roberta reminded him. "Khan is a tough customer, with plenty of smarts and manpower on his side. He wasn't going to let us just waltz in and shut down his precious

germ warfare program." She sat down in an upholstered wooden chair opposite Seven's desk. "Look at
it this way. This is twice now we've stopped someone
from spreading that nasty flesh-eating bacteria. Not a
bad track record."

"And all it's taken is two nuclear explosions," he
pointed out dryly.

Roberta shrugged, determined to lift Seven's spirits. "What's a couple of nukes between friends, especially considering all the times we've prevented
World War Three? I figure history owes us a mushroom cloud or two."

"Let's hope the Aegis agrees," Seven said. He appreciated Roberta's sunny attitude more than ever
these days. "The more worrisome part, of course, is
that Khan is still out there. We won a costly battle at
Muroroa, but not the war."

"True, but look at all the other power-hungry supermen who have bit the dust." She ticked them off
on her fingers. "Hunyadi, Amin, Gomez, Morrison,
Arcturus. Unless I've forgotten somebody, Khan is
the only one left with any real following."

"And Morning Star," he reminded her. "Don't forget that." Although he had contingencies in place
should Khan ever attempt to carry out his ultimate
doomsday scenario, Seven was all too aware that even
the best of plans could go awry. As long as Morning
Star remained in orbit, carefully watched and guarded
by Khan's fanatical underlings, Earth's entire ozone
layer remained at risk.

Until now, the world's superpowers had kept their
hands off Chandigarh, for fear of provoking Khan's
wrath, but, as news of the close call at Muroroa in-

evitably made its way through the intelligence networks of the United States, Russia, China, and their various allies, how much longer would it be before someone took the risky step of calling Khan's bluff?

Seven sensed time running out, all the more so because he knew one thing that he feared the rest of the world didn't.

Khan wasn't bluffing.

CHAPTER TWENTY-FOUR

"CONGRATULATIONS ON A JOB WELL DONE!"

Shannon O'Donnell applauded enthusiastically as Dr. Carlson uncorked a bottle of Château Picard and began filling everyone's glasses, slopping a bit over the rim in his eagerness to make sure everyone got a drink. The rich bouquet of the expensive French wine teased her nostrils, tempting her lips.

The entire team—O'Donnell, Doc Carlson, Walter Nichols, Jackson Roykirk, and Shaun Christopher—had gathered in the conference room for an informal celebration. Brightly colored streamers brightened up the dull wood paneling of the room, while helium-filled balloons, bearing the images of stars, comets, and nebulae, bobbed against the ceiling. A frosted white cake in the shape of the DY-100 occupied a place of honor upon the oblong table, prompting Shannon to wonder where Carlson found a baker with that high a security clearance.

"Toast! Toast!"

Blushing slightly, Carlson cleared his throat. "Our esteemed president talks a lot about a bridge to the twenty-first century, but it took everyone in this room to actually build that bridge—and with five years to spare! At the beginning of this decade, an impulse-powered sleeper ship was just a dream, but you have all helped to make that fantasy a reality. Lady and gentlemen," he said proudly, raising his glass, "I give you the DY-100, the first true interstellar spacecraft—and the prototype for many more to come!"

"Hear! Hear!" Shannon and the others chorused enthusiastically. Even Jackson seemed to be caught up in the spirit of the occasion, the usually dour and antisocial cyberneticist grinning just as giddily at the rest of them. Shannon sipped her wine, feeling a warm glow of accomplishment and camaraderie. To think, after all these years, slaving away in secret, the ship was finally ready!

Too bad Helen can't be here, she thought wistfully. But, aside from Carlson, the rest of the team remained unaware of the help they had received from the mysterious older woman. *We couldn't have done it without her, though.*

"I don't know about the rest of you," Shaun declared, giving Walter a hearty pat on the back, "but I can't wait to give that baby a test-drive."

Shannon held up her hand like a traffic cop. "Hold on there, flyboy! We still need to run a few tests on the navigational systems, make sure we've gotten all the kinks out."

"Oh, you just don't want me to make it into space before you," he teased her. "Don't worry, I'll leave you a few planets to explore . . . maybe."

"Dibs on Alpha Centauri!" she joked back. The wine was already going to her head, adding to her elation. "Besides, the DY-100 doesn't need a pilot anyway. We're all just going to snooze our way to the stars!"

"Ouch!" Shaun winced, clutching his heart as if he didn't already know that the sleeper ship was capable of flying under full automation, while its crew rested in suspended animation. "Obsolete already!"

Seriously, though, she couldn't imagine a better test pilot for the DY-100's initial trials than Shaun Christopher. She looked forward to watching him blast off in just a few short days, then maybe joining him years from now on a manned mission to Saturn and beyond. "Well, if you're good, we'll think about letting you land the ship once we get where we're going."

"After all our hard work," Walter interjected with a chuckle, "I could use a thirty-year nap in a hibernation niche!"

Jackson snorted. "I still think manned missions are a waste of time and money." He pointed to a nearby poster of Viking II, ascending into space atop an expendable Titan-Centaur rocket. "That's the future of space exploration: unmanned robotic probes." Cold-blooded and aloof, he sounded a bit like a robot himself. "Sending people into deep space is a sentimental anachronism."

"Are you kidding?" Shaun asked, appalled. "Where's the fun, the adventure, in that?" He gesticulated wildly, causing the wine in his glass to slosh precariously. "Do you think Columbus would have been happy sending an empty boat to the New World, with maybe a friendly note from Queen Isabella tacked to its mast?"

Oh God, Shannon thought, rolling her eyes. *Not this old argument again.* Shaun and Jackson had debated the pros and cons of manned versus unmanned space probes since the day they first met, and she didn't expect that the pilot and the robotics expert would ever see eye to eye on the issue. At times she wondered why Jackson even deigned to work on the DY-100, given his views, but figured that Area 51's unlimited budget and resources pretty much answered the question. Where else would Jackson get a chance to examine captured alien hardware?

"Boys, boys!" Carlson chided them in an avuncular manner. The elderly scientist approached the ship-shaped cake with a stainless-steel pastry carver in hand. "Stop quarreling and have some of this delicious cake."

Sounds good to me, Shannon thought, her mouth watering already. She was just stepping forward to help Carlson with the cake when, unexpectedly, the pen in the breast pocket of her lab coat vibrated against her chest. *What?* she thought in surprise. *Now?*

The pen vibrated again, with apparent impatience. "Excuse me, guys," she improvised hastily, "but I have to make a pit stop." Bent over the cake, Carlson peered at Shannon over the tops of his bifocals, as if suspecting something was up, but the younger men seemed to take her at her word. "Save me some cake!" she told them as she slipped out of the conference room.

She hurried down the hall to the nearest ladies' room, one of the few places at Area 51 that was not (she hoped) under twenty-four-hour surveillance. Hiding out in a stall, relieved to discover that she had the rest room to herself, Shannon pulled up the vibrating silver pen and held it near her lips. "Helen?"

It was silly question. Who else contacted her via a fountain pen?

The voice of the woman Shannon knew only as "Helen Swanson" emerged from the pen. *"I need to see you right away,"* she said without preamble, unusual for the typically gregarious mystery woman. This alone worried Shannon, never mind the obvious stress she heard in Helen's voice. Has something gone wrong? The redheaded astronaut trainee had always been afraid that this cloak-and-dagger business would blow up in her face someday.

"Where?" she asked hesitantly. Now was really not a good time to be leaving the base.

"Not far," Helen said, with a trace of her usual humor. *"Meet me at S-4, Launch Control."*

Huh? Shannon couldn't believe her ears. She felt like one of those slasher movie victims who suddenly discovers that a threatening call is coming from inside their own house. "Are you serious?" she asked the pen.

"Serious as an ozone alert," the other woman quipped. *"Don't be long."*

Putting away the pen, which had ceased vibrating once Shannon had answered Helen's insistent page, the young aeronautics engineer took a second to assimilate what she'd just heard. *S-4? What in the world was Helen doing there?*

At least Shannon didn't have far to go. A high-speed underground monorail connected this part of Area 51 with the facility code-named S-4, a concealed hangar and launch pad built into a spiny mountain ridge overlooking a dry lake bed known as Papoose Lake. On the surface, it was thirty-minute trip by Jeep, but the monorail got her there in less than ten.

The guards posted at the entrance to S-4 knew Shannon by sight, but still asked to see her ID before letting her proceed. "Just can't stay away, huh?" asked one of the guards, Sergeant Steven Muckerheide, who had been working security at the base for years.

"Guess not," she replied as lightly as she could manage. It dawned on her that, by coincidence, Muck had been on duty the first time Helen broke in to Area 51, back in 1986. Then the mystifying stranger had stolen a "phaser" and a "tricorder" (as Shannon had later learned they were called). Shannon couldn't imagine what Helen was after now.

After passing the usual fingerprint and retina scans, Shannon took an empty elevator cage up to Launch Control. Despite her mounting anxiety about this unscheduled (and highly illegal) rendezvous, she couldn't help but admire once more the underground hangar's most impressive occupant.

Gleaming brightly, the DY-100 rested upright upon the reinforced concrete launch pad. Over four hundred feet high, the completed prototype resembled a missile with mumps, the spacious hibernation compartments bulging outward beneath the sleeper ship's bullet-shaped prow. Four fusion-powered deuterium boosters were strapped onto the vessel's lower fuse-lage, ready to help the DY-100 achieve escape velocity as soon the first flight test was approved. Its heat-resistant, blue ceramic finish gave the prototype an appropriately shiny, right-out-of-the-box luster.

The DY-100 was more than state-of-the-art, it was a sneak preview of a brand-new era Shannon hoped to be a part of. Its revolutionary "impulse" engine, based on alien technology observed at Roswell, with an uncredited assist from whomever Helen Swanson was working for, was theoretically capable of achieving velocities thrillingly close to the speed of light. Built-in hibernation niches, improving upon Walter Nichols's original cryosatellite designs, promised to hold some eighty-five passengers in suspended animation while the fully automated computer system (Jackson Roykirk's pride and joy) piloted the sleeper ship to unknown worlds light-years from Earth.

The sight still took Shannon's breath away. *Too bad this whole project is still so hush-hush,* she thought. She wanted to show the magnificent starship off to the entire world. *Maybe someday, once all the secrecy is lifted, billions of television viewers will watch a DY-100 take off for the stars.*

The elevator lurched to a halt and Shannon exited the cage, right outside a door labeled: S-4. LAUNCH CONTROL. Another guard should have been standing watch over the entrance, so she was surprised to find the door unattended. *Curiouser and curiouser,* she thought, as she slid her own key card into the lock and entered today's password into the electronic keypad. "Hello?" she asked uneasily, as the door slid open.

It was past eleven on a Friday night. With the earliest lift-off date still days away, Launch Control should have been completely deserted. And, indeed, rows of unoccupied computer control stations looked out on the launch site through a gallery window made of six-inch-thick transparent aluminum, strong enough to withstand even the tremendous heat and force of a blast-off. The consoles were all switched off, giving the launch gallery a sepulchral feel, lacking its usual flashing lights and humming circuitry.

But the control room was not entirely empty. Helen Swanson, wearing (of all things!) an orange NASA flight suit, lounged in one of the rolling bucket seats used by the launch technicians, her booted feet resting atop an inactive keyboard. Next to her, in the adjacent seat, a uniformed guard snored contentedly, his head slumped onto the console in front of him. An inane grin was plastered on his face, and a tiny river of drool trickled from the corner of his mouth.

"Don't worry about him," Helen assured her, nodding at the oblivious sentry. His gun, Shannon noted, was resting on another console, safely out of arm's reach. "Trust me, he's having very pleasant dreams right now."

Tell me about it, Shannon thought, having been on the receiving end of one of Helen's weirdo tranquilizer beams back in '86; she had never slept quite so well in her life. "What's this all about, Helen?" she whispered urgently. "What are you doing here?"

She didn't even bother asking Helen how she had managed to sneak into S-4, despite all of Area 51's plentiful security. The enigmatic older woman (whose honey-blond tresses, Shannon suspected, held a great deal of dye) had long ago proven that she could more or less come and go as she pleased; even still, for Shannon's peace of mind, if nothing else, they had usually arranged to meet in Vegas, far from the vigilant eyes and ears of the base's military guardians.

Helen grimaced, as if reluctant to divulge the purpose of her visit. "I have a very big favor to ask of you," she began, flinching in anticipation. "I need the DY-100. Tonight."

What? The shocks just kept on coming. "You have to be joking." Shannon stared at Helen's orange NASA flight suit, hoping it was all part of some twisted practical joke. "You want the ship?"

"Tonight," Helen echoed. She got up out of her chair and walked over toward Shannon, who saw that the self-proclaimed blond "go-between" was carrying a translucent green paperweight, which she fidgeted with nervously as she spoke. "Look, I know it's a lot to ask—"

"No!" Shannon blurted, venting her sudden anger and confusion. "It's more than a lot, it's insane." Her upset voice crept up an octave. "We're talking about a one-of-a-kind, multi-billion-dollar spaceship, the result of decades of ultra-top-secret research and experimentation. I can't just loan it out like the keys to my old Subaru!"

"Actually, it wouldn't really be a loan," Helen admitted sheepishly. "Once it leaves, it ain't coming back." Overcoming her apparent embarrassment, she addressed Shannon in all seriousness. "Listen to me. I wouldn't ask this if it wasn't a matter of extreme importance. I can't explain it all to you now, but, believe me, the fate of the entire planet, of every living thing, depends on you helping me steal the DY-100 tonight."

Am I dreaming this? Shannon wondered. The whole thing felt like some sort of crazy nightmare. "Believe you? I don't even know who you are!" She threw up her hands in a paroxysm of emotion. "What do you need me for anyway? Why don't you just whisk the ship away the same way you got in here?"

"I wish!" Helen said, ignoring the bitterness in the younger woman's tone. She peered through the see-through aluminum at the massive spacecraft on the launch pad. "Too much mass, plus way too much high-tech electronic surveillance around here." She shook her head. "I was pushing my luck just to, er, 'whisk' in here tonight."

Helen gave Shannon a sympathetic look, seemingly full of compassion and concern. "Besides, I wouldn't want to swipe the ship without at least talking to you."

"Oh yeah?" Shannon shot back, not buying the other woman's show of consideration. Dire suspicions rushed into her mind. "How do I know this wasn't your plan all along? That you haven't been 'playing' me all these years?"

She snuck a peek at the narcotized guard's revolver, lying not too far away. If she made a sudden grab for it, she might be able to catch Helen unawares. *Maybe it's finally time to come clean with the authorities,* she thought. *The FBI might be very interested to find out Helen's connection to the project.*

Helen fiddled with her paperweight, a crystalline green pyramid, as her eyes entreated Shannon. "I sincerely hoped it would never come to this," she divulged. "And it's not like I'll be completely snatching away all of your hard work and progress. You'll still have all the blueprints and diagrams and such. You can build a new sleeper ship. Heck, you can construct a whole fleet of them if you like." She spoke softly and distinctly, as if getting through to Shannon at this critical moment were all-important. "But that ship out there is needed elsewhere, for a mission that could save this entire planet from a disaster of global proportions."

Windows 95? Shannon thought irrationally. Despite the utter insanity of the very notion, she found her initial anger and skepticism melting away, succumbing, perhaps, to the overwhelming sincerity—and the fear—she sensed in the other woman. It occurred to her, against her better judgment, not to mention every last shred of her common sense, that there would have been no DY-100 without all the priceless scientific hints Helen Swanson had passed on to her over the years. *Wasn't I just thinking the very same thing, back at the party in the conference room?*

"I don't know, Helen," she murmured, wavering.

"Roberta," the blond woman said. "My name is Roberta Lincoln." She shrugged the shoulders of her orange flight suit, as if the revelation was no big deal. "I can't expect you to trust me this far, not unless I trust you, too."

Oddly moved by this disclosure, Shannon gave an only slightly hysterical laugh. "What the hell? I've been a double agent for years now. Why not a starship rustler, too?" She wiped a spontaneous tear from the corner of her eye. "What do you need me to do?"

Helen—no, Roberta—grinned, and Shannon felt

the genuine relief radiating from the other woman, who gestured at the expensive hardware and empty seats all around them. "Congratulations, you're Launch Control."

If Shannon still had her wine, she would have done a spit take into her glass. "Come again?" She wiped a bang of bright red hair from her face. "Now you're really talking crazy. I mean, look at all these stations. You need a whole team to coordinate a launch. One person can't do it alone!"

"You can with the right equipment," Roberta said, giving Shannon a mischievous wink. She laid her crystal pyramid on top of the nearest computer console. "Get hopping."

At first Shannon thought Roberta was addressing her, then she realized the older woman was talking to her paperweight. To her amazement, the miniature pyramid, which was no bigger than a Rubik's Cube, suddenly emitted a cool emerald glow. A second later, all the consoles in the control room came alive at once, their multicolored switches and displays lighting up like Christmas decorations. The hum of two dozen computerized work stations suddenly revving for action was even enough to briefly rouse the tranquilized guard. "Sssh!" he admonished the inconsiderate hardware, managing, if only for a moment, to lift his head from the saliva-covered console. "Tryin' to get some shut-eye . . ."

"Don't worry," Roberta instructed him, gently pushing his head down. "Go back to sleep."

The glowing crystal beeped. "Override protocols engaged," the pyramid announced in an impudent tone. "All relevant programs assimilated."

Apparently, that was just what Roberta wanted to hear. "Resistance is futile," she said with a smirk, as though enjoying a private joke. "Anyway," she informed Shannon, giving the crystal pyramid an affectionate pat. "All of your launch systems are now slaved into this little guy. Just tell him what to do, and trust him to keep an eye on everything else." She paused, making sure she hadn't forgotten anything, then snapped her fingers as one more thought occurred to her. "And, oh yeah, don't be annoyed if he gets a bit snippy with you. Artificial intelligences always seem to come with a touch of attitude."

While Shannon struggled to lift her metaphorical jaw from the floor, Roberta went on to explain the rest of her plan. "Got that?" she asked afterward.

"I think so," Shannon said uncertainly. She'd never aided and abetted a starship heist before. Her shell-shocked gaze drifted over Roberta's bright orange NASA attire. A rectangular plastic name badge identified the blond woman, surreally, as SALLY RIDE. "Is that authentic?" Shannon asked absently. Not that it really mattered . . .

"Nope," Roberta admitted. "Left over from Halloween several years back." She tugged at the insulated orange fabric over her hips. "Thank goodness I can still fit into this thing."

Alone with the sleeping sentry, Shannon watched tensely from the launch gallery as a tiny orange figure ascended to the capsule at the top of the DY-100. A few minutes later, the intercom crackled to life. *"All right, I'm all strapped in,"* Roberta's voice came over the speaker. *"Let's get the show on the road."*

Shannon swallowed hard. "Okay," she said into the launch supervisor's microphone. Too stressed-out to sit down, she paced back and forth in front of the supervisor's station. "The ship was designed to be able to take off with the entire crew, including the pilot, tucked away in suspended animation, so everything is totally automated. In theory, you shouldn't have to do anything at all, just enjoy the ride."

She wasn't sure if she was explaining this for Roberta's benefit or her own. *Probably the latter,* she admitted.

Feeling faintly ridiculous, she addressed the tiny green pyramid. "Initiate pre-launch procedures."

"Acknowledged," the pyramid replied promptly. Shannon heard the whir of specialized equipment responding to her command. *Maybe we can actually pull this off,* she thought, crossing her fingers. Fortunately, the boosters employed nuclear fusion technology so there was no long fueling procedure; the boosters were already filled with an adequate supply of nonvolatile deuterium.

Down below, on the other side of the impervious window, metal arms retracted from the DY-100, which remained upright due to the stabilizing weight of the booster rockets. "Initiating pre-burn sequence," the pyramid informed her. "One minute to lift-off."

Shannon couldn't believe how fast this streamlined countdown was going; the blinky little pyramid was way too efficient as far as her nerves were concerned. She couldn't help remembering that this was, after all, the first launch of an untried, experimental spacecraft—being supervised by a tiny talking piece of crystal! The faces of Gus Grissom, Christa McAuliffe, and the other tragic martyrs of the space program flashed through her mind; she didn't want Roberta to join that distinguished pantheon.

"Attention: Launch Control!" An irate voice blared over the PA system. *"Cease unauthorized operations immediately. That's an order!"*

Shannon groaned, startled but not too surprised by the warning. There was probably no way they could get this close to a lift-off without someone noticing what was going on at S-4. She had a sneaking suspicion that she was hearing, in the stentorian intonations of that cease-and-desist order, the sound of her NASA ambitions going down the tubes.

No turning back now, she thought.

"Attention: This is Dreamland High Command." Shannon visualized the apoplectic face of General Wright, beet-red with fury. *"You are committing an act of high treason. Stand down at once!"*

"Kill the sound," she ordered the pyramid, and the incensed voice fell silent.

Someone was pounding heavily on the door to the control room, which Roberta had thoughtfully welded shut before heading down to the launch pad. "Open up!" Muck shouted, as rifle butts slammed against the reinforced steel door. Shannon kept her gaze glued on the awakening spacecraft below. Plumes of white-hot steam jetted from the tails of the booster rockets. Shannon figured the threat of imminent immolation would keep the base's security forces out of the hangar until the blast-off was terminated, one way or another.

"Open the hangar doors," she instructed.

"Already in process," the pyramid responded, with a bit of that attitude Roberta warned her about.

High above their heads, camouflaged doors slid away, offering Shannon a glimpse of a starry Nevada sky. The automated launch procedures would take the DY-100 beyond Earth's atmosphere before requiring further instructions from Roberta; she wondered where the enigmatic go-between was planning to take the ship next. Mars? Moscow? The Ferengi home-world?

"Thirty seconds to lift-off."

Without warning, the pen in her pocket started vibrating again. By now, though, Shannon was beyond surprises, so she simply plucked the pen, which Roberta had given her years ago, from her pocket and lifted it to her face. "Yes?"

"Thought I'd use our private line," Roberta said via the pen, *"in case anyone was listening in. I just wanted to let you know that I really appreciate all your trust, not just tonight but for the last few years. If you ever want to do this stuff full-time, just give me a ring."*

I may need a new career after this, Shannon thought realistically. "Thanks, but let me think about that." It was an interesting offer, but, deep down inside, she doubted that she really wanted to cope with this much suspense and tension on a regular basis. "Bon voyage," she wished Roberta. "Give my regards to space."

"Will do," the other woman promised.

"Ten seconds to lift-off," the pyramid announced. "Ten, nine, eight, seven . . ."

Shannon counted along, like she was in Times Square on New Year's Eve.

". . . six, five, four, three, two, one . . . Ignition!"

Despite Walter's boasts, she could still hear the roar of the engines through the thick transparent aluminum. Before her awestruck eyes, the DY-100 lifted off its launch pad, ascending into the midnight sky atop an inverted geyser of flame and smoke. One way or another, she realized, her wide brown eyes tracking the rocket's ascent until it flew out of sight, a new era of space exploration had begun.

She just wished she knew, really, who was behind the wheel.

The pounding on the door halted for a breath or two, as even the determined soldiers paused in rapt contemplation of the launch. Then the relentless hammering resumed again, and she saw the door's cast-iron hinges begin to give way.

There was only one more thing to do. Shannon wasn't looking forward to this part, but she knew it had to be done. "Initiate exit protocol," she ordered the pyramid, bracing herself for the tranquilizing energy blast that Roberta had sworn would not harm Shannon permanently. The pyramid would not be so lucky; it was programmed to self-destruct.

"Acknowledged," the obedient gizmo said with a beep.

There was a blinding flash of light and then, for the second time in her life, all her worries went away.

At least for another hour or so.

CHAPTER TWENTY-FIVE

KHAN WATCHED HIS WORLD COME APART ON A dozen different video screens. Multi-tasking was not a challenge for a mind such as his; accepting the ugly truths conveyed by the monitors was almost too painful to endure.

Riots raged on the streets of Chandigarh as his troops battled hordes of angry demonstrators, provoked by the most recent round of arrests and assassinations. Libelous charges of corruption and economic malfeasance, regarding the justifiable diversion of state funds to certain questionable military projects, most notably the now-incinerated base on Muroroa, with its expensive black-market missiles and biological weapons facilities, had forced Khan to jail the entire editorial staff of a popular opposition newspaper, and order the covert executions of any and all suspected whistle-blowers in his administration. Alas, such Draconian measures had only sparked greater unrest among the common people, who unfairly blamed Khan for the wretched inadequacies of their sordid little lives.

Savages! Malcontents! Khan cursed the fickle, ungrateful populace revolting against his rule. *They should have been happy to have been governed, at long last, by a truly superior leader, rather than by one of their own feeble kind. Yet look how they repaid me for my noble efforts to bring peace and order to an unhappy world! Slack-witted imbeciles!*

"Damn you, Chen Tiejun," he muttered bitterly. If not for Chen and her accursed amazons, his flesh-eating bacteria would have already rid the world of the puerile masses now ravening at his very door. Instead he found himself trapped upon a wretched planet overpopulated by inferior, unreasonable beings. *Perhaps,* he thought, *it was time to put the Earth out of its misery?*

Khan slumped against the velvet padding of his seat, gripped by a melancholy of heroic proportions. A simple crimson uniform, free of medals and decorations, suited his mood, while the P226 automatic pistol holstered at his hip provided more comfort and reassurance than any number of crowns, scepters, or fawning courtiers. Unbound and unturbaned, his dark hair fell behind him like a lion's mane, only this lion felt more hunted than hunter at the moment.

His master control room, in the lowest reaches of his palace, had expanded dramatically as security concerns increasingly forced him to take refuge deep beneath the surface, like some joyless Plutonic king condemned to rule eternally over the underworld. Now an entire wall of video screens, monitoring his fortress, his territories, and the world, not necessarily in that order, shared the subterranean chamber with his last and greatest weapon: the targeting controls for Morning Star.

"Your Excellency! Look!" Joaquin, ever faithful, unlike ninety-nine percent of the worthless human race, pointed to a series of monitors keeping watch over the luxurious grounds and ornate rooftops of the palace above. Khan watched, his face immobile, as special forces commandos, in pitch-black night gear, parachuted into the fortress, immediately exchanging fire with what remained, after weeks of resignations and desertions, of Khan's palace guardians. Russian Spetsnaz, Khan guessed, or perhaps Mossad.

Exon warriors, in their proud crimson uniforms and silver sashes, fought as well as Khan might hope, but the relentless Special Operations forces had soon penetrated the palace itself, leading to hand-to-hand combat and scorching firefights amidst the antique tapestries and marble-inlaid walls of Khan's opulent residence. He had no doubt what the foreign commandos' ultimate objective was. Indeed, he had been expecting just such a surprise attack ever since the thermonuclear destruction of his deadly germ-warfare initiative. Apparently, the so-called "legitimate" governments of the world now considered it more dangerous to leave him alone than to confront him. Hence, tonight's clandestine incursion: a search-and-destroy mission aimed at Khan himself.

Warning sirens, belatedly responding to the lightning-fast raid, whooped hysterically. Titanium blast doors slammed into place, sealing off the lower levels from the attack above, at least for a time. "Your Excellency!" Joaquin blurted in alarm. "You're in danger! We must flee!"

Khan dismissed the bodyguard's fervid pleas with an airy wave of his hand. "To where?" he asked fatalistically. "With my fortress violated? My island destroyed?" He shook his head in doleful resignation. "I have been a prince, with power over millions. I will not be reduced to hiding in some squalid, festering rathole, while my enemies place a bounty on my head."

You may my glories and my state depose, he mused darkly, finding bleak solace in the tragic verses of the Bard. *But not my griefs; still am I king of those.*

"Lord Khan!" Suzette Ling came running into the control room, from the radar and tracking station outside. She clutched a crumpled printout in her hand. "We have confirmed reports of American B-52s en route from Pakistan. We believe they intend to bomb the fortress!"

Khan laughed out loud, the sheer accumulation of disaster providing morbid amusement. "Bombs and commandos both?" he asked rhetorically, feeling almost flattered by the degree of overkill implied. *Is this a coordinated international effort,* he wondered, *or does the Russian bear not know what the American eagle is up to?*

It mattered little. Even if he managed to repel these twin onslaughts, and quell the bloody rioting in the streets as well, that would not bring an end to the murderous attacks upon his realm and person. The world's leaders now knew of his ambition to purge the world of its superfluous billions; they would not rest until he was dead or captured, his power broken beyond repair.

The dream is over, he realized. Now all that remained was retaliation. "My sentence is for open war," he murmured angrily, abandoning Shakespeare in favor of the more satanic poetry of Milton, "which if not victory is yet revenge."

The world would pay dearly for thwarting his destiny.

Ament glided into the control room, her gentle tread as light as ever. Amber eyes rapidly took in the multifarious conflicts displayed upon the flickering panoply of video screens. "Lord Khan," she addressed him forcefully. "Perhaps it is not too late to negotiate a peaceful resolution to the present crisis. You can still contact the American president, persuade him to call off his bombers." In keeping with the severity of the occasion, she wore a simple indigo sari that fell past her ankles. Her long black hair, similarly unadorned, hung straight down her back. "For the sake of your soldiers and subjects, if not for yourself, do not let your exalted reign end in nothing but fire and blood."

Khan rose imperiously from his seat before the monitors, his eyes narrowing in disdain as he confronted the peace-loving Egyptian counselor. "I should have known you would suggest as much," he said coldly. How dare she recommend that he humble himself before his enemies! After all these years, did she know him not at all? His forbidding gaze swept the faces surrounding him. Steadfast Joaquin, anxious Ling, inscrutable Ament, all looking to him for a deliverance, and a happy ending it was not within his power to deliver.

"Out! Out, all of you!" The ire and frustration of years exploded within him and he banished them all with a sweeping wave of his arm. "I would be alone with my thoughts."

Ling retreated quickly before his wrath, but the senior members of his court were not so easily dismissed. "But, Your Excellency—!" Joaquin protested. His stricken expression betrayed his despair at the thought of leaving Khan unprotected at such a time.

Such stalwart devotion touched Khan, despite the fury in his heart. "Simply wait outside," he instructed the worried bodyguard, his tone softening for a moment. "I will be safe with you at the door."

Mollified to a degree, Joaquin left the chamber at last. Ament, however, showed no sign of departing.

"Did you not hear?" he asked her brusquely. "I desire solitude."

"For what purpose, my lord?" Her gaze shifted knowingly from Khan to the control station for Morning Star, only a few paces away. "Forgive my bluntness, Lord Khan, but I do not think it wise to leave you alone in this place, not in your present state of mind."

You think you know me, do you? Khan smirked cruelly. Perhaps it might be amusing to show her just how little she truly understood of the Machiavellian workings of his mind. "Very well," he said curtly. "Perhaps it was a mistake on my part to shield you from the harshest necessities of power." He strode with confidence over to the computer governing Morning Star. The lighted display tracked the killer satellite's steady procession over the rectangular map of the world. "Watch and learn, my lady."

His hands clasped behind his back, he spoke crisply to the machine. "Morning Star, begin targeting sequence. Command authorization: Hammurabi-1792."

Sophisticated voice recognition software was yet another recent improvement to the control room's capabilities. For surety's sake, the computer was programmed to respond only to select code words, known exclusively by Khan, and only if those codes were delivered by Khan's own voice.

"Command authorization approved," the machinery responded in Punjabi. Disk drives whirred in obeisance. "Please select target."

Ament looked more alarmed than he had ever seen her. "My lord!" she exclaimed, stepping hurriedly toward the satellite controls. "Please, in the name of sanity, do not do this thing."

Khan ignored her entreaty, as, indeed, he had been ignoring her counsel for some time. "Global targeting," he specified. "Gomorrah scenario."

This, as its name implied, was Morning Star's most apocalyptic option, spelling the total destruction of Earth's entire ozone layer. On the illuminated map, a bloody crimson tint spread over continents and oceans alike, condemning the whole of the planet to the killer satellite's unchecked depredations. "Target selected," the computer confirmed impassively. "Moving into position."

On the global display, Morning Star, now symbolized by a flashing yellow dot, adjusted its orbit to zero in on the North Pole, where Earth's magnetic field was strongest. From there, it could begin the process of stripping away the planet's first line of defense against ultraviolet rays. "Arming satellite," the computer announced. "Ten minutes until Gomorrah position."

"No!" This was obviously too short a countdown as far as Ament was concerned. Squeezing between Khan and the satellite controls, she shouted decisively at the computer. "Morning Star, halt targeting sequence. Command override: Bubastis."

She glanced back at Khan over her shoulder. "My apologies, Lord Khan," she said with what sounded like genuine sorrow, "but I cannot permit this."

"Command override rejected," the computer stated flatly. "Nine minutes until Gomorrah."

The look of shocked chagrin that appeared on her lovely face pleased Khan even more than he had anticipated. "What?" she blurted, her distraught gaze swinging from the recalcitrant computer to Khan himself. "I do not understand—"

"Really, my lady?" Khan gloated, *tsk-tsk*ing her in his most patronizing tone. "Did you truly believe that I would not discover your presumptuous installation of an emergency override command in Morning Star's programming, implanted, I believe, when I was lost at sea in the Adriatic, and thus temporarily out of touch with Chandigarh?" Taking hold of her shoulders with both hands, he effortlessly moved her away from the satellite controls. "I stumbled onto your perfidy shortly after my return from Europe, and changed the command codes, granting me sole control of Morning Star."

Unrepentant, Ament tried once more to avert the coming apocalypse. "Command authorization Hammurabi-1792," she called out, parroting Khan's code phrase from moments before. "Halt targeting sequence."

The computer was not impressed. "Termination command rejected. Eight minutes to Gomorrah."

Khan shook his head disparagingly. "No use, my lady. Once the Gomorrah scenario has been initiated, it can be halted solely by a second code phrase, which I alone have knowledge of."

"Please, Khan," Ament pleaded, dispensing with any honorifics, "why not accept defeat gracefully? Do not make the entire world suffer for your crushed ambitions."

Khan responded by citing Milton to her, spitting out Lucifer's immortal words with rancorous passion:

> "What though the field be lost?
> All is not lost; th' unconquerable will,
> And study of revenge, immortal hate,
> And courage never to submit or yield."

Cutting off his soliloquy, he sneered at Ament with sardonic amusement. "Resign yourself to the facts, O lady of little faith or fidelity. Within minutes, Morning Star will herald the beginning of the end for the corrupt and venal human race, and nothing you can say will dissuade me from this course."

"Then perhaps you will listen to me," a new voice interrupted.

Khan looked away from Ament in surprise, just in time to hear a familiar electronic hum coming from right outside the control room, where Joaquin stood watch. A moment later, a lean old man in a dark suit strolled into the futuristic-looking chamber. Sparks leaped between the twin antennae of his servo, while vaporous tendrils of blue plasma swirled about his ankles, wafting in from the radar and tracking room beyond.

"Hello, Khan," Gary Seven said. "We need to talk."

Instinctively, Khan reached for his P226, drawing the Swiss-made handgun with preternatural speed. "Stay back," he warned Seven menacingly. In theory, there should have been nothing the meddling American could do to derail Gomorrah, but Khan was not inclined to take chances where Seven was concerned. "Do not come any closer."

Nodding in acknowledgment, the older man deactivated his servo and laid the silver instrument down on a convenient countertop, adjacent to the open doorway. "I am not here to do battle," he explained in calm, measured tones. He remained where he was standing, slowly raising his hands to display empty palms. "As I said, I just want to speak to you. One last time."

Sensing sincerity in the man's word, Khan felt less threatened by Seven's sudden appearance. He had the advantage, after all, as long as he retained sole control of Morning Star; even if Khan was somehow incapacitated, Seven could not halt the satellite's doomsday directive without the necessary code phrase. Like Ament, Khan realized, Seven could do little more than make a futile appeal to the vengeful superman's unheeding conscience. A pointless exercise, in Khan's judgment; it had been many years since Seven's words had held any influence over him.

Let him talk until senility sets in, Khan thought scornfully. *It will avail him nothing.* Although he declined to lower his gun, Khan relaxed enough to take stock of his unexpected visitor. With the Lincoln woman carrying out Seven's manipulative agenda by proxy, it had been a long time since Khan had actually beheld his onetime mentor in the flesh.

Seven's short, neatly trimmed hair was entirely silver now, while the lines of his craggy face had grown deeper and more severe with age. His intellect and vitality, however, appeared undimmed by the passage of time. Khan saw enduring cunning and purpose in the American's cool gray eyes, while his erect bearing betrayed little trace of infirmity.

For a second, it struck Khan that there was something he could not quite place missing from the man's appearance, then he realized what he had been unconsciously looking for. *The ubiquitous black feline,* Khan recalled, noting the animal's conspicuous absence. No doubt Seven's four-legged familiar had long since gone to its eternal reward. . . .

"The years have been kind to you," Khan granted magnanimously, his P226 aimed squarely at the other man's breast. He dipped his head slightly in salute, while not letting his gaze leave the enigmatic old spymaster for a heartbeat.

"And you, Khan," Seven replied in turn. His eyes grimly surveyed the humming, blinking hardware filling the control room, lingering at last on the mounted map of the world, now rendered incarnadine by Morning Star's targeting processors. "Although I regret that we must conduct this reunion under such ominous circumstances."

"Eight minutes to Gomorrah," the computer reported, oblivious to the tense encounter in the control room. Khan was gratified to see a flicker of apprehension cross over Seven's bony face at the automated announcement. *How does it feel,* he wondered mercilessly, *to see all that you have worked for come to ruin?*

"I confess I am curious about how you managed this timely visit," Khan admitted, glancing briefly at Seven's feet. At this point, the last wisps of the ectoplasmic blue fog had dissipated entirely into the climate-controlled atmosphere of this subterranean level. He tilted his head quizzically. "My force field?"

To his surprise, Ament supplied the explanation. "I lowered the shields, Khan," she said simply. Stung by her betrayal, he turned to berate her—but the elegant Egyptian woman was no longer there. In her place was a sleek black cat with gleaming amber eyes.

Her ebon fur glossy and impeccably groomed, the impossible feline meowed once before leaping into Seven's arms. "Hello, doll," he addressed her fondly. "I've missed you, too."

Eyes and mouth agape, Khan stared at the cat in unalloyed astonishment. An ancient memory, long neglected, intruded into his consciousness: of that final night at Chrysalis, over two decades ago, when a much younger Khan, no more than four years old, had seen the same black cat transform into an exotically beautiful woman. *I had thought that but a dream,* he marveled, *a childish fantasy born of the trauma and confusion of that fateful evacuation.*

"Can this be true?" he murmured. Had so fantastical a creature truly been working beside him, under his very nose, for all these years?

"For shame, Khan," Seven chided him, stroking the head of the purring feline cradled in his arms. "The name, Ament, means 'hidden goddess,' and is just one of many alternative names for the Egyptian goddess, Isis." He and the cat enjoyed a joke at Khan's expense. "She's been hiding in plain sight for quite some time."

Khan's mighty brain raced to keep pace with these startling revelations. "But—I had thought her one of my own kind, another child of Chrysalis?"

"That's what you were meant to believe," Seven explained. "After you surprised me in Moscow several years ago, I realized that you might someday attempt to round up the rest of your scattered, superhuman siblings. Consequently, I deliberately added the false identity of Ament to the Beta 5's database on the Chrysalis Project, just in case you ever succeeded in appropriating that information, as indeed you did." Reaching into his pocket, he offered the cat a special treat of some sort. "When you 'recruited' Ament shortly thereafter, you provided me with a valuable informant inside your inner circle."

"I see," Khan said venomously. As he gradually recovered from the mind-jarring shock of Ament's miraculous transformation, other mysteries became clear at long last. He suddenly realized who had helped Roberta Lincoln escape from Chrysalis Island four years ago, who had alerted Seven to Khan's plan to attack Dubrovnik by submarine, and even how Chen Tiejun had learned about his precious stockpile of flesh-eating bacteria. *Yes,* he thought, with growing resentment, *many things make sense now.*

"O tiger's heart wrapped in a woman's hide!" he hissed, glaring balefully at the treacherous feline. "But why play this card so late in the game?" he asked Seven. "Why wait until now to have your Trojan horse"—Isis squawked in protest at the equine allusion—"bring down my fortress walls?"

Seven held on to the cat protectively, lest Khan succumb to an entirely understandable desire to wring the duplicitous beast's neck. "In matters of espionage," he elaborated, "it is often necessary to sacrifice temporary advantages to preserve a long-term asset. 'Ament' was my ace in the hole, held in reserve all this time to provide me with constant intelligence on your activities. There was also the hope," he added ruefully, "that she might be able to steer your unquestioned brilliance toward more constructive ends."

He regarded Morning Star, blinking its way toward the Arctic Circle, with a look of resigned disappointment. "Now, though," Seven allowed, "with the fate of billions at stake, the time had clearly come to use every resource at our disposal, in order to prevent you from making one of the most calamitous mistakes in the history of the human race."

Khan found Seven's hectoring tone galling in the extreme. "My apologies for not living up to your exalted standards," Khan sneered, "but I fear your priceless words of wisdom come a trifle too late." With his free hand, he addressed Seven's attention to the encrimsoned map, its tainted coloring bearing testament to the dire fate awaiting all mankind. "I will have my vengeance, regardless of anything you can do or say."

"Five minutes to Gomorrah," the computer stated, seconding Khan's sanguinary assessment of the situation. *The phyloplankton will perish first,* Khan surmised, wiping out the marine food chain at its base. Then would come the crop failures, and the cancers, until, finally, the unchecked ultraviolet rays began to break down proteins and DNA on a molecular level. . . .

Seven persisted in the face of Khan's defiance. "What if I could offer you a better alternative?" he asked emphatically, too intent on reaching Khan to continue stroking his remarkable cat. "A more attractive destiny?"

"Such as?" Khan asked dubiously.

Seven gestured toward the wall of video screens, where even now scenes of turmoil and violence predominated. Spetsnaz commandos, wielding Russian AK-47 assault rifles, fought their way through the fierce resistance of several dozen remaining Exon warriors, while beyond the sandstone walls of the fortress, rioting protesters clashed with Khan's personal police force. Khan saw his once-proud flag, with its silver moon and golden sun, torn apart and set aflame by an angry mob. "With your permission?" Seven asked, tactfully refraining from commenting on the televised pandemonium.

"By all means," Khan said, an edge in his voice contradicting the graciousness of his words. "But do not attempt anything clever or foolishly heroic."

"Let's hope that won't be necessary," Seven answered. With exaggerated caution, he lifted his servo from the countertop and aimed it at the stacked video screens. The slender device hummed briefly, and the disparate scenes of chaos and conflict were replaced by a single image, appearing on every one of the multitudinous monitors: a cylindrical space vessel drifting in orbit somewhere high above the Earth. The ship, which somewhat resembled a submarine, complete with a finlike conning tower, was unfamiliar to Khan, who had not known of any such spacecraft in the works.

"The DY-100," Seven offered by way of introduction. "Until recently, a top-secret creation of the United States of America, but now available to you, under certain conditions." He looked over at Khan to see if he had the other man's attention. "Are you familiar with the concept of a sleeper ship?"

Khan nodded, his gaze glued to the astounding image on the monitors. "I know the theory, but do you mean to say that such a vessel actually exists?"

"You're looking at it right now," Seven assured him. He put down his servo again so as to allay Khan's worries in that direction.

Nonetheless, Khan suspected trickery. "How do I know this vessel actually exists, and is not simply an illusion created by special effects." He peered at Seven with great distrust. "You can hardly expect me to throw away my rightful vengeance for a few minutes of footage from some forgettable piece of science fiction."

Seven indicated the radar and tracking station just outside. "You can certainly verify the ship's presence overhead once I give your people the appropriate coordinates, but, for the sake of argument, consider this: what if I gave you the DY-100 in exchange for your promise to leave Earth's ozone layer intact?"

"Three minutes to Gomorrah," the computer alerted them, adding extra urgency to Seven's last-minute negotiations.

"You have a choice, Khan," he insisted. "You can go down in flames, taking the entire world with you,

or you and your people can make a new life for your-
selves somewhere beyond this solar system." He
placed Isis at his feet, the better to concentrate on
convincing the skeptical younger man. "Think of it,
Khan: the challenge of conquering an alien world, of
forging a new civilization where no man or superman
has gone before. You could be a new Columbus,
found a new dynasty light-years from Earth."

Khan did not know what to think. It all seemed so
unbelievable and yet . . . He considered the secretive
old man and his unnatural pet. Was what Seven offered
any more implausible than a luminous blue fog that
bent time and space, and a beautiful woman who could
transform into a cat at will? "I do not know," he conceded. "Your proposal is intriguing, but I am unsure."

"One minute until Gomorrah."

"Choose wisely, Khan." Seven spelled out his options bluntly. "An ignominious death in a bunker, the
useless slaughter of your most faithful followers, and
eternal infamy as the man who inflicted generations
of suffering upon the planet, or a chance to plant
your seed on a fresh and untamed world of your
own?"

"Thirty seconds to Gomorrah." On the map, the
flashing yellow blip turned the same pestilential
shade of red as the rest of the world. After shielding
Earth's fragile creatures for over six hundred million
years, the ozone layer faced oblivion.

Khan considered his alternatives. What, truly, did
he have to lose, save for the malignant pleasures of
revenge. He thought of Joaquin, and Suzette Ling,
Vishwa Patil, Liam MacPherson, and all the rest of
his loyal subjects, who would surely battle to the

death on his behalf. Perhaps he owed them, and the noble dream of Chrysalis, something better than a final bloody massacre?

"Morning Star, halt targeting sequence. Terminate Gomorrah scenario. Command authorization: Caesar-44BC." He walked away from the satellite controls and pocketed Seven's discarded servo. His wary eyes promised immediate retribution should Seven prove to be deceiving him.

"Tell me more about this ship," he commanded.

CHAPTER TWENTY-SIX

THE SHIP WAS ALL SEVEN HAD PROMISED: A MARVEL of futuristic technology and design. As an engineer, Khan wanted to take the ship apart to see how it worked. As a sovereign-in-exile, he pronounced it satisfactory.

"Excellent," he declared, looking about him. The habitation decks of the sleeper ship were surprisingly roomy for a spacecraft, perhaps as a precaution against claustrophobia during boarding and disembarking. Blue steel bulkheads, constructed of a durable alloy that Khan did not immediately recognize, offered sturdy protection from the airless void outside, so that the dreams of the ship's slumbering passengers would not be troubled by fears of structural collapse or minor meteorite collisions. The built-in hibernation niches were paired two by two, bunk bed style, which made Khan feel rather more like Noah than Columbus, although this ark was mercifully free of yowling livestock; according to Seven, all of the ship's ample provisions, transported aboard in preparation for the coming voyage, were conveniently nonanimate.

"Quite spectacular," Liam MacPherson confirmed, his eyes aglow with excitement. The red-haired astrophysicist could barely contain his enthusiasm for the DY-100. "The technology is generations ahead of every other spacecraft in development."

With Khan's consent, Seven had transported the cream of Khan's followers, some eighty-three supermen and women, aboard the orbiting starship, its total capacity. Limited to only seven dozen niches, including his own, Khan had been forced to make some difficult choices; ultimately he had practiced a brutal form of triage, leaving the most seriously wounded of his Exon fighters behind, so that he could begin rebuilding with the fittest and least damaged of his loyalists. The sexual ratio, alas, was less than ideal, with 55 men to 31 women, promising a certain amount of strife down the road. *Nothing I cannot deal with when the time comes,* Khan decided confidently.

"So, the ship still needs a name," Roberta Lincoln pointed out. Khan had been less than surprised to find the American woman already aboard the DY-100 when he and Seven had first teleported aboard. Ironically, she was clad in the same imitation NASA flight suit she'd been wearing on that Halloween night in 1984, when Khan first visited Seven's original office in New York. "Any thoughts?" she asked Khan.

A name, Khan pondered. It should be something

appropriate, conveying both the gravity of his exile from Earth as well as his grand aspirations for the future. *The Phoenix? The Ark?* No, those were too obvious. *The Mayflower?*

He wandered over to the primary computer station, a bulky transistorized console built into the bulkhead not far from the empty sepulcher Khan had chosen for himself. According to the navigational scanner, the unchristened ship was currently orbiting the Earth over one thousand kilometers above the continent of Australia. A landing monitor showed him the magnified contours of the Gold Coast and Botany Bay.

The latter, he recalled, was the site of Australia's first European settlement: a British penal colony, peopled by transported convicts, that eventually led to the conquest of the entire continent. *An omen of sorts?* Khan wondered, impulsively arriving at a decision.

"The *S.S. Botany Bay,*" he informed Roberta, who promptly entered the name into the ship's computer. Almost immediately, liquid-crystal display panels flaunted the DY-100's new designation throughout the ship and upon its outer hull. "A fitting name," Khan observed, pleased with his choice, "foretelling both struggle and triumph."

"Indeed," Seven agreed, as he escorted MacPherson over to his designated niche and prepared him for cold storage. The aged American was busily supervising the disposition of the ship's passengers, saving Khan and (at the bodyguard's insistence) Joaquin for last. The crowded hibernation deck gradually thinned out as his people took their places in the niches, so that the chamber soon resembled a space-age catacomb, packed with living corpses. Lighted indicators, positioned above the upper left-hand corner of each niche, revealed which cavities were now occupied. One by one, each light came on.

Khan found himself deeply moved by the faith in his leadership that these courageous men and women had so unequivocally demonstrated, accepting this outlandish new enterprise with nary a complaint or qualm. Their loyalty alone convinced him that he had made the correct decision in accepting Seven's offer. *Such superior beings should not be wasted in a Pyrrhic orgy of revenge,* he resolved. *I shall see to it that their faith is rewarded one-thousandfold in my empire to come.*

After seeing to MacPherson, Gary Seven joined Khan by the computer station. "I have programmed the ship to carry you and your people to an uninhabited solar system roughly 100 light-years from Earth. At full impulse power, just below lightspeed, the journey should take a little over a century, while all of you remain in a state of suspended animation."

Khan did not bother asking Seven how he knew this solar system to be uninhabited; what was one more mystery amidst the constellation of enigmas surrounding the shadowy older man and his secrets? He could not help being daunted, however, at the prospect of so protracted a voyage. "Over one hundred years," he repeated in awe, "more than a lifetime, spent in frozen slumber!"

"I must warn you, Khan," Seven added, his somber expression growing graver still, "that this trip is not without dangers. The DY-100—excuse me, the *Botany Bay*—is an experimental spacecraft after all, so

I cannot guarantee that it will not malfunction in some way. In addition, space itself is full of hazards: asteroids, radiation, space–time anomalies, and so on. There is a very real chance that this journey could end in disaster."

Khan waved away Seven's warnings. "It has been said that to conquer without risk is to triumph without glory." He shrugged nonchalantly; with his course now set, he saw little point in dwelling on worst-case scenarios. "I do not fear the unknown. I welcome it."

"An attitude that may serve you well," Seven granted, no doubt relieved that Khan took his warnings as philosophically as he did. "In any event, I have also programmed the computer to wake you first should there be any manner of emergency."

"That is as it should be," Khan approved. He inspected once more the intricate garment, constructed of fine golden mesh, that Seven had provided Khan and his fellow emigrants; according to Seven, the delicate fibers were designed to monitor the passengers' vital functions as they slept. The gilded raiment clung tightly to his body, feeling cold and metallic against his skin.

"Now then," Seven reminded Khan, "it is time to complete your side of the bargain." He rested his fingers upon a keyboard attached to the communications terminal. Isis, apparently content to remain in feline form after her lengthy undercover assignment, curled atop a heat-conduction pipe running along a nearby bulkhead. "The self-destruct codes for Morning Star?"

Khan nodded in assent. "It is a two-step process," he began, resolved to honor his pact with Seven.

"First, I must deactivate the force field protecting the satellite, then I can transmit the self-destruct directive." He gestured for Seven to step aside from the keyboard. "If you will permit me?"

Seven turned over the terminal to Khan. After contacting Morning Star via the correct frequency, Khan commenced to key in the encrypted command to shut down the force field, which, ironically, was based on technology he had pilfered from none other than Seven and Roberta. *Strange are the twists of fate,* Khan thought.

"No, Your Excellency!" Aghast, Joaquin cried out to Khan before he could input the final self-destruct code. "Do not cooperate with these saboteurs and traitors!" Clenching his fists, he glowered murderously at Seven. "We should seize control of this vessel and return to Earth!"

The bodyguard's outburst did not surprise Khan. Joaquin had been in a sullen mood ever since he had recovered from Seven's tranquilizer beam. That the older man had managed to surprise him back in the sub-basements of the palace understandably disturbed Joaquin, who was also openly suspicious of everything connected with the *Botany Bay* and its proposed voyage; unlike Khan and the rest of the passengers, he had not yet donned his own gold-mesh outfit, currently lying rejected and ignored within an empty hibernation niche. The ferocious bear's head upon the bodyguard's customized brass belt buckle seemed to match Joaquin's belligerent attitude.

"Return?" Khan echoed, mere seconds away from ordering Morning Star to self-destruct. "To a planet that fervently wishes us dead and buried?" This, he knew, was no longer an option; news reports from the planet below, monitored from the *Botany Bay*, confirmed that his fortress in Chandigarh had already been reduced to rubble by the American bombers. *Does the world already think me dead?* he wondered. *Doubtless, the world's leaders will claim that their bombs ended my life, rather than admit that I escaped their wrath.*

"Do not trouble yourself, my old friend," he said gently, sparing a moment to reassure Joaquin. With the press of a button, he sent the coded transmission that ended the threat of Morning Star forever. "Accept my wisdom in this."

"Yeah, Lenny," Roberta Lincoln added mockingly. "Go find yourself some rabbits to play with." She snatched up Joaquin's discarded golden outfit and thrust the wad of glittering fabric at the bodyguard's brawny chest. "Better yet, hurry up and get dressed for beddie-bye."

Foolishly, the insolent blonde turned her back on Joaquin as she walked beneath a metal archway toward Seven. Khan watched with interest, his adamantine face betraying nothing, as Joaquin drew forth the serrated throwing knife concealed in his ursine belt buckle. Gary Seven, preoccupied with monitoring Morning Star's disintegration via the scanners at the computer station, did not notice Joaquin raising his knife to throw it straight at the unsuspecting woman's back. Khan held his tongue, remembering the many times the Lincoln woman had been a particularly irritating thorn in his side. After all, he could always disavow any knowledge of Joaquin's intentions later on. . . .

The outraged bodyguard drew back his blade.

"Roberta! Beware!"

One moment, an alert black cat sat curled atop a comfortably heated conduit. The next, a glamorous dark-haired woman threw herself between Roberta and her would-be assassin.

Snarling, Joaquin hurled his knife anyway. The blade flashed across the deck of the starship, lodging between the catwoman's breasts. Roberta spun and stunned Joaquin with her servo, but it was too late for Isis/Ament, who crumpled to the floor.

Seven and Roberta both rushed to their companion's side. Seven, his aged bones moving with remarkable speed, knelt beside the wounded woman, while Roberta scanned her raven-haired counterpart with the tip of her servo. The older woman shook her head sadly, even as Ament looked up at them both and purred her last words: "What? Not curiosity after all?"

A heartbeat later, the still form of a small black cat lay lifelessly upon the floor of the hibernation deck, the brass hilt of a knife protruding from its velvety chest.

"No!" Seven uttered, his voice hoarse with grief and anger. He yanked the killing blade free from the cat's remains, then smashed the knife against the steel floor, shattering the bloodstained blade in an impressive display of strength. "I'm sorry, doll," he murmured. "You deserved so much better than this."

Roberta looked speculatively at the nearest empty hibernation niche, intended for Joaquin himself. Seven shook his head. "Even if she could somehow be revived," he explained mournfully, slowly rising to his feet, "she would be waking, wounded and at the mercy of her enemies, into an unknown situation and environment. We would be doing her no favor by trapping her spirit in expectation of such a dire resurrection."

His blazing eyes focused on Joaquin, now slumping in a narcotized state against one of the ship's sturdy bulkheads. Khan was curious to see whether Seven would compromise his vaunted principles long enough to exact bloody vengeance on the insensate bodyguard. "His life, of course, is yours," Khan volunteered, unwilling to scuttle his pact with Seven, even to save Joaquin from the consequences of his rash attack upon Roberta.

Seven glared at Joaquin for a long moment, while Roberta looked on apprehensively. Then he whirled around and marched toward Khan, his lean and angular face angrier than Khan had ever seen it. "Damn you, Khan!" he raged, venting his frustrated rage. "Does no one's life mean anything to you?"

Khan looked coldly at the feline corpse on the floor. "Do not expect me to mourn one who betrayed me," he informed Seven bluntly. "It is perhaps simple justice. Twenty-two years ago, you and your operatives were responsible for the death of my mother; now my servant has cost you your shapechanging familiar."

"Your mother's death was her own doing," Seven shot back. His fists were clenched tightly at his sides as he struggled visibly to rein in the bitter hatred seething in his veins. "But right now, part of me is wishing that I had let you and all of your power-mad siblings be exterminated at Chrysalis years ago."

Empty words, Khan thought. Now that it was apparent that Seven could not be tempted to murder, no matter what the provocation, Khan found himself growing bored with the encounter. "No matter," he declared haughtily, turning his back on Seven and walking away. "Let us conclude this transaction with all deliberate speed."

If nothing else, Seven and Roberta were now understandably anxious to depart the *Botany Bay,* so the final arrangements were conducted swiftly and with little discussion. Khan himself prepped Joaquin for hibernation and single-handedly installed the massive bodyguard within his niche. A rectangular hatch closed over the recess, sealing Joaquin in for long decades to come. A transparent window afforded a glimpse of the slumbering superman, lying supine like a mummy in its crypt. "Sleep well, my friend," Khan whispered. "When we wake, we shall have a new world to win."

Then, without ceremony or trepidation, Khan climbed onto the metal shelf protruding from the bottom of his own niche. He stretched out on his back, feeling the hard, uncushioned surface of the shelf beneath him, with only his unbound dark hair providing any padding for his skull. "You may proceed," he instructed Gary Seven, not deigning to glance in the aged American's direction.

Hidden conveyors retracted the shelf, drawing Khan into the waiting cavity. His chin held high, he looked straight ahead at the illuminated ceiling of the nook, less than ten centimeters away from his face.

"Farewell, Khan Noonien Singh," Seven addressed him from just outside the niche. His voice still held a bitter ring. "May you make better use of your second life."

Khan sneered in reply, unmoved by the old man's

typically self-righteous leave-taking. *I answer to no judgment but my own,* he thought. The hiss of hidden hydraulics sounded in his ears as the hatch rose, cutting him off from both Seven and his peroxided amanuensis. The two Americans, he knew, planned to transport back to Earth once they were certain that neither Khan nor any of his underlings were capable of turning the *Botany Bay* back toward Earth. They would exit as they arrived, leaving the computerized sleeper ship to begin its epic pilgrimage across the stars.

For himself, Khan had no regrets about abandoning the world that had rejected him. Even with Morning Star destroyed, he doubted that the planet Earth would survive long without him. Inferior humanity would surely destroy themselves of their own accord, without his having to raise a hand. *My curse upon them all . . . !*

Frigid gases filled the niche. Khan took a deep breath, in preparation for the sleep to come. As a chilling numbness spread over him, slowing his thoughts as well as the beat of his magnificent heart, he looked forward to conquering a lush and virgin planet . . . someday.

'Tis not too late, he mused, recalling the immortal words of Tennyson's Ulysses, *to seek a newer world . . .*

To strive, to seek, to find . . .

And not to yield.

CHAPTER TWENTY-SEVEN

"YOU CAN COME IN NOW, SHANNON."

A somber Jeffrey Carlson let her into his office, then closed the door behind her. Moving slowly even for a man his age, as if he weren't at all looking forward to this meeting, he sat down behind his cluttered mahogany desk, opposite Shannon. A scale model of the DY-100, the only version of the ship still remaining at the base, sat atop the desk, reminding them both of exactly why they were here. Removing his bifocals, he rubbed his aged eyes wearily before addressing Shannon again. "Thank you for dropping by," he said softly, sounding uncertain how to begin.

It wasn't like she had a whole lot of choice. For the past two weeks, ever since the spectacular departure of the prototype, Shannon had been under house arrest, confined to her own quarters at Area 51 while an intensive investigation had been conducted into the startling and mysterious events of January 5. She had endured numerous debriefings, trying to cooperate as much as possible while clinging to the cover story she and Roberta had concocted, all the while wondering what sort of consequences she was ultimately going to face. *Guess I'm about to find out,* she speculated.

"No problem," she said meekly. Most of all, she regretted all the grief and upset she had caused Doc Carlson and the rest of the DY-100 development team. Kept in isolation, she hadn't even had a chance to talk to Shaun and the others about what had happened, not that she could really tell them all that much. *It's been two weeks,* she reflected, *and the world hasn't come to an end. Does that mean that it was all worthwhile?*

"I don't need to tell you what the last couple of weeks have been like," Carlson continued, smiling wanly. "You have no idea how tempted I've been to start smoking again." He spoke gently, making an obvious effort to put her at ease. "Thank you for your patience while everything was being sorted out. I'm sure you've been concerned about what all this means to your future."

If I even still have one, Shannon thought bleakly. She half-expected to spend the rest of her life in solitary confinement somewhere. Antarctica maybe, or the moon.

Carlson's wrinkled face took on a more serious expression. "Before I inform you of the final decision resulting from our investigation, I feel obliged to ask you one last time: Are you still standing by your original story, that you were the victim of insidious Ferengi mind-control?"

Shannon nodded, feeling bad about lying to Doc Carlson, of all people. "It's the only explanation that makes sense," she dissembled once more, for the umpteenth time; at this point she practically believed the fabrication herself. "The last thing I remember is being in the conference room with the rest of you, then suddenly feeling an irresistible psychic compulsion to go to the launch bay. After that everything is a blank; the next I knew, I was waking up in the infirmary, with about a half-dozen armed MPs watching over me."

That much was true. True to Roberta's word, she had recovered from the stun-blast with no ill effects, except, perhaps, to her reputation and career.

"I see," Carlson said thoughtfully. Shannon couldn't tell if he believed her or not. "Fortunately for you, there is no hard evidence to contradict that interpretation of events. All videotapes and audio recordings from that evening were apparently erased by the same electromagnetic pulse that rendered you unconscious."

Thank you, little green pyramid, Shannon thought gratefully. As far as she knew, no trace of the crystalline gadget had survived its self-destruction.

"Nevertheless, a multi-billion dollar, top-secret spacecraft has gone missing, and I'm afraid that someone has to take the fall." Carlson offered her a sympathetic look that belied the severity of his words. "If it's any consolation, General Wright and most of the Air Force brass wanted to lock you up and throw away the key, regardless of the lack of evidence, but, not without some effort, I managed to talk them into a slightly less drastic decision."

Taking a deep breath, he launched reluctantly into the disciplinary phase of the meeting. "As of this moment, all of your security clearances are officially revoked. You are no longer employed at this base, and your career at NASA is over as well." He slid a clipboard, bearing a densely typed piece of paper, across the desktop. "By signing this document, you agree never to discuss any of your work at Area 51, on pain of criminal prosecution."

Shannon felt numb all over. Even though she knew this outcome was the best she could hope for—probably better, in fact—it still came as a blow. Years of hard work and personal progress, along with all her childhood dreams of going into space, evaporated forever. With a lump in her throat the size of a Viking space probe, she signed the confidentiality form without even reading the fine print. Ironically, she used the same shiny silver fountain pen that had gotten her into all this trouble; despite the recent investigation, nobody had ever guessed that it was more than just a fancy writing implement.

"Thank you, Dr. Carlson," she said, sliding the signed form back to him. Her voice, which was notably husky at the best of times, was rendered even hoarser by the powerful emotions surging through her. "I want you to know that I appreciate everything you've done on my behalf, both before and after the Incident. It's been a privilege to work with you."

Unsure whether her rubbery limbs would support her, Shannon stood up and headed toward the door.

"Please give my regards to Shaun and the others. Tell them I'm sorry that things turned out the way they did."

"Shannon, wait." Carlson rose and gestured toward the chair she had just exited. "There's something else I want to say, off the record." He waited for her to sit down again, then took a deep breath before speaking. "I'm not sure I'll ever really know why you did what you did, but I may understand a bit more than you might imagine. You see, I know that sometimes simple humanity, and our own private consciences, have to take precedence over the demands of science and so-called national security." He lowered his voice to a conspiratorial whisper. "How do you think Quark and the other Roswell aliens escaped in the first place?"

Shannon's eyes widened. "You?"

"Don't give me that old 'Ferengi mind-control' alibi," he told her with a knowing grin. "I invented the Ferengi mind-control alibi.

"Or, to be more exact, my wife did."

A black stealth helicopter was waiting to take her away from Area 51. Still reeling from Doc Carlson's unexpected confession, she trudged across the tarmac, bearing a small cardboard box full of personal possessions. It was a chilly winter morning, the desert air cold and crisp.

To her surprise, she found Shaun Christopher waiting for her by the helipad. "Hey there, stranger!" he said with forced levity. "You didn't think I'd let you leave without saying good-bye?"

"To be honest, I wasn't sure you were still speaking to me," she confessed. The helicopter pilot, wearing a khaki uniform conspicuously devoid of any identifying insignia, took her box from her to load onto the 'copter. "Apparently, I lost a spaceship or something."

Shaun gave her a gleaming smile, doing his best to defuse the awkwardness of the moment. "Hey, it's not your fault. We should have known those sneaky Ferengi would pull something like this. Guess they don't want any competition from us uppity Homo sapiens." His clean-cut, all-American face took on a determined cast. "But I'll tell you one thing: this isn't the end, not by a long shot. We're not going to let those rat-faced E.T.'s yank the rug out from beneath us. We're going to rebuild." Stubborn brown eyes looked past Shannon into the future. "One way or another, I'm making it to Saturn."

Shannon never doubted it for a minute. "I know you will," she told him.

"Excuse me, miss," the 'copter pilot interrupted. His breath frosted in the air between them. "Time to go."

A clumsy, heartfelt hug later, Shannon waved goodbye to Shaun, and Area 51, from the passenger seat of the sleek black helicopter. As she adjusted her seat belt, something in her pants pocket jabbed her uncomfortably. Investigating, she pulled out the silver pen Roberta Lincoln had bestowed upon her. *You again?* she thought wryly.

Its propeller blades spinning almost silently, the 'copter lifted off the tarmac. Shannon took one last look at Area 51, her home away from home for over a decade, then contemplated the silver pen—and the job offer Roberta (a.k.a. "Helen Swanson") had made to her the night of the blast-off.

Did she really want to join Roberta's mysterious organization? Now that she had said good-bye to NASA for good, she had literally no idea what she wanted to do with the rest of her life. Maybe she ought to take the older woman up on her offer? As long as she had the pen, she knew, she could always contact Roberta.

No, she realized, coming to a decision all at once, with surprising certainty. *That's not going to happen.* She glanced back ruefully, unable to even see the top-secret desert base anymore. Being a double agent had cost her far too much already.

Feeling completely confident about the choice she had just made, if about nothing else, she tossed the silver pen out the window of the helicopter. "Excuse me, miss," the pilot asked her, looking more perplexed than upset. "What was that?"

Shannon shrugged, brushing back a strand of her auburn hair. "Nothing I'm going to need anymore."

A new millennium, it occurred to her, was only four or five years away, depending on how picky you were about the math. *Maybe by then,* she thought hopefully, *I'll have found a new life for myself.*

And a new dream to pursue.

CHAPTER TWENTY-EIGHT

ISLE OF ARRAN
FEBRUARY 2, 1996

"You realize, of course," Roberta said, "that we've unleashed Khan on the rest of the universe?"

"The universe has survived worse than Khan," Gary Seven observed. "Earth might not have been so lucky."

True enough, she conceded. In her heart, she knew that they had handled the Khan crisis the best way they could, except for what had happened to Isis, that is. At times, though, she couldn't help wondering what Khan would be up to once he finally woke up, a hundred-plus years from now. If nothing else, it gave her something to think about besides what was just about to take place.

Gary Seven stood in front of the open transporter vault, his bags packed. Sunlight peeked through a window in the farmhouse's venerable stone walls, offering her a glimpse of violet hills and clear blue skies beyond.

"So you're really going?" Roberta felt herself getting misty-eyed already, and she reached for a box of Kleenex atop Seven's—scratch that, *her*—oak desk.

Seven nodded. "It's time," he told her gently. He wore a simple black bodysuit that Roberta assumed was in fashion back on a certain cloaked planet light-years away. "My aging musculature would prefer a lower-gravity environment, and, to be honest, a change will help me get over the pain of Isis's death." A bittersweet tone crept into his voice as he mentioned his once-constant companion. "Besides, I know Earth's future will be in good hands, Supervisor 368."

Roberta would have blushed if she hadn't been too busy being weepy. "Thanks," she replied, still mildly flabbergasted by the promotion. She wiped her eyes, hoping to avoid crying over her favorite downy blue pullover. "But how am I supposed to police this entire planet by myself?"

A cryptic smile appeared on Seven's crinkly face. "Arrangements have been made," he assured her. "In fact, I believe that's being taken care of right now."

As if on cue, the transporter controls on the inside of the heavy vault door started flashing and beeping. A cloud of glowing blue plasma materialized within the vault, rapidly filling the entire cavity.

What the heck? Roberta wondered, her gaping eyes struggling to penetrate the swirling azure fog. *Seven didn't tell me we were expecting company.*

At first, she couldn't spy anyone in the mist, then she realized that she was looking too high up, as their unexpected visitor came padding out of the vault on all fours. A fluffy orange Persian cat, with yellow eyes and an adorable pushed-in face, stepped onto the carpet and meowed hello.

"Roberta Lincoln, meet Ramses," Seven said by way of introduction. "He's your new partner."

"He?" She gave the long-haired feline a careful once-over.

"Yes," Seven answered dryly. "As a matter of fact, Ramses is a tomcat."

Roberta arched her eyebrow. *This could be interesting,* she thought.

First, however, there were some difficult good-byes to get through. Roberta got up from behind the desk and, being careful not to trod upon Ramses, gave Seven a heartfelt hug. "Don't be a stranger," she urged him. "Remember, I'm always a subspace call away."

"Good to know," he answered warmly, putting down his luggage long enough to hug her back. "And who knows? I may find reason to brave Earth's gravity again, whether there's a brewing interstellar emergency or not." Letting go of her at last, he stepped back so he could look her squarely in the eyes. "In any event, I want you to know just how proud I am of everything we've accomplished together over the years. You're living proof that the human race is worth preserving—and that you don't need genetic engineering or selective breeding to produce a superior human being."

On that note, he picked up his bags and, smiling back at her over his shoulder, stepped into the same roiling blue plasma that had disgorged Ramses, which suggested, if you thought about it, that he might be going exactly where the apricot-colored Persian had just come from.

Or not.

Roberta watched his familiar figure disappear into

the mist, then kept on watching until the fog itself had entirely evanesced, leaving her alone in the antique stone farmhouse with her brand-new feline companion. "I don't know about you, buster," she said, dabbing at the corner of her eye with a tissue, "but I still think we need some new blood. After all, who's going to do all the running around I used to do?"

Roberta still had her hopes regarding Shannon O'Donnell, but was starting to doubt whether that was going to happen. *After all she's been through,* the older woman thought, having discreetly checked on Shannon's situation in the weeks since the great spaceship heist, *I can't blame her if she doesn't want to get any deeper into the extraterrestrial spy biz.*

That still left Roberta, though, with the problem of finding a qualified new operative. *What am I supposed to do?* she asked herself rhetorically. *Take out an ad in the* Village Voice?

A knock at the front door of the farmhouse took Roberta by surprise. Hastily closing the transporter vault, and hiding it behind an authentic-looking cedar armoire, she scurried down the stairs to the foyer, with Ramses hopping down the creaking wooden steps behind her. "Hang on!" she called out to the increasingly insistent knocker. "I'm coming!"

She undid the latch and tugged open the door. There upon her threshold, caught in mid-knock, was a slim, dark-haired, young woman who Roberta had never seen before. The stranger, who looked to be in her mid-twenties, wore a striped woolen sweater and an excited expression. Vibrant brown eyes peered at Roberta from beneath a pair of unusually animated eyebrows.

"Oh, thank goodness someone's home!" she said breathlessly, her raspy voice carrying a trace of a New York accent. "Listen, please don't think I'm crazy, but I've got to talk to you!" She stuck her foot in the door just in case Roberta felt like slamming it in her face. "My name is Rain Robinson, and I'm with SETI—you know, the Search for Extraterrestrial Intelligence? Anyway, I was manning the radio telescope at Griffith Observatory a couple weeks ago, when I spotted some sort of bizarre spacecraft, like nothing I've ever seen before, in orbit above the Earth! Now, officially, according to NASA and all, there was nothing up there, but I tracked it for hours—and then I detected a strange kind of concentrated energy burst, sort of like a cross between a laser beam and a radio wave, zapping from the ship to the Earth. And you want to know where that beam ended up?" she asked Roberta exuberantly, answering her own question before the older woman even had a chance to respond.

"According to my calculations, right here! This island, this house, right in the middle of nowhere, no offense." Dangly white earrings rocked back and forth as Rain practically bounced up and down on Roberta's doorstep. "So, you want to explain to me why an advanced spacecraft of unknown origin is beaming down some sort of transmission to a quaint little cottage on an island that's primarily inhabited, as far as I can tell, by loads of freakin' sheep?"

Finally running out of breath, she looked expectantly at Roberta, who didn't know whether to be appalled or impressed. Clearly, the eager young astronomer had spied the *Botany Bay* during its brief stay in orbit. What's worse, she had even picked up on Roberta and Seven transporting home right before the hijacked sleeper ship took off for parts unknown.

Pretty good detective work, Roberta admitted, admiring Robinson's obvious spirit and initiative. In some ways, Rain reminded her of another excitable young woman, a wide-eyed hippie chick who had once found a job as a secretary for a small New York firm specializing in encyclopedia research. . . .

"So," she asked Rain right back, "you interested in saving the world?"

EPILOGUE

Captain's log, stardate 7004.2.

The Klingons have departed, for now. With the Paragon Colony's force field and protective dome repaired, the immediate crisis appears to have passed, with the only casualty being the Columbus-2, which did not survive its prolonged encounter with the planet's deadly atmosphere. Thankfully, Lieutenant Lerner and I managed to avoid the shuttle's fate by successfully beaming into the colony through the temporary gap in its force field.

Still, my original mission remains: should I recommend Sycorax for membership in the Federation, despite or because of its expertise at human genetic engineering? As I conclude my historical survey of the Eugenics Wars, I confess that my mind is far from certain on the matter. . . .

KIRK CLICKED OFF THE COMPUTER TERMINAL THAT the colony had thoughtfully provided him with, finished at last with the comprehensive data files he had brought with him from the *Enterprise*. He leaned back in his chair, stretching his arms behind his head. Thanks to a shower and a clean uniform, he was none the worse for wear after his harrowing shuttle flight earlier that day, although he was aware that things could have easily turned out very differently.

"Well?" McCoy asked him. "Made up your mind yet?"

The doctor sat in a comfy easy chair in the northwest corner of the Paragon Colony's deluxe VIP suite. Varnished walnut panels adorned the walls, while the bioluminescent ceiling, another product of applied genengineering, provided more than adequate lighting. Hardwood floors and oak furnishings, along with the ivory switches and knobs, also displayed the colonists' preference for organic materials.

A dog-eared medical journal rested upon the lap of the *Enterprise*'s chief medical officer, who had graciously volunteered to sit up with Kirk while the captain prepared for his final meeting with Masako Clarke and her advisors tomorrow morning. Lieutenant Lerner, exhausted from his trials aboard the *Columbus-2,* had already turned in for the evening. Kirk momentarily envied the young security officer, who was not responsible for deciding the future of an entire colony—and perhaps the Federation itself.

"I just don't know, Bones," he admitted. "Khan's infamous career, not to mention our own nearly-fatal run-in with him, make a strong argument against genetic supermen." A phantom pain tweaked his lungs as he remembered how Khan had tortured him in the *Enterprise*'s own medical decompression chamber.

"But what about Gary Seven, who stands as a compelling example of an enhanced human being who accomplished a great deal of good? And is it fair to punish the Paragon colonists for the sins of a previous generation of superhumans?"

"I wouldn't be so quick to take these folks entirely off the hook," McCoy observed candidly. "True, they're not the monster Khan was, but they've got a bit of the same attitude when it comes to us lowly, inferior human beings. You and I have both felt it. Who's to say they wouldn't get even more overbearing, and perhaps even dangerous, once they're accepted into the Federation?"

A scary thought, Kirk conceded, even while continuing to play devil's advocate. "I'm reluctant to condemn an entire people just because they're a trifle high-handed. I seem to recall that our not-so-distant ancestors originally found the Vulcans a bit condescending and aloof." A smile crossed his lips as he recalled some of the more amusing anecdotes he'd heard about Jonathan Archer's early dealings with the Vulcans. "But today human–Vulcan relations have never been stronger."

His light tone evaporated as his thoughts turned back toward the Eugenics Wars. "The question is: what made Khan a monster, his DNA or his times? Remember, Khan was a product of both genetic engineering *and* twentieth-century barbarism. That was three hundred years ago. Perhaps our civilization has evolved to the point where we can absorb this sort of superhumans into our society, without all the wrenching turmoil Earth went through in the 1990s?"

"Well, you know what I think," McCoy commented, never reluctant to express his opinion. "I'm all for responsible gene therapy when it comes to preventing and curing hereditary illnesses and mutations, but tampering with the very stuff that makes us human?" He shook his head uneasily. "Three hundred years or not, I don't believe we're ready for that kind of power, Jim."

Kirk knew exactly how he felt, but there were also other issues to consider. "What about the Klingons?" he asked. "We know that the Klingon Empire most definitely does not want the Paragon Colony to join the Federation, but is that a good enough reason to overturn a centuries-old ban on human genetic engineering?"

McCoy shrugged. "I'm a doctor, not a defense minister. The whole thing still makes me leery, no matter what the Klingons or the Romulans may be up to." An unintended yawn escaped his lips. "Sorry about that," he apologized. "It's been a long day."

Kirk glanced at the coral-and-ivory timepiece mounted on the wall; it was almost 11:05, local time. "You might as well get some sleep, Bones," he urged the doctor. "I suspect I'm going to be burning the midnight oil on this one."

"Well, far be it from me to ignore sound medical advice," McCoy said, rising slowly from the seasponge padding of the easy chair. He passed by Kirk's borrowed work station on the way to his own guest quarters. "Do yourself a favor, Jim," he offered as one last bit of doctorly wisdom. "Don't let this eat you up inside. You've already saved the universe from Khan once. You don't have to do it again."

Let's hope not, Kirk thought sincerely.

A pregnant silence fell over the suite after McCoy exited the room, as Kirk wrestled with the thorny issues presented by the Paragon Colony and its inhabitants. Masako Clarke was expecting his answer in the morning, knowing that whatever Kirk recommended would likely determine the Federation's policy toward the colony.

He paced across the polished teak floors. Tomorrow Spock would send down a fresh shuttle to pick up Kirk and the rest of the landing party. Kirk wanted to leave Sycorax knowing that he had made the right decision. Was it possible to condone human genetic engineering without risking another round of Eugenics Wars?

"Dr. McCoy is quite right, you know," a surprising voice interrupted his thoughts. Kirk reached for his phaser, resting on a carved wooden end table next to the couch, before he recognized the stranger stepping through the open doorway to the adjacent bedroom.

Gary Seven looked much older than Kirk remembered, more like he was depicted in the latter sections of the historical files Kirk had just been reviewing. Considering that those events took place almost three centuries ago, the silver-haired gentleman intruding on Kirk's privacy struck the captain as remarkably well-preserved.

"Mr. Seven," Kirk acknowledged, lowering his phaser. Although he and Seven had certainly had their differences in the past, mostly regarding Seven's inherent disregard for the Prime Directive, especially where primitive Earth was concerned, Kirk no longer regarded the alien operative as a threat. "To what do

I owe the privilege of this unexpected visitation, time travel or extreme longevity?"

"A little bit of both, Captain," Seven said cryptically. He was wearing, Kirk noted, a dark gray suit of twenty-third century design, such as a particularly colorless Federation bureaucrat might don. Moving easily under his own power, the older man approached the chair McCoy had vacated not long before. "Do you mind if I sit down?" he asked.

"By all means," Kirk responded, finding Seven's geriatric state oddly unnerving. He was used to thinking of himself and Seven as being roughly the same age, albeit three hundred years apart. "I was just reading about some of your experiences during the Eugenics Wars," Kirk commented. "My condolences regarding your cat."

"Thank you, Captain," Seven said, settling into the easy chair. "That was some time ago, objectively and subjectively."

Kirk felt a headache coming on, so he made an effort to overlook any and all temporal paradoxes for the time being. "I take it this visit is no coincidence."

"Hardly, Captain." Seven looked over at Kirk with a concerned expression. "I am aware of Sycorax's petition to join the Federation, with all its troubling implications, and thought that you might welcome another perspective on the subject, from someone who lived through the worst of the Eugenics Wars."

Kirk's pride was briefly wounded by the suggestion that he might benefit from the other man's advice, but he swiftly overcame his irritation, recognizing that it could hardly hurt to hear what Seven had to say. *Spock,* he reflected, *would no doubt encourage me to keep an open mind—and take advantage of all available resources.*

"You said you agreed with Dr. McCoy," he stated, wondering just how long Seven had been eavesdropping on their conversation. "Does this mean that you disapprove of accepting the Paragon Colony into the Federation?"

"Very much so," Seven said gravely. "Despite all the truly commendable progress humanity has made since the 1990s, we are not yet ready to take our genetic destiny into our own hands."

Kirk could not help noticing that, somewhere along the way, Seven had lost his occasionally annoying habit of referring to the human race as something different from himself. *Nice to know he's joined the club at last,* he mused, *and that people can change for the better.*

"I need more than that," he told Seven, not too harshly. "An explanation, not just a blanket statement. Give me a reason to believe you."

Seven's eyes were full of hard-won experience. "The greatest danger of eugenics, Captain, is not the enhanced abilities of people like Khan; it's the assumption that those enhancements somehow make certain people intrinsically superior to others, on the most fundamental level conceivable."

He glanced at the coral-shell computer terminal where Kirk had recently studied the unsettling annals of the past. "You've seen what happens next. Once you accept that assumption, that certain people are intrinsically more advanced than others, then you end up with megalomaniacs at one end of the spectrum and dangerously frightened people at the other. Look at what Khan became. Look at the violent backlash of General Morrison's militia. Eugenics programs, no matter how well-intentioned, invariably become just another way of turning 'Us' against 'Them.' "

Kirk found himself playing devil's advocate again. "But maybe it doesn't have to be that way anymore. The Federation already embraces scores of diverse alien races and life-forms. Why not two separate strains of humanity?"

"Sometimes it is easier to accept diversity among aliens than among our own kind. It's not necessarily logical, but it's true nonetheless." Seven spoke as though he'd seen a great deal of illogic in his time, whenever that was. "Genetic engineering is not like warp technology or even artificial intelligence. When you talk about DNA, Captain, you're provoking a very powerful emotional response, one that hits people at the very core of their identities, no matter how civilized they might otherwise be." He gave Kirk a pointed look. "Even in the enlightened world of the twenty-third century."

Part of Kirk, whose lungs still ached from the memory of Khan's torture, wanted to agree with Seven, to have a good excuse for banning forever the technology that created Khan, but another part—less fearful, more optimistic—felt compelled to defend the people of his own era.

"I'm not sure I accept your premise: that modern humans would react the same way people did back in the 1990s. You may be underestimating us, just like Khan did." Crossing the room, he peered out a window at the streets and gardens of the thriving colony; everything certainly seemed harmless enough. "Give me one good reason why human genetic engineering would be a terrible mistake."

"Because what truly matters can't be found in the genes," Seven said forcefully, as if he couldn't stress the point strongly enough. "Superior strength. Superior intelligence. These are all useful traits, but, in the end, they don't necessarily make superior people. Character. Compassion. Courage. Those are learned qualities, not encoded on any chromosome, but, ultimately, they are what will truly advance the human race."

His gray eyes turned inward as he looked back across the gulf of time. "Khan thought that he was more than human, but, over the years, his arrogance and lack of empathy ate away at his humanity, turning him into the monster you encountered. Roberta Lincoln. Shannon O'Donnell. Those were the truly superior humans, and what made them special did not come out of a test tube." Returning to the present, he leaned forward in his chair. "Trust me on this, Captain. If humanity goes looking for its future in strands of altered DNA, it will be heading in the wrong direction."

The captain nodded, paying close attention both to Seven's words and the obvious passion behind them. "And what about the Klingons?" he asked.

Seven sighed wearily. "For better or for worse, I suspect the essence of the Klingon soul will remain the same, no matter what genetic bells and whistles they may or may not add to their DNA. In any event, don't let an unreasoning fear of the Klingons, or any other alien adversaries, scare mankind away from its own humanity."

Because if we abandon that, Kirk realized, *then we'll have already lost the most important battle of all.* Remembering how he and his crew had just foiled Koloth's genocidal schemes, and without any augmented DNA, he felt much more confident about the human race's ability to take on even genetically engineered Klingons or Romulans. "Thank you, Mr. Seven," Kirk said sincerely. "You've given me a lot to think about."

He helped the older man out of the easy chair, then watched as Seven walked back toward the open doorway, where a shimmering cloud of blue plasma awaited him. "Good luck tomorrow, Captain," he said. "I know you'll make the right decision."

"And if I don't?"

Gary Seven just smiled as he stepped into the fog.

The next day, in Masako Clarke's office, Kirk wasted no time informing the regent of his decision.

"The good news is that I intend to strongly recommend that the Federation place the Paragon Colony under Starfleet protection, thus deterring any further assaults by the Klingons and other hostile parties. Starfleet engineers can help you upgrade your planetary defenses, and we may even decide to establish a military outpost in orbit around Sycorax, enforcing the quarantine."

"Quarantine?" Clarke asked. The regent sat behind a coral desk while her top advisors, including a grim-faced Gregor Lozin, listened to Kirk from their own chairs flanking their chief executive's desk. Chartreuse sunlight, filtered through the restored chlorodome, entered the office from a balcony to the left of where Kirk now stood, delivering his final verdict on Sycorax and all it represented.

"Yes, Madame Regent," he said. "Beyond the protection I spoke of, I am also advising the Federation to have nothing more to do with the Paragon Colony. Full membership in the Federation will be denied, the planet declared off-limits, and the ban on human genetic engineering will remain intact."

McCoy and Lerner waited at the back of the room, ready to accompany Kirk to the shuttle that would return them to the *Enterprise*. Kirk suspected that McCoy was considerably relieved and gratified by his decision, just as Gary Seven would be, wherever and whenever he was now.

"I'm sorry, Regent Clarke," the captain declared. "I wish you and your colony continued health and prosperity, but, after much consideration, of the past, the present, and the future, I do not believe that it is in the Federation's best interests to re-embark on a perilous course that once nearly destroyed humanity. The Romulans and the Klingons are a serious threat, yes, but even more dangerous than alien competitors is the possibility of a second Eugenics War."

Never again, Kirk vowed, fervently hoping that the foreboding specter of Khan Noonien Singh had been laid to rest at last.

AFTERWORD

Historical Notes on *The Eugenics Wars,* Volume Two

Unlike the world wars of the past, the Eugenics Wars were shadowy conflicts, fought behind the scenes of current events, against elusive, conspiratorial enemies whose genetically engineered origins remained largely unknown to the general public. Although the existence of the Eugenics Wars was well-known by the twenty-third century, most citizens of the late twentieth century were not even aware of the global struggle against Khan and his fellow supermen, seeing only scattered brushfire wars and random acts of terrorism.

Due to the covert nature of the Eugenics Wars, trying to find accurate contemporary accounts of the events described in this volume is like searching for a pacifist Klingon. Nonetheless, certain facts and references in this volume are corroborated by the "official" records of the era. . . .

Chapter One: Roberta is not exaggerating when she frets about the civil wars and unrest plaguing the world in 1992. By that summer, war was raging in Liberia, Peru, Afghanistan, Bosnia, Somalia, Sudan, and elsewhere. There had been food riots in Albania, race riots in Los Angeles, and ongoing chaos in the former Soviet Union. In hindsight, it's difficult to determine just how much of this global turmoil was caused and/or exacerbated by Khan and his genetically engineered confreres, but Mr. Spock was also on the money when he described the 1990s as "a strange, violent time" in Earth's history.

On the brighter side, France did suspend nuclear testing in April 1992, shortly before Khan secretly took possession of the Centre d'Experimentation du Pacifique. The French government had fought a running battle with environmentalists over their South Pacific bomb tests, which may explain the Greenpeace logo Roberta found carved into that detention cell on Muroroa.

Chapter Two: A twenty percent increase in the size of the Antarctic ozone hole was indeed noted in the summer of 1992. Officially, the expansion was blamed on the eruption of Mt. Pinatubo in the Philippines the summer before, but this was obviously just a cover story, intended to keep the general public from guessing the existence of Khan's ozone destroyer.

Meanwhile, a United Nations peacekeeping force was definitely stationed in Bosnia that summer. Undermanned and overwhelmed, they were certainly in harm's way, even if Khan hadn't instigated a plot against them to keep Seven and Roberta busy.

The European Remote Sensing Satellite (ERS-1), Europe's first environmental satellite, went into orbit in 1991. ERS-2, launched three years later, was capable of charting Earth's ozone layer every seventy-two hours, thus allowing those nations to watch out for any sign of Morning Star at work.

Chapter Three: Roberta's efforts to protect Windsor Castle were only partially successful. On November 20, 1992, less than a month after Khan's commandos raided Gary Seven's headquarters in London, a portion of the castle did catch fire, causing nearly sixty million dollars in damage. An overheated spotlight was blamed for the disaster, no doubt to avoid alarming the British public. We can perhaps thank Roberta that the entire edifice did not go up in flames.

Chapter Four: It is unsurprising that the destruction of Seven's bookshop was blamed on the Irish Republican Army. IRA bombings were sadly common in London during the early nineties.

Likewise, the intercaste conflict that Khan notes in India was very much an issue at the time, costing the lives of several suicidal upper-caste protesters.

Chapter Five: Amidst much hype, the Biosphere II experiment, mentioned by Shannon O'Donnell, began in October 1991. Although not entirely successful, this ambitious attempt to create a sealed, self-sustainable living environment provided data on artificial habitats that no doubt influenced the construction and cargo of the *S.S. Botany Bay.*

The existence of Area 51, as well as the details of the infamous Roswell incident, have been well-documented elsewhere, including Volume One of this history.

Chapter Six: The attendees at Khan's superhuman summit are all too typical of the various revolutionaries, gurus, terrorists, and warlords who made the nineties such an interesting and tumultuous era.

Chapter Seven: Although it has nothing to do with the Eugenics Wars, Spock's innovative battle strategy was, as he admits, inspired by the actual historical exploits of Jasper Maskelyne, a noted British stage magician who used his skills as an illusionist to assist the Allied cause in World War II. The searchlight trick he used to defend the Suez Canal in 1941 was just one of several bits of wartime prestidigitation carried out by Maskelyne and his notorious "magic gang."

Chapter Ten: The catastrophic earthquake that struck Maharashtra early in the morning of September 30, 1993, came as something of a surprise given that the region had previously been considered aseismic. Speculation afterward focused on the Lower Tirna Reservoir, approximately ten kilometers from the center of the quake, where it was theorized that the reservoir's contents exerted too much loading on an underlying fault. (Only Khan and his inner circle, however, guessed that the quake had actually been triggered by an underwater concussive charge.) Death tolls attributed to the 1993 quake vary widely, ranging from nine to thirty thousand fatalities; given the widespread devastation, Khan can certainly be forgiven for assuming the worst.

Chapter Eleven: The Dunes Casino, later re-created holographically on Deep Space Nine, was open for business from 1955 to 1993. It was demolished in a controlled implosion on October 27, 1993, a few weeks after

Roberta and Shannon had their final rendezvous there. As far as we know, Khan had nothing to do with the casino's destruction, although I wouldn't bet the farm on that.

Chapter Twelve: Why a sub attack? Khan had few other options, given United Nations Security Council Resolution 781, adopted in October of 1992, which banned military flights over Bosnia-Herzegovina. Subsequently, Resolution 816, adopted March 31, 1993, allowed NATO to shoot down aircraft violating the no-fly zone, severely curtailing Khan's ability to launch an air strike against Vasily Hunyadi's Bosnian headquarters.

The experimental Shkval (Squall) torpedo, which Khan employed so successfully against Hunyadi's attack sub, was indeed developed by the Russians during the late seventies. Later on, desperate for hard cash, Russia is rumored to have sold improved versions of the Shkval to such nations as France, China, and Iran. Not to mention the Great Khanate, of course!

Chapter Thirteen: Contemporary historical records contain no mention of the submarine battle between Khan's and Hunyadi's forces, suggesting that all involved succeeded in keeping the deadly encounter out of the press, much as Gary Seven hoped. On the other hand, it was then pretty much impossible to open a newspaper or turn on the television without hearing about the well-publicized scandal involving Olympic ice skaters Tonya Harding and Nancy Kerrigan. What with Tonya and Nancy occupying the news, not to mention O.J. and Amy Fisher, it's no surprise that the average American never noticed the Eugenics Wars.

Chapter Fourteen: Even by Indian standards, the summer of 1994 was a scorching one, with temperatures reaching as high as 50 degrees Celsius in New Delhi; small wonder Khan felt so uncomfortable posing in his garden.

He was also entitled to feel pessimistic about the state of the world that year. His despairing litany of geopolitical hot spots and crises, from North Korea to Rwanda to the Middle East to the Balkans, was all too well-informed.

Just as on-target were Ament's timely warnings of inflation and unemployment in large parts of India, as that struggling nation endured a painful transition from pseudo-socialism to a more free-market economy.

Chapter Fifteen: Militias such as the Army of Eternal Vigilance were becoming a serious threat by 1994, convincing tens of thousands of Americans that evil government forces were plotting to steal their freedom. Thankfully, most of these private armies were not led by a genetically engineered superman, but they still managed to inspire the likes of Timothy McVeigh. (For a terrifying and eye-opening look at the rise of the militias, check out *A Force Upon the Plain: The American Militia Movement and the Politics of Hate* by Kenneth S. Stern.)

Chapter Sixteen: By August of 1994, NATO was threatening another round of air strikes against Serbian positions in Bosnia, with the full sanction of the United Nations. It was the continuing threat of these strikes that surely prompted Vasily Hunyadi to confront the U.N. in Geneva.

The nerve gas assault on the Palais des Nations anticipated a similar attack that occurred in Japan not long after. In March 1995, members of Aum Shinrikyo, an apocalyptic cult, released sarin gas in crowded rush-hour subway trains in Tokyo, killing a dozen innocent commuters and injuring countless more. (An earlier trial run, in June 1994, killed another seven people.) Thankfully, neither event claimed as many casualties as the attack in Geneva.

Concocted by German scientists in the 1930s, sarin was also used by Saddam Hussein in the 1980s, against both Iran and the Kurds. Twenty-six times more deadly than cyanide gas, it works by inhibiting the production of cholinesterase, an enzyme produced in the liver that causes contracted muscles to relax. With no cholinesterase, muscles stay contracted, resulting in suffocation, paralysis, and eventual death. (Dr. Beverly Crusher, of the *U.S.S. Enterprise,* later diagnosed the cause of Claire Raymond's death as an "embolism," suggesting that the sarin caused some sort of fatal clotting in the unfortunate woman's brain.)

Giving credit where it's due, it should be noted that Walter Nichols's revolutionary cryosatellite technology has an absolutely astonishing record of success. Not only did it preserve Khan and several dozen of his followers way into the twenty-third century, but it also allowed Claire Raymond and two other twentieth-century Americans to be revived nearly a hundred years later, in the time of Captain Picard. Those twentieth-century cryonics units were obviously built to last!

Chapter Seventeen: As Roberta suspects, Seven was no doubt busy in the summer of 1994 monitoring the tense situation in Southeast Asia, where North Korea had threatened to turn its long-time rival, South Korea, into a "sea of flames" in response to U.S. accusations that it was attempting to develop nuclear weapons by diverting plutonium from power plants to bomb-making. Attempts to mediate the situation by former President Jimmy Carter (with perhaps the covert assistance of Gary Seven) were complicated by the sudden death of North Korea's long-time dictator, Kim Sung, leaving it unclear as to who was in charge in Pyongyang. A tentative accord was finally achieved in October of 1994, but only after many months of anxious uncertainty that surely occupied much of Seven's attention.

Chapter Eighteen: The symptoms exhibited by the late Dr. Donald Williams, although artificially accelerated, correspond with the known effects of necrotizing fasciitis. For more information on this very real, but thankfully rare, syndrome, check out the Web site of the National Necrotizing Fasciitis Foundation at: http://nnff.org.

Chapter Nineteen: As Seven observed, the Eurotunnel running beneath the English Channel (popularly known as the Chunnel) officially opened on May 6, 1994, when Queen Elizabeth II took the train to meet French President Mitterrand at Calais, but did not begin carrying regular passengers until November 14 of that same year. I'm guessing General Morrison was tempted to attack the gala opening in May, but may have decided that the security surrounding the Queen was just a little too tight; hence, he waited for real passenger service to begin.

Eight years in the building, the Chunnel cost over $15 billion and was one of the most ambitious and expensive engineering projects this side of the Millennium Gate.

Chapter Twenty: The less said of the John Bobbit castration scandal of early 1994, the better.

Chapter Twenty-one: Believe it or not, there really was a flesh-eating bacteria scare in June 1994, especially in England where the London tabloids hyped the "epidemic" for all it was worth. A high-ranking government official was finally obliged to deliver a live address on national television in hopes of calming the panic. Naturally, he didn't say anything about Phoolan Dhasal's germ warfare experiments.

Chapter Twenty-two: Contemporary accounts confirm that a 10-kiloton nuclear explosion occurred in the South Pacific on September 5, 1995, provoking a storm of international protests. Little did the world know that France's apparent resumption of nuclear testing was just a cover story Gary Seven arranged to account for the atomic destruction of Khan's germ warfare capability.

Chapter Twenty-three: One of the first genetically engineered foodstuffs to be approved for human consumption, "Flavr Savr™" tomatoes were test-marketed in Chicago in the summer of 1994, and could be found on sale in the United Kingdom by spring 1995.

Like the Great Khanate, they were not a total success.

Chapter Twenty-four: Rumors of a top-secret UFO hangar and testing facility, codenamed "S-4" and located in the rocky hills overlooking Papoose Lake, south of Area 51, have circulated for years among UFO researchers and conspiracy buffs. Unfortunately, like so much of the Eugenics Wars, no definitive proof of its existence can be found in the official histories of the time.

Chapter Twenty-five: Nineteen ninety-six was an election year in India, full of heated rhetoric and charges of political corruption, so it is perhaps no surprise that resentment against Khan's heavy-handed tactics finally bubbled over into open revolt that year.

Following his bombing of Khan's "terrorist base" in Chandigarh, U.S. President Bill Clinton later launched similar bombing raids on Afghanistan, Iraq, Sudan, and Serbia. The air assault on Chandigarh was a singularly effective one, with the result that no trace of Khan's fortress can now be found anywhere in the vicinity.

Chapter Twenty-six: Despite the mysterious disappearance of the original prototype, the DY-100 class sleeper ships became the mainstay of mankind's continuing exploration of space, until innovations in sublight propulsion rendered them obsolete by 2018. The final fate of the *Botany Bay*, of course, was not to be discovered until Captain Kirk and the Starship *Enterprise* found the ancient vessel floating derelict in space some three hundred years after the Eugenics Wars. It is unclear how the *Botany Bay* ended up in the Mutara Sector and why it never reached its original destination, but, as Seven warned Khan, spaceflight is not without risk; we can only speculate about navigational malfunctions, wormholes, quantum filaments, or any number of other unforeseen hazards.

Chapter Twenty-seven: Although Shannon O'Donnell's stint at Area 51 remains undocumented, like everything else related to that top-secret base, it is known that she later married a man named Henry Janeway and played a crucial role in the inception of the famous Millennium Gate project of the early twenty-first century.

So much for the 1990s! Only seven more years until Shaun Christopher lands on Saturn . . .

—Greg Cox
January, 2002

Look for STAR TREK fiction from Pocket Books

Star Trek®

#90 • *Belle Terre* • Dean Wesley Smith with Diane Carey
#91 • *Rough Trails* • L.A. Graf
#92 • *The Flaming Arrow* • Kathy and Jerry Oltion
#93 • *Thin Air* • Kristine Kathryn Rusch & Dean Wesley Smith
#94 • *Challenger* • Diane Carey
#95–96 • *Rihannsu* • Diane Duane
    #95 • *Swordhunt*
    #96 • *Honor Blade*
#97 • *In the Name of Honor* • Dayton Ward

Star Trek®: The Original Series

The Janus Gate • L.A. Graf
    #1 • *Present Tense*
    #2 • *Future Imperfect*
    #3 • *Past Prologue*
Errand of Vengeance • Kevin Ryan
    #1 • *The Edge of the Sword*
    #2 • *Killing Blow*
    #3 • *River of Blood*

Star Trek: The Next Generation®

Metamorphosis • Jean Lorrah
Vendetta • Peter David
Reunion • Michael Jan Friedman
Imzadi • Peter David
The Devil's Heart • Carmen Carter
Dark Mirror • Diane Duane
Q-Squared • Peter David
Crossover • Michael Jan Friedman
Kahless • Michael Jan Friedman
Ship of the Line • Diane Carey
The Best and the Brightest • Susan Wright
Planet X • Michael Jan Friedman
Imzadi II: Triangle • Peter David
I, Q • Peter David & John de Lancie
The Valiant • Michael Jan Friedman
The Genesis Wave, Books One, Two, and Three • John Vornholt
Immortal Coil • Jeffrey Lang
A Hard Rain • Dean Wesley Smith
The Battle of Betazed • Charlotte Douglas & Susan Kearney
Novelizations
    Encounter at Farpoint • David Gerrold
    Unification • Jeri Taylor

Enterprise®

Novelizations
   Broken Bow • Diane Carey
   Shockwave • Paul Ruditis

   By the Book • Dean Wesley Smith & Kristine Kathryn Rusch
   What Price Honor? • Dave Stern
   Surak's Soul • J.M. Dillard

Star Trek®: New Frontier

New Frontier #1–4 Collector's Edition • Peter David
   #1 • *House of Cards*
   #2 • *Into the Void*
   #3 • *The Two-Front War*
   #4 • *End Game*
   #5 • *Martyr* • Peter David
   #6 • *Fire on High* • Peter David
The Captain's Table #5 • *Once Burned* • Peter David
Double Helix #5 • *Double or Nothing* • Peter David
   #7 • *The Quiet Place* • Peter David
   #8 • *Dark Allies* • Peter David
   #9–11 • *Excalibur* • Peter David
      #9 • *Requiem*
      #10 • *Renaissance*
      #11 • *Restoration*
Gateways #6: *Cold Wars* • Peter David
Gateways #7: *What Lay Beyond*: *"Death After Life"* • Peter David
   #12 • *Being Human* • Peter David

Star Trek®: Stargazer

The Valiant • Michael Jan Friedman
Double Helix #6: *The First Virtue* • Michael Jan Friedman and Christie Golden
Gauntlet • Michael Jan Friedman
Progenitor • Michael Jan Friedman

Star Trek®: Starfleet Corps of Engineers (eBooks)

Have Tech, Will Travel (paperback) • various
   #1 • *The Belly of the Beast* • Dean Wesley Smith
   #2 • *Fatal Error* • Keith R.A. DeCandido
   #3 • *Hard Crash* • Christie Golden

#4 • *Interphase, Book One* • Dayton Ward & Kevin Dilmore
Miracle Workers (paperback) • various
    #5 • *Interphase, Book Two* • Dayton Ward & Kevin Dilmore
    #6 • *Cold Fusion* • Keith R.A. DeCandido
    #7 • *Invincible, Book One* • Keith R.A. DeCandido & David Mack
    #8 • *Invincible, Book Two* • Keith R.A. DeCandido & David Mack
  #9 • *The Riddled Post* • Aaron Rosenberg
#10 • *Gateways Epilogue: Here There Be Monsters* • Keith R.A. DeCandido
#11 • *Ambush* • Dave Galanter & Greg Brodeur
#12 • *Some Assembly Required* • Scott Ciencin & Dan Jolley
#13 • *No Surrender* • Jeff Mariotte
#14 • *Caveat Emptor* • Ian Edginton
#15 • *Past Life* • Robert Greenberger
#16 • *Oaths* • Glenn Hauman
#17 • *Foundations, Book One* • Dayton Ward & Kevin Dilmore
#18 • *Foundations, Book Two* • Dayton Ward & Kevin Dilmore
#19 • *Foundations, Book Three* • Dayton Ward & Kevin Dilmore
#20 • *Enigma Ship* • J. Steven and Christina F. York
#21 • *War Stories, Book One* • Keith R.A. DeCandido
#22 • *War Stories, Book Two* • Keith R.A. DeCandido
#23 • *Wildfire, Book One* • David Mack
#24 • *Wildfire, Book Two* • David Mack
#25 • *Home Fires* • Dayton Ward & Kevin Dilmore

Star Trek®: Invasion!

#1 • *First Strike* • Diane Carey
#2 • *The Soldiers of Fear* • Dean Wesley Smith & Kristine Kathryn Rusch
#3 • *Time's Enemy* • L.A. Graf
#4 • *Final Fury* • Dafydd ab Hugh
Invasion! Omnibus • various

Star Trek®: Day of Honor

#1 • *Ancient Blood* • Diane Carey
#2 • *Armageddon Sky* • L.A. Graf
#3 • *Her Klingon Soul* • Michael Jan Friedman
#4 • *Treaty's Law* • Dean Wesley Smith & Kristine Kathryn Rusch
The Television Episode • Michael Jan Friedman
Day of Honor Omnibus • various

Star Trek®: The Captain's Table

#1 • *War Dragons* • L.A. Graf
#2 • *Dujonian's Hoard* • Michael Jan Friedman